RELIC AND RUIN

RELIC
AND
RUIN

WENDII McIVER

wattpad books

wattpad books **W**

An imprint of Wattpad WEBTOON Book Group.

Content Warning: magic, necromancy, violence, ghosts, undead, language

Published in Canada by Wattpad Books, a division of Wattpad Corp.

36 Wellington Street E., Toronto, ON M5E 1C7

www.wattpad.com

First Wattpad Books edition: June 2022

ISBN 978-1-98936-535-9 (Hardcover original)
ISBN 978-1-98936-543-4 (eBook edition)

Library and Archives Canada Cataloguing in Publication information is available upon request.

Printed and bound in Canada
1 3 5 7 9 10 8 6 4 2

Cover design by Greg Tabor

For everyone.
All my love, Wendll

INITIUM

GRIM REAPER: The personification of death in the form of a cloaked skeleton wielding a large scythe.

NECROMANCER: One who conjures the spirits of the dead via the conduction of the souls of the dead back into their former bodies for purposes of communicating with them.

ZOMBIE: The body of a dead being given life again, but mute and without will.

HUMAN: None of the above.

IN THE BEGINNING

This is how the feud began. And how good and evil came to be.

It is an old tale of two brothers, not of blood but brothers nonetheless: Grim and Neco.

The two possessed strange abilities, though they did not know it at first. They worked in the wheat fields of a world unlike yours. It was Grim's job to cut away the wheat with a scythe, while Neco dug and churned the earth.

There was also a girl. No one remembers her name, or how she came to know the brothers. Both fell in love with her, though she was entranced by only one. And on the day that they came of age, Grim asked her to marry him. The woman accepted, for she loved him back, oblivious to the younger boy, Neco, who was left with only heartbreak and jealousy.

On the night of the wedding, inside a large barn filled with family, friends, and the bride, beautiful and pure in her long white gown, Neco finally snapped. Through blind jealousy and hatred, his strange abilities finally manifested.

The ground beneath them trembled and an almighty crack echoed across the Nethers as things—creatures—crawled up from the earth. Attendants screamed and fled as the undead, rotting and foul, hauled themselves from the soil. The corpse-like beings rallied before Neco, soldiers awaiting orders.

Neco commanded his army to kill them all, sparing only his brother and his brother's bride.

Before either Grim or his bride could muster a cry, the undead soldiers spread over the farm like a plague. Every last one of the attendants was chased down, the monsters breaking upon them in a sickening fury of teeth, talons, and godlike strength. Children, elders, husbands, wives—the fields were awash with their blood.

Having returned to Neco, the undead soldiers pushed Grim to his knees and held him there, beneath the arch under which he was to be wed.

Neco beckoned to the woman. When she didn't move, he took her by the arms and, despite her struggles, dragged her to the center of the aisle, in front of Grim.

Ignoring her curses, Neco took her by the chin and raised her head.

"Why would you do this?" he asked. "Why would you tear us apart like this?"

"I don't know what you're talking about," she replied.

"Why would you do this?" he said, gesturing to the massacre that surrounded them. "Was I not kind enough? Smart enough? Funny enough? Did I not work *hard* enough?" He dug his fingers into her cheeks, but she gave no reply, refusing to meet his eyes.

How could she not choose him?

Grim screamed in protest as Neco's hand moved to her throat. The younger brother held up a hand dismissively, not taking his eyes from the girl. She spat curses and words that would transform into hellfire if only she could muster the magic to do so. She wanted her words to hit, to break, to burn.

But as the last words left her lips, Neco's grip tightened.

Grim yelled and tried to lunge out of the soldiers' grip.

Neco ignored him. The soldiers gnashed their teeth in unison, a chorus of *click, click, click*. Neco looked down at the woman, smiled, and threw her into the waiting arms of his soldiers.

Her screams—accompanied by the sounds of tearing flesh and talons raking across bone—filled the barn. Blood seeped into the floorboards below. Soon her screams stopped, leaving only Grim's.

The world seemed to slow then. Grim managed to stand and, shrugging clear of the monsters, reached out the nearest window and grabbed his harvesting scythe—the very same he'd used while working alongside Neco. The wooden handle changed with his touch, turning from faded, water-swollen wood to glowing black metal. The blade curved and grew longer, morphing into a deadly, pewter blade that reflected the moon like a mirror.

Grim made his way to Neco, cutting down every rotting creature standing between him and his brother. One after the other, at the faintest slash of Grim's blade, the soldiers burst into dust. Grief and rage consumed Grim, swirling around him in dark, mist-like tendrils.

Neco turned, still expecting his brother to be restrained, and the blade of Grim's scythe cut straight down his face—a bone-deep gash through his left eye. Neco howled and stumbled backward, tripping into the pews. Grim advanced to the group of undead still crouched around his would-be bride's disemboweled body.

Before he could bury his scythe into the first creature's brain, Grim was shoved from behind by Neco, who'd barreled into him. He spun and faced his brother. Neco, blood gushing from his face, smashed his older brother over the head with a long floorboard.

Grim stumbled back, vision turning black. Dark tendrils of power zapped about him like lightning. The scythe burned his palm. He could feel Neco's power, as if he was standing too close to a fire. Grim roared and raised his scythe—ready to cut his brother down. Neco did the same with the plank of wood.

Everything slowed once more as their weapons clashed, and all went silent. It was as if the world had sucked in a huge breath—and then a roaring explosion knocked both brothers off their feet.

Grim landed flat on his back, winded, looking up at the black curtain of the night sky—not the barn. He sat up, confused. The earth in front of him dipped, revealing a deep, smoldering crater. The trees that had once surrounded the barn were now mere piles of ash. The barn—what remained of it—consisted of only a few chunks of charcoaled wood and the sizzling, melted, metal arch under which he was to be wed.

For a long time, Grim stood there, watching the smoke dance in the air. Then he sat down and cried. Eventually, eyes swollen and red, he looked at his hands. They were scorched and blistering.

The scythe.

He stood and turned to see his scythe half-buried in the ground, its blade reflecting the moon's light. The long blade was jagged in parts, serrated with beautiful patterns. A large pointed hook curved out its back.

He approached the weapon, pulled it from the ground, and held it in his hands. He knew then what power he had. And he would do whatever it took to avenge his family and his love.

He would destroy his brother.

PART ONE

NECROMANTIC

CHAPTER ONE

COULROPHOBIA – FEAR OF CLOWNS

The pendant rested warm and pulsing against the hollow of Nyx Lahey's throat. It flashed every few steps to assure her she was going in the right direction.

Detectors were rare and extremely valuable but also stubborn, and they didn't always work. When she was seven, Nyx found the plump ruby—a priceless gem the size of her eyeball—in the trunk of a dead tree behind her grandmother's house. She had discovered it while landscape workers were on break after cutting down the tree.

Her father, a Reaper who specialized in the study of detector stones, fashioned a golden, braided chain for it, and encased the ruby in a matching frame. He'd trained the stone to flash when its wearer approached their prey, the stone pulsing faster and faster the closer they got.

The pendant threw off another beam of light as Nyx continued walking. It had been taught to flash in the presence not only of zombies and Necromancers, but also creatures that belonged to the Inbetween: things neither zombie nor human.

The detector flashed again.

Sickly yellow, artificial light poured from the deteriorating carnival stalls to either side of her. Which would have been fine had this place actually had any power. But the park had been abandoned for years. Something, or someone, was causing this.

She climbed into an abandoned ice-cream van and checked the cupboards and drawers, even behind the door, searching for anything that might give her an idea of what they were up against.

On their way in, before they split up, her father had outlined everything from the academy's email: five girls had been found murdered in the park—gutted, actually, some with the backs of their heads caved in, others wrapped tightly with barbed wire. Some even had limbs sewn to different parts of their bodies. Each was found hanging from the park's entrance, their mouths sliced into long, bloody grins.

The police had found nothing—no motives, no suspects, not a trace of evidence. Meaning the crime was likely supernatural in nature. It was then that the Misten Academy stepped in and took matters into their own hands. They sent Reapers to hunt down whatever had killed those girls.

They sent the Laheys.

The Laheys weren't actually Reapers—not technically. They were an old family of Necromancers caught up in a never-ending war between Necroes and Reapers. Hundreds of years ago, their ancestors had switched sides. Lahey children were sent to the Reaper Academy, where they were given scythes and taught to handle items meant only for Reapers. All while dealing with their necromantic powers, and the social pressure of being "the enemy."

The ruby flashed again, illuminating the inside of the ice-cream truck. Nyx covered the stone with her hand and jumped to the crunchy, trash-covered ground outside.

One of the stalls cast a golden square on the ground—lit from within. Nyx blew the black hair away from her face. They always did this to try and scare you off—a flickering light, something thrown at you from across an empty room. A single light shining in a house filled with broken bulbs. A whisper from above.

Each Inbetweener had their signature. They were smart like that.

A row of painted porcelain clown heads hung inside the stall, their mouths open midlaugh, heads swinging from left to right. Some had been smashed or spray-painted. Glitchy, repetitive carnival music screeched from a busted speaker above the awning.

To her left stood the entrance to the rides—a huge black tunnel guarded by a mechanized clown statue in a multicolored jumpsuit, bolted to the ground. One side of its face was smashed in, revealing broken shards of porcelain, metal, and exposed wiring. Its remaining face, scratched and faded by the sun, showed rosy cheeks, exaggerated blue eyes, and full red lips.

One of its mechanical arms moved up and down, waving. From a speaker hidden inside its mouth, a garbled, "*Hello! Hello! Hello! Hello!—*" echoed.

The ruby flashed again. Nyx gave the robot one last look before moving toward the black tunnel.

"Can I have some light, please?" she asked, squinting into the darkness. The ruby obliged, casting a red glow into the tunnel ahead.

The robot voice continued to sputter. "*Hello! Hello! . . . Goodbye.*"

Nyx slowly turned around. The clown no longer waved, no longer spoke. Its smile was now a frown, with pointed teeth sticking out from beneath blood-red lips. It'd turned and now faced the entrance of the tunnel.

The ruby flared.

Nyx continued forward, her boots echoing with each step. Hands over her shoulder, she pulled her scythe from its holster.

"*Good-bye*," the robot sputtered once more, giving her a murderous stare.

She swung, bringing the blade up in a quick arch. The upper half of the statue slid diagonally away from the rest, landing with a thump and a clang. She'd cut straight through the power box.

Around her, lights flickered and music jolted. The Inbetweener's power stumbled for a moment. Nyx looked back at the statue before returning to the tunnel, scythe still in hand.

It wasn't the prettiest thing, especially in the ugly red glow of the detector. Bronze metal, with copper-colored barbed wire wrapped around parts of the blade and angry, wild sections of serration.

As a Lahey, Nyx was able to handle the otherwise toxic Reaper Iron. But since she was the enemy, her scythe had been chosen for her by a bunch of snot-nosed parents on the academy board who offered only the most horrendous looking bit of gear they could find in the back of the scythe cupboard.

Nyx's footfalls softened as the tunnel ended, and she came out the other side onto dead grass. The tracks of a giant, rusted roller coaster twisted and turned above and around her. Farther down, a Ferris wheel was silhouetted against the lights in the distance, creating a web of metallic spires. More stalls and buildings lined the litter-covered path ahead.

Nature had taken over the area. Trees twisted in and out of the metal, roots growing through the concrete while weeds and vines scaled the rides and pavilions. The detector flashed red once more, assuring Nyx that she was headed in the right direction. She passed an empty purple tent with "Magic" inscribed across an old, frayed banner. Lined up along its outside walls were mirrors of various shapes that distorted Nyx's reflection in myriad ways. No matter how tall, fat, or short she appeared, the details were the same: black hair, cut in jagged layers and half-curled; bright, orange eyes; mud-stained jeans; and boots. A multitude of gleaming Reaper Iron hung from her many belts and straps. Bronze scythe in hand, gun on her hip.

Nyx continued working her way down the center of the park, rummaging through every open building, pop-up van, and tent. Across the park, she could hear her parents doing the same. Following a bend in the path, she came to another run-down building. She kicked in the door and found herself peering into a tiny, messy storage room; a single smashed window filtered in light.

As her boots hit the metal floor, the ruby started to strobe. She spun around, scythe at the ready. She saw only the shadows of the trees as they danced in the weak wind. There was a clank to her left. Paper rustling.

Stay calm.

She backed into the room, holding the scythe in front of her. Four quick flares from her detector. She kept her eyes trained on the door, expecting something to come barreling around the corner. But nothing did.

She dropped her arms and turned to look at the contents of the room: stacks of old boxes, dirt, bug shit, and cleaning chemicals scattered across a steel floor. Nyx noted a deep, empty echo beneath her feet as she stepped forward. She stamped her foot and felt the floor shake under her weight. The building was at ground level but the world below had been hollowed out.

She sheathed her scythe and began to clear the space as best she could. Finally, she found what she was looking for: a gleaming hatch, its outline clearly visible in the dirty floor.

The detector warned her once more as she pulled the hatch up, revealing a staircase descending into darkness. She pulled the gun from her hip and aimed it into the pitch black. The pendant around her neck brightened to light the way as she trudged forward.

At the bottom, Nyx found herself staring down rows of hanging fluorescent lights. Cement pillars held the ceiling in place while huge hooks hung from chains suspended from the low ceiling. It looked as if someone had turned an underground parking lot into a meat locker.

In the center of the room was a long steel table, right out of a butcher's shop. Surrounding it were several smaller wheeled carts containing knives, small saws, and other instruments used to delimb animals. The cold of the room seeped through Nyx's clothes almost instantly.

There was a long, loud shuffle to her left, from around the corner. She flicked the gun safety off and hugged the wall. The ruby flared like a beacon.

This is it, she thought, glancing at the chain around her neck, waiting for the pendant to signal green—to alert her parents out in the park.

Nothing happened. She frowned. There was more shuffling, followed by a distinct and echoing:

Click. Click. Click.

She pressed herself against the wall and edged closer.

Click. Click. Click.

The edge of the wall was at least four feet away. She needed to get closer. She put the safety back on and shoved the gun into its holster before opening a worn leather pouch hanging from the side of her belt. It bore the golden stitching of her aunt Maura, one of the family Seers. Inside were numerous charms and protectors, amplifiers and warding items—things like wolfsbane or peacock iris set in amber to protect—gems of every color to help amplify one's strength and power. Ancient bits of jewelry to bring luck.

Nyx dug through the contents, looking for one item in particular.

Black pearl? No.

Tiger's tooth? No.

Dragon's eye? *Yes.*

From the bag, she pulled a small, spherical, cloudy, jade-colored gem. The dragon's eye, according to Maura, was to "See shit you can't see on your own."

Crouching, she rolled the gem across the concrete floor. It came to an abrupt stop in the shadow of the butcher's table. Her vision flickered. From its position, the eye allowed her to see the space on the other side of the wall. Directly across from the table, an iron sliding door was set in the wall. It was slightly ajar. Beyond it, she could hear more *click, click, clicking*—someone, or something, was on the other side.

She blinked and her vision returned to normal. Crouching down and holding her hand to the ground, she watched the eye roll back obediently. Nyx dropped it back into the pouch and, grabbing her gun again, crept around the corner. She flattened herself against the wall, pistol to her cheek.

Three more steps.

Click.

One.

Click.

Two.

. . .

THREE.

Just as she was about to hook her foot around the door and slide it open, it slid back, and Nyx came face to face with the source of the noise—a boy.

The ruby flared brighter than ever, practically searing her skin. She had her gun level and cocked in milliseconds. It was then she realized that he, too, had his gun ready.

The boy looked just as startled as she felt. "Watch yourself," he warned.

She stared at him, confused. Detectors only *ever* gave off warnings when something supernatural was around. While some hunters had theirs specialized to detect other forms of prey, Nyx's was tuned to seek zombies and Inbetweeners made from dark necromantic magic—the bad things for which a Necromancer was responsible.

When a Necromancer performed a raise, it was never perfect. They might be able to call a soul back from the Other Side, but they could never fully restore a body and mind as it once was. They simply placed the soul back into a rotting body—they restored *life*, nothing more.

This boy wasn't dead. He wasn't decaying or falling apart or something intangible. He wasn't throwing shit at her. He wasn't screaming so high and loud her ears bled. He wasn't trying to eat her or project himself into her body. No orange eyes, no fangs, no tail, no demon's wings.

A perfectly normal-looking human. Tall, dark-auburn hair, a pair of heavy eyebrows set disapprovingly above two peculiar eyes—rich, lapis lazuli blue, spotted with gold. He wore a long black trench coat, its hem dusty and starting to fray. The legs of his jeans were covered with straps and holsters sporting blades.

"What are you doing here?" he said, pulling back to look at her.

"What are *you* doing here?" she shot back. Neither of them moved. His jaw twitched as if resisting the urge to smile. "What's your name?"

There was a long pause. "Erebus," he answered suspiciously.

"Are you seri—that's actually your name?"

"No, I just said so for the fun of it."

The ruby on her chest grew warm but didn't light. A whisper then. A name.

Eros.

Nyx gripped her gun tighter. The boy looked off to one side, having heard the same thing. He looked clouded, confused.

"What?" Nyx asked. "Eros? Is that your name?"

He looked at her darkly. "No, I told you, it's *Erebus.*" He tightened the grip on his gun. "Who are *you*?"

"Nyx," she replied.

"Well, Nyx, you need to leave."

"*Excuse me?*"

He shoved the gun back in its holster. "Can you please vacate the premises immediately. Like, right now," he said politely, looking straight at her. He turned back into the cold room he'd come from.

Past him, Nyx could see a large metal barrel with several other guns sitting on it—the *clicks* were magazines being loaded. He finished the last few. A duffel bag on the floor next to the barrel was filled with gleaming, silver items.

"What are you doing down here?" She lowered her gun.

The boy continued as if she hadn't said a word. "You need to be out of here by nine," he said bluntly. "It's currently eight fifty. I suggest you run."

Annoyance bubbled up inside of her. Nyx pointed her gun at him again. "I'm not going *anywhere*, and if you're not going to move your ass then you might as well tell me who you are, what you are, and what the *hell* you're doing here."

He checked his watch again. "Look, it's now eight fifty-one—"

"So I guess that only leaves you nine minutes."

He looked at her. "No."

Her pendant flared again, although he didn't notice. Nyx leveled the pistol at his head.

"*Look*," he said, stepping toward her, "I don't need some trigger-happy kid running around here while I'm trying to do my job."

"*Your* job? I was called—"

"I don't know what kind of costume party or whatever it is that you're dressed up for," he continued, "but I assure you, it's *not* here, so you might as well leave."

"What? I—"

"Please, just leave." He sighed.

"You know what?" she snarled. "Make me."

In a flash, his hand was at her neck. He tightened his grip, looking for a pressure point. Nyx's pulse raged. Time slowed.

Erebus's eyes widened suddenly, glimpsing the orange of hers. Something only found in her kind.

Necromancer.

He sighed again. "Ah fuck."

He loosened his grip enough that she was able to flip the gun over in her hand and bring it down on his skull. Erebus dropped to the ground.

"*Asshole*," she said, hooking her hands under his arms and dragging him back into the freezer. The small box of a room could hardly hold him.

He needed to be out of the way when her family finally found what they were looking for. And Nyx didn't need her mother killing some random boy because her detector lit up.

She eyed a duffel bag atop one of the barrels. Inside, there were boxes of bullets, extra guns, knives, and a dirty cloth. She tipped the contents out onto the barrel's top, scrunched the bag in her hands, and lifted Erebus's head, sliding the bag beneath it as a pillow.

She stood again, wiping her hands on her jeans. A quiet alarm sounded. She scanned the room, spotting a watch and a piece of paper atop the barrel.

The watch read 8:59. The paper, worn, fold lines brown and dirty, read:

> - *Killed five girls.*
> - *Girls hung up out front.*
> - *Sanderson's Amusement Park.*
> - *Strong enough to power entire park.*
> - *CANNOT be killed by a bullet. Can only be killed by a blade made of Starbone Metal.*
> - *Every night at 9:00 p.m. enters meat room, where girls are disfigured before being killed.*
> - *Extremely dangerous.*
> - *BEWARE the trickster with emerald eyes.*
> *Be careful, Erebus ~ M*

In a few seconds, Nyx became sure of three things:

1. Erebus obviously was a hunter, sent here by someone to slay the creature at the park.

2. Starbone Metal was another name for Reaper Iron. Which meant Erebus was able to handle the iron. Which meant . . . what exactly? If he was a Reaper her detector would have let her know, as it would have had he been a Necromancer. A human would have burned up the second they *touched* a weapon made of Reaper Iron.

3. If the being that powered the park came to this room every night at nine, then . . .

Nyx quickly turned and shut the sliding door. That's when she heard them—footsteps, echoing above. Moving toward the stairs.

Can only be killed by a blade made of Starbone Metal.

"Get my mother here *now*," Nyx whispered to the detector, which was finally flashing green.

The sliding door didn't close all the way, so she put her eye up to the crack and peered into the other room, waiting for the creature to enter her view. The lighting made it impossible to make out anything but a silhouette: tall, wide, hunched over. It trudged toward the large butcher's table in the center of the room, dragging someone behind it by the ankles.

There was a bang as the creature hauled the limp body up and onto the metal table—a lifeless, hollow sound. Then it sauntered over to the power box embedded in one of the walls. With a bang of its fist, the lights flickered and grew bright.

Nyx finally saw what they were up against.

The creature wore a full-body costume: ruffled neckline and cuffs, pom-poms down the front—white with multicolored polka dots—big white clown boots and white gloves, and a dirty, frizzy yellow wig. Its face was painted a shocking white, with small pink circles smudged on both cheeks and small lines drawn above and below both eyes. Its mouth, completely black and filled with razor-sharp teeth, stretched into a wide grin.

Like the ones he cut.

All this white—the suit, the boots, the gloves, its chin—was stained red.

The person on the table—a young girl—stirred as the clown turned toward her. Duct tape covered her mouth and bound her wrists, knees, feet. She wore a white blouse with an emblem on the left breast and a blue pleated skirt. A school uniform.

Nyx shoved the pistol into its holster and drew her scythe. The blade was made from pure Reaper Iron—the only kind of metal that could harm Inbetweeners.

The girl was fully awake now, panicking, trying to scream through the tape over her mouth while tears ran down her face. Overhead, Nyx heard faint footsteps—her parents were in the storeroom above, being careful not to make too much noise. The emerald bracelet around her mother's wrist would lead her down here.

While the Inbetweener sorted through a tray of utensils next to the butcher's table, Nyx silently opened the iron door and squeezed out, sliding it closed behind her. She moved carefully around the room, keeping to the shadows, making sure the creature's back was to her at all times.

It didn't see her.

But the girl did.

She screamed louder, staring at Nyx with teary, urgent eyes. Nyx held a finger to her lips; the girl nodded and quieted. The clown faced her again, a long scalpel in his hand, bronze eyes full of sadism.

Nyx slipped behind one of the cement columns. Out of the corner of her eye, she saw her mother enter with long, twin daggers in hand. The blades were slim, wavy, made of Reaper Iron and with handles of polished rosewood. Her father was next, and he brandished an enormous sword. The blade was made of a rare type of Starbone Metal—thick and black, shaped like a ridged bovine horn. Nyx's mother came around behind her while her father rounded the opposite side of the room, moving toward the table.

From where she stood, Nyx could see the clown's partial transparency—definitely unnatural. It glared down at the girl, showing its full, sharp-toothed, black-lipped smile.

With a single curt nod to Nyx and her mother, Nyx's father moved toward the center of the room. The girl kept her eyes trained on Nyx's father as he rose up behind the Inbetweener.

Her father lifted his blade as the clown swung around with a frightful hiss, then brought the sword down swiftly, attempting to bury its tip in the creature's chest. But the clown swung wildly, knocking the sword off course. A hollow scream resounded as the blade slashed the Inbetweener's hip. The clown lunged forward, snarling, knocking Nyx's father to the ground.

"Help the girl!" her father yelled through the commotion.

Nyx ran to the table and ripped the tape from the girl's face. She sobbed loudly, and Nyx began unwinding the tape around her wrists while her mother worked on the girl's ankles. Nyx noticed then she was shaking but no longer crying. The sound had changed. The girl was shaking with laughter.

Hysterical laughter.

Nyx's mother met her gaze, both of them confused.

The girl continued to laugh, her entire face reddening. Nyx thought she might pass out. She gripped the sides of the metal table—it screeched as it bent in her hands.

"Nyx," her mother said, slowly backing away from the table.

The girl opened her eyes. They were brilliant emerald.

"Fools," she gasped.

BEWARE the trickster with emerald eyes.

It was a trap.

The girl stopped laughing, the corners of her mouth pulling down as if being yanked by invisible hooks. Nyx backed away as the girl swung her legs over the table. Her skin bubbled and boiled, turning from fair to lava—orange and yellow and red, radiating heat. Her red hair singed away, as did her nose and ears. She grinned at them, showing off her full set of long, white, razor-sharp teeth.

"You Laheys are a real embarrassment to your kind. You know that, don't you?" The girl took long strides toward them, pretending to inspect nails she no longer had. "You will no longer slaughter your own kind; you will no longer stand in our way." Her voice seemed to echo within itself. "We will wash over the earth like a plague until there is nothing left of the Reapers you think yourselves to be. You have betrayed your kind. We are going to *rise* with *the great Young God* as our leader."

Before Nyx could absorb her words, the creature closed the space between them. There was a loud crack, and her mother was thrown across the room, smashing into the cement wall there.

The creature spun and faced Nyx, but Nyx moved just as fast, slashing down with her scythe and carving a deep groove in the girl's chest from which thick liquid, black and bubbling, poured. Steam rose from the wound.

Reaper Iron working its magic.

The girl growled at her, eyes fierce. She lunged, slapping the scythe from Nyx's hands and sending it skittering across the floor. Nyx had two seconds to grab the knives strapped to her legs and brace herself before the girl came crashing down on top of her.

Burns, cuts, bruised heads, bites, knees to the stomach, and elbows to the face. In the chaos of it all, the girl froze. When Nyx was able to focus her eyes again, she noticed one of her daggers buried up to the hilt in the side of the girl's neck. Nyx tore it out again and black, gooey blood burst from the puncture. Nyx kicked her away but the girl's blood was already running—and burning—down Nyx's arm.

The girl lay on the ground, squirming, hands to her neck. Nyx could see the wound healing. She needed to completely take her out and focus on the Inbetweener—what they had *actually* come for. She needed to take away the source of her—of anyone's—power: the brain.

As Nyx scanned the room for her mother, the girl began to rise. Nyx's mother was still limp and unconscious on the floor—she wasn't going to be much help. Then Nyx saw it: the staff of her scythe, on the floor some thirty feet away. But the girl was already sprinting toward it.

Scrambling to her knees, Nyx darted for it too. The girl made a sound somewhere between a wail and a laugh, her claws scraping the rubber soles of Nyx's boots as she skidded, catching the scythe in her hands. Nyx turned and slashed at the air.

A lifeless head, spurting black blood, landed at her knees. She looked up just in time to see the girl's headless body slump over in front of her. Blood pooled around Nyx, burning into her jeans.

Nyx blinked and the girl's remains burst into ash.

Getting to her feet again, Nyx's attention quickly turned to the snarling to her left. Her father was standing over the Inbetweener as it lay on the ground.

"Who sent you here?" Her father spat, panting heavily, blood dripping from his brow.

The creature tried to wriggle free on broken legs and arms, hissing and growling like a feral animal.

Her father brought down his blade and buried it deep in the Inbetweener's chest with a crack. All that remained after he pulled the sword from its body was a pile of wet, decaying leaves and party streamers.

They stood for a moment, finally able to catch their breath. As the pile of streamers dissipated, Nyx's mother stirred in the background. They turned to see her slowly hoisting herself up. Most of her black hair had escaped its tie and fell around her in a voluptuous cloud. A nasty bruise was forming on the side of her head, and her eye had begun to blacken.

"Geez, honey," she said to Nyx's father as he rushed over to her. She held her head and scanned the room, confused. "Did you take a wrong turn or something while I was asleep? How far off are we?"

Nyx's father looked at her. She shrugged.

"From where, Mae?"

Mae looked at him incredulously. "Vegas, Christophe. Vegas. Did you—are we lost? Nyx, are we *lost* right now?"

She had obviously taken a bigger hit than they thought. Nyx tried not to laugh.

"Okay, honey," Chris said, taking her arm. "Let's just get you in the car and take you home, hey?" As they walked to the stairs, he leaned over to Nyx and whispered, "I'll take your mother to the car. Make sure we didn't leave anything behind."

Nyx nodded and resheathed her scythe. As soon as her parents were out of earshot, she bolted for the heavy door to the freezer and slid it open.

Erebus was gone, as was his weaponry.

"Shit," she breathed, walking to the center of the room, searching for any clue as to how he could have just disappeared. She checked every shelf, knocked the walls with her fist.

It was all cement walls—no secret doors.

Nyx turned to leave, annoyed. Crossing through what little light there was, she paused, catching sight of something shining on the floor. She knelt down and reached for whatever was just under the nearby shelving. When she pulled out her hand again, she held a shiny, silver locket. She found the seam of the pendant and pressed her nail into it, trying to see if it would open. It didn't budge.

Nyx sighed and stood up again. She looked around the room once more, then slid the pendant into her pocket as she made her way out.

She'd had a sister once. A twin. They'd looked nothing alike. Nyx was bold and dark—dark hair, orange eyes, freckles, and skin like soil. Nyx was like their mother, completely. Tellus, on the other hand, had their mother's curls, but had inherited nothing else. Tellus was all sun matter. Dusty-red hair, green eyes, splays of dark freckles along cheeks of gold.

Tellus was the day and Nyx was the night—so completely opposite that strangers found it hard to believe they were even sisters. But despite their differences, they were utterly inseparable.

And now, all Nyx had left of her were scattered dreams in which Tellus would come and visit.

Tellus had died a few days after their fourteenth birthday. After months of pain in her abdomen, doctors had found a tumor the size of a tomato tangled in her bowels. In less than six weeks she had died in her sleep.

If anything, that experience—the worst days of Nyx's entire life—had proved one thing: that despite everything in their seemingly indestructible nature, creatures like the Laheys weren't bulletproof.

Now, six years later, Nyx's mind had created its own coping mechanisms. The dreams were always in a dreamscape Nyx wasn't sure actually existed in the real world. Tellus and Nyx would sit under the same oak tree overlooking the same misty lake. Tellus was always different, though. Not once did she ever look the same. Sometimes she showed up looking more zombie than Necromancer, with rotting flesh that exposed her teeth through her cheek. Her hair would be wild and full, filled with twigs and dirt. Her dress would be tattered and yellowed. She wouldn't speak much.

She might look at the tattoo on Nyx's thigh and recite the verse over and over again: *Fire, metal, blood, and bone. Protect thy haven from creatures that roam.* The Reaper's Oath. Other times, she might catch birds flying past and break their wings, or set the tails of squirrels on fire. Sometimes she appeared in an immaculate white gown, skin glowing, a crown of flowers braided into her curls.

They would talk for hours. About school, about family. She'd ask about Nyx's training, about their younger cousins Bethany and Persephone.

Tonight was like that. After the hunt, Nyx sat at the base of a tree, braiding long blades of grass in her hands. Behind her, she heard the hush of feet on grass and noticed the familiar scent of Tellus's homemade rose soap.

Tellus came and sat next to her, kissing the top of her hair. Nyx smiled at her, feeling quite proud of herself for being able to re-create her sister's image so perfectly in her mind.

Tellus didn't speak at all. Not until the very end, before Nyx woke. "I'm so proud of you, Nyx."

"What for?" Nyx asked.

"I'm really proud of Erebus too. You should be so proud of yourselves."

"Who?" And then Nyx remembered the locket and the boy from the park. "What are you talking about? I don't know him."

"Not yet." Tellus smiled. "But you will, soon."

Nyx's eyes snapped open then and she became instantly aware of a heavy, warm weight across her legs, down at the end of the bed.

"Bjørn," she mumbled. "Get off, my legs are asleep." She tried wriggling her toes to annoy the hound.

Bjørn had been a third birthday present from their aunt Maura. She'd crafted him from pine needles, stones, opal, and spring water. Over the last seventeen years he'd grown into a Goliath of a wolf. Fur the color of pitch and storms, eyes like Saharan sand.

"*Bjørn*," she repeated, nudging him again.

Nyx noticed it then—he was growling. She sat upright and focused on his large figure in the darkness. Bjørn was staring out the glass wall of her bedroom and into the backyard. Lips peeled back, hair on end.

"*Bjørn*," she whispered, trying to calm him. "*Shh, shh, shh.*" She looked out the window then and saw it—a giant, jet-black raven sitting atop the veranda only a few feet away. Its face was disfigured by a large scar across a single milky eye and a mutilated beak. Its other eye was the bloodiest red she'd ever seen.

And it just sat there.

Staring at them through the window.

At Nyx.

CHAPTER TWO

ONEIROPHOBIA – FEAR OF DREAMS

Chasity Lahey glared at her cousin from the end of the table. Curly blond hair stuck out around her face. Purple seer eyes nestled deep underneath dark brows. She had a blanket around her shoulders, hands wrapped around a mug of brewing herbs, and was surrounded by lit candles. And she was staring at Nyx.

Behind her, in the kitchen, Nyx's mother and her sisters were crowded around the sink. They wore their long, winter pajamas; curls all out and filling the space between each other. To the left of them, the sun had just begun to rise over the treetops, streaming through the kitchen window. Normally, the entire house would still be sound asleep—her mother's sisters and their seven daughters, Nyx's cousins.

But today was not a normal day.

At 3:37 that morning, Chasity had woken the entire household screaming bloody murder.

Nyx wasn't even fully awake when she swung out of bed and sprinted down the hall, Bjørn hot on her heels. Standing in the open doorway was Eris, the eldest cousin. She looked over her shoulder at Nyx, tired eyes so wide they were frightening.

Inside, Chasity continued to scream, while the voices of Nyx's mother, father, and aunts all spoke over her, trying to calm her down.

Nyx's father and Chasity's mother, Maura, held Chasity by her hands and feet as she lashed about on the bed, eyes glazed.

"Holy shit," Eris yelled, stepping away from the door. "Do we need to call, like, an exorcist or something?"

Maura looked up, panting from the struggle. "This is no time for jokes, Eris Lahey!"

"Please, Eris." Nyx's father looked up from his task. "Can you go and get some hot water and a towel? She's all clammy."

Eris nodded and, with one last look at Chasity writhing on the bed, bolted down the staircase. At age three, Chasity had been confirmed as having the seer strain, which her mother had also inherited. For the next fifteen years, Chasity could be found bent over a potions book, wiping a blown concoction from her clothes, or accidentally setting the drapes on fire as she trained.

But what no one had mentioned in the job description were the night terrors.

They'd started after her twelfth birthday, happening every six months or so. They shook Chasity to her very core. She wouldn't speak, wouldn't eat, wouldn't venture from her bed for days.

But they'd never been *this* bad.

Chasity's screaming was torturous, desperate. Around her, the bedroom was in complete disarray: pillows and quilts thrown to the floor, a lamp smashed, fingernail scratches in the bedside table.

Chasity's younger sister, Hunting, with whom she shared a room, clung to Nyx's mother.

Eris rushed back in with a bucket of steaming water and a terry-cloth towel. Christophe took the damp towel and put it to Chasity's face. "Chazz," he said, trying to get her attention. "Chazz, can you hear me?"

Chasity continued to scream so loudly Nyx felt the pressure between her ears begin to build.

"Chazz! Come on, darl, just listen to me—"

Chasity stopped almost instantly, staring at Nyx's father with wide eyes. Without so much as a blink, she snapped her head in Nyx's direction and, in two unnaturally quick movements, shoved Chris aside and was on her knees, perched at the end of the mattress, inches from Nyx's face.

"I know you have it, Nyx. Where is it?" she demanded.

In her peripheral vision, Nyx saw her mother looking at her.

"Chazz," Maura said, slowly approaching her daughter, "what are you talking about? Where's what?"

Chasity didn't even flinch at the sound of her mother's voice. "I know you know, Nyx." She was almost growling.

"What are you talking about?" Maura repeated.

"A silver went missing." She spoke as if to no one in particular. *A silver went missing.*

"A silver went missing, and Nyx knows where it is."

Nyx's mother cast a look in her direction. Chasity was still watching her, waiting for her to say something. Chasity grabbed Nyx's forearms, yanking her closer.

"No, Nyx, no!" she screamed.

Eris tried to lift Chasity's fingers away even as her nails broke Nyx's skin. Nyx didn't know what to do. She couldn't move.

"No! No-no-no-no, Eris, no!"

"Chasity, let her go!" Maura yelled.

"No!" Chasity's eyes glazed over as the others finally managed to pry her away. She slashed at Eris's face before she was pushed back onto the bed.

"Chazz, you need to calm down! Let the terror pass!" Maura screamed.

"He already knows where we are! The ravens will come looking for the silver! He's going to follow them, Nyx!" Her eyes were glowing.

A silver has gone missing.

"You need to leave the room, Nyx." Her father spoke in a low voice.

Nyx stared at Chasity.

"He's going to get you!" she yelled.

"Get *out*, Nyx!" Eris roared, snatching her bleeding arms and dragging her from the room. She shoved Nyx into the hallway and pulled the door shut behind them.

"What is she talking about?" Eris hissed.

Nyx wiped at the blood on her arms with the end of her shirt. "I don't know—"

"Did you steal something?"

"*What?*"

"Like, I don't know—a silver cup, or a fork, or a fucking *earring*? I don't know, what the fuck is '*a silver*'?" Eris hissed.

"How am I supposed to—" And then it clicked. The silver locket from four nights ago.

Eris stared, expectantly. "What?" she said.

"I've no idea," Nyx said, shaking her head.

"So, you don't know what she's talking about?"

Don't you lie.

"No."

"Nyx, are you ready for school?" Mae leaned away from her sisters to look at her daughter.

Nyx tore her eyes from Chasity. "Yeah, I just need to go get my bag," she replied, standing. Approaching the staircase, she felt her mother at her back.

"Hey," she said quietly, touching Nyx's shoulder. Mae stared at her bandaged forearms. "You okay?"

Nyx took a deep breath. Over her mother's shoulder, Chasity was still staring. "Yeah. I'm fine. How's Chazz doing?"

Mae sighed and pushed some of her hair behind her ear. It bounced right back out. "She's going to stay home today. She won't even talk to Maura about what she saw. It must have been pretty bad."

"So she's not saying anything?"

Mae shook her head. "Nothing—she's pretty shaken up about it. Do you know what she was talking about?"

Nyx glanced at Chasity and shook her head. "Uh, no, I'm not sure."

Mae nodded softly. "Okay, honey."

"Where's Dad gone?"

She yawned. "He's in Chasity and Hunting's room, trying to put Hunting's bed back together."

"Back together?" A voice from behind. Alice. She sauntered downstairs, red curls pulled back in braids.

"Chasity kicked it into the wall and popped out some of the bolts," Mae said.

Alice made a face. "Geez, okay."

"You're going to keep that on today, aren't you?" She pointed to Alice's black, hooded coat.

Alice rolled her eyes. "Yes, Aunty Mae."

"Good. We don't need any more calls from the academy about fires or scorched backpacks."

Alice had inherited the Ignis strain, meaning she had the power to control and create fire. Her mother, Harring, had discovered Alice at three days old, lying in a smoldering crib surrounded by burning curtains, having triggered the smoke alarms.

Alice had been completely unscathed.

And so, Maura crafted a fireproof hood that contained Alice's powers, and which she wore every day.

"I know," Alice replied. "It's not going to happen again."

"It better not, kiddo."

Behind Alice, Eris slowly trudged down the stairs wearing her trusty leather jacket. "Everybody ready?" she asked. Alice nodded while Nyx ran upstairs to get her bags.

"Chasity's staying home today, but the others are already out front. Hurry, don't miss the bus," Mae said, kissing each of their heads as they walked past.

Alice looked down at the black marble tiles and whispered, "What do you reckon she saw?"

They passed by the kitchen. Nyx could feel Chasity's eyes boring into her back.

Eris gave her a sideways glance. "I'm not sure."

Outside, Hunting and Alice's twin little sisters, Bethany and Persephone, were already waiting. Hair back in buns and braids, backpacks strapped on tight. All of them looked tired.

"Where's Lilith?" Alice asked, looking around as the sound of pounding boots on gravel came from behind them. They turned to see Lilith running toward them.

"What were you doing?" Eris asked.

"Peter wants to get Chazz some flowers but he couldn't find the key for the greenhouse. I went to unlock it for him."

"Oh, that's sweet of him." Alice smiled.

Lilith Lahey had inherited one of the rarest strains known to their kind. Being an Artifex meant that she was able to create life and objects from anything. She could create weaponry or food or absolutely whatever she wished for with a mere thought. Their house had been filled with invisible people—characters from books, people from portraits—ever since Lilith mastered her gift. While the rest of the family couldn't see them, they were definitely there—accidentally bumping into them in the halls, fighting over the showers, trudging mud upstairs.

Lilith's best friend was Peter, whom she'd taken from J. M. Barrie's book. Considering how many years he'd been with them, he was family, even if only Lilith could see him.

"Anyone know what the deal with Chasity is?" Lilith asked, her wide, pale eyes contrasting with her dark skin.

Eris didn't answer. Storm clouds brewed overhead.

Alice, being her cheery self, said, "No, but I'm sure she'll be better by this afternoon. Poor thing, I think this one really shook her up."

"Yeah," Lilith agreed, glancing at the cobblestone below. "I hope she'll be okay."

"Me too," Nyx said, watching the three younger girls play tag in front of them. Their town, Misten, was generally as quiet as the road ahead. The Laheys lived in an old Victorian estate called Ebony Manor because of the black wood that made up its exterior. It was set away from the center of town, where the academy stood.

Alice pulled her hood over her head as rain began to drizzle. They stopped at the corner. It wasn't long before the headlights of the Reaper Academy bus came into view.

The normal pit of dread settled in Nyx's stomach at the sight of it. The bus slowed and one of the girls in the back flipped them off through the window. Typical Reaper-Necromancer interaction.

Alice whispered, "I was hoping the bus had crashed into a tree somewhere and everyone had been burned alive."

"Same," they answered in unison.

Alice's fingers twitched toward her hood. "That can still be arranged," she said, hopefully.

Eris gave her a sharp look. "Not today, Alice."

CHAPTER THREE

PHASMOPHOBIA — FEAR OF GHOSTS

I become insane . . .

"Erebus."

. . . with long intervals of . . .

"Are you even listening to what I'm saying?"

. . . horrible sanity.

Sigh. "You're not."

Erebus couldn't remember how many times over the last couple of hundred years he'd heard Damien Tate recite his plans to redesign and renovate their warehouse home. To be completely honest, Erebus wasn't actually interested in changing anything.

Approximately four stories high and the length of half a football field, it was a monster of exposed metal, gridded floors, and tall industrial windows. Over the years, all five of its inhabitants had gathered every utensil, appliance, and piece of furniture on their own. Nothing worked well together, and Erebus loved it.

Damien, not so much.

Erebus sat at their dining table, fiddling with spare bolts that one of the others had left lying around. Damien, cross-legged on the table, looked expectantly at his friend.

"I'm sorry." Erebus slid the bolts away. "I'm listening. Tell me again?"

Damien sighed dramatically. "*Well*, do I get to start over?"

Erebus winced. "*Fine.*" It had been four days since his encounter with the Necromancer. Erebus had shown up at the warehouse with a swollen face—his vision foggy and his legs falling beneath him—as he stumbled through the doors with his bags. Damien had been the first one there, running down the stairs to the doorway to pick Erebus up off the ground.

Following Damien was Max, their caretaker and owner of the building, in his robe and fluffy slippers, with the silhouettes of the other two boys running close behind. Erebus passed out again, and continued to slip in and out of consciousness for the next three days.

Damien turned, pointing to the metal grid ceiling above and the second story beyond that. "And then, in the kitchen, I was thinking that we could—" He dropped his hands, unimpressed. "Erebus! Seriously?"

Erebus straightened. "*What?*"

"I can tell when you aren't listening. I'm asking you to just pay attention for, like, two minutes."

Erebus was about to speak when Max shouted from the upstairs kitchen. "Erebus! Have you gone to see the Legion Council yet?"

Erebus closed his eyes. "Not yet!" he yelled back.

"And when do you plan on doing that, exactly?" The older man stood at the top of the stair, staring disapprovingly over his wire-framed glasses.

Erebus grabbed the bolts and twirled them between his fingers. "I'll go this afternoon."

"Good. Taeto isn't very happy about what happened," Max repeated for what felt like the hundredth time. Even Damien rolled his eyes.

"I know, Max. I'm sorry, I had no idea she was going to be there."

"I don't think her being there is what's bothering him."

"He still should have checked that none of the academies had sent out Reapers of their own—*that's* Taeto's fault," Damien said, pointing at Max.

Taeto operated the Dewmort Legions, of which the boys were all members. They were a group of Necromancers and Reapers occasionally sent topside to dispose of rogue creations or their masters.

Max nodded. "Yes, that does fall on Taeto's shoulders. But both he and the Legion Council are bothered by the fact that you, Erebus, having been trained to do this for hundreds of years, were knocked out by some girl who's been training for what—fifteen, sixteen maybe?"

From behind: "What I don't understand is how you managed to not notice her eyes. Necromancer eyes tend to stand out."

Erebus looked up as Mason Sørensen pulled out the chair next to him. "She had her back to the light," Erebus said. "It was dark and I couldn't see her eyes."

"Do you have any idea who she was?" Mason asked.

"She was a Lahey," Max answered. Everybody who was anybody knew about the Laheys. They were the only Necromancer family in history to have changed sides in the war.

"What's her name?" Mason asked.

"Nyx," Erebus answered, and Damien giggled. "What?"

Max pulled out a chair opposite Erebus. "Let's just hope that she forgets all about it and doesn't ask questions."

"Yeah," Damien scoffed. "I'm sure she'll forget all about it by next week."

Erebus grimaced. "Actually . . ."

The others fell silent, eyes snapping to Erebus. The ground shook below; banging echoed throughout the building.

"Actually?" Max pressed.

"She kind of . . . she has my necklace," he said, expelling a breath.

Damien looked at Mason. Mason looked at Max. Max stared at Erebus.

"How exactly did she acquire that?" Max asked.

"I think it fell out of my pocket."

"How do you know she has it?" Damien queried.

"I went back there this morning and it was gone. She's the only one who would have been down there looking for something."

"You don't know for *sure*, though, right?" Mason asked, glancing desperately between Damien and Max.

Max cleaned his glasses. "We cannot afford another incident with her, Erebus. She's already seen you—she knows you're not normal."

"Do you think she'd just give it back?" Damien asked. Erebus made a face. "Realistically, we don't know she has it for sure. I mean, anybody could have been down there in the last few days. People love abandoned places."

"I think it's most realistic that the girl has it," Max cut in.

"I'm not sure what I should do," Erebus said.

Max stood. "Here's what we're going to do. First, we're going to make sure she has it, and if so, where. If it's inside their home, we need to figure out how to get it without anyone knowing." He frowned at each of the boys; they nodded. "Go as soon as you can," Max said. "But, Erebus, I don't want you missing your meeting with Taeto. Just get that over with firs—"

Bang, bang, bang.

"*First.* And don't mention anything about the necklace—you didn't lose it; she didn't find it. Nothing—"

Bang, smash, smash, bang.

Max looked toward the stairs to the basement, annoyed.

Bang, bang, bang, bang!

"Ridley Channing!" he roared, stomping his foot.

The banging stopped and was followed by the *thud* of a sledgehammer being dropped. Seconds later, looking unimpressed, Ridley Channing came up from below, safety goggles askew atop his head, black hair spiked out, a dust mask around his neck.

He narrowed his eyes at the old man. "Can I *help* you, *Maximus?*"

"Would you be so kind as to leave your project for the day and join us for a conversation?" Max gestured to the table.

"It's going to take *all* day?" Ridley made a face.

Max shut his eyes. "No, but I need you to go on an errand with the others."

Ridley sat down on the end of the table. "What did you guys do now?"

"The girl has Erebus's necklace," Mason said, running his fingers along the tabletop.

Ridley's face dropped. "Are you serious?"

"Yes." Erebus clenched his jaw.

"Shit," Ridley breathed, scratching paint from his eyebrow.

For the last forty years, Ridley Channing's sole purpose in life had been demolishing and refurbishing the huge cathedral below the warehouse. None of them were sure of its age—it was all vaulted ceilings, gold trimmings, polished oak pews, and beautiful painted scenes. Some days, like today, Ridley went at it with a sledgehammer, removing rotten walls or benches.

Others, he sat on the floor in complete silence, tracing over long-faded biblical scenes with a paint brush no larger than a toothpick or cutting bits of stained glass to fit into mosaics. Sometimes, he simply played music from a monstrous organ set into the front wall.

"We'll get it back," Ridley said. The others nodded in agreement.

Erebus could feel Max watching him. They *all* knew how important it was to him, Max especially. Hundreds of years ago, when Erebus first appeared in the city, he arrived with nothing but that necklace. No name. No recollection of who he was, where he'd come from. Even *what* he was. He had simply appeared on the streets of Dewmort, unconscious. A few volunteers from one of the town's hospitals had collected him and left him in a room until he woke.

Max was the first person Erebus Salem laid eyes on. Back then, Max even looked younger—though that should have been impossible considering he hadn't aged. Stethoscope around his neck, white coat in place, glasses new and shiny.

"Ah," Max had said, placing a medical chart at the end of the bed as Erebus sat up. "I was wondering when you were going to wake." He extended a hand to Erebus. He had introduced himself as Dr. Maximus Brais, and asked Erebus if he remembered his name.

Erebus shook the man's hand silently. His brain reeled, trying to find some possible reply. Names ran through his head as he tried to find something that sparked some kind of remembrance.

Erebus struggled for words, his heart falling as he realized he couldn't find a name.

Max nodded. "That's not unusual, it may take a day or two for it to come back to you."

"What's going on here? I literally have no idea where I even am

right now. Like, what is this building or . . ." Erebus trailed off, touching the stethoscope around Max's neck.

Max offered a concerned look. "This is a stethoscope, my boy. And this"—Max gestured to the room—"is one of Dewmort's hospitals. We help people like you with the transition."

Erebus's face was hot; he remembered nothing. He rose from the bed and looked out the window. Before him was a great city of old buildings and stone streets.

Dewmort, Max revealed, was what some people called the Second City, or the City of Souls. When a supernatural person passed to the other side, normally their soul dissipated—wafting up into the clouds and disappearing. But sometimes, when a person's death was particularly brutal or unjust, they ended up in Dewmort. A city of unfinished business.

White noise rang in Erebus's ears. "What? What are you trying to—"

"Congratulations, my boy." Max interrupted him. "And I'm sorry. You're dead."

CHAPTER FOUR

DIDASKALEINOPHOBIA — FEAR OF SCHOOL
OR GOING TO SCHOOL

"Dead bangers!" someone yelled from the academy gardens.

The Misten Reaper Academy was home to over three thousand boarding students—three *thousand* Reapers. All Ivy League– worthy, polished, steel eyed, and sharp.

The academy itself had stood since before Misten was even a town. In its early days, it was located within a great forest. It rose with huge columns of stone and iron, sparkling spires, and great lead-lined windows. Around them, humans hurried down the footpath, completely oblivious to the monster of a building beside them—and the monsters filing off the bus.

Outside, the academy had defined boundaries. As huge as it was, it was nestled deep within a large flat piece of estate land. Manicured shrubs and trees and pearl-lined paths paved the green block, and gardens and butterfly houses dotted the corners, while stone training arenas circled the academy walls.

Inside, however, the academy was endless—a constant maze of ever-changing halls and staircases. The elder Reapers claimed the building was alive, and that if you mistreated it, its magic halls would make you disappear forever.

Necromancy was so profoundly banned inside school grounds that the plaque outside the gates practically screamed.

WARNING

THIS SCHOOL DOES NOT TOLERATE THE FOLLOWING:

1. Any use of necromantic magic once within the gates.
2. Raising of the dead.
3. Speak of raising of the dead.
4. Threats of raising the dead.
5. Rumors of raising the dead.
6. The use of any necromantic gifts.
7. Chewing gum.

Not only was the practice of necromancy itself banned, but any second gifts that a Necromancer inherited were banned as well. Reapers, unlike Necromancers, didn't inherit gifts—they were Reapers and that was all there was to it.

The Laheys had been homeschooled on all things necromantic due to their family's Reaper transition. By the age of two, the Lahey children were able to control their powers, whereas before they would accidentally raise dead birds and mice when upset. Once they became aware of their abilities, the girls were asked to search through the gardens of Ebony Manor to find something dead.

Alice had found a beetle, Lilith a small bird, Chasity a snake, Eris a baby raccoon, and Nyx a butterfly. The creatures were each placed in their own separate jars and set on shelves in their bedrooms where, once a fortnight, the girls would raise them and release the buildup of their necromantic power. After a day or two, their mothers would make them siphon their excess life, and the creatures would be corpses again until their next resurrection.

At home, they were just Necromancers who took Reaper classes. At the academy, they were second-best Reapers—*things* that needed to be watched. Even as they walked the halls, there were always eyes on them. Someone was always stationed nearby. They were only guests here, and they knew it.

And so, out of spite, they always found ways to get sent to the headmaster's office. Eris might secretly resurrect a hive of bees, sending them flying through the halls. Alice might singe someone's hands or hair. Lilith's invisible friends would sometimes follow her to school—Fred and George Weasley tripping people in the halls, Gandalf refusing to let people pass through classroom doors.

"You know," Lilith whispered during first period, using her brush to paint the long black feathers of a bird on canvas, "I really don't know what the point of this class is."

Beside her, Alice nodded, watching the other students paint in silence. "I honestly don't understand how I'm meant to give a shit about this class when I have a battle exam next."

Nyx watched Lilith painting, staring at the flicks of Lilith's brush as she shaped the wing of a bird.

"You okay?" Lilith asked.

Nyx looked at the brush in her hand then at her own blank canvas. She faked a smile. "Uh, yeah. Why?"

"*Shhh*," someone hissed.

Lilith frowned. "Oh, just that you haven't done anything . . . I thought you liked this class?"

"Sorry." Nyx blinked. "What'd you say?"

"Are you sure you're okay?" Lilith asked again. "You're not still thinking about what happened this morning, are you? You know it's just one of her dreams."

Lilith painted a white oval, mixing with the black of the bird to create a light gray.

"What? Of course I'm not," Nyx lied, still fixated on Lilith's painting.

"Okay, good," Lilith said. "I don't want you to think it's your fault or anything." She painted a thin white line that stretched to the bird's mouth.

Nyx's face felt hot. "What are you painting?"

Lilith looked at her. "Oh, lately I've been seeing this big, black raven around the house. Poor thing looks like it's lost an eye. And last night I had a dream about a raven—I'm not sure if it's the same one—flying off with a locket like this." She pointed to the gray oval.

A silver has gone missing. "So, you've seen that bird?"

Lilith nodded. "Yeah, I don't know if it's sick or has a broken foot or something, it's always hanging around. You've seen it too?" she asked, highlighting the edges of the locket with bright white.

Nyx swallowed. "Um, yeah. A few times. It likes to sit outside my window at night."

Madame Lorel, seated at the front of the class, sighed and set down her newspaper. "*Who* is talking?" she asked.

A girl behind them cleared her throat. "It's Nyx and Lilith Lahey, madame."

Madame then picked up her paper again. "That's all right, girls, just keep it quiet."

Lilith smiled to herself and continued painting. The girl huffed in annoyance.

"Why does she always do that?" said a voice from the row behind them. "If it had been any of us, we would have been screamed at in front of the entire class. I'm *so* over her favoring them."

Alice scoffed, not turning from her canvas. "It's *favoring*, Alicia. Jesus. Are you sure you're even smart enough for this class?"

Alicia continued, "One day, they're going to find out about this bullshit and hopefully kick your ugly ass out of school."

Another girl piped up. "Honestly, I don't know why they're even letting these things come to the academy."

"Yeah, like, do you guys even know the Reaper's Oath?" Alicia laughed.

Nyx swung around and faced them. All three were pale, with light, strawberry-blond hair. Alicia sat in the middle, smiling. "You know *what*—"

Lilith grabbed the corner of Nyx's jacket and swung her back around. "Calm down," she whispered through gritted teeth.

"*You* know *what?*" Alicia laughed. "You're lucky someone was ever stupid enough to give your family a chance here. They should have just killed you like the rest. Save our school looking like a joke."

"Don't listen to her," Lilith whispered.

"No," Alicia said. "You should know. No one wants you here. This is what everyone thinks of you. Your family is vile."

A fizzing sound quietly filled the air.

"It's actually embarrassing seeing you come here every day. Embarrassing for you. Embarrassing for our school. And while you're at it . . . what is that noise? Jessie, can you hear that?"

The noise grew suddenly louder, and a sudden bang reverberated throughout the room. Alicia and her friends screamed, chairs scraping backward as they stood. Nyx swung back around and saw the burst paint cans, aluminum canisters sizzling, boiling paint splattered all over.

Alicia held her face, screaming, as red-hot paint ran down her cheeks. Half of the class ran out of the room.

Nyx looked at Alice. She simply stared at her canvas. Hood off.

—

"For how long?" Eris asked, speaking around a mouthful of peanut butter.

Nyx sighed, leaning forward. "A day."

Alice sat next to her, silent. Lilith watched her from across the lunch table, seated next to Eris. The younger girls sat on the grass nearby, engrossed in their own conversation. They had all been suspended for a day and taken out to the front of the school to wait for Maura to pick them up.

"Dibs not mopping the house tomorrow, then," Eris said, followed by six more dib-nots.

"Lilith, you were the last one." Hunting laughed, pointing.

Lilith shrugged. "I have friends who love cleaning. Those animals from the *Snow White* movie."

Watching Lilith, Nyx couldn't stop thinking about her painting. A raven. A necklace. The silver necklace was in her jeans pocket at that moment—she was paranoid about someone finding it in her backpack.

The wind beat against Nyx's ears. She scoured the school grounds, searching for a boy in a black coat coming to hunt her down and take back what was his. Bird wings beat overhead, louder than they should have been. She looked up.

And saw a flash of black in the branches above.

CHAPTER FIVE

EPISTEMOPHOBIA – FEAR OF KNOWLEDGE

There was a bird at the window again.

It was big, with the same blue-black, oil-slick feathers as the first one. But this bird had pea-green eyes; its face was completely unscathed. It watched from outside as Nyx resurrected the butterfly within the jar.

They'd returned home that afternoon only to have to sit through another lecture from their mothers about the importance of laying low. Later, Nyx found a note, written in Chasity's cursive, slid under her bedroom door:

We need to talk. I'll come see you tonight.

Chasity hadn't spoken a word or even glanced Nyx's way all night. Maura and Nyx's mother both said she seemed fine, but Nyx thought otherwise. Chasity knew something. Whether it was about Erebus, the raven, or the locket, she knew something. And right now, something was better than nothing.

Nyx glanced at the clock on her bedside table: 11:42.

Tap.

The raven outside shuffled closer. He turned his head side to side. Bjørn growled from the end of the mattress.

"What?" she said to the raven.

Tap.

"What do you want?" She waved it away. It briefly leaned backward before tapping once more. Then it placed its beak to the window and scratched the glass, around and around until a clear, lopsided circle appeared in the frost.

Nyx raised an eyebrow. The raven leaned back again to assess its work.

"I hope you don't expect me to understand what that's supposed to be," she said. The raven answered with an irritable squawk. Nyx stared at the squiggles on the glass, which reminded her of Lilith's painting. The necklace and the raven. *Erebus's* necklace.

"What are you, his pet?"

The raven tapped the glass.

Chasity burst through the door, causing both Bjørn and the bird to jump. She closed it behind her. The raven inspected her. Bjørn sat up, tail wagging.

"Hey," she said, facing Nyx. She spotted the bird. "Nyx, what are you doing with that?" Chasity crossed the room and went right up to the window. "Get out of here," she hissed, followed by some seer curses.

The raven flapped clumsily and flew up into the trees. Chasity glared until it was no longer visible.

Nyx gave Chasity a less-than-impressed look. "What was that for?" She peered out the window, trying to find the bird in the trees.

"I don't like them," she said.

"Since when?"

Chasity sat down on the edge of the bed, tucking a strand of curly blond hair behind her ear. "I honestly don't know. The vision I had last night . . . I, uh, I saw a lot of them."

"Ravens?" Nyx asked. Chasity nodded. "Any idea why?"

Chasity shook her head. "Sometimes I'd see a boy—a few boys, different faces each time. One second they would be there, and then the next there were just these big black birds in their place. I kept getting caught in between. Seeing them half man, half bird. Beaks on human faces—I don't know, it just scared me."

Nyx cleared her throat. "So, what did you want to talk about?"

Chasity narrowed her eyes. "You know *exactly* what I want to talk about. I know you have the necklace, Nyx. The vision showed me the amusement park. I saw you pick it up."

Nyx swallowed and looked out the window.

"So, do you have it here?" she asked. Nyx stared at her for a long second before nodding. "Can I see it, please?"

Nyx stood and went to the bookcase. She pulled out a shelf and held it as she retrieved the silver locket, which she'd shoved behind a row of books.

Outside, a raven called, and Chasity glanced out the window. Nyx sat back down on the bed and held out her hand, the silver coiled in her palm.

Her cousin backed away, raising her hands. "Oh, no, I don't want to touch it."

"Why?" Nyx asked.

"Just . . . because." She turned her head, birdlike, inspecting the jewelry. "So, what's he like?"

Nyx looked at her, confused. "Who?"

"Erebus Salem," she said, not taking her eyes from the pendant.

"How do you know him?" Nyx asked.

"I *saw* him, Nyx."

"What, the other night?"

She nodded. "The vision showed me where you met. And then some."

"What do you mean?"

"He's going to come back. He's going to find out you took this—if he hasn't already." Her eyes welled with tears.

"You're freaking me out. Why are you so worried about this? It's just some kid—"

"He's *not* just some *kid*, Nyx. I don't know about you, but I could feel how not normal he was. There's something wrong with him, and I don't want you anywhere near him."

Nyx knew what she was talking about. Her detector had warned her over and over that night—something *was* wrong with him.

"What else did you see?" Nyx asked, whispering, afraid of what she might say.

Chasity sighed. "I heard people yelling, screaming. The sound of fire crackling and smoke so thick I almost choked." Her eyes were wide and blank, like she was reliving her vision. "Then you're standing with Erebus. He's got his hands raised, blood all over him. You're crying and holding a blade at his chest. There's blood all over you too. It's dripping from your chin, the ends of your hair. I can't see where you are; I don't recognize any of it."

Nyx blew out a puff of air. "Anything else?"

"A lot of birds. Ravens, anyway. Trees full of them. And then it's a group of boys, watching me, and there are daggers and staffs and these different symbols that I don't know, but they made me feel physically ill. Then a woman with red eyes, smiling—"

"Not Eris?" Nyx asked.

"No, this one had horns."

"*Horns?*"

Chasity nodded. "I'm always seeing doorways, gold and red ones. An albino snake sitting on the shoulders of a man as he leans into frame. I can't see his face, either, but I know he's, like, waiting for someone."

"And you don't recognize anyone?"

Chasity shook her head. "I have no idea who they are, but I know they're important—or, at least they *will* be, to you."

Nyx nodded, and the two of them fell silent.

"And . . . was that the end of it? The man at the door?" Nyx finally asked.

Chasity stared out the window. "No."

Nyx watched her, waiting.

"The last thing I see is you, alone, on a floor. There's blood and golden dust all around you. Your wrists and ankles are bound, and you're just *sitting* there, crying. People are screaming for you, and I just get this feeling like . . ."

"Like what?" Nyx pressed. Her cousin didn't answer. "*Chasity,*" she hissed.

Chasity looked up, eyes wet, and Nyx knew what she was about to say.

"Nyx," she began. "It felt like you died."

CHAPTER SIX

WICCAPHOBIA — FEAR OF WITCHCRAFT

"What the *fuck* is she!?"

Damien Tate landed in the snow in an explosion of black feathers and thick, black suede. He had all but fallen over as they sat atop the mountains, watching dawn break.

Erebus and Ridley laughed.

"No, guys, I'm serious," Damien said, flustered. "I was literally just *hissed* at. By a *girl*—she hissed at me like a demon. How does a noise like that even come outta someone?"

Ridley said, "She's obviously a Seer, Damien."

Mason nodded. "That's just something they do. Kind of like how lionfish flare their fins when threatened."

Ridley grabbed a palmful of snow. "So, getting back to what you actually went there to find out: Does she have it in the house or did she leave it at the academy?"

Damien shook his head. "It's there. She had it out. They were talking about it, I think."

Erebus looked at him. "They were *talking* about it? That doesn't sound good."

"If they're talking about it, they're more than likely talking about *you*," Mason said.

"Her detector knew, straight up, that there was something wrong. I could tell she was confused," Erebus said.

Damien sat down. "Do you think she'd tell people?"

"No idea. I know nothing about her—I don't know what she's going to do."

Mason stood. "Well, we obviously need to get that necklace back ASAP."

"Where you going?" Ridley asked.

"I'm going to go talk to Max, see what the protocols are about being around Upsiders. See what we can do to get it back." Mason crouched in the snow, jumped, and his coat spun a flurry of fabric and blue-black feathers from which emerged a raven who disappeared into the clouds.

The other three sat, staring quietly across the range as the lilac of dawn broke across the snow-capped tops. Somewhere beyond the forest at their backs, Nyx Lahey slept, Erebus's necklace in her grasp.

CHAPTER SEVEN

AICHMOPHOBIA — FEAR OF SHARP OBJECTS

She was like a ribbon, Eris Lahey decided.

If she were to let loose a ribbon in the wind, its twists and turns would match Nyx completely. From where she sat, above the arena, Eris decided that Nyx was the ribbon and the Reapers she faced were rocks—heavy, slow, and sure to sink.

The boy standing before her, dripping with sweat, was sluggish and heavy footed. The grip on his scythe wavered, arms shaking as he clumsily swung the weighty weapon. Nyx, on the other hand, danced on her toes—jumping and swiping and spinning on the spot. The scythe Nyx held was ugly, small, and jagged, all copper and rusted barbed wire; all the odds were against her, but Nyx always came out on top.

Always.

The Reaper boy was soon on his back with a copper blade to his throat. He shoved Nyx aside as a whistle sounded, and went back to sit on the sidelines. The whistle blew again and another challenger was pushed into the arena with Nyx. This one was tall, gangly, all arms and legs.

"Johnson," the coach said gruffly. The boy nodded and removed his thick glasses and shoes. "Shirt, Johnson," the coach added, and the boy rolled his eyes and lifted his gray shirt over his head.

"Here." One of the Reapers passed Johnson his scythe:

emerald green with sparkling, raw crystals at the staff's tip. Eris thought it looked heavy in his arms. Nevertheless, he heaved it up before him, mirroring Nyx's stance.

"Good luck, Stick," one of the Reapers yelled from the sidelines. "Her left side is weakest."

Eris smirked in the darkness above. *Nyx doesn't have a weak side.*

"Commence," said the coach.

Stick lunged forward, driving the blade of his scythe toward Nyx's side. She spun away and came back around to slash at him, slapping the flat of her blade against his back. He was jolted forward, an angry red mark appearing across the small of his back. A groan echoed through the watching crowd.

Stick spun the staff in his hands, creating a windmill effect, trying to distract Nyx. It didn't work. She cut in, stopping it with the blunt end of her staff while swinging the bladed end at his other side. She nicked his hip, and he jumped away.

Stick hesitated, then thrust his blade forward once more. But Nyx came back quicker, smashing his scythe away. Stick reeled to the right and swung back around unnaturally fast. He brought his staff down onto Nyx's and was suddenly on top of her.

The entire arena went silent as Stick stood over her, using his weight to push down on the two scythes. Nyx struggled, the weight of it making her arms shake.

"Come on," Eris whispered.

The boys in the seats below whistled and cheered.

"*Come on, Nyx,*" Eris muttered to herself.

Stick bit his lip, arms shaking. Eris watched the way her cousin's arms creased in certain places, muscles bulging against the added weight.

Suddenly, the pressure too much, Stick's arms dropped, and

Nyx rolled free. He fell as she got to her feet again, lifting one leg before planting her foot into his back and sending him slamming into the brick.

Everyone gasped. Nyx dropped her scythe, panting, and wiped the sweat from her face. Other Reapers leaped over the barrier into the arena and knelt down around Stick, lifting his head.

"Shit, man, you okay?"

Stick nodded, wincing.

"All righty, then," the coach announced. He looked at Nyx, whose hands were on her hips. "Looks like Lahey's won another day."

She smiled at the coach. No one cheered for her, though. That's what it was always like.

Eris, determined that Nyx would always have someone there who cheered for her, snuck into the arena each afternoon to secretly watch her cousin. Always backing her. She would always be there, whether Nyx knew it or not. She arrived before everyone else and would be the last to leave. No one was aware of her presence.

"Good job today, Lahey." The coach smiled and shook his head.

Nyx wiped her face with a towel. "Thank you, sir."

The Reapers had already filed out of the arena, and Nyx and the professor followed closely behind. Once the lights were turned off, Eris gathered her things and made for the exit. Stepping outside, her heart all but skipped a beat at a billow of wings and a loud squawk—a raven taking off from one of the windowsills that looked in on the arena.

Eris narrowed her eyes at the sky as the raven flew out of sight.

CHAPTER EIGHT

AGYROPHOBIA — FEAR OF CROSSING STREETS

Erebus Reid Oram Salem.

Eros.

That was it. All he was. The only tie he had to his life before Dewmort.

Erebus had gone to see Taeto. After they'd discussed what happened, Erebus had been sentenced to two weeks' probation. No traveling to the human world, no assignments—nothing.

He was only two days in and was already bored. He tossed the name around in his head over and over again, trying to remember those words coming from his mother or father. Of course, he didn't know who they were. But he was sure that he'd known them at one point.

What a great thing it was, to have a name but no memory of it ever being used. Erebus rolled his eyes and sat upright. He stared at the piles of borrowed library books, papers and files scattered across the floor. Ridley's laptop screen had gone black during Erebus's timeout. He wiggled the mouse, trying to find the page he'd been reading.

Mason and Damien had been given an assignment by Taeto— an Inbetweener had been spotted somewhere in Zambia, raising lions to terrorize villages in the area. Since they'd been gone,

Erebus had been searching through the Dewmort records for any reference to other Salem family members. If he could find just one, he could go to them. He could learn *something* about his previous life.

But there were no other Salems.

Searching the internet, he found information about the witch trials and Arabian horse breeds, but that was it. He even tried asking the city's oldest members if they remembered seeing him on the road the day he arrived.

Nothing.

Ridley was downstairs again, smashing at the old walls at the back of the cathedral. Max, meanwhile, was lost somewhere else in their monolith of a warehouse.

Standing, Erebus gathered up everything and went to return Ridley's things. He paused, catching his reflection in the mirror in Ridley's room.

A scar on his right hand, another on his chin. A birthmark that looked like a leaf above his left hip just above the waistband of his sweatpants. A great tattoo of a snake eating its own tail stretching across his bare shoulder blades. He wanted to know where they came from. But Erebus wasn't hopeful. He'd been here for years now and hadn't remembered a single thing on his own.

He trudged downstairs, pulling on a shirt and his long, black coat. He knocked on the wall of the cathedral. Ridley turned, dropping his sledgehammer and removing his dust mask. He was still in his pajamas, the bird tattoos on his chest visible through the fabric of his shirt.

"What's up?" Ridley asked.

Erebus held up the borrowed books in a burlap sack. "I'm going to run to the library, in case Max asks where I am."

Ridley nodded. "Cool, no worries." Erebus turned to leave.
"Hey."

Erebus turned back. Ridley was walking toward him.

"Are you all right?" Ridley asked.

Nope. Erebus nodded. "Uh, yeah? Why?"

Ridley looked sympathetic but shook his head. "Just wanted to check."

The warehouse stood in the center of the French Quarter. Outside were colonial verandas drowning in plant life, pots hanging from ceilings, vines weaving in and out of cast iron railings. All around Erebus were brightly colored manors, stone streets, and old, oil-run street lamps.

Walking alongside him, standing on their balconies, and filling the entire city, were all manner of supernatural creatures: women with horns—ram, deer, antelope—adorned with ancient jewels; men with leaves along their hairline, wildflowers growing between cobblestones wherever they walked; children with blue and pink skin swimming in the river that bisected the streets, pearls in their hair, long colorful tails swishing beneath the surface.

He squeezed through the gaps between buildings, holding the sack of books close to his chest, trying not to accidentally step on children playing tag or get hit in the head by a seraph racing across the sky. He made his way to the library in the center of the district.

Music flowed through the air, always, be it from a busker on a corner or a parade or a bar down the road. A great church shadowed the horizon ahead of him, a square with a fountain before it. Erebus remembered Ridley appearing there when he came to Dewmort the night he died.

They had all arrived at different times. Some had come to the city back when Dewmort was nothing more than a great forest. Mason had been a Viking, and he'd arrived at a castle. Damien grew up during the witch trials, and woke in Dewmort when it was still just a large village. Ridley, on the other hand, came during the time of flower power and painted Kombi vans. They'd watched it change throughout the centuries—from a medieval fortress to the New Orleans lookalike it was now.

When Erebus first arrived, Max had explained to him that Dewmort was merely a reflection. And this—the old man had gestured to the city—was how Dewmort had chosen to depict itself.

After returning the books to the library, Erebus slipped round the back of the building, arriving at two tall doors set into the ancient brick of the structure—one, golden and shining, rippled with carved patterns and a great dragon head that glittered in the sun.

This was, as all of the dead of Dewmort knew, the door to the human world. To their pasts, their families—the golden life they'd once had.

Erebus glanced at the other door, only a few feet from the first. Red and rusted, dents in its frame, bent edges, holes where the rust had all but eaten through it. It had been locked for millennia. Even Dewmort's oldest members were unsure if it had ever been opened. For thousands of years people had tried to open it. To pry it, curse it, burn it, smash it down. Now, though, in this age, no one paid it any mind. It was simply part of the scenery.

Erebus gave it no more than a quick glance as he approached the golden door and slipped inside, pulling his coat tight around him. This was against Taeto's rules—Erebus had lost his right to travel through the door for at least a fortnight. But he had to try his luck with the Reaper academies. Maybe in their libraries he'd find something.

It was said that the Reaper academies held most of the world's records: birth records, death certificates, stories and epics, news articles, and conspiracies. Each academy had their own pieces. And Erebus was determined to find out whether or not any of them were about him.

Erebus knew the chances of finding anything were slim—he figured that they saved the pages in archives for information on kings and great people, and great things great people did.

Not some random dead boy.

Nevertheless, Erebus trudged down the dark streets of Misten toward the Reaper Academy. It had just rained, and its aftermath still pooled in the gutters and in the center of the road where the old asphalt dipped. Lampposts glowed weakly on street corners, looking as if they'd fall over if anyone so much as breathed on them.

The wrought-iron fencing of the academy rose up from the sidewalk. Before long, the great gates of the school appeared, its crown of spires brushing against a canopy of trees. A great iron scythe rose proudly—the centerpiece. A large golden lock kept them shut tight.

Erebus sighed, staring at the lock. He rested a hand upon the metal, shaking his head. He looked through the gate, to the large wooden doors of the academy.

I need to at least try.

He closed his eyes and put his hand on the lock. He felt his body grow light, then stepped forward, the iron bars passing through him like thick liquid. Erebus held his breath—he always did. With another step he was on the other side of the fence. His weight and tangibility returned to him.

"What . . . the fuck?" someone gasped.

Erebus opened his eyes to find none other than Nyx Lahey standing before him. Scythe still in hand, backpack over one shoulder.

"Oh—my God," Erebus spluttered. *Holy shit, she actually just saw that.* He contemplated disappearing into a cloud of feathers. "What are you doing here?"

Nyx laughed, and the stone around her neck flared. "What am I doing here? I go to school here! What are you doing here, and what the *hell* was that?"

Erebus held up his hands and stepped forward. Nyx's detector flashed once more, and she raised the blade of her scythe in his direction.

"I can explain," he pleaded.

"What are you?"

Erebus sighed, "I don't know if I can actually tell you that."

Nyx laughed sourly. "Well, you better try, because what I just saw . . ."

"Like, I really, *really* don't think it's a good idea—"

"You're not a Necromancer and you're not a Reaper. You're not an Inbetweener or *anything* . . . so, what are you?" Nyx slowly approached; scythe still raised. "I swear to God, if you don't—"

He threw up his arms. "I am . . . a . . . uh, ghost, I guess."

Nyx blinked, her scythe dropping slightly. "A what?"

Erebus grimaced like the words stung. "A ghost."

"How?"

"I died, I guess?" Erebus halfheartedly shrugged.

"How is that possible?"

I am in so much trouble, he thought to himself. "I honestly don't know, but I woke up in the city and there were others already there so I—"

"What city?" she persisted, moving closer.

Fuck. "Our city." He slowly lowered his hands. "The one we go to when we die. Dewmort."

"You're serious, aren't you?"

"Unfortunately."

"Then why were you in the freezer that night?"

"Dewmort has its own hunters, the Legions. They send us out sometimes when they think it may be a bit too . . . *revealing.* They don't want you questioning anything you don't need to be questioning."

"How many of you are there?" she asked.

"I couldn't tell you. Hundreds, maybe thousands?"

"And where is this city?"

As she spoke, Erebus caught sight of a small girl hiding behind the corner. She peered out at Nyx, smiling. She was no older than five and definitely not old enough to have classes so late.

Erebus pointed past Nyx. "Uh . . ."

Confused, Nyx looked around. Holding her scythe behind her back, she bent over. "Are you okay? Are you lost?"

The little girl fiddled with the empty slot at the front of her mouth from a lost tooth. She shook her head. "My mommy said that dead people aren't allowed in the school."

Nyx stood straight. Erebus's mouth dropped, and he felt the urge to turn and fly away again.

"What was that?"

"That dead boy. He's not allowed in my school. My mommy said dead people are bad." The girl stared intently at Erebus.

Nyx looked at Erebus. "Oh, no, he's . . . he's not dead—"

"Yes, he is," she whispered. "Did the Old Necromancer send him here?" Her face flushed with excitement.

"Who?"

She lowered her voice as if it was a secret. "My mommy told me a story about the Old Necromancer who knows all the dead people in the whole world. Maybe he sent that dead boy here to steal our school."

The Old Necromancer? Erebus thought to himself.

Nyx almost laughed. "Oh, no, darling, he wasn't here to steal our school. He was just . . . visiting."

"Ooh," the girl said. "Did you bring the dead boy here? Because you're a Necromancer?"

"Oh! No, no, no, no, I didn't bring him here. He's not, uh, dead." Nyx felt a wave of panic at the thought of a younger student walking around telling kids the Necromancers had brought a dead person onto school property. "Let's not tell people that, okay?"

"Okay," the girl agreed, immediately forgetting what she'd said.

Nyx held out her hand. "Why don't we get you home, hey? Before your mommy starts wondering where you are?"

There was a crash then, and a door swung open around the corner. The laughter of boys filled the air. Nyx pulled back quickly and dropped her voice, looking over her shoulder in the direction of the noise.

"You need to leave," she whispered, turning back to Erebus.

He started to back away.

She locked her eyes with his, nodding at him with her blade. "This isn't over," she said. "Now go, get out of here."

Erebus nodded and fell back two paces before he felt his legs drop away and let his thick coat envelop his body. He seemed to melt into the black suede until it swirled and shrank. Feathers emerged from the fabric and, in an instant, a raven took his place and beat its wings into the air.

Nyx stared, dumbfounded as Erebus flew into the distance. She continued to stand there even after the other late-class students rounded the corner, their conversation hushing at the sight of the Necromancer.

Her mind reeled. Had that really just happened? Was he crazy? Was she crazy for thinking she'd just seen him turn into a bird?

The girl tugged her toward the side gates, and Nyx looked up at the sky.

This was definitely not over.

A pale man with orange eyes smiled in amusement at the globe before him. It turned in the middle of the room, a great sphere floating in the air as misty clouds rolled off. At its center, an image of Nyx Lahey, hand in hand with a Reaper child, walking through the academy gates.

A voice beside him: "It's funny, isn't it? How our stories sometimes come up in the most peculiar of places."

The man moved aside. A woman stood beside him, leaning on the railing as she looked down into the well of the room. The scent of incense and jasmine enveloped them both.

The woman's red eyes reflected the glow of the sphere. "I remember when the first travelers went to that world and spread our stories to the Reapers and the Necromancers—even the humans heard bits and pieces. For centuries they knew our names. But it's rare to find ones nowadays who know of us."

"We seem to have gone out of fashion." He kept his eyes trained on the beauty beside him, with her pale skin, long dark ringlets, garnet eyes, and shiny black horns spiraling up from her hairline. She was primordial—something to behold.

She pointed at the slowly fading image of Nyx Lahey. "You're sure about these two?"

"Erebus and the Lahey girl? I'm positive. I can see the power radiating from the pair of them. I don't think either is aware of it yet. Erebus doesn't even have his memories from before he died."

The woman looked at him, a glint of sadness in her eyes. "Even now? After all this time?"

"Not a thing. Nyx, on the other hand . . . her powers are so repressed that I don't know how she hasn't exploded."

She could see the pain in his eyes, seeing one of his own kind so bottled up and caged. So unaware of the power she held. He wanted to help her, but in order to do that, the girl needed to be ready to receive it.

"She's not ready. These things take time," the woman said.

"I know, Ira. I just . . . we could help the pair of them so mu—"

"And we will." Ira placed a hand on the man's arm. Neither Nyx nor Erebus was ready to hear the truth about who they were. Or what they were and what they could do.

Ira smiled. "But, hey, seems like you might be coming back into fashion. 'Old Necromancer.'" She laughed.

Mortem chuckled.

CHAPTER NINE

SOMNIPHOBIA — FEAR OF GOING TO SLEEP

Ridley knocked on Erebus's door. "What?" Erebus called.

"I'm coming in," Ridley announced. He stepped inside and looked around. The floor was covered in loose pages, open books, and notes. "What the fuck have you been doing?" he asked.

Erebus looked up at him from the floor, where he was sitting in nothing more than track pants. He waved his hand. "Would you mind closing that, please?"

"Seriously, what is all this?" Ridley asked, standing at the edge of what seemed to be Erebus's universe.

"It's uh, just a bit of research I'm doing." He continued to scan the laptop screen in front of him.

Ridley knelt down and picked up a piece of paper. "About what? Fairy tales? What is this?" He flipped the page around for Erebus to see. Erebus reached across and snatched the paper away.

"The Hallows" it read in medieval script. Below it, a picture of a beautiful dark-haired woman with horns, and beneath that, a short poem about a fabled kingdom.

"Haven't you heard the stories?" Erebus asked, finally looking up.

Ridley shook his head. "As you seem to have forgotten, I thought I was human for eighteen years. I'm afraid I'm not familiar with supernatural lore."

"It's just stories that the people here and topside know about. Apparently, once upon a time, there was a way to travel to the country where the gods lived. The country was known as the Hallows. But, according to myth, thousands of years ago the doors to the country were sealed and no one has ever been back."

"Okay . . ." Ridley sat down and crossed his legs, mirroring his friend. "Did you miss the part about it being just a story? I mean, why are there literally three hundred pages on your floor right now about this?"

Erebus grunted in retort. Ridley looked around at the countless leather-bound books piled on top of each other; the bookshelves that lined the room were now mostly empty. "What's so important that you've spent the last three days doing this?" Ridley asked.

"I think I may have found somebody who might know what happened to me. Who might know why I can't remember *anything.*"

Ridley nodded, doubtful. "And who's that?"

Erebus sighed and held up a finger as he scanned the chaos. He pulled a book from the middle of one of the piles. Ridley cocked his head to read the gold foil on the cover: *Explorer Dr. Leveti's 1537 Journey Across the Heavens.*

Erebus turned to a particular page. "This guy was permitted to visit the kingdom. Here, he quotes a chapter of a text he found within an *older* explorer's guide, telling him about this guy called the Old Necromancer . . ." Ridley nodded, and Erebus continued, reading directly from the text. "'The man was tall and pale, with gray skin and hair like snow. He was covered in strange, rust-colored markings. During my brief time in the Hallows it had slipped my mind to ask what they had meant. But I assumed they had something to do with the man's powers. He appeared to be the same as others of the necromantic kind. But the man also seemed to specialize in the keeping of information regarding the dead. It seemed the Old Necromancer was connected with the lives of the living (and, therefore, the dead) in a way that many may never come to understand. Truly a remarkable character, and I do wish to see him again on my next visit.'"

Erebus looked up.

"And . . . what does that mean, exactly?" Ridley asked.

Erebus shut the book. "I went topside the other day—"

"Didn't Taeto put you on lockdown?"

"He *did*. But I figured this was more important. So, I went to the academy in Misten . . ."

Ridley rolled his eyes.

". . . and I was going to try and get in, but as soon as I walked through the gates, someone saw me—"

"Oh great! First, you try to break into the Reaper academy, then you let a Reaper see you. Awesome. How'd you try to get yourself out of that one?"

"Well, thankfully, it was only Nyx."

Ridley shook his head. "It was the Lahey girl? Seriously, of all people?"

"Yeaaah, but there was also this little kid."

"Oh Jesus."

"*Anyway*," Erebus went on, "the little girl said something about this Old Necromancer and how he apparently knows *all* of the dead people. Maybe that means me too."

Ridley waited for more, but Erebus had finished. "That's it?" he said. Erebus nodded. "So, some kid mentions him, and now you think he's real?"

"I've been doing a lot of research, Rid—"

"And I could do a lot of research on Valhalla but that doesn't make it real!"

Erebus glared at him. "Why are you being so shitty to me?"

"Because you're wasting your time and getting your hopes up for nothing!"

Erebus set the book down, then straightened the pile.

Ridley sighed. "Look, Eb. I'm *sorry*, but I really don't think this is the best use of your energy. I know it's hard, but I don't think chasing fairy tales is the right way to go about this."

Erebus ignored him, searching for something in the pockets of his track pants. He retrieved a folded piece of paper and threw it.

"What is this?" Ridley asked, catching it.

"Just open it," Erebus said quietly.

Ridley unfolded the thick piece of parchment. His eyes narrowed in confusion: *Erebus Salem, when the time is right you will know all the answers you desire. The Hallows looks forward to meeting the two of you. Regards, the Old Necromancer.*

Ridley glanced up. "Where'd you find this?"

"When I came back down from the academy, through the golden door, this was sticking in the frame of the other one." Ridley stared at him. "That's what the red door is, Ridley. It's the opening to the other country—the Hallows or *the Hallows*, whatever they call it."

Ridley folded the paper again. "How do you know someone isn't just messing with you? And what does it mean by 'the two of you'?"

"I don't know about the 'two' part, but who would write that? No one even knows about this. I only just found out myself."

Ridley made a grim face. "Well, someone knows about the girl."

"What girl?"

"Nyx Lahey. Damien said he's seen someone shadowing her."

"And? That family probably has hundreds of enemies."

Ridley shook his head. "Damien says it's a raven, like us. Who do you know who has access to that kind of magic apart from legion members?"

Erebus thought quietly. "They're watching her?" he said.

Ridley nodded. "He thinks they're threatening her too . . . I don't know, Eb. What if it's all a setup? What if this other raven is trying to get your necklace too? And using *this*"—Ridley held up the paper—"as a trap?"

"Who would want to do that? What have *I* done to anyone?"

"Erebus, you don't know who you were before. You could have been anyone. For all you know, you could have enemies too."

"Do you think I could have been a bad person?"

Ridley didn't answer. He couldn't bear the thought of Erebus Salem being anyone less than who he was right now. But no matter who Erebus turned out to be, to Damien, Mason, Max, and Ridley, he would always be their dreamer. Their brother.

"I *think* you should be careful," Ridley said. "And until we find out what this other raven wants, I think we should look out for Nyx." Erebus nodded; Ridley continued. "I know we don't know, but if she's been dragged into something because of your pendant . . . we need to make sure nothing happens to her." Ridley paused. "What happened with her the other day? Did you at least get your locket back?"

"She saw me pass through the gate. All of it. The whole thing.

She freaked out. I . . . I didn't even think to ask about the locket. She just started asking a heap of questions."

Ridley made a pained face. "And what did you do?"

"I told her the truth. But I don't know if she believes me or not."

"Good, maybe we should try to keep it that way. Try your best to not run into her anymore. Hopefully, once we get your locket back, whoever is following her will just leave her alone, and we can forget about this."

Erebus remembered Nyx's words: *This isn't over*. He doubted that she would just forget about anything.

"Yeah, okay." Erebus shut the laptop.

Ridley rose from his spot on the floor. "You should get some sleep. I'll check the house tonight. If I see the raven, I'll try to find out who it is." Ridley paused. "Do you think it's Taeto? Do you think he knows what happened?"

Erebus shook his head. "No, I don't think so. He's here all day and night, dealing with the Legions. He's not interested in my mess-ups anymore. But . . . I do think it's got to be one of the Legions' members. No one else has that kind of magic."

"And if it's not?"

"Then maybe I really do have enemies."

Erebus had clambered into Damien's clean room and promptly fallen asleep as Ridley began placing books back onto shelves and collecting loose pieces of paper from the floor of Erebus's room. When he could finally walk across the floorboards, Ridley knelt in the center of the room and picked up the laptop. He opened it and started closing tabs one by one until only the last remained.

On the open tab was a sketch of a man, shirtless, slender. His skin was gray and he had long, white hair hanging to his ribs. He had dark lips, pointed ears, and orange eyes that matched the Lahey girl's. His stomach was covered in tiny, intricate tattoos. His arms, from the elbow down, were wrapped in black leather and chains. In his hand he held a Necromancer staff.

At the bottom of the sketch, a caption: The Old Necromancer, a.k.a. Mortem.

CHAPTER TEN

PIGMENTUMPHOBIA – FEAR OF PAINT

There had been a raven in Nyx's room a night ago. Not outside the window, but *in* the bedroom. One eye crimson, the other milky white and scarred. It was an ugly thing with old, festering skin around its eyes and beak. The same one she'd seen after the amusement park.

She and Bjørn had walked in to find it rummaging through her schoolbag. Bjørn had lunged for it, and the bird made a horrible screeching sound as it flapped into the air, its talons just missing Nyx's face as it shot past her and out the bedroom door.

Bjørn bounded after it, growling. There were shrieks from downstairs as the bird tried to find an exit. Eventually, someone opened the back door, and the bird took off. Nyx watched from the window as Bjørn chased it to the edge of the trees.

She had gone to close the door. Swinging around again, she saw the main compartment of her bag overflowing with ripped, loose pieces of paper. But nestled there, at the bottom, was the locket.

Bjørn had chased the raven from the house, but it was here now. In her dreams, watching from the branches of a scraggly, dead tree. Nyx could feel its eyes on her back.

She was surrounded by tall, dead trees. They towered over her, their branches like long, bony fingers silhouetted by the full moon. A thick layer of fog covered the dead pine needles on the ground. The fog swirled and thickened as a bird dropped from the sky. It twisted and grew before landing as a man, his feathers folding into a long, black trench coat. He was an apparition, but she knew him.

Before her stood the spirit of Erebus Salem. His eyes burned bright, the skin around them darkening. His dark russet hair shimmered with gold. A ghostly crown of blood-red flowers sat curled within his hair. They bloomed and unbloomed as he breathed. Faint bronze lines appeared over his face in the pattern of a skull.

"What are you doing here?" Nyx asked.

He looked at her as the flowers in his hair bloomed, their golden centers glowing. He said nothing and turned, walking away.

In the background, Nyx became aware of Eris calling her, telling her to get her ass out of bed.

"Hey!" she yelled as the fog began to thicken.

Erebus glanced over his shoulder, jaw set. He faded away.

"Time to wake up, Nyx."

CHAPTER ELEVEN

DECIDOPHOBIA — FEAR OF MAKING DECISIONS

A world away, Erebus Salem was also dreaming.

The dreams had started two nights after meeting the Lahey girl. In them, he was at the red door. It was dark, with no moon or stars in sight. A single street lamp at the alley's opening emitted a weak light.

Erebus was shaking. Sweating. Panting. *Had he been running?* He reached out to touch the door.

The nightmare jumped—a record scratch, pulling him to a new scene. Now he was in a dark room. He caught the edges of what looked like judges' benches—seven of them. They encircled him. He could hear voices—murmurs in the shadows. Adjusting to the dark, he saw that each bench had a golden nameplate.

One read Jack, and straw and hay lay scattered about the floor in front of the bench. Above, perforating the darkness, two glowing, triangular shapes floated in the air above a big, glowing, razor-like smile. Looking almost like . . . a *pumpkin*.

"What the hell," Erebus whispered aloud.

"Ah"—a velvety female voice echoed through the room—"he speaks."

Hans & Greta was engraved on a double-wide bench. This one was covered in sweets of all kinds—baskets of chocolates, hard-boiled treats, lollipops, and cupcakes. A heavy-looking axe leaned against the wood.

A Russian voice whispered from behind a bench that read Chef. A thick silver steak knife was wedged into the wood next to his nameplate. Vegetables and roasted meats of all manner were spread around the base of his bench. The murmurs continued.

"Enough, all of you." The velvety voice echoed again and the whispering ceased. "We are the representatives of this *council*, and I believe we should act accordingly."

Her voice came from behind a pedestal marked IRA, decorated with animal horns and antlers that created an almost spiderweblike structure. Erebus saw the glint of blades between them, and small tea light candles.

More murmurs around the room. The voice spoke again. "Don't you think so, Hatter?"

"Oh! *Yes!*" someone said, giggling nervously behind the bench labeled HATTER. Scattered and toppled about it were teacups, small cakes, and a large white teapot. There were bloody handprints all over the pot and the dining ware.

"Yes, I thought you might."

Another deep, accented voice cut through the shadows. "Can this boy even hear us? Does he know we're here?" Small glass vials of powders were everywhere, jars of dried flowers and snake skins hung from strings. BAYOU was engraved on his plate, sigils painted on the wood surrounding it.

"Oh, he can hear us," a new voice said.

The last pedestal. MORTEM stood out bright and bold. Skulls and gems and dirt were scattered about the floor and hanging from the bench. In the shadows, two orange eyes stared out at Erebus.

Erebus spoke up: "Where am I?"

"Oh, my *dear* boy, you're in a *dream*," Ira said.

"Is this on the other side of the door? The red door?" he asked.

"Yes, darling. Anyone can get through as long as we permit it," Ira drawled.

Erebus turned to the MORTEM pedestal, pointing to the shadows there. "*You.* You're the one who wrote the letter. *You're* the Necromancer."

There were murmurs and grunts of surprise. Mortem's eyes didn't waver.

"You talked about the Hallows. Is this it?" Erebus gestured around the small room.

"*Erebus Salem.*" Ira sounded sympathetic, drawing his attention back to her. "This is nothing more than a dream to see if you are ready."

There was silence. Erebus felt the floor beneath his feet begin to sway.

"And you are," she said. The room started to spin—a swirling tornado of broken teacups, dust, knives, and sweets. The benches and the occupants behind them disappeared in the chaos.

Ira's voice echoed: "You will find your way to the Hallows in due time. Don't worry. We only wait for your counterpart. She isn't ready. You need to wait for her."

The world continued to spin.

"Eros," Ira's voice whispered through the mess. "Oh, how he looks like his mother . . ."

"Erebus"—the Old Necromancer's voice boomed in his head—"it's time to wake up."

CHAPTER TWELVE

NYCTOPHOBIA — FEAR OF THE NIGHT

"Just jump!"

Alice gave Nyx an incredulous look. "Can't I just go downstairs and out the back door?" she whined.

"Have you *heard* the way you walk?" Eris whispered. "It's like you're *trying* to wake the entire house. Just jump!"

Alice looked down at the one-and-a-half-story drop before her, clutching and unclutching her hands as she balanced on the balcony railing. It was after much debate that she had persuaded Eris and Nyx to let her come with them to a party just a few blocks away. And, so far, they regretted that decision immensely.

Eris and Nyx had gone every year since Nyx was sixteen. It was so crowded each year that no one ever noticed two strange-looking girls in attendance. No one knew them, no one even looked their way—they blended into the throng of people.

Alice sighed. "What do I do when I hit the ground?"

"Just tuck your legs under and roll. Otherwise you'll jar your ankles."

"You guys are paying my hospital bill."

Eris and Nyx stood under Alice's balcony, which overlooked the family graveyard. It was Eris who'd woken Nyx earlier. Undoubtedly, the dream had shaken her, and Eris had noticed.

But she didn't ask questions. Nor did she say anything as Nyx pulled a silver locket from her schoolbag and placed it around her neck. Watching Erebus suddenly change from man to bird the other afternoon had made her all too aware of just how many ravens had been sauntering around the house lately. Maybe one of them was him.

Nyx needed to know more about these "ghosts" and the city that Erebus spoke about. She needed to know if he was crazy or if there was something going on that they were all oblivious to. And if she had to coax him out of the trees, she would.

"Three," Eris counted, bringing Nyx's attention back to the matter at hand.

Alice bent her knees, bobbing up and down.

"Two . . ." they both said.

"One!" Alice pushed off the railing, landing on the ground a second later, and rolling into the bushes.

Blocks away, a boy leaned against the side of a frat house. Hundreds of mingling voices and the sound of laughter filled the air, while music made the wall vibrate. Dark hair blew across blue eyes as he stared down at the half-crumpled piece of paper in his hand, the names *Erebus Salem* and *Nyx Lahey* written messily.

He'd heard rumors. Whispers among soldiers and village people. The names seemed to carry all the way through the Hallows, from the ranges to the sea, the desert people to the sky dwellers. People were growing hopeful. But the Council had said nothing so far.

But Cole needed to know. He needed to see them for himself. He needed to know whether this hope was even worth it.

—

"Wait, which one of these guys is actually throwing the party?" Alice asked as they approached the veranda of the frat house. People trickled in and out, and the floors were slick and sticky with spilled drinks. Music and hundreds of conversations caused her ears to buzz.

Eris made a face. "Oh, I have no idea. I bet half of these kids don't know who's throwing the party."

No one even seemed to notice them as they walked in, slipping seamlessly through the crowd to the backyard where there was a pool, party lights, and a bar. And beyond that, a thick, dark forest. People squealed as they tackled each other into the pool, and the smell of barbeque was strong, filling the air.

Grabbing three cups from a girl walking around, Eris turned back to Alice and Nyx, and handed them over.

Eris sighed, her shoulders drooping several inches. "Here's to a night where no one knows our names. And thank God! I've been looking forward to this for a whole-ass year."

They clinked their glasses together as the party thrummed around them.

"Here's to being no one for a night," Alice said.

CHAPTER THIRTEEN

HYLOPHOBIA – FEAR OF FORESTS

A man stood in the forest, surrounded by clawed, spindly brambles. He was a horrid beast with a scar that turned one eye white, the skin around it festering, and another that disfigured his nose and mouth.

The man listened. Silent. Still.

A chaotic noise could be heard in the distance. A jumble of laughing, thumping music, and chatter. But of all the voices, the man was able to discern the few he sought:

The ghost. The young man with a clouded mind, trying to remain unnoticed.

The little Necromancer with the fierce orange eyes and an even fiercer power.

He, too, had heard the rumors. The Relics were back. He'd been observing them for weeks to see if what he'd heard was really true. And he could feel it—the stench of their power radiating from them. The girl was far more repressed than her counterpart—it had taken him quite a while to really catch the scent on her.

But the boy . . . the boy was ripe with power. All that potential, and they didn't even know it. But the man did. And he knew what he had to do.

He raised his arms and screamed, *"ARDU!"*

RISE.

For a moment, nothing happened. Then the soil shifted. It turned over and bubbled as something climbed from its depths—a hand clawing its way from the soil. The air was suddenly filled with the moans and growls of the dead.

The man addressed his army, grinning venomously. *"BEATHA!"* he cried.

FEED.

No one paid much mind as Erebus materialized at the edge of the forest and slinked across the lawn. Light and music and bodies surrounded the house as the late hours set in.

Ridley, Damien, and Mason had been taking turns scoping out the Lahey house, trying to catch a glimpse of the strange raven that had been lurking around. Erebus had always followed along, too, though none of the others knew that. He needed to know if this mystery person knew him, and what they wanted. And if they were following Nyx around, then maybe she knew something.

He'd heard the girls talking about the party, so he knew where to find Nyx. It wasn't long before he caught a glint of silver through the crowd.

She was standing in a small circle with two others. Even at a party full of people, they occupied their own space. Erebus could sense their magic.

Nyx keeled over laughing at something one of the others said, and Erebus's eyes fell on a figure standing behind her—a boy leaning against a nearby wall. The space around him was different too. It wasn't stagnant air, like that hanging around the humans.

This space was darker, almost shadowed. From the dark jacket pulled tightly around his arms to his black tousled hair, something about him was different.

And he was watching Nyx.

Without thinking, Erebus found himself moving around the room. But before reaching him, the stranger's eyes locked with his own.

The boy smiled, stood up straight, and held out his hand. Erebus was taken aback.

"Hey, man, how's it going? I'm Cole."

Erebus regarded the outstretched hand a moment before warily shaking it. "Erebus."

The boy wore the briefest visage of disbelief. "Erebus . . . that's a different name, man, where'd your parents get that?"

Erebus decided to play along. "No idea," he replied, truthfully. "You know anyone here?"

Cole shook his head, bringing a red cup to his lips. "Nah, I just heard about it through the grapevine. Thought I'd check it out. What about you?"

"Same, just heard about it from some friends." He felt it then, across the room—Nyx Lahey's eyes had landed on them. She said something to the other girls and started moving through the crowd. Erebus looked at Cole as Nyx neared.

"Looks like someone's recognized you," Cole said, laughing.

Nyx popped out of the crowd beside them. She looked pretty, and small, next to the two of them. "Hi, do you mind if I steal this one for a bit?" she asked, grabbing Erebus's arm.

She was strong, Erebus thought. And *angry*. A strong, angry, pretty thing, he decided.

Cole shook his head. "By all means. Nice to meet you." He turned and disappeared into the crowd.

Nyx let go of Erebus's arm. "What on earth are you doing here?" she asked softly, though like she had expected him.

Erebus wasn't about to tell her about the strange raven. He shrugged. "Heard there was a good party tonight."

Nyx rolled her eyes, and Erebus saw his necklace around her throat. He gave a halfhearted chuckle. "That looks nice on you."

Nyx dropped her eyes to her chest. "Shit, this is yours, isn't it?" She reached around the back of her neck and undid the clasp.

"It is," he admitted as she handed it to him. Just like that. He closed his fist around the locket and regarded Nyx warily, unsure of what she was going to do.

"Is that why you came here?" she asked, one brow raised.

Erebus nodded. "Yeah—well, no."

"Good," she said. "Because I'm not done with our talk."

"Oh that." Erebus made a face.

"Were you telling the truth?" she asked.

Erebus deflated. This broke almost every rule the Dewmort Legions had. "I wish I wasn't, but I kind of had to after you watched me walk through a fence, you know?"

Nyx was still unsure. "Come outside?" she asked, pointing with her cup to the open back door.

Erebus followed her through the crowd as Nyx led him into the garden, stopping under the branches of a massive cypress pine, where the noise of the party wouldn't drown them out.

She sat on the stone wall surrounding the garden. "Can you do it again?" she asked, looking up at him.

"What?" he asked.

She pointed with a nod. "Walk through that tree."

Erebus glanced over his shoulder. "In front of all these people?"

She shrugged. "I don't think they're paying you much attention."

Which was true; no one had even looked his way. "All right then. You're explaining it if I get caught, though."

"Deal," Nyx agreed, and watched as he stepped into the garden. He glanced back as he approached the tree, stepping gingerly over small clumps of flowers.

He slid his hands into his coat pockets and looked at Nyx. "What, you want me to just walk through, that's it?"

Nyx looked amused. "Yep."

"Fine," Erebus replied, giving the party a final once-over.

He closed his eyes and took a breath. He felt his body lighten, and he stepped forward, growing lighter still with each step as his body moved through every ring of the tree. It felt rough as he moved against the grain, until, finally, it all dropped away.

Erebus opened his eyes; the tree was behind him now. He turned and faced Nyx; her face had grown serious.

"Good enough?" he asked, stepping over the flowers again.

Nyx nodded as he sat down next to her, swinging his legs against the stone wall. She spun and faced him. "So how come you don't just fall through this wall here?"

"I control what I want to phase through. Right now, I don't want to, so I just don't think about it. But like, if I . . ." Erebus raised his hand, watching Nyx. She did the same. Erebus closed his eyes as Nyx brought her hand to his. A breath, and Erebus could feel her palm press against his. And then—she fell through it, her hand moving through his.

Nyx was wide eyed with wonder. "If I think about it, I can move through anything," he said. Nyx pulled her hand away and his tangibility bounced back.

Nyx shook her head. "What about the raven thing? With your coat? Is that just a ghost thing too?"

"No, that's our uniform in the Legions—the hunters. The coats let us transform. As ravens we can get away when we need to while remaining inconspicuous."

Nyx looked at the ground as she took it all in. The wind blew her inky hair in her eyes. "How did it happen?" she asked.

"How did what happen?"

"How'd you die?" Nyx cringed.

"Oh." Erebus raised his brows, surprised. "To be honest, I'm probably one of the only people in Dewmort who can't remember."

"Anything?"

"Not a thing. All I know is I woke up in the city one day with this"—he held up the locket—"and that's it. And I can't even open it."

"That's why you wanted it back so badly. I'm sorry, I shouldn't have taken it," Nyx said sadly.

Erebus shook his head. "It's okay, I'm the one who dropped it. You had no idea what it was. And it's not so bad there—in Dewmort, I mean. I've got a family there now. Three other guys who are like my brothers. We live with this old guy named Max. They've helped me try to find out who I am."

"And have you learned anything?"

Erebus shook his head. "People in the streets have come up to me and said I look familiar, but they can't figure out why. That's about it. I knew after a while that my name was Erebus, but it wasn't until that night at the amusement park—"

"Eros."

"Yeah, Eros. It was a nickname. I don't know who gave it to me. But it stood for my initials. Erebus Reid Oram Salem." Erebus frowned. "But I have no idea how I heard it that night."

Nyx had heard it, too, the night at the amusement park. Like a whisper on the wind.

Erebus remembered the dream he'd had earlier. The benches

in the dark room. Ira speaking that name. It had all felt so familiar.

"Your brothers," Nyx spoke, pulling his attention back. "These ones you have in Dewmort, are they like you—hunters? With the coats?"

Erebus nodded. "Yeah, why?"

"Does one of them have a red eye and a scar?" Nyx drew a finger down one of her eyes.

Erebus felt slightly sick. The stranger. The other raven. "No, that's not one of us. We're not—"

Nyx moved suddenly, kneeling, and holding a finger to her lips. She inhaled deeply and then glanced at him, noticeably paler. "Can you smell that?"

Erebus was about to shake his head when the wind blew once more, filling his face with the stench of . . .

Rot.

He stood, and they looked at the tree line—past the darkness and swaying branches.

Nyx grabbed his arm, pulling him back toward the house. "We need to find the others."

CHAPTER FOURTEEN

APOTEMNOPHOBIA — FEAR OF PERSONS
WITH AMPUTATIONS

The inside of the frat house was chaos. Nyx could hear her heartbeat as she scrambled through the crowd of bodies. Glancing over her shoulder, she could see Erebus hot on her heels, face stricken.

Nyx dodged a group of boys catching each other as they jumped from staircase railings, her gaze settling on a flash of red hair and a black hood. "Alice!" she yelled.

Eris appeared then, pushing her way downstairs at the sound of Nyx's distressed voice.

"Eris." Nyx grabbed her arm at the bottom of the stairs.

"Bub, what's wrong?"

"There's something in the fore—" She paused, watching Eris's face change as the stench rolled through the house.

That's when the screaming began.

Through the window, Nyx saw the crowd outside turn toward the tree line. Toward the screams. Her blood pumped in her head, her breathing loud and ragged. Eris grew paler by the second. Erebus looked grim.

No one moved.

Then: howling. A chaotic symphony of moans and hellish

wailing surrounded the house. Nyx looked at Erebus. He gave a single stiff nod. "I'll be back," he said before disappearing into the crowd once more.

The horrid smell now invaded the house like a thick fog.

Alice took her cousin's arm, eyes wide. "Nyx . . ."

The howling hit a crescendo. The crowd of humans littering the backyard started to stir. Nyx's eyes remained fixed on the tree line.

The wails ceased as a man appeared, stepping through the trees. He was flanked by four other men. He was tall, dressed like a naval officer of some sort, in a broad hat with a single long feather, a sword, and boots. The man removed his hat and swept into a deep, flamboyant bow.

A boy on the lawn burst out laughing. His friends soon joined in, albeit nervously. "What the hell do you think this is, man?" the boy shouted before turning away. "Go home! Halloween's not for another month!"

Nyx looked closer. The man's skin was a sickly looking blue-gray. His clothes were tattered, covered in mud, dirt, and dark, dried stains. His sunken cheeks set his jaw at an odd angle.

Zombie.

She looked at the men behind him. Two of them were also sailors, another a blood-stained baker missing his lower jaw, the last a businessman in a tattered suit and tie, blood and gunk dried on his face.

Nyx watched as the captain reached into his coat, a wicked smile spreading across his face. In one long-nailed hand, he produced something red, dripping, and gooey. He reared back and flung the red mass toward the laughing boy and his friends. It hit the boy between the shoulder blades and slid down his back before landing on the cement with a wet splat.

The boy slowly turned and looked at his feet. Those around him screamed and jumped away.

Bile climbed up the back of Nyx's throat. It was entrails. Stomach and intestines. But *whose*.

"Oh shit." Eris covered her mouth. Alice turned around, mouth slack, eyes full of fear. She mouthed Nyx's name, shaking.

Nyx looked at the captain again. His mouth was set in a stiff, flat line. He reached into the pockets of his coat once more and pulled out a piece of folded cloth.

He held it up to the crowd. It unraveled with a single jerk. It was a plain blue pullover, covered in blood.

"Hey," said someone in the crowd, "isn't that Troy's shirt?"

The captain grinned and threw the bloodied shirt to the ground, then people started to scream and run. One by one zombies emerged from the shadows to stand along the tree line: sailors, pilgrims, elderly people, and others without any remnants of clothing, some so old they were mere skeletons. They quickly surrounded the house.

Through the chaos, the captain's yellow eyes found Nyx. The corner of his lip twitched, rising to a grin. He bent at the knees, hands growing claws as he roared. His teeth became fangs and his yellow eyes flashed milky white.

They charged.

"Everybody run!" Eris screamed to the humans still standing there, watching the oncoming swarm "Nyx!" she yelled. "What are we going to do?"

Nyx felt a rush of heat and looked over at Alice—hood gone, and a pair of folded war fans pulled from the folds of it. With a flick of her wrists, the fans opened and ignited. The flames traveled up her arms and engulfed her entire body. Within seconds she was walking fire. She began to dance the way she'd been taught in battle strategy—to jump and flip and spin toward the enemy, making a show, distracting them while others readied their weapons. She flipped and landed atop one of the tables, right in front of the enemy line. She flung the fans at the ground, in front of the monsters. Small sparks and slivers of flame erupted, forming a thick barrier in front of the zombies.

Those who didn't halt quick enough ran into the flames and disintegrated. The captain snarled and shielded his milky eyes from the light.

Alice brought an arm down in an arc. The sound of fire rose, becoming an incredible cacophony. She danced alongside the barrier, sometimes within the flames. The arc followed her movements, obliterating countless monsters in her wake.

"Nyx, this isn't going to last long!" Eris yelled. "They're going to find a way around. And what about the others?" She was talking about the horde of zombies still surrounding the house.

Before she could answer, someone yelled Nyx's name from across the house. She turned and saw the boy with the dark hair Erebus had been talking to earlier in the kitchen ripping through drawers and cupboards.

"Come on!" he yelled, and waved them over. Eris and Nyx dug through the drawers, pulling out knives and scissors, and anything sharp or heavy that they could find.

Nyx turned to the boy. "Who are you?"

He kept his eyes trained on Alice as she danced outside. "My name's Cole. Where's Erebus?"

Alice screamed, "Eris!" She continued to bend the fire, but her voice was strained, eyes fixed on the tree line. The zombies had found a way around by backtracking through the forest—one in particular, who happened to look like a paramedic, had pulled a fire blanket from his soggy bag and was dousing a section of the barrier. They were coming now from two points.

Alice continued, bending multiple arcs of fire, setting most of the monsters ablaze. But they soon closed in and her flame was dying out. Nyx was busy shoving knives into her pockets when Cole threw her an iron chair leg that he'd taken off one of the pool chairs. He passed another to Eris, then, when Alice retreated to their position, he handed her a meat cleaver.

"What the hell are *these* going to do?" Eris whispered. "We *need* Reaper Iron."

Nyx's heart was thumping. "I know."

The zombies were dawdling now, slowly closing in. The captain watched the Necromancers, mouth slack, green saliva dripping down his chin. His eyes were clouded and hungry.

It was the first time in her life that Nyx had feared monsters. She'd hunted and killed thousands. But never had she *feared* them. She glared at the captain. Smashed the iron chair leg down on one of the other chairs in front of her.

"Come on!" she screamed. He snarled in response and charged, closing the space between them.

Suddenly, something barreled past them. Blurred shapes shot out from behind the group and tackled the oncoming zombies. The entire front line was taken to the ground, halting the ones behind them.

Dogs. Growling, yelping when the monsters clawed at them. The one nearest to Nyx ripped a zombie's throat out with its teeth.

"Shit!" Eris yelled.

It was only then that she noticed the patchy skin and fur of the dogs. *Wolves.* The white, glazed, orb-like eyes. Visible rib cages and femurs. These were dead wolves. *Zombie* wolves.

A second wave of dogs shot out from behind them and took down the next line of zombies. Nyx scanned the pack's tracks through the house to the front door, which had been knocked off its hinges and thrown into the lounge.

Nyx spun back around as a black blur thumped to the ground in front of them. Blond hair and a long black coat, tall wooden scepter in hand. A glowing green stone was embedded at the top. A single blue-black feather floated down in front of Nyx's face.

Ravens.

The man in the trench coat turned, spinning the staff in his hands. The world seemed to stop as, using all his strength, he slammed the butt of the staff to the ground.

A shock rolled over the yard, rippling into the distance. The stone in the man's scepter flared a bright lime green. The earth churned and another wave of animals burst forth from the tree line, crawling up from the ground.

The Necromancer faced the Laheys and Cole while his creations ravaged the marauding monsters. A splay of freckles across his nose, dark eyes contrasting starkly with his pale skin and blond hair. He broke out in a smile and bowed. "Nice to meet you lot."

"Who are you?" Alice shouted, but he ignored her and was off.

To the right, a group of zombies fell, their skin sizzling. Another boy in a dark coat stood behind them. Shaved hair and a long, dark scythe in hand, its blade glowing orange and dripping with zombie gunk.

A Reaper. *No,* Nyx said to herself, *look at his eyes.* They were golden.

The second boy gave a wicked, bloodlust-ish smile and

disappeared into the swarm of monsters. The backyard and surrounding forest were now completely packed with zombies. The noise was an incredible thing—growls, screams, ripping flesh, clashes, moaning, and heavy thumps. The army was overwhelming.

And now two Necromancers were running around, weapons out, while Nyx just stood there. She growled and yanked her jacket off. "I'm not just standing here all night."

"Nyx, there's nothing we can do, we have no proper weapons," Alice said.

"Nyx," Eris warned.

Erebus appeared then, chest heaving, and tossed a duffel bag to the ground. He pointed to it with a blade of his own. Inside, Nyx caught the glint of weaponry.

"Take your pick."

CHAPTER FIFTEEN

HEMOPHOBIA – FEAR OF BLOOD

A zombie was running toward her, moving faster than the usual type. Nyx reared back and flung the chair leg at its head. The hollow, broken end burrowed deep into its eye socket with enough force to knock it off its feet. It lay on its back as she ran up and buried a fire poker hilt deep in its chest. Then, one of Erebus's swords in hand, Nyx stood over it and brought the blade down on its throat, separating its head from its neck.

Nyx pulled the sword free and moved on, cutting her way through countless others. Her clothes and skin quickly became slick with black blood. Zombie spines were so brittle she could split them clean in half when she got in a good swing.

She felt constant flares of heat above her, meaning Alice was back at work. The wolves still darted among the madness, streaked with blood and zombie gunk.

Another group caught her attention. As they neared, she heard a shot, and the line of five zombies in front of her dropped, blood spraying her face. An arrow hung from the head of the last one. Reaper Iron—five zombies killed with the same arrow.

Behind them stood another trench coat–wearing boy. One side of his head was shaved, the other longer and tangled with blood. He held a crossbow in one hand and a long sword in the other.

"Sorry." He laughed at the fact that he'd almost hit her, and then continued with his attack. Over his shoulder, Nyx spotted Erebus shoving a dagger through a dead nurse's head while spinning around and cutting another zombie in half with his sword. Behind him, Cole shot with a compound bow atop one of the barbeques, picking them off one by one.

Something burst through the bushes farther down the tree line. A Brauge. Her whole body turned cold at the sight of it.

There were two types of zombies. Most common were things that used to be human, that had felt both physically and emotionally. Then there were Brauge. Stick thin and pale, with massive black eyes and hundreds of tiny razor teeth. They were never human. They were created from dark and forbidden Necromancer magic. Just one could substitute for an entire army. Their goal: maim, feed, and destroy.

There were ten of them now, crawling from the forest like spiders.

Erebus breathed. "Fuck." And then, spotting something, he shouted, "Mason!"

Mason, the blond one, was oblivious to the monsters behind him as he pulled a blade from a pile of ashes that was once a zombie. One of the Brauge latched onto his back and buried its face in his neck. Mason screamed.

The three other boys sprinted toward their friend. The one with the crossbow shot at the creature. "Ridley! Hurry up!"

The one called Ridley cut down two other Brauge attempting to join the attack. He spun and jammed the blade of his scythe into the attacking Brauge's back. The zombie howled and released Mason, who fell to the ground, pale and unmoving.

Nyx ran to him.

"Nyx!" Eris screamed. She felt the heat of Alice's fire as her arcs followed Nyx across the yard, fending off attackers. Nyx skidded to a halt, tripping in the mud and falling to her knees. Frantic, she rolled Mason onto his back. There was blood all down his neck and chest, holes where the Brauge had ravaged his skin.

"Mason," she called. He didn't open his eyes. "*Mason.*" Heavy footsteps approached. Nyx spun around, sword at the ready, but it was Cole. Mason tried to open his eyes.

The boy with the crossbow appeared then and glared at Cole. "He's hurt," Cole said. "Let me take him inside. He'll be okay."

The boy nodded stiffly and ran back into the mess. Cole reached down to pick Mason up.

"Nyx!"

She spun back around. Ridley and Erebus both danced among the horde, dark scythes in hand. The one with the crossbow yelled, "Take the ones around the back!"

Nyx began dispatching normal zombies while the others took apart the Brauge. There were still six left. Alice's flame remained overhead at all times while she fought alongside them, brandishing a blade of her own. The hunters began to cut them down.

A scream from behind Nyx, followed by a shout. "Damien!" It was Ridley, yelling at the Reaper with the crossbow. His face was panicked as he looked back over his shoulder while trying to fight off what was before him.

Nyx looked over to see Erebus locked in a duel with one of the Brauge, his scythe holding the full weight of the creature above him.

"Go, Lahey!" Cole yelled, having returned. Nyx was closer, so she sprinted back toward the Brauge. She almost made it before Erebus's arm gave out and the zombie fell upon him.

Somewhere behind her, Ridley screamed for his friend. Nyx raced toward the growing mess of blood and teeth. Erebus tried to keep it away, but the creature simply chewed his hands, as it did the rest of his body.

Nyx brought her sword down in the middle of the monster. White talons found their way out of the mess and smacked her in the chest, sending her flying into a Ping-Pong table. Her head hit the concrete with a thud. She opened her eyes again and watched as another Brauge crashed down onto Erebus.

Nyx scrambled to her feet again, vision blurry. She couldn't breathe.

Both Cole and Damien shot at the creatures from afar. The ringing in Nyx's head from the fall was too loud to hear anything. But she heard Erebus—his shouts, his struggle.

And then, suddenly all was silent. Nyx was almost on top of them before they were shot off their feet, a wave of electricity rippling through the air. She landed back on the concrete; air pushed from her lungs. She rolled to see a wave lift the Brauge from Erebus. Everyone was knocked onto their backs.

Erebus got to his feet. He wasn't bleeding anymore—not a single cut or graze. His tattered, blood-covered shirt hung from his torso, but beneath, Nyx couldn't see any marks on him.

The stunned Brauge rolled into a crouch. It lunged, with an unnaturally sharp movement, and Erebus uppercut the creature with the blade of his scythe, for a moment holding it in the air by its jaw.

The final razor-toothed Brauge rose, snarling, as Erebus dropped his scythe to release the other dead monster from its blade. He turned, and Nyx gasped at the distortion on his face.

Adorning his skin was the skull she'd seen in her dream earlier that day—shimmering bronze lines, dark circles trimmed with copper around both eyes. Magic and power rolled off of him like fog.

The space around Erebus seemed to slow. The final monster lunged, talons outstretched. Erebus brought his weapon up in a counter-clockwise swing, blade to the moon. He curved it around and brought it straight through the monster's abdomen. Both halves dropped to the ground with wet thuds.

Nyx stared, as did the others as they clambered to their feet.

"Erebus," Ridley said, hands on his knees.

Erebus didn't respond.

"Are you okay?" Damien yelled.

Erebus still said nothing. The scythe fell from his hands. He looked at Nyx—the marks on his face were gone. His eyes were bright with fear before they rolled back and his knees gave out.

"Oh fuck!" Damien darted to him with Eris close behind. Alice gathered her hood and ran after them.

Nyx knelt down next to Ridley and whispered, "If you guys need to go, just go. Get Erebus and Mason back, I can cover for you."

Ridley looked up at her and nodded a thank you, then turned to yell over his shoulder. "Damien! Go get Mason, we need to get them back to Max." Ridley scooped Erebus into his arms and stood.

"Wow, you guys are just leaving?" Eris said.

Ridley looked at her. "We can't stay."

"You're not even going to tell us who the fuck you are?"

"Nope." Ridley walked past her, straining with Erebus's weight.

Eris spun, ready to follow him, only to find that he'd disappeared. She swore and faced Nyx again. "Where's the other one?" She pointed to where Cole had been standing. Nyx looked over her shoulder—he, too, was gone.

"Do you know them?" Eris asked.

Nyx looked her dead in the eye, her face hot. "No."

Sirens grew on the wind. "We can talk about this later," Alice said. "We need to go."

CHAPTER SIXTEEN

ALGOPHOBIA — FEAR OF PAIN

They walked in silence, ripped and bloodied, dirt under their fingernails and grass in their hair. Alice threw one of the kitchen knives she was still holding into a neighbor's bin.

The moon was still high over the mountains of Misten that morning as they walked through the front door of Ebony Manor. In the foyer, they encountered Nyx's mother, Maura, and Harring—Alice's mother—all seated at the base of the staircase. At the sight of their daughters, all three stood.

"We heard the sirens," Harring said, pulling her crocheted shawl around her shoulders.

Nyx's mother enveloped the three of them in her arms. Eris made a face.

"The police said there was a disturbance and some injuries. People were talking about zombies coming out of the forest and attacking kids at a party," Maura said.

Eris pulled back. "And you're not mad that we snuck out? Why?"

"You're kids, we need to let you mess up and be able to sort it out on your own. We can't act like we never did any of this. I can't even count how many times we snuck out on Granny Deanna and accidentally raised some—"

"Oh wow, no." Alice shook her head. "This wasn't us. We just went to the party; we didn't raise anything."

All three mothers made the same face. "*Oh* . . . we thought . . ."

Nyx stepped forward. "No, someone else did this. We were the ones who got *rid* of them. Whoever did this raised *Brauge*—we don't even know how to do that."

Her mother's face went slack. "Brauge?"

"Who would do that?" Maura whispered.

"How many other Necromancers were at the party?" Nyx's mom asked.

"None, it was just us," Nyx said, without thinking.

Eris shot her a look. "Well, there were two others . . ."

"I've never seen them before," Alice added.

"And they helped us get rid of them—I don't think they made them."

"Shit," Maura whispered.

Nyx's mother took her daughter's face in her hands. "And you're sure you got rid of them all? Did anyone get hurt?"

Nyx thought about Mason being taken down by the Brauge, Erebus falling to the ground. And then she remembered the innards the captain had thrown. The bloodied shirt he'd unraveled.

Nyx swallowed. "Someone may have been hurt. I don't know . . ."

Her mother took a deep breath. "All right, let's not jump to conclusions just yet. The police are there. Let's just see what they come back with. Whoever did this, it sounds like they were putting on a show."

Harring turned to them. "You girls go get some sleep, and we'll sort this out when the sun is up, okay? Let's not worry until we know we have something to worry about."

The three of them nodded before Mae ushered them upstairs.

As they passed, they overheard Harring whispering to her sisters, "We need to find out who did this."

Maura added, "I'll put some extra guards around the house. I'll get Nuy to help me."

"This had to have been a targeted attack," Mae said. "No one would just attack a bunch of human kids. Someone knew our girls were there. This had to have been a hate crime."

A hate crime. Against them, because of their name.

Nyx wiped the fog from the bathroom mirror. The face that stared back was sunken, tired. She had a gash along her chin and another on her cheek, and a bruise on her forehead. Her slick hair stretched to her collarbone and dark circles were starting to form over burned patches of skin.

She scrunched her hair with the towel as she walked down the hall. Looking over the railing into the foyer, she could see the great golden clock: 3:30 a.m. Her bedroom was lit by the light of the moon streaming through the windows, silver washing over everything. Bjørn, atop the bed, opened a single eye.

Nyx's gaze settled on the large bird sitting outside the window, staring into the forest. She felt almost sick at the sight of it, remembering what Erebus said—that he had no idea who the scarred bird was. Nyx tried to calm her growing panic as she approached the window, eyes on the latch.

She extended a hand slowly and, as if on cue, the bird turned its head slightly to the side. Her fingers turned the latch, and she pushed the window open. It swung out, and the bird suddenly vanished. In its place was Erebus.

Nyx dropped to the bed, sighing heavily.

"Sorry if I scared you," he said, taking a seat on the verandah and crossing his legs. Bjørn, tail wagging, tried to push past Nyx to see who was outside.

"What are you doing here?" she asked, shuffling closer.

"Ridley wanted me to come and check that you all made it back safe. The others are looking after Mason."

"How is he?"

Erebus winced. "He's pretty bad. He's got some deep wounds but he should be all right." Bjørn jumped out the window to the verandah and proceeded to sniff Erebus's boots.

"How does that even happen? If he's a ghost, how can he get hurt?"

"I know, sometimes it doesn't make sense," he said. "As long as we're tangible, we can be hurt. Especially by things like Brauge."

"But why not just do what you showed me? You could've walked through everything without getting hurt, couldn't you?"

Erebus shook his head. "It doesn't work like that. To do that we have to be completely focused, not distracted by anything. There was simply too much going on. Besides, if we had, we wouldn't have been able to pick up any weapons."

"What happened to you tonight?" Nyx asked. "At the end."

He paused, scratching Bjørn's ears. "Honestly, I have no idea. I can hardly remember it."

"You literally shot us off our feet and then killed two Brauge quicker than I can blink," she said, eyes wide.

"I know . . . I've never done *that* before."

Nyx had goose bumps at the mere thought of his face again—the gleaming skull she'd seen in her dream. It was unnatural, even for their world. "Do you know what you were before you died?" she asked.

He shook his head. "I mean, I don't have the Reaper's Oath tattoo. But I don't really look like a Necromancer, nor have I ever been able to raise anything. But whatever I did tonight—that doesn't sound like either of them anyway."

Which was true. Never once had Nyx heard anything about Reapers or Necromancers being able to do what Erebus had done. The sheer amount of power and magic that had rolled off him was unlike anything she'd ever seen or heard of.

He looked up. "Do you know who could've been responsible for all of that?"

Nyx shook her head. "I don't even know anyone *capable* of raising Brauge. I don't know if Maura or my mother would be skilled enough to raise *one* let alone a whole *horde* of them."

Erebus nodded. "It's got to be related to the raven we've been seeing around here. Someone has been keeping an eye on you."

"My mom thinks it was an intentional attack. Like a hate crime," she added quietly.

Erebus looked confused. "Against who?"

Nyx sighed. "Us. My family is the only one in history to go against our own kind. Other Necromancers don't take too kindly to that. We were away from the family so we were easy picking."

"I don't know . . ." Erebus said. "I mean, if that was the case, how could they transform like me? To have access to magic powerful enough to make just one of these coats *and* also be strong enough to raise a whole swarm of Brauge—this has got to be some next level necromancy." He looked at her. "I just feel like there's so much more to it."

CHAPTER SEVENTEEN
TERATOPHOBIA — FEAR OF MONSTERS

A world away, a blue-skinned girl hurried through a great castle. Electricity charged around her as she ran, gliding down staircases and thundering across the floor. Blue-black hair, slick as oil, trailed behind her as she rounded a corner. Assortments of pins and glowing threads were entwined in her strands. She raised her palms to the closed door ahead of her and slammed into it. The door swung into a vaulted room. The people standing inside looked her way with a start.

The girl searched for her breath as another woman stood. Long black hair and two towering antelope horns—Ira, the Great Horned Witch.

"Kita, what is it?" Ira said, rounding the table.

Kita, still gasping, closed her mismatched eyes. "He's attacked them," she huffed.

"Who?" someone said from behind Ira.

"In the woods, he raised an—an army, and he tried to kill them."

Ira took Kita's face in her hands. "Who, darling?"

"Bellum," she blurted.

Ira pulled away, face morphing with disgust. The room chilled.

"Oh, dearie me." Someone giggled among the gasps.

"Are you sure?" Ira asked.

"When was this?" asked another Council member.

"Just now. Cole sent word—he was there."

Ira shook her head. "Wha—Cole? Why was he there?"

"That doesn't matter right now," boomed a man's voice. He walked toward them. His skin was gray and marked with hundreds of tiny tattoos, and his hair was white and tied at the nape of his neck. Dark brows stern over fiery orange eyes.

Mortem.

"If he's attacking them, then he knows who they are. They're not safe anymore, Ira." He looked at Kita. "Are they hurt?"

She shook her head.

"What are we going to do?" Ira asked.

"We've no other choice. We need to bring them here. They don't yet know what they are."

"The girl isn't ready," Ira protested.

"If we wait any longer, he might kill her." He turned to the others. "Hatter," he said, and a ginger-haired boy with angry-looking face paint stepped forward. The one called Hatter pulled the antique tailored suit he wore tight, adjusting the battered top hat atop his curls. He smiled a manic-looking grin, mismatched eyes on his leader.

"Yes, sir," he replied, snickering.

"Go and get the girl. Ira, you get the boy. The rest of you, get everything ready. Kita, I want you to bring me every bit of information you have about the attack. And starting now, I want someone in the globe room on constant lookout for any activity from Bellum."

The room scattered. Mortem turned back to the witch.

"Okay," Ira said, standing with her partner. "We're really doing this."

Mortem nodded. "Finally."

CHAPTER EIGHTEEN

ECCLESIOPHOBIA — FEAR OF CHURCHES

The boys were in *so* much trouble.

They had returned home carrying a limp and bloody Mason and an unscathed Erebus.

Max had lost his shit.

The Legions had summoned them the very next morning, furious with them for abandoning their duties and interfering with the Living Ones. They'd been asked about the fifth boy, Cole. All of them had shrugged, saying that they knew nothing.

"I mean, he was cute and all, but I've never actually seen him before," Damien had commented.

They'd all been temporarily suspended from hunting and weren't permitted to travel through the doors. Which meant they were stuck in Dewmort until their suspensions were lifted.

Which meant none of them were able to find the strange raven. But Ridley had a feeling that a mere double suspension wouldn't stop Erebus.

It was almost six in the morning, and Ridley was in the middle of repainting one of the main pieces of the underground cathedral—scenes from the Garden of Eden merged with the Romans burning Christ on the cross, and, above and below it, depictions of heaven and hell accompanied by angels and demons—when there was a loud creak and the doors of the church opened. Erebus entered, making his way past the old pews.

Ridley made a small curving movement with his paintbrush—a black horn for a devil. "Don't sit there," he said without looking. Erebus moved away from the pew he was about to sit in. "I ran out of nails for the floorboards so I had to pull them from that pew. Sit there and you'll be staked."

Erebus settled on the dusty floor while Ridley rinsed his paintbrush. Ridley could hear Erebus fiddling with pieces of broken plaster.

"I'm sorry," Erebus said quietly.

Ridley set his paintbrush in the water and faced Erebus. He was still in his pajamas, boxers and a long-sleeved shirt. "For what?"

"For bringing you into this. I lost the pendant. If I had just been more careful, none of this would have happened. I should have just—"

"No." Ridley shook his head. "You did the right thing. They needed help. None of us want anything to happen to her or her family."

Erebus was silent.

"Are you going to tell me what happened?" Ridley asked. He'd seen Erebus change—they all had. For a moment, he had turned into something none of them had ever seen before. Something *else*.

"You saw my face?" he asked.

Ridley nodded. "I think we all did."

Erebus thought about how frightened Nyx had looked. He didn't know what they had seen, only that it had stayed with them all. "I don't know what it was. I was being held by the Brauge and it was just getting heavier, and I felt like I couldn't breathe. And then I got hot all of a sudden. I had this surge of adrenaline, and suddenly I wasn't sore or tired. I just felt strong."

"Dude, you literally didn't have a scratch on you when you got up. And there was all this . . . stuff coming off you—like mist or steam or something. And your face . . . I don't know. It looked like it was glowing." He paused. "Do you think you could do it again?"

Erebus shook his head. "I don't even know what it was, let alone how to bring it on."

"Do you think it has something to do with your life before you died?"

Erebus didn't know. He was so full of this not knowing that he felt numb. As if it was all out of his control. Which it was. "Rid, I don't know *who* I am. Let alone what. And what happened . . . I don't know what that was. Neither does anyone else by the sounds of it. And it fucking scares me."

Ridley's eyes softened. "Hey, it's going to be all right." He reached over and touched Erebus's arm. "How about we go and try to do some research or something? I mean, if I saw a sketch or a picture of what your face was like, I'd be able to recognize it."

Erebus couldn't help but laugh. "Ah yes, let's start in some beast manuals, hey?"

Ridley smirked. "Pretty fitting, you *are* a fucking freak. But what do you think?"

Erebus shrugged. "I guess. If we do find something, I can start piecing this shitstorm together."

"Sounds like a plan."

Ridley opened the doors to the library, revealing a vast interior of towering shelves and a painted, domed ceiling. Chandeliers hung from the ceiling, aglow with magic. The building was silent as the two boys made their way through the center aisle. Shelves of mahogany to both sides of them held hundreds of books.

In Dewmort, the library held all information from human evolution to '80s pop culture to the war between the faeries and the sea people to the war between the Necromancers and the Reapers. Ridley was hopeful they'd have something—anything— to help Erebus.

"Is that you, Ana?" someone yelled from the front of the room.

"Even better!" Ridley called as the librarian peered out from around one of the shelves near the bronze service desk, a stack of books in arm. She was a Necromancer. Eyes like fireflies and hair tied at the nape of her neck in two curly, orange buns.

She frowned. "Oh . . . sorry, I thought you were my relief. Can I help you two find something?"

Ridley smiled dashingly. "We were wondering if you could show us any of your beast manuals?"

"Beast manuals?" She raised an eyebrow. "Er, they should be . . . shelf sixty-four, over there." She pointed behind them, to one of the golden plaques at the end of an aisle.

"Thank you." Erebus smiled.

They collected at least ten books each and sat at a table not far from where the librarian was busy stacking returns. Erebus had so far found nothing apart from anatomy sketches of a centaur and a pixie, and instructions on how to plant dryad-baby seeds.

Erebus sighed, closing his book and setting it aside. He looked over. Ridley was watching the librarian as she moved back and forth from her cart of books.

Erebus cleared his throat and Ridley snapped to. "Have you found anything?"

"Nothing so far—just myths about dragons and shit," Ridley said.

"Yeah, I'm pretty sure I picked up another book about extinct supernatural creatures. Maybe there's something in there? I *have* been dead for a long time, so who knows."

Ridley pointed at the librarian. "Does she have a tattoo?" he whispered.

"What?"

"On her neck, right there. Is that a tattoo?"

Erebus squinted. Above the collar of her shirt, he could see that yes, there was some kind of script along her neck, below her ear. "I mean, yeah, I think so . . ."

Ridley stood abruptly, chair screeching across the marble floor. The librarian spun.

"Rid!" Erebus hissed.

"I'm sorry, but that tattoo on your neck . . ." Ridley pointed.

She brought her hand up and brushed her neck. "What about it?"

"It's the Reaper's Oath, isn't it?" Ridley approached her slowly.

She took off her glasses and glared at him. "Yes, it is, and?"

"You're a Necromancer," Ridley stated. She took a step back and crossed her arms.

"Ridley, what are you doing?" Erebus asked.

Ridley turned, giving a halfhearted chuckle. "Erebus, she's a *Necromancer*."

Erebus paused.

Ridley looked at him expectantly. "What Necromancer family would have that tattoo, Erebus?"

"Holy shit," Erebus said. "You're a Lahey."

The Lahey shifted uncomfortably.

Ridley laughed again. "How the fuck? I can't believe this."

Erebus stepped forward. "Wait, who is Nyx to you?"

"You know Nyx?" she asked.

"Yes!" they said in unison.

"How? If you're both here in Dewmort . . ."

Erebus's smile faltered. "Well, yeah, that's a long story."

The girl regarded them. "Nyx is my younger cousin. My little sister is Eris—I don't know if you know her. My name's Die."

Ridley turned to Erebus. "Eris was at the party, right?" Erebus nodded.

The front door of the library opened suddenly. "Hellooo, sorry I'm late, love!" a woman yelled.

Die lowered her voice. "Look, I'm about to finish my shift. Borrow what you need and come with me to my place. I might be able to help."

"How do you know what we need help with?" Erebus asked, suddenly wary.

Die rolled her eyes at him, and he realized now how much she did look like Eris. "I just . . . I'm pretty sure I know what you're trying to find, okay?"

Ridley and Erebus followed Die through Dewmort. They spoke briefly, introducing themselves as she led them to her home. It wasn't much—a little loft above a corner café, painted black on the outside. It reminded Erebus a little of Ebony Manor. She took them up a set of wooden stairs at the back of the café, where she fumbled with the door.

"And here we are," she huffed, dropping her backpack and hanging up her keys as she walked in. Erebus looked at the high-peaked triangular ceiling, all exposed wooden beams. Die had strung fairy lights everywhere, leading from the small kitchen to the bed in the center of the room, to a large triangular window that took up the whole back wall.

"Have a seat, if you want," she said from the kitchen. She pointed to two beanbags by the window. Ridley and Erebus sat, library bags in hand. "So," she continued, pouring herself a glass of water, "how did you meet them?"

"I met Nyx on a hunt," Erebus said. "We ran into each other. Her detector started going crazy, and she freaked out. I didn't know she was a Necromancer so I freaked too. And . . . she pistol-whipped me."

Die almost did a spit take. She set down the cup. Erebus continued: "I actually dropped something there, and Nyx found it."

"What was it?"

Erebus pulled the chain from under his shirt to show her the locket. "I don't have any of my former memories. This is all I had on me when I showed up in Dewmort."

"Could you remember your name?" she asked, sitting cross-legged in front of him.

"Yeah, but that was it. It was actually Nyx who helped me remember my whole name."

Die made a face. "How would she know?"

Erebus shrugged. "I have no idea. We met and then two seconds later, we heard it all of a sudden, like someone had whispered it to us. I don't know if that sounds crazy or—"

"Stop," Die said, holding up a hand. "Don't move."

"What?" Ridley asked.

Die got on her knees and leaned in closer, squinting as she studied Erebus's face. "Not crazy at all . . ." she said at last.

"What?" Erebus asked.

Die sat back on her heels, laughing. "Oh my God. No wonder her detector was going off."

Erebus gave Ridley a nervous glance. "Yeah . . . it's because I'm dead, right?" Erebus asked.

Die laughed again. "No. Here, get up." She stood, then held out her hands. He took them and she hauled him to his feet before leading him to one of the mirrors on her wall.

"Stand here," she said, standing behind him and gripping his shoulders. "I want you to look into your reflection. And I mean *really* look into it. *Lean* into it. Keep looking until your eyes strain."

"Why?" Erebus asked, turning to her.

She took his head and forced him to face the mirror again. "You need to see what I can see right now. It can be difficult for people to learn how to do it. To see someone's Underneath. You have to basically peel away the layers to see what's there. Every little hair, every freckle, every line on your skin or scar. Tear it all away."

As she spoke, Erebus watched himself, still unsure. He stared until his eyes started to sting. He resisted the urge to blink and felt himself starting to fall forward, into the mirror. His eyes devoured the image of his face. He looked deeper until his features started to blur. Stripping and fading away until they were gone.

He gasped and stepped back, closing his eyes.

"What!" Ridley yelled.

"Did you see it?" Die asked excitedly.

Erebus didn't know what he had seen. It had been dark.

"Open your eyes. Look again," she said.

He didn't want to look. But he did. A single eye open, Erebus found in his reflection a stranger. His face was clouded, lines crisscrossing in the shape of a skull. Encircling his eyes were deep pockets of shadow, trimmed with shimmering bronze. His lips were etchings of teeth, each gleaming with sunlight.

"What is it?" Ridley asked.

Along his hairline, thick red peonies opened and closed. Blooming and unblooming. Their luscious centers glowed golden like tiny tea light candles were nestled among the petals. They sat atop his head like a crown. This had to have been what Nyx and Ridley had seen at the party. He laughed out loud. He couldn't believe what he was seeing. Die appeared in the reflection, beaming at him.

"I have flowers in my hair," was all he could say.

"You have flowers in your hair," she agreed, smiling.

"What the *fuck* are you two talking 'bout?" Ridley asked.

Erebus focused on Die. "He doesn't see it, does he?"

Die's smile faltered. "For some it comes naturally. Others can take years to learn. But sometimes it can, like, *leak* out. Especially if you're emotional or full of a lot of energy or power."

That explained how they had seen it at the party. "What does it mean?" he asked. "How come you can see it?"

Die sighed. "Well, that's a long story too. The short version is, before I died, I was a little bit like you." Erebus and Ridley stared expectantly. "I never got to know the full story of what I was," Die continued. "I was a pretty strong Necromancer—my ability to raise was alarming to my family. Our goal is to repress our powers, not grow them. It wasn't until I got older that I started having dreams of this . . . other place. I started meeting people while I slept, and they weren't like us. They were different, creatures I'd never seen before. A whole kingdom of them, and they were ruled over by this council. They told me I was different. And important."

Erebus's stomach dropped at the mention of dreams and councils.

"I had these dreams every night for about a year, and my powers were slowly getting out of hand. I'd been kicked out of school for accidentally raising an eighty-six-year-old grandmother from her grave on the other side of town."

"Across town?" Ridley asked, impressed.

Die nodded. "That night, one of the people I'd dreamed about appeared in my room and told me it was time to go, that I was getting too strong. He said he knew how to help me and could explain everything. His name was Mortem."

"Oh shit." Ridley looked at Erebus.

"Do you know him?" Die asked.

Erebus felt sick. "Well, no—but I've been experiencing the same thing. Dreams, all the time. I've seen the Council. Mortem has talked to me, and he left me a letter—"

"Is he dangerous?" Ridley interrupted.

Die shook her head. "Absolutely not. Mortem *did* help me."

"What happened?" Erebus pressed.

"There's more to it than what we know. The universe isn't just Dewmort and the human world. Mortem sent one of his Council members, Hatter, to bring me to their world—the Hallows. I know, it sounds ridiculous. But the Red Door? *That's* where it goes. There's a whole other *world* on the other side of it."

"What's it like?" Ridley asked.

Die smiled like she didn't know where to start. "It's the most amazing thing I've seen. All these stories that we hear as kids of magical places and creatures, it's *all* there. Every kind of magic you can think of, every god or goddess you've heard about. Everyone in the Hallows has an Underneath, that's where I learned to see them. Everything is colorful and crazy and the wrong way around, but it's amazing, you know? Mortem trained me to be a real Necromancer. They let my powers run free—I raised every day, and with every raise I got stronger. I didn't feel like I was going to explode anymore."

Die fell silent then. Erebus cleared his throat. "So how did you . . . you know, end up here?"

"One night, I went to sleep and just . . . never woke up again. Well, I *did*, but it was here. Not in the Hallows. The hospital found me, and told me I was dead. They couldn't tell me *how* I had died, though." She paused. "Mortem found me after a few days. He was hysterical. My throat had been slit in my sleep. They didn't know who was responsible."

"After I died, I lost all my new abilities and went back to being a regular Necromancer," she said sadly. "Mortem came with me to visit my family afterward, but he made sure no one could see us. That was probably the hardest part, having to come back and face what I'd left. I had to watch Eris breaking down—still, every day. She didn't know why I'd left her—she was too little to understand why I wasn't there. And my mom, she blamed herself. She thought for such a long time that I'd run away because of the family—because of our rules. There was no way to comfort them."

Ridley shifted uncomfortably. Erebus remembered Max taking Ridley to his own funeral. Invisible in the background while his family mourned. It had been the hardest thing he'd ever had to watch.

Die shrugged. "So I moved in here and started working at the library to kill time. I still go to the Hallows sometimes. And I still go visit at the Manor. I even sleep in my old bed some nights, in the room I used to share with Eris."

"And you never found out why Mortem took you to the Hallows?" Erebus asked.

Die shook her head. "He never actually said what I was becoming. He said that there were people in the world who knew what I was and would want me dead. I think he just wanted me to be free."

Erebus narrowed his eyes. Die's skin was suddenly blurring and starting to peel . . . "You still have your Underneath," he said.

Die looked embarrassed. "Oh, you can see it? Sorry, talking about my family makes me sad sometimes."

"No, don't be sorry," he replied, taking in her new, shimmering visage. Her skin was blue, with flaming orange hair and blood-red eyes. Gold paint shimmered over her eyelids and trailed down her cheeks like molten tears. Symbols and etchings in another language adorned her forehead, jaw, and arms in symmetrical patterns that sparkled as if painted with the blood of stars. Her ears grew longer, as did her eyelashes. And atop her head, amid a shining tangle of golden wire, grew two deep-red horns.

"I lost my powers when I died, but I kept this," Die said, gesturing to her body.

"Which I don't understand, by the way." Ridley piped up. "If you lost yours when you died, how are Erebus's powers only just coming in?"

"I don't understand that either," Die said. "But I'm sure once you meet the Council, they'll be able to explain—hopefully."

"So, what now?" Ridley asked. "We just wait until the Council is ready for him? Or *decides* they want to tell him what the fuck is going on?"

Die sighed. "I've got no idea. I'm sorry I can't be any more help."

Erebus replied, "No, no, no, you've got no idea how much you've helped me. You've told me more about myself in the last half hour than I've learned in the last few hundred years. Thank you."

Ridley smiled at her, and the two of them made their way to the door.

"Just promise me one thing," Die said behind them.

Erebus turned, hand on the doorknob. "What's that?"

"If Nyx is somehow tied up in all of this, look after her, please?"

"Of course," they said.

Die laughed. "Good, 'cause if my baby cousin gets hurt, I'll have to break your soul."

CHAPTER NINETEEN

ANATIDAEPHOBIA – FEAR THAT YOU ARE
BEING WATCHED BY A DUCK

The Young God stood in a cottage, in the depths of the woods. Gray brick and a thin thatched roof, partially caved in. Rubble and pieces of broken glass, pottery, and splintered wood littered the hard-packed dirt floor. Mother Nature had entangled herself within the house. Vines grew up the walls in the old kitchen and across the windows. Wild grass sprouted through the cracks in the floor. Pastel flowers decorated the greenery.

The man bowed to walk under a fallen beam, glass crunching beneath his feet. Four old paintings hung on the brick wall above the hearth. One was of a woman—a portrait of a pale-haired, orange-eyed Necromancer lounging in a lagoon atop a bank of pearly skulls, one in her hand.

Ossa—*bones*—the eldest of the Original's three children.

To the right of her was a portrait of a boy. Black hair and red eyes. Arms spread wide to welcome the rushing wind. Dozens of white eyes behind him—his army of dead awaiting his order.

Bellum—*war*—the youngest, the son, of the Original.

The Young God stared longingly at the young boy in the painting. Hair black as night. Face smooth and unmarked. His eyes burning and his hands red with power.

He had been so young then.

Then, a woman much like the first. Cutem—*skin*. Silver eyes like the moon, her beautiful face snarling as she raised her fist in the air. Her white dress was stained with the blood of their enemies.

The Young God stood in front of the old, dusty hearth and glimpsed the final portrait, askew and faded: a dark, stormy sky surrounding a tall, cloaked figure wearing a great horned helmet atop his head.

There, in all his might stood Great Neco, brother of Grim and the father of necromancy.

The Young God knelt before the hearth and bowed his head. "Don't fret, Father. You will rise again. I will not fail." He stood then, and listened: a rustling in the leaves outside. He turned to see a woman ducking under the rubble of the half-fallen house.

"Hurry, Bellum," the woman hissed. "My husband will be back soon."

The Young God—Bellum—dug around in his pockets. His fingers found two pieces of paper. "Here," he said, handing them to her.

His sister snatched the photographs from him.

Ossa's gray skin and porcelain hair, usually down in long, wavy locks, was held atop her head in a bun of golden chains, pins, and trailing jewels. Her orange eyes filtered through thick layers of dazzling kohl and gold dust. Her lean body was covered by a long gown of sea green, and at the hollow of her throat sat a golden pendant—a locket in which a single ruby was embedded.

Bellum frowned at it. From her lovely husband, no doubt. His sister covered the pendant with her hand as she studied the photos.

"It's lovely to see you too," he grunted.

Bellum wondered what had happened to her over the years. All that time spent in the Hallows with *him* had changed her. What had happened to the Ossa who would march onto a battlefield even after she was already covered in mud and blood? For years she'd used glamour and magic to hide her true identity. Bellum could see it now, shimmering around her like a cloak made of summer light. But over the years it seemed that perhaps Ossa had let this glamour run more than skin deep. Bellum didn't like it. Bellum didn't like *him*—the one who had managed to make her soft.

Ossa smiled, a hint of her old evil shining through. "Yes," she said, handing back the photos. "I know who they are."

"Even the boy?" Bellum mused, waiting to see if she would recognize him.

Ossa smirked. "Oh yes, the little Salem who got away. My husband expects them here soon. He's been watching them. He says they're only growing stronger. I take it you had no luck with your attack?"

Bellum shook his head. "I didn't even get close. The boy is already too strong for what I had at the time. I can smell his power—it reeks."

"Listen, brother," Ossa purred. Bellum looked up. "If I were you, I'd try to put an end to them before they make it here."

"Why?"

"Once they get to the Hallows—both of them, together— they'll be the most protected things in the whole kingdom. Mortem will have his eyes on them at all times. I won't be able to get anywhere near them."

Bellum went to speak but his sister cut him off, shooing him before she vanished into the air.

"And you're running out of time."

CHAPTER TWENTY

TETRAPHOBIA — FEAR OF
THE NUMBER FOUR

A dark room. Large and circular, with a vaulted ceiling and raw rock walls that dripped with moisture and glowed with bioluminescent moss. In its center, an enormous diagram of the Earth. The planet rotated slowly, its light bathing the room in blue.

Mortem watched the globe carefully. He could hear the click of boots approaching the cavern entrance but did not turn to see who entered.

Two sets of footsteps now. They stopped behind him. A flowery, incense-like perfume wafted through the air—Ira. Beneath that, the leathery scent of Thorn, the head guard.

"You haven't left yet, I see?" Mortem called over his shoulder.

"Show me the princes," Ira commanded.

With a wave of his hand, Morten replaced the globe with an image of the Nethers—the collective name for the Hallows, the ghost city of Dewmort, and many other kingdoms.

Four scenes—for four brothers—formed in front of them.

There was Keelie, the eldest, held in a prison in a great snowy mountain, weighed down by ancient iron chains. His bare back was ridged with whip scars and burns—marks from centuries of torture.

Then Sage, the youngest of the fair-haired twins, frozen under a lake for hundreds of years. Mortem could see the chains and cuffs that held him prisoner, a forgotten prince in the barren, abandoned wilderness. Mortem regarded these two lost princes sadly. For eons the Council had tried to find them, save them, set them free. But their locations could never be determined.

Then there was Ander, the eldest twin. Stripped of skin and voice, the remnants of his body hidden away by the Council after his death. His shimmering bones were home to thin vines and tiny pink flowers. The castle brick could be seen behind the pile of them. Only Mortem and Ira knew where they'd been hidden.

Finally, there was Erebus. The second eldest. He'd suffered possibly the worst torture of all—amnesia. Stripped of all memories the moment Bellum took his life. Still, Mortem could see it, the power he held even now as he laughed with his new brothers in Dewmort. It rolled off him in dark waves, the winding shapes of skulls slashed by scythes. Tendrils of dark power just waiting to erupt.

The same dark powers that had consumed Grim.

Four brothers.

Four princes.

One Relic.

"Bellum has made no advances?" Ira asked.

"We don't know; we can't seem to locate him," Mortem answered. He could tell she was worried. They'd hunted the Young God, son of Neco, for centuries, but he continued to escape their grasp. And he knew about the Relics.

"I'll go and get Erebus. Hatter has already left to get the girl," Ira said. "Hopefully once they're here we can put an end to this mess Bellum has created."

CHAPTER TWENTY-ONE

LEPORIPHOBIA — FEAR OF RABBITS

Alice blared Hozier from the speaker in her room. It was six in the morning but she had no intention of turning down the volume. "How long do you think they're gonna keep us up here?" Eris asked, lying in Alice's bed with the covers pulled up to her chin.

By sunrise, the inhabitants of Ebony Manor were awake and nervous. Nyx's mother and her aunt Nuy, Eris's mother, sat at the kitchen table with a radio and a laptop between them, both searching and waiting for any news about the attack.

They'd sent the girls upstairs until they knew what was going on—they didn't want them to hear anything until they were positive there was something to worry about. And whatever they learned, the women wanted the children to hear it from them, not the local news.

"I don't know," Alice huffed. Nyx leaned back against the wall and rested her legs over Eris's, creating a plus sign with their bodies.

Lilith sat next to her as Alice spoke. "Do you think it was real? The blood on that shirt and the stuff that he threw?"

The door swung open and in walked Chasity, still half asleep and in her pajamas. She rubbed her face and shuffled toward the bed. "Alice, I'm going to smash that speaker when I find it." She flopped onto the bed, lengthways like Eris. Bjørn came through after her and rested his head on the edge of the bed, big eyes waiting for someone to pat him.

Nyx turned back. "I don't know. Hopefully not, but I guess we'll find out soon enough." She could still hear the faint wail of the radio downstairs. She had no idea what would happen if someone had actually died. They would probably be kicked out of the academy. Run out of town by the Reapers.

"So how did you guys get out of there?" Chasity asked.

Eris and Nyx exchanged a glance. "We got help," Alice blurted before they could stop her.

"From who?"

"There were other Reapers there," Nyx said. "Obviously from out of town or something—I've never seen them before."

Chasity opened a purple eye and looked at her suspiciously. "I heard there were Brauge? How did you guys get through them?"

"Oh, one of the other Reapers was, like, weird," Alice said. "He somehow threw a heap of them into the air and, like, shape-shifted or something."

Chasity eyed Nyx again as she sat up. "What?"

The door swung open. Harring appeared and asked them to come downstairs.

Two people had died. The police had found their shredded remains in the woods not far from the frat house. "We haven't heard anything from the academy just yet. We'll let you know if we do," Mae said. "Right now, let's just all stay calm. We'll get through this."

Nyx lay in bed that night with the weight of Bjørn on her

feet. If they hadn't been there, no one would have died.

She rolled over, trying to shake it from her head. The pale moonlight was harsh as she looked into the trees beyond their backyard. Nyx pushed the window open, inviting the mountain breeze into her bedroom. There was a glint of feathers in the treetops. She closed her eyes.

And as she finally felt herself starting to drift, there was a thud. Followed by a loud bang, as if someone had dropped a sack of books onto the floor. Bjørn whimpered excitedly at the foot of the bed. She flipped over and looked.

Glitter was suddenly everywhere, covering the entire bedroom floor. The doors of the wardrobe across the room were open slightly, and a bright light flooded out. A single teacup sat atop the chest of drawers next to it.

"What the fuck?" Nyx jolted upright, quickly reaching behind the headboard for her scythe.

The wardrobe door widened. Someone inside grunted in annoyance amid the clanging of china and coat hangers.

"Who on earth makes a . . . a *portal* in a wardrobe, my goodness . . ."

Her heart pounded as the door opened fully to reveal a man tangled in one of her sweaters. He was holding a stack of saucers and teacups, and a porcelain teapot. There were dried, bloodied handprints over everything.

He cleared the cupboard and the entanglement of clothes and sighed at the ceiling. He was a flurry of auburn colors—deep reds, oranges, and burgundy, wearing what looked like an antique suit and a patterned top hat atop frizzy, chili-red hair. He faced Nyx's chest of drawers and set his things down. Glitter glinted in his curls.

"What . . . are you doing?" She pointed her scythe at him like a shotgun. He paid her no mind as he poured himself some tea. "Who are you?"

He slammed his empty cup and saucer down. Dabbed his mouth frantically with a napkin. "Oh, you're quite right, how rude of me." He spun and threw out his hand. "I'm Hatter."

Nyx stared at it: white skin, long fingernails. "Uh, okay . . . I'm Nyx." She didn't miss the angry red tattoo on his wrist—*Wrath* written in a chaotic scrawl.

"Oh yes, I know," he replied, returning to his teapot.

She caught sight of the other wrist then, the word *Purge* written in the same angry script.

"How?" she asked, scythe still raised. His eyes were neon blue and green. Full heterochromia—mismatched. They were encircled by dark-red stains that ran down both cheeks, like painted tears. Underneath all this, though, Nyx could see the boy he really was.

He turned back around, staring out the window as if searching for something in the trees. "Mortem sent me," he said quietly, voice suddenly serious. "I was to come and collect you while Ira got Erebus."

Nyx dropped her scythe. "Erebus?"

But Hatter's attention remained elsewhere. He leaned down, glaring harder through the trees. "Something isn't right here. We have to go." He grabbed the staff of Nyx's scythe and hauled her from her bed without hesitation. Bjørn jumped up, tail wagging.

A raven called outside as Hatter grabbed another of his teacups from the drawers and threw it to the ground. Instead of smashing against the floorboards like Nyx expected, it dissolved, turning into a swirling purple mass at their feet, glittering with stars.

A portal. He pushed Nyx toward it.

"Wait, no!" She turned around and pushed back. "Where are we going?"

"It isn't safe here. We have to find Ira and Erebus. She's in Dewmort, we'll go there. He can't get to us there."

"Who?" Nyx demanded. "Dewmort? I'm not dead; I can't go there!"

"Well, I am, and I'm your chaperone." He spun her back around, pushing her closer to the hole, Bjørn bounding happily at their feet.

"What—I can't just leave!"

But Hatter paid her no mind, and with a final shove Nyx disappeared into the hole in the floor.

CHAPTER TWENTY-TWO
ANGROPHOBIA — FEAR OF ANGER
OR BECOMING ANGRY

"Sorry, I don't allow random people into my home. Not even random women," Damien said, blocking the warehouse's entryway while staring at the hunched-over woman hiding a horned witch beneath her glamour.

"You don't seem to understand the importance of my being here, Damien Tate," Ira insisted. "You *must* let me see Erebus."

"I'm sorry, Miss Lady, but—"

"No! I need to see him! *Erebus!*" Ira held open the door with a strength that Damien couldn't withstand. Her voice echoed through the warehouse.

Upstairs, recognizing the smooth, velvety voice, Erebus bolted for the staircase. Reaching the bottom, he found Damien fighting over the door with an old woman. He frowned—he was *sure* that voice belonged to Ira, the horned woman from one of his dreams.

The woman spotted him over Damien's shoulder. "Oh, thank the *gods*."

Erebus watched her face shimmer as she shoved Damien aside. Two spiraling horns in her mess of long hair rose as her skin suddenly became smooth and unmarked.

Ira was breathing heavily, cheeks flushed, hair windswept. "Erebus," she said with severity, "we need to leave. *Now*."

Bellum watched from the edge of the forest as Hatter left a note atop Nyx's dresser, along with one of his cups, before he, too, disappeared into the abyss. The portal closed behind him.

Bellum was shaking. Furious. He'd gotten there as quickly as he could. His sister had been right—it would be almost impossible for her to rid the world of the two of them if they made it inside. He'd missed his chance at the Necromancer by mere seconds. If he'd just been faster, he could have disposed of her before the Hatter had even arrived. He wouldn't hear the end of this—Ossa would have to deal with Nyx now.

Dark smoke curled from his coat, extending to the surrounding brush, and setting it on fire. He had ravaged the forest, hoping to maybe catch them. The forest burned to the ground in his wake. He heard the calls of owls searching for their young; the desperate galloping of deer as they ran to escape, and their pain as flames licked at them.

He eventually found himself standing at the back of Ebony Manor once more. Bellum narrowed his eyes at Hatter's letter. His feet slipped out from underneath him as his coat enveloped him. His tiny raven body slipped through the window and went to the top of the drawers, accidentally knocking some of the teacups to the floor. Using his beak and talons, he tried to peck the letter open, grasping it in his feet.

Suddenly there were footsteps in the hall outside. The door opened before Bellum could escape.

"Nyx?" a girl asked, opening the door and slowly entering the room. "I heard banging, are you okay—"

She spotted him. The scarred raven she'd seen so many times before. Her face contorted as she hissed. In his mind, Bellum snarled pure rage. The girl opened her mouth to scream.

But it was too late.

CHAPTER TWENTY-THREE

BASIPHOBIA — FEAR OF NOT BEING ABLE
TO STAND OR WALK

The portal opened again, launching Nyx face first into a brick wall, scythe still in hand. Bjørn landed with a yelp. Hatter barreled into the side of a dumpster amid a mixture of curses and laughter.

Nyx peeled her cheek from the rough surface and looked around. They were in an alley crammed between two tall buildings. Dumpsters lined either side, stains marking the concrete. Across the street were French Colonial–style homes, pastel in color, with winding vinery and wrought iron rails. The sun was only just setting.

This wasn't Misten.

Bjørn sniffed along the walls, while Nyx went over to Hatter, lying on the ground and laughing. She grabbed his collar and hauled him to his feet. He continued to laugh even after she threw him against the wall.

"What the *fuck*?"

Hatter wiped away tears. "A man just tried to kill you and your puppy dog."

She slammed him against the wall again, pointing her blade at him. "*Hatter*!"

"Okay, okay." He held up his hands defensively and took a deep breath. "SothisguynamedBellum.He'shuntingyouandErebus—he's*also*abird—andhewasjuststandingatyourwindow.Waitingtokill youinyoursleep."

"What?"

"And now, I'm here to take you to the Hallows, to keep you safe."

The Hallows.

Hatter stopped smiling and leaned in close, his expression sinister. "An ancient Necromancer who wishes to destroy the Nethers and the Relics has just discovered you're no longer home." He looked up to the sky and smiled. "And he's not very happy about it."

Nyx glared at him. "Take me back."

"Oh no. He won't spare time for your family. He's already looking for you in the woods. He'll be at the door before long."

"The door?"

Hatter gestured behind her. She turned, still clutching his collar. In the alley wall were two doors. One rusted, chained, boarded, and nailed shut. The other golden, polished to a shine.

The golden door was trembling.

"There are hundreds of doors in the human world that it goes to. *But*! Don't worry. Bellum cannot enter Dewmort or any part of the Nethers. Not anymore."

"This is Dewmort?" Nyx asked, stepping back. "What the hell is the Nethers?"

Hatter gestured around him. "*This* is Dewmort. City of the Dead. The Nethers is its conveyor."

Nyx glared at him. "What do you mean 'conveyor'?"

"Dewmort is carried *within* the Nethers." He laughed again.

"Stop with your stupid riddles, Hatter!" she snarled. "Are we safe here?" Hatter nodded vigorously. "And you're keeping me here?"

Hatter shook his head. "No. In the Hallows under the protection of the Council."

Council? "Why? Why can't you just keep me here? Why do I have to go to the Hallows?"

"Because, my dear, Bellum may not be able to cross into the Nethers now. But he will find a way. And the safest place for you right now is the Hallows."

"What about Bjørn?"

Hatter looked at the wolf seated at their feet, wagging his tail and watching them fight. "Suuuuure he can come. Chef *loves* puppy Bolognese."

Nyx glared at him as footsteps rounded the corner. As they looked toward the mouth of the alley, Erebus appeared, walking next to an old woman. As they watched, the old woman rippled and shimmered. Her skin peeled away, revealing a tall, leather-clad, raven-haired woman. Smooth, pale skin, and long, ridged antelope horns. Her eyes were dark red and surrounded with silver paint or glitter that covered her lids and flicked out over her temples.

"Hatter," she said, calling Bjørn to her side and taking Nyx around the shoulders. "Open the door."

Nyx looked at Erebus as the woman angled her toward the rusted door. She hugged her scythe to her chest. He gave her an encouraging smile.

"What's happening?" Nyx asked.

The rusted door trembled under Hatter's gaze. One by one, the bolts flew out. The chains disintegrated, and the boards shot away.

"There is no time to explain right now, love." Ira kissed Nyx's forehead and quickly hugged Erebus, then stood on the side of the now-open door with Hatter on the other. Bjørn sat at their feet. Darkness lay ahead.

"We'll see you on the other side," she said.

Hatter laughed. "Hopefully you'll make it out . . . *alive*."

Nyx had no time to scream before darkness enveloped them and the ground dropped out.

CHAPTER TWENTY-FOUR

ANTHOPHOBIA — FEAR OF FLOWERS

Lilith ran her fingers through Hunting's hair, following with a comb. For Hunting, being a Flos meant that all sorts of plant matter grew from her scalp. They tangled themselves with her white-blond curls.

Lilith plucked the last rose and placed it on her bedsheet with the others. "How's Chazz been lately? No more night terrors?"

Hunting, seated between Lilith's feet, answered without looking up from her coloring book. "She's still going on about ravens when she sleeps. Sometimes she talks about Nyx."

Vivid night terrors were commonplace for Seers. Chasity hadn't had one since the night she screamed at Nyx and all but destroyed her and her sister's room. Chasity's baby sister, Hunting, took these outbursts hardest.

"Do you think they'll let us go to school tomorrow?" she asked.

Lilith braided Hunting's hair as she spoke. "I don't think so, sweetie." Scared to send the girls to school after what had happened, the entire family had stayed home that day. It was just a waiting game to see if the academy would even allow them back.

Hunting huffed. "Fine. But tomorrow can Pete play hide and seek with me?"

Lilith smiled and looked over her shoulder. Peter Pan sat on the windowsill, head against the glass. He smiled and nodded, invisible to everyone but Lilith.

"Yeah, Pete can play."

"Yes!" Hunting clapped.

"Come on," Lilith said, tying off the end of Hunting's braid. "It's late. You've got to get to bed." She led Hunting out of the room and down the hall, then tucked her into bed. She paused on her way out and frowned at Chasity's empty bed. Her stomach twinged at the thought of her cousin wandering around the manor in a trance.

Tiptoeing back to her room, she noticed the strangest smell. Warm and pungent, it came from Nyx's room at the end of the hall. Lilith approached the slightly ajar door and pushed it open. Inside, large black feathers littered the ground, as if a cat had fought a bird—and won.

She spotted movement.

A raven pecked and jumped on something atop the bed. Lilith peered into the dark, waiting for her eyes to adjust.

Blood. Skin ripped open. A body staring back at Lilith with empty, dead eyes. Stomach ripped, innards decorating the ground. Staining the sheets. Painting the walls.

Hanging from the ceiling fan.

The ugly, scarred raven pecked at the almost-hollow insides. It gave a single ragged call, beak dripping, before flying through the open window with the girl's remaining intestines in its talons.

Lilith screamed.

CHAPTER TWENTY-FIVE

DEMENTOPHOBIA — FEAR OF GOING INSANE

Mason jumped on the balls of his feet, trying to keep himself warm as they waited in line. His wounds from the frat party had healed quickly under Max's supervision.

Damien, having already gotten his food from the van, sat on the curb shoveling noodles into his mouth. It was dark in the French Quarter, but the streets were alive with music and parties. Ridley still hadn't spoken to him after the events of that afternoon. He had been downstairs with his earmuffs on, smashing away at some rotten pews when Erebus had left.

Damien hadn't stopped him, and the woman didn't even let him say good-bye. Ridley understood that this was huge—that in the previous few days Erebus had learned more about his past than he had in hundreds of years. He knew that this Council would be able to help Erebus become whole. But that still didn't change the fact that he was livid that Erebus had just disappeared.

"Cold tonight," Mason noted, trying to break the tension between the other two. Ridley shrugged and lowered his chin into his scarf.

"Ey!" Damien yelled around a mouthful of food. "Look!" He pointed down the street to where a body was slowly falling to rest in the center of the road. A new citizen of Dewmort.

"Another one," Ridley noted, unsurprised.

"No, it's not . . . it can't be," Mason said. Damien and Ridley gave him a look. "That's—holy shit."

"What?" Ridley asked, but Mason was already sprinting toward the body. Damien and Ridley were hot on his heels, noodles forgotten.

Mason leaned over the girl. He raised her up, leaning her against his chest. She was still asleep but he recognized her well enough.

Ridley and Damien stopped in their tracks. Damien covered his mouth and backed away. "Oh my God," he said.

It was Chasity Lahey.

"Where *the fu—mmhnnn!*" The doctor covered Chasity's mouth before she could scream.

The boys waited in the hall outside, watching through the window. Damien spread the blinds with his fingers as Chasity threatened death to the doctors restraining her wrists and ankles. She'd been asleep for hours, yet had no trouble remembering who she was. The moment she woke she'd demanded to know where she was, and that she be allowed to leave immediately.

Damien pulled away as Ridley snapped the blinds shut. There was a thump as Chasity threw something at the doctors, yelling in seer tongue.

"Ma'am, you just need to calm—" *Thump.*

Mason's eyes widened. "I am *not* fucking going in there."

"You *are*," said Ridley.

"You know we're going to be the *last* people she wants to see, right?" Damien said. He slid down the wall, sitting on the floor in the hospital hallway.

Then a shrill sound—metal crashing.

"No, miss," said a nurse. "You can't go up there!"

Ridley watched Die Lahey round the corner, stepping over rolling metal dinner plates that had clattered to the floor.

"Where *is* she?" Die demanded.

Mason leaned over and whispered in Ridley's ear. "Um . . . who is she?"

Ridley whispered, "One of the Laheys."

"Where is she?" Die repeated.

Ridley pointed at the door just as it opened. The doctor appeared, regarding them wearily.

"She's ready to see you," he said, ushering them in.

Ridley peered around the door before slowly walking through. The others trailed behind.

Chasity took one look at him and narrowed her eyes. "*You!*" She lunged forward only to be jerked back by the restraints. "I've seen you. With Erebus. In the visions. What the *hell* am I doing here? Where's Nyx?"

The boys remained silent as Die entered the room. Chasity stared at her for what felt like forever. Her face crumpled.

"No, no, no, no . . ." Chasity shook her head. Die came to her side and wrapped her arms around Chasity's small shoulders. She pulled her close, smoothing her hair.

"Where's Erebus?" Die asked quietly, looking at Ridley. He said nothing. "They came," she noted.

Ridley nodded. "And Nyx too."

Chasity pulled away once more and looked at the ghost of her older cousin. "No, this—this isn't right. What's wrong with me?"

Die's eyes welled up. She held Chasity's face. "Chazz . . . you've died."

Chasity's wail echoed throughout the hospital.

CHAPTER TWENTY-SIX

BAROPHOBIA — FEAR OF GRAVITY

Nyx landed on her back in water.

Drowning. She was drowning. Her cheeks hurt and her lungs burned.

She opened her eyes. She was in a pool. She scrambled for the surface and burst through, gulping down air. She realized then the water was barely three feet deep. Embarrassed, she stood, drenched, and hugged herself.

She was in some sort of beauty spa, judging by the white floor, walls, and ceiling. Soft music played from speakers set above. The smell of oils and moisturizing balms filled the air, and chairs lined the pool's edge. In one sat a large woman with a towel around her head, cream on her face, and cucumbers on her eyes. Another rested her head on the side of the pool as she floated there, her nails a bright Ferrari red.

White-clad workers walked past carrying trays of fruit and cocktails. Others tended to the beauty needs of various customers.

Nyx waded to the edge of the pool. She pulled herself up and out, and was making her way to the door with a green sign above it, hoping it was the exit, when someone grabbed her arm. She looked and saw the woman from the pool's edge, her chubby fingers wrapped around Nyx's wrist.

"Staaaaaaaay," she hissed, forked tongue darting through serrated teeth. The woman's eyes had turned black and were sinking into their sockets, cucumbers falling to the ground. Her skin began to crinkle and discolor.

Zombie. Nyx yanked her arm away, and the woman's hand crumbled. Nyx looked around wildly. Staff and customers watched her hungrily. The woman who had been in the water now took a predatory stance, ready to sprint. A hole had formed in the flesh on her side—fluids leaked into the pool water.

One staff member dropped her plate of fruit. Her bottom jaw dropped to her collarbone. Her razor teeth gleamed in the overhead lighting.

"Staaaaaay," they moaned in unison, shuffling slowly toward Nyx.

Nyx turned to the exit and came face to chest with a masseur. Maggots crawled in the open cavity of his chest, devouring the remnants of his lungs. She yelped, pushing him aside and sending him tumbling into the pool.

She ran for the exit, narrowly missing flailing claws as she grabbed the handle, flung open the door, and threw herself outside.

Nyx landed with a thud on cold floorboards and rolled into the wall. The spa door slammed shut behind her before anything else could come through. She pulled herself up and looked around, noting that her clothes had somehow dried. Windows behind her showed only darkness outside. Small chandeliers overhead lit the dark, polished hall. Doors lined both walls.

A rumble like thunder. The windows trembled and the chandeliers shook—even the paintings on the walls shifted on their hooks.

A whisper tickled her ear: *run*. Without thinking, she pounded down the hall. The rumble grew louder overhead while doors around her slammed open and shut. Vases and paintings became missiles, launching and smashing into pieces midair.

A portrait crashed against the wall, the shattered glass of the picture perforating her leg. Nyx screamed and tried to pry the giant shards from her thigh as she continued to run. She caught snapshots of scenes as she passed the rapidly opening and closing doors:

A man with long white hair.

A boy frozen beneath a lake.

Another chained and whipped.

A pile of bones so long forgotten that it had become a shell, moss and flowers growing between.

She saw Cole, the stranger from the frat party. And Erebus, laughing. As the noise around her peaked to a crescendo, she saw an image of Lilith looking over at someone's mangled body. Nyx screamed and covered her ears, continuing to sprint as best she could with the glass in her leg. Nearing a rusty door ahead, Nyx saw one final vision: herself, a thick cloth gagging her, her face red and grimy, cheeks shining with tears.

A flash of gold streaked across her vision and wafted away like smoke as she came face to face with the door. Nyx kicked it open, ran forward, and fell into darkness again.

She bolted upright a moment later, gasping for air. Above her, Hatter smiled, and behind him, Ira was beaming.

Bjørn was in Nyx's lap, asleep. "Where am I?" she sputtered.

"You've made it; you're in the Hallows," Ira said, stepping forward.

It didn't look like much. They were in a tiny, brick-walled room with nothing but a few gloomy, green lanterns.

"Where's Erebus?" Nyx demanded.

Hatter looked to his right, at the unconscious Erebus. "He hasn't arrived yet."

CHAPTER TWENTY-SEVEN

HIPPOPOTOMONSTROSESQUIPEDALIOPHOBIA – FEAR OF LONG WORDS

Erebus's eyes flashed open. He jolted, feeling as if he was falling.

Springs squeaked as he landed atop something soft. He looked around and saw pastel-blue walls and white curtains framing a window, the night sky just outside. Pillows surrounded his head—he was lying on a large, soft bed.

Erebus noticed the tiny, dark-headed Nyx lying next to him. Her back was to him, and she lay curled into the curve of his torso. She stirred, turning over to face him. She rubbed her eyes, then sat up and smiled.

"Hey," she said.

Erebus admired her messy hair and sleepy eyes. "Hi?" he replied, confused.

Nyx leaned closer. "You okay?" She cupped the side of his face.

"Y-yeah . . ."

She giggled. "Well, that's good."

Something is so very different about her . . . something's wrong . . . But Erebus could not take his eyes from her.

Nyx put her forehead to his, noses touching. Green eyes staring at him. She shifted closer and—

Green eyes.

Erebus grabbed Nyx's hands and leaned back. "Nyx doesn't *have* green eyes."

Instead of looking surprised, the girl growled. Her skin burned and crinkled like paper on fire. Erebus rolled off the bed and stumbled to the bedroom door as the girl's skin continued to burn, setting the sheets afire. The smells of singed flesh and linen filled the room.

He found the door handle as the girl lunged from the bed, landing on all fours. Her nails raked across the floorboards as Erebus opened the door and stumbled through.

He slammed into something hard, cold, and slippery—like glass or crystal or—

Ice. He was lying on a sheet of ice. Hands burning, he carefully pushed himself up only to see what lay beneath: blond curls, frozen midsway. Pale skin, dark freckles. A dagger hanging from a red ribbon around a neck.

Erebus stared in awe at the boy beneath the ice. The prisoner's eyes snapped open. They were the palest green. He regarded Erebus in horror and started beating against the ice, screaming, bubbles roaring from his mouth.

The ice began to crack. Erebus didn't have a chance to react before it broke and he fell.

He landed hard on a cold stone floor. Erebus let out a winded groan as he tried to adjust his eyes to the dark.

The sounds of chains and clinking metal dragging along the stone floor.

In the distance, Erebus heard screams coming from elsewhere. There were bars on either side of him and a dark, slouched heap at the end of the room, on the other side of the bars. Bloodied, weak, with long black hair that hid their face. Strong, tattooed arms chained to the brick high above, thick cuffs cutting into their wrists.

Erebus pressed his face to the bars. "*Hey!*" he hissed.

The slouched man jerked awake. "Who's there?" he asked.

Erebus waved an arm through the bars. "Over here!"

"Your name?" the man asked.

"Erebus," he whispered as a thick chain wrapped itself around his neck and yanked him back into the shadows of his cell. As Erebus fell he could hear the man crying his name. He landed seconds later on cold, hard tiles and rolled onto his back. Tapestries covered tall brick walls. Thick, red velvet curtains draped across large windows, and burning torches lit the hall ahead.

A castle.

He got up and dusted off his clothes. A voice came from down the torch-lit hall. Erebus listened. It was a voice he knew well.

Somewhere within the castle, Nyx Lahey was screaming. It was pained, desperate. Real or not, Erebus wasn't going to risk waiting. He shot down the dimly lit stone corridor, hurrying toward her. As he ran, he felt some familiarity. He'd run these halls before. With this same desperation, this same sting in his throat. Like his life depended on it. He'd *done this before.*

"Ereb—" And then Nyx's voice cracked.

He flew around a corner, slamming his shoulder into the brick. "Nyx!" he shouted.

A rumble sounded overhead, followed by devilish laughter: "*You're too late, boy! Once again . . .*"

Nonononononononono . . . Sweat stung the corners of Erebus's eyes. He listened for something, *anything* from Nyx that might tell him where she was.

Eros. Run.

And he did, faster than he ever had. He flew down a hall of slamming doors. Images passed in front of his eyes as he ran: A golden sarcophagus. A wheat field. A throne made of bones and a white-haired man seated atop it.

Nearing the end of the hall, Erebus spied a rusty red door. It seemed to pull him toward it. As he ran, more images flashed from doors to either side: Mason slamming his staff into the ground, breaking the earth. Making it churn as monsters crawled from its depths.

Nyx, hair pearl, face decorated with a skull—her Underneath. Large white magnolia flowers in her hair. She was dancing in the street. A long, white dress billowed around her as she spun.

The last image Erebus saw before he barreled into the door was Nyx again. Gagged, cuffed, and chained. She scraped her knees against a stone floor as she tried to crawl. Erebus felt so helpless but he didn't know why. Why he was so afraid for this girl he hardly knew?

Erebus braced himself but the door fell to pieces before he could touch it, opening into darkness.

He fell again.

Erebus's eyes snapped open and he gasped for air. Nyx crouched above him. Behind her stood Ira and Hatter. Erebus grabbed Nyx's arms. He stared at her. Nyx gave him a sad look. Erebus let his head drop to the ground, exhausted. Behind him, the others let out sighs of relief.

Nyx squeezed his arm. "It's okay. We're here now."

Erebus nodded and touched her hand, disorientated.

"It's okay," she repeated.

She's okay. We're okay.

CHAPTER TWENTY-EIGHT

PYROPHOBIA — FEAR OF FIRE

Eris swore she had never heard something so harrowing in all her life as the sound of Lilith screaming. The rest of their family poured from their rooms. Eris was at the door in seconds. She scanned the room, reflexively yanking Hunting away from the sight. She felt the wind leave her body as she pulled her tiny cousin's body into her own.

It was Chasity. *Everywhere*. Eris recognized her body immediately. She watched as Nuy made it to the door and covered her face. Aunt Mae was next, and then Alice, trying to push back her younger sisters, Bethany and Persephone—they couldn't see this.

No one should ever see this.

And then there was Maura, bolting up the staircase. Marga, Lilith's mother, turned and held her hands up to her sister. "Maura, no." But Maura pushed past only to lay her eyes on the horror inside. She fell to the floor.

Eris heard Mae screaming over everyone: "Where is Nyx?"

Christophe waded into the room and immediately spotted the note atop the dresser.

Eris found the teacup. "They came again." She was numb.

Mae turned to her. "Who?"

Eris didn't reply. She watched as Christophe opened the letter.

"Who?" Mae yelled again.

She was numb.

Christophe's legs looked to almost give way as he passed the note to his wife. He leaned against the dresser, his chest heaving with an ungodly heartbroken sound. He couldn't bear to turn around.

"No." Mae's voice was airy, like she had lost it in the wind.

They'd seen this before. Eight years ago, leaving behind nothing but a china teacup, Die Lahey had vanished into the night.

I'll do better this time. I promise.

~ H.

CHAPTER TWENTY-NINE

NYCTOHYLOPHOBIA — FEAR OF FORESTS AT NIGHT

"Follow us," Ira said as Nyx helped Erebus up. Bjørn sniffed around the edges of the small green room. The old bricks were slick with water. They followed Ira and Hatter through the door and down a dimly lit hall.

"What was that back there?" Erebus asked.

Ira glanced over her shoulder as she walked. "Part dreams, part visions. Your fears, your memories, visions of your future. Everyone's first time is different. Some people don't ever wake up—you two are lucky."

"Where are we going?" Nyx called.

"To the castle!" Ira replied.

Nyx looked to Erebus. "Is this still Dewmort?" she whispered.

He shook his head. "I don't think we're in Dewmort anymore."

Bjørn walked next to them as orange leaves appeared ahead, scattered along the ground. Nyx stood on her toes, looking over Hatter's hat and Ira's horns. There was an orange glow at the end of the hall.

The leaves grew in abundance, becoming thick, crunching beneath their boots as the brick walls became the trunks of towering trees, orange, red, and burgundy leaves floating on the

air like confetti. Through the gaps above, Nyx could see the rose-
and gold-colored sky.

Bjørn bounded after the leaves with glee while Hatter and Ira
carried on their chatter, as if everything was completely normal.
Nyx looked at Erebus. He'd stopped in the middle of the path,
gaping at the trees surrounding them. Fireflies floated among the
branches while snarling jack-o'-lanterns sat at the base of the
trunks.

"Come on, you three!" Hatter yelled at the crest of the path.
Bjørn bolted toward him, and Erebus and Nyx followed.

Ira smiled at them as they neared. "Erebus, Nyx, I'd like to
welcome you to the Hallows."

They looked to the bottom of the hill. In the mountains
opposite, Nyx could see a giant castle silhouetted by the setting
sun.

"Welcome to Kyra. Village of Ghouls."

Erebus, Bjørn, and Nyx followed Hatter and Ira down the slope.
The sounds of crackling leaves and rustling wind disappeared
as they descended into an eerie stillness. The dirt path became
uneven cobblestones as the forest turned to fields of pale-green
grass on either side. A washed-out wooden sign swung gently at
the edge of the town.

WELCOME TO KYRA. The O's had been replaced by painted
skulls.

Two great maples stood on either side of the path, marking
the entrance to the town. Surrounding them was a cluster of
uneven, lopsided tombstones. Among the graves were more
jack-o'-lanterns of all sizes, snarls, and smiles. Nyx felt someone
watching them.

Ira fell back. "Most of the towns are on the other side of the mountain range," she whispered, pointing at the mountainous land on which the castle sat. "Kyra is a very small village in comparison, also one of the oldest." She gestured to the dull, pilgrim-like housing.

Erebus looked around. "Where are all the people?"

"Not people, ghouls," Ira said. "A cross between the dead and the living dead. They're almost harmless, but you want to do your best not to wake them. Especially the older ones."

"Wake them?"

"Yes, dear. The Hallows runs on a different system to yours. Here, life begins when the sun goes down. We're nocturnal." Ira looked at the violet sky. "We haven't much time before they wake. Come on, faster."

"What will they do?" Erebus asked.

"Oh, nothing much, dear. Most of them are fine. But the *oldies*, they're slightly . . . lost. They lean more toward the zombie side of things. Not really sure where they are or what they're doing—they'll just follow you around. It's annoying. The younger ones take care of them until they eventually perish."

As they made their way through the village, Nyx noticed its inhabitants starting to stir: lights in houses, eyes watching them from slightly drawn curtains. Hatter led them through the town square, at the center of which was a large fountain. Atop the pedestal stood a scarecrow statue, dressed in a trench coat. Its hands were cupped in offering. From them spurted not water, and not blood (which, truthfully, Nyx had expected), but fine golden dust that rained into the bowl below, filling the fountain's bottom with a glow that bathed the surrounding buildings.

A plaque at the scarecrow's feet read JACK.

"Quick, quick, quick." Ira hurried them.

They twisted and turned through the village, past small houses and dusty antique shops. At the edge of town, they passed one final house. On the veranda stood a tall, lanky ghoul. He held a pitchfork in his hand. His skin was withered, his cheeks sunken into deep groves and shadows. He wore plain farmer's clothes, and his feet were bare and grass stained. He watched them silently as they passed, following their movements.

He gave a stiff, curt nod before the forest swallowed them again.

"Uuuugh!" Hatter stopped in the middle of the path and stared up at the steep mountain path ahead.

"Come on, Hatter," Ira said, passing him. "It's just a few minutes more."

"Carry me, *please*," Hatter whined. "Don't expose me to such torturous practices."

Ira laughed. "No. Now come on."

Nyx followed Ira, keeping her eyes forward and head down, starting up the deep incline. But when she turned around, she saw Erebus piggybacking the Hatter behind them.

Ira and Nyx waited at the top of a crest. Hatter smiled happily. Using Erebus's shoulder, he perched his chin in his palm and watched the scenery pass. Erebus's cheeks were flushed.

Ira started again once they neared. Nyx waited. Erebus reached the crest, breathing heavily.

To their right was a sheer cliff. To their left, a towering wall that surrounded the castle. The dirt and pine-needle path on which they walked curved to follow the arc of the wall.

Ira waited for them at the end. She stood in front of a giant, closed entry—a double gate carved with various scenes from old fairy tales.

"Erebus, Nyx, Bjørn. Welcome to your new home. Here, you will train, you will learn, and your powers will flourish."

The doors opened wider, and Nyx spotted a group of people waiting on the other side. Hatter wriggled down from Erebus's back to stand with Ira.

He grinned wildly. "We, the Hallowed Council, welcome you to Castle Monstrum."

CHAPTER THIRTY

ILLYNGOPHOBIA — FEAR OF VERTIGO OR DIZZINESS WHEN LOOKING DOWN

Bellum waited patiently. He'd knocked three times, still no answer. He shrugged, pulling the collar of his coat tight to fend off the icy wind. He'd flown there straight away, as soon as he'd finished at Ebony Manor. Snow smothered the ground in a thick blanket of gray and white, the rocky side of the mountain rising behind the small hut.

Bellum gave it three more blows. There was a crash inside, followed by a string of mumbled curses. Bellum smashed on the door again.

"*Hör auf mit deinem Geballer!*" Two angry German voices yelled back at him before someone flung open the door.

Before Bellum stood twins, Luto and Petram—the Blind Witches. Long ago, in the depths of the Black Forest, the witches had built a house of sweets that they had used to lure young children into the forest—an endless supply of everlasting youth. Even now, they could be mistaken for a pair of fair-haired teens—however, it was their glowing golden eyes that revealed them to him. They were two of the oldest witches in the world, and contained information not held by even the most ancient of texts.

Bellum spied the dark inside of their hut. Bones hung from strings, and jars of bugs, snakes, and other creatures lined the dusty shelves. Vials of sparkling potions and powders littered the table, circling a thick spell book.

Luto scowled. "Ugh, what do you want?"

"I need you to get me into the Hallows," Bellum said reluctantly, wanting to be *anywhere* but there.

Petram grinned. Luto looked unsure. "What's in it for us?" she asked.

"Mortem's head," Bellum said quickly. "And my father's unquestioned gratitude, when he finds that you aided in his raising."

Petram grinned still. Luto stepped forward, hesitant. "What has happened, Bellum, for you to be so eager to risk entering the Hallows?" she asked.

"The Relics have been found. They've made it inside."

PART TWO
HALLOWED

CHAPTER THIRTY-ONE

ARACHIBUTYROPHOBIA — FEAR OF PEANUT BUTTER STICKING TO THE ROOF OF YOUR MOUTH

The gates opened, revealing two rows of guards standing in a large courtyard. At their head was a tall, brooding man dressed in thick black armor. Long, dark hair entwined with shards of metal, beading, and sharp feathers fell all the way to his hips. Symmetrical patterned scars covered both cheeks, and a winding purple tattoo wrapped around his left arm and up to his red eyes.

The armored man watched them intently. The men behind him were dressed head to toe in black chain mail, helmets covering their faces and necks. Multiple weapons of havoc hung from their belts. They didn't so much as breathe.

Ira laughed as they approached, swinging her thin arm around the man, and giving him a slap on the back. "Come now, Thorn, try not to be so intimidating."

The man—Thorn—broke into a crooked smile. He gave a long, deep bow to both Nyx and Erebus. "Your Highness, m'lady."

Erebus frowned. Nyx scrunched her face.

One by one, the men lined up behind him and fell to one knee, bowing their heads.

Nyx glanced around the courtyard: hard, packed ground;

weapons and wooden beams leaned up against the wall in one corner while the stone path led to another, smaller door. Above and around them were huge arched windows used for spying on those below.

She felt the eyes of many watching as they made their way to the door.

"Come," Ira said. Hatter jumped excitedly.

There was a loud crash from somewhere inside the castle, followed by Russian curses.

"*Dummkopf!*" someone yelled back.

Ira banged on the smaller, wooden door beneath an arch at the end of the path. The sound of feet crashing down stairs was immediately followed by a small metal panel in the door sliding open. Two pale eyes peered out beneath a shock of white hair.

"Ira!" The voice was muffled but Nyx still heard the trace of a German accent. "Is this them? Are these the Relics?"

"Yes," Ira sighed. "Now, let us in."

"What's the password?"

"*Hans!*" Ira snapped.

Hans stopped laughing and opened the door. He stood aside and bowed. When he reached out to shake their hands, Nyx saw the Reapers Oath tattooed on his wrist.

"Nice to meet you both," he said. "I'm Hans. Greta's brother."

Ira started upstairs. "The boys will show you around," she said. "I have some work to do before Mortem returns. I know you're confused, but I promise, everything will be explained soon."

Nyx nodded, turning back to the others. "Hans—Hansel . . . from the fairy tale?" He nodded.

"Well, now that that's out of the way . . ." Hatter patted Hans's head then linked arms with Nyx and Erebus and started forward. "Come, *I'll* show you the house."

"Hey!" Hans took the steps two at a time, coming up behind them. "Hatter, I'm trying to introduce myself!"

"Don't care! I saw them first."

Hans made a face. "*So?*"

Hatter stopped, turned, and glared. "So that makes them mine. My friends. Not yours."

"You can't play the 'mine' thing with people, Hatter."

"*Watch me*, bread boy."

Hans rolled his eyes as Hatter pulled them away.

At the top of the stairs was a spacious brick kitchen with enormous ovens, high ceilings, towering shelves lined with bags of ingredients, and walls strewn with copper pots and pans. In the middle of it all was a long table covered end to end with a monstrous display of sweets: crystal bowls of custard, jelly, ice cream, and various puddings; silver cake stands overflowing with cupcakes and fudge. Bjørn held his nose to the edge of the table, sniffing, tail wagging happily.

"*Holy shit*," Erebus said.

Hatter clapped and jumped on the spot. "Welcome to my table! Oh, we simply must have some tea! Come, please, sit. Oh! Greta! Good, you're back, please come sit with us."

A girl appeared in the arched doorway at the end of the great kitchen. She was white haired and tanned, like Hans. Small and athletic, she reminded Nyx of Chasity.

Her jaw dropped. "Oh my gods. . . ." She looked at Hatter. "The Relics?" He nodded. She ran over and wrapped her arms around Nyx. "I can't believe you're here!" She hugged Erebus next. "It's so good to finally meet you both. I'm Greta."

"So . . . you've been expecting us?" Nyx asked.

Greta nodded. "This is probably a bit weird, huh? We were able to contact Erebus a lot easier than you. We would have explained what was happening before you came, but it was too dangerous. At least you're safe *now*. Once Mortem and Bayou get back, we'll tell you everything you want to know."

"Come on!" Hatter yelled over chocolate cake. "Come and sit!" He patted the table excitedly.

Erebus whispered to Hans, "Is this why he's so hyper?" He gestured to the sweets.

Hans whispered back, "It's not the sugar." They sat down and Nyx leaned her scythe against the table. "He's . . . troubled."

"How?" she asked, though it was quite evident that something was definitely troubling about Hatter as he busily stacked teacups covered in bloodied handprints.

Hans dropped his voice again. "He can hear the voices of things on the astral planes—he's a Beacon. When he was alive, spirits flocked to him, made him think he was going crazy—his parents too. They had him committed. Medication didn't help— if anything it made it worse, as did the shock therapy. He ended up drowning himself in the hydrotherapy room."

Greta added, "Mortem thought he'd be useful on the Council. Beacons are a rare thing to come across. When he got here, he read *Alice's Adventures in Wonderland* and was obsessed with it. He got us to start calling him Hatter instead of Jake." She smiled at Hatter at the end of the table.

"Here we go!" Hatter passed them each a saucer and a cup.

Nyx set hers down—it was empty. She glanced at Erebus, who stared into his own, unsure.

Hans smiled. "Just play along."

"Drink up, guys! And help yourself to the food! Chef has done a *wonderful* job, hasn't he?" Hatter grabbed a piece of caramel cake and set it on his saucer.

Nyx leaned over to Greta. "Is the food safe? It's not, like, made of dirt or anything?"

She laughed. "Oh, no. Chef makes Hatter a tea party on special occasions, like his birthday or Christmas. He made this"—she gestured to the sweets—"so Hatter could have a tea party with you two."

"Chef?" Erebus asked, to which Greta and Hans grimaced.

"Hans and I went into the woods one day," Greta said, "and found a trail of blood leading deep into the forest. Since we'd been trained as Reapers, we followed the trail for hours, planning to turn back when it got dark—you know, the whole bread trail thing. Then we saw the house: chocolate walls, icing trims, candy buttons dotting the door . . ." She sighed. "The house magically pulled us in. We didn't even have time to scream for help.

"The witches—there were two of them—were known around our village as the Blind Witches. They were sisters—twins: Luto and Petram. They fed on the flesh of the young in order to stay so themselves. They kept Chef as their personal slave, and he cooked whatever they lured into the house. Once inside, we were force fed for five days before being cooked alive in an oven."

"How'd Chef get here?" Erebus asked.

"I ran away," came a deep, Russian voice. They turned and saw a burly man in a dirty white apron. He had a fat face and rosy cheeks beneath a bushy beard, eyes that thinned when he smiled, and a tattoo of a scythe on his large forearm. "For forty years, I was forced to lure, feed, and cook innocent children for those hags. I built them a house of sweets, enough to lure even the most stubborn of children. In time, the supply of children began to dwindle. The witches were forced to conserve their energy and slept for long periods of time.

"One day, I cut my chains and fled into the forest. I'd grown old and weak, and eventually collapsed from running. I woke in the Hallows, surrounded by Ira, these two"—he pointed to the twins—"and Mortem."

"So," Nyx said, poking at some grapes, "who's Ira then?"

"She's head of the Horned Witches," Hans said as he bit into a peach. "She is also the sister of Krampus."

"Of what?"

Greta laughed. "He's like this hairy, horned goat man."

"I don't think my brother would appreciate the title Hairy Horned Goat Man."

They turned to see Ira laughing in the doorway.

"I see you've met almost everyone," she said. "Come now, let us explain this mess."

CHAPTER THIRTY-TWO

CARTILOGENOPHOBIA — FEAR OF BONES

"Now," Ira began, her voice echoing as they followed her through the dark tunnels of the castle, "you're both going to hear things that may confuse you. All I ask is that you hear us out."

Nyx glanced over at Erebus. He reached out and touched her arm without looking. They approached another set of large double doors, these ones marked by wrought iron strips and bolts. Greta smiled reassuringly as Ira shoved them open with an echoing groan.

"Come," she said as she was swallowed by the darkness ahead.

They followed her. When their eyes adjusted, they saw seven large judges' benches set in a perfect circle.

"Nyx, Erebus," said a voice from somewhere within the room. The detector at Nyx's throat buzzed. She stepped into the circle, Erebus beside her.

Each bench had its own name plaque—CHEF, HATTER, JACK, GRETA & HANS, BAYOU, MORTEM, IRA—and an array of items and valuables spread around it.

The last bench read Mortem. Two orange eyes stared out from behind it.

Necromancer.

"Erebus," Mortem said, "it's good to see you again. And Nyx, it's a privilege to finally meet you."

He seems nervous, Nyx thought to herself.

Mortem continued, "Let's start off with something simple. What is it you want to know?"

Nyx looked up. "Why are we here?"

Ira cleared her throat. "At first, we had our eye on only Erebus. It took us a long time to realize that he was in Dewmort and had no memories of his former life. We had been looking for him for years. And it just so happened that he had been seeking us out as well."

Erebus watched Nyx, studying her reaction.

"But we realized something was different with him. And then you came, Nyx, and we finally found what we'd been missing. You two are very special."

"You are the Relics," boomed a deep voice from behind the bench marked Bayou.

Then, from behind the one labeled Jack, "There are only ever two Relics at a time: one to represent the Reapers, the other the Necromancers."

Greta said, "These Relics are so called because they possess abilities handed down from their ancestors. Powers beyond any other Reaper or Necromancer. The Relics are given the powers of the Originals—of Neco and Grim."

Nyx felt sick. Everyone knew the story of Grim and Neco. Everyone knew what Neco had done.

"Historically, in the end, Relics destroy each other," Ira said. "Either from hate or love. Romeo and Juliet . . . their demise was fueled by love and not bloodlust. It wasn't just a story—William wrote it as a warning."

"Sometimes millennia can pass without a Relic ever being born," Hans said, changing the topic.

"Or"—Greta looked at her brother—"the power can be passed from one dying Relic to another of the same family."

Ira leaned forward. "That is what happened between you and Die, Nyx. She was the Necromancer Relic, but when she died, her power passed to you."

Oh God. Die. How had she missed it? The teacups? The letter? Die had disappeared, and now so had Nyx.

"You were brought here because someone very powerful wishes you both dead. We are doing our best to track this . . . individual, but for now this is the only safe place for you," Mortem said. "We'll train you, teach you, and enable you to fully harness your powers."

"Who is it?" Erebus asked. "Is it the same person who attacked the Laheys?"

Mortem glanced down. "His name is Bellum. The Young God. One of Neco's children. He knows what the two of you are and he wants to use you. And yes, he has already attempted to do so."

Nyx gave him a stunned sideways glance. Of course—no regular Necromancer could have raised Brauge, and so many of them at that. But a child of one of the Originals . . .

"Now," Ira said, rising and making her way down to them, "there are just a couple of things you should know before we start your training. First, as your powers start to manifest, you will start to grow a second skin of sorts. If you haven't already." Ira opened her hand, her nails extending into talons. She raised her hand and, as she did, a mirror rose from the black tiles before the Relics.

"It's called your Underneath. It represents who and what you are and will cover you in times when your emotions or magic are at their highest. If you look hard enough, you might be able to find it."

Nyx didn't need to try. In the mirror stood a girl with curly white hair. Nyx's skin was still her own, only now it glowed from the inside out, a shimmering pearlescent hue. A crown of magnolias wrapped around her head. Her radiant face was underlain by a skull of shimmering silver lines. Marks over her lips looked like stitches. Her eyes were surrounded by large shining circles outlined in flower petals. They burned like molten silver.

Her Underneath.

She looked at Erebus in the mirror. His markings were the same as she'd had seen previously. A shimmering skull of black and bronze, cheeks hollowed, and lines down his neck and spine—all molten bronze. The crown of peonies along his hairline bloomed and unbloomed, their golden centers glowing.

Ira leaned against the mirror and smiled. "Erebus, you are what's known as the Wraith. In mythology, they are ghosts who act as sorcerers. They feed on the souls of the living—much like the humans' interpretation of the Grim Reaper—and appear to those who have just died. And, of course, your current . . . living situation . . . will impact your powers.

"And Nyx," she turned, "you are known as the Banshee. In Irish fables, she is a wandering spirit, often found washing the clothes of those about to die. In other mythologies, the Banshee marks the death of a person with an ear-splitting scream. You will gain powers no other Necromancer could ever dream of—you will become more powerful than even Mortem." She paused. "We cannot say how exactly this process will change either of you—"

"Why not?" Erebus asked.

Ira sighed.

"Because no other Relics have ever survived that far into their training," Mortem said.

CHAPTER THIRTY-THREE
CRYSTALLOPHOBIA — FEAR OF CRYSTALS OR GLASS

"So, everyone else has died, and you just want us to start training?" Erebus said.

Mortem ignored the question. The rest of the Council members filed out of the room.

Nyx saw Mortem fully for the first time as he descended. Her eyes traveled the length of his white hair and leather-clad arms to the bird skull at the hollow of his throat. She eyed the scars and tattoos across his stomach.

From where he stood, Erebus could only make out a few of the tattoos: a pentagram; the feathery, sharp tail of some kind of bird; a zombie. The rest were hieroglyphs that he couldn't make out.

But, by the look on her face, Nyx could. She regarded Mortem like he was something dirty, and tightened her grip on her scythe. Mortem pretended not to see it. He stood next to Ira as her mirror dissolved back into the ground.

"Now, Nyx, if at any time during this you need me to stop, just say the word, okay?" Mortem looked her dead in the eyes.

"What are you doing?" Erebus asked, only to be ignored.

"Don't worry about me," Nyx said, still glaring at Mortem.

"It's my *job* to worry about you from now on. You've been suppressed your entire life. You've led a life where you've been *forced* to forget your heritage—what you *are*. You've never been exposed to *real* necromancy. But now you are going to eat, breathe, sleep, and *live* the practice, and it's going to shock you."

"What exactly are we doing? We just got here," Erebus asked impatiently.

Mortem held his hands behind his back. "We are going to bring Nyx's necromantic self to the surface. It's been muzzled to the point where it needs to be forced out. This needs to happen before we can do anything else."

"Erebus, your training won't start until tomorrow," Ira said. "For now, you can just observe."

"Okay, Nyx." Mortem spread his hands out in front of him. "Try to be calm, okay?" His hands trembled, then a clear wall rose in front of Nyx, forming a barrier between her and everyone else in the room.

"What are you doing?" Erebus demanded. Nyx looked around, furious.

Mortem spoke without looking away. "The Banshee is more violent than the Wraith by nature. In a moment, she's going to get quite angry. We'll use this wall to keep her contained while she calms down. It's basically impenetrable."

"Why?"

"Because you are a Reaper. She is a Necromancer. You're natural enemies. We're hitting her now with something she should have had years to adapt to." An orange orb like a fireball appeared in Mortem's hands. "I've already conducted the spellwork needed to bring it out. We've just got to throw it her way."

Nyx nodded. Mortem hurled the ball at her. "In time," he continued, "she will learn to control it—overcome it—but for now, she's going to want to rip your throat out."

Erebus watched as Nyx's orange irises were swallowed by black. "Fuck," he breathed.

She was still for a long time. Like she was listening. Smelling. Thinking. Then, suddenly, her face contorted. A low growl grew from not-Nyx's throat. She kept her face down and slowly crept around the edge of the wall like a lioness, dragging her scythe behind her.

"There's nothing around for her to raise, is there?" Erebus asked, concerned.

Mortem shook his head. "Nothing she's strong enough to raise—not yet. We're safe here."

Nyx slowed as Mortem spoke, then quickly spun, snarling, and slammed the blunt end of her scythe against the glass, right at Erebus's face. A webbed crack appeared.

"*Fucking impenetrable*!?" Erebus jumped back.

"Yeah, well, I said *basically* impenetrable!" Mortem was clearly startled. "Ira," he continued, "I think that maybe you should take Erebus outside. I'll take care of Nyx."

It took some persuasion but eventually Erebus left with Ira. Not-Nyx's eyes followed him the whole way out.

For the rest of the night, Erebus heard Nyx's groans as she and Mortem went back and forth. Ira had to stop him from barging back in. Eventually, she put a spell on the door so that he couldn't open it.

Erebus sat at the table with Hans and Hatter. "What's he doing to her?" he asked.

"He's trying to wear her out. She's just had years of power

released into her system. He needs to break it down. Break her," Hatter said.

"The spell Mortem is casting not only releases her instincts, it will also help her hone her powers after a while. Just a few more hours and she'll be able to calm herself down," Hans said.

Downstairs, Nyx snarled again. Erebus wanted her out of there.

"If she gets out, Erebus, she'll kill you," Hatter said.

"You do realize I'm already dead, right? I don't think there's much she can do."

"Ah, don't say that. Even the dead can die again." Hatter smiled darkly.

Nyx lay on the ground. Exhausted, surrounded by broken glass, splinters of wood, and her discarded scythe. The dawning sun glinted off the shards of Mortem's barrier.

She and Mortem had fought for hours before the Banshee finally calmed. At the end of it all, he'd been cut and burned by the Starbone Metal of her scythe. Meanwhile, she was scuffed and bruised from his magical blows.

Mortem pulled his knees to his chest as he slid to the ground, exhausted. Nyx could hear Bjørn whining and scratching on the other side of the door.

Slowly, Nyx hauled herself into a seated position. She heard footsteps in the hall outside. Mortem raised his head as it flew open. Nyx felt the other, newer part of her growl internally.

Stranger.

The woman burst into the room in shades of blue and green. Skin like opals and hair black and slick. Flickers of electricity charged around her. She was panting, distressed.

"Kita, what is it?" Mortem asked. "You're not meant to come—"

"He's attacked again," she blurted, almost crying.

Nyx looked at Mortem in confusion. His face dropped. "Where? Why? But we have them here?"

The girl looked tearfully at Nyx. "Her family . . ." she sobbed.

Something in Nyx shifted. She felt her stomach plummet as she tried to push herself to her feet. "What's happened?" she asked, blood rushing to her head.

"Nyx . . ." Mortem rushed forward to keep her from stumbling.

"What happened?" Nyx said again.

Mortem sighed, sensing something Nyx could not. "It's Chasity, Nyx. He got Chasity."

Ira ran into the room with Hatter. She hurried and caught Nyx as her knees gave away.

Chasity was dead.

The Banshee came undone.

Ira and Greta carried Nyx up the stairs of the tallest tower, where attendants bathed her. Bayou's Brides, they'd been called. Colorful and mismatched. She didn't flinch as they stripped her and led her to the center of the room, where she was placed in a pearl-white tub. She laid her head back in the scalding water, still crying. She didn't speak, staring blankly as the strange, glowing women, peacock-blue beings of feathers and pins, tended to her.

She was exhausted. Broken.

Finished, they helped Nyx from the tub, wrapped her in a terry-cloth robe, and returned her to Ira and Greta. Together, they climbed above the clouds to where the tower walls were iced over.

At their destination, Ira reached for the ice-coated door latch and opened the door to a circular bedroom.

Nyx was engulfed by the warmth of the room. The floors, wall, and ceiling were onyx, and great pillars and rivulets of burning amber streaked beneath every surface. Nyx dully ran a hand over a thick, tawny ribbon embedded in the stone. She could feel its heat. At the heart of it all was a large, circular bed, its covers also streaked with orange heat.

Ira led her to the bed. Nyx was shivering still—her wet hair, puffy eyes, and bruises made her look sickly.

Ira tried to smile. "This is the Lava Room. It's where you'll be staying."

Nyx said nothing. She climbed into the massive bed and nodded. Ira backed away silently and watched as the most broken girl she'd ever seen succumbed to sleep.

CHAPTER THIRTY-FOUR

HYPSIPHOBIA — FEAR OF HEIGHTS

Nyx woke to knocking. Raising her head from the pillow, she could feel the damage that had been done. Her eyes were swollen from crying, her throat was raw, and every muscle in her body was exhausted. Her head was still cloudy with disbelief. The Hallows, the Banshee . . . Chasity. It couldn't be real.

Someone knocked again. Nyx pushed herself up. "Come in."

The door opened slightly and Erebus peered through the crack. The corners of his mouth picked up ever so slightly as he tried to smile. Bjørn's dark nose tried to push through his legs. The Banshee inside stirred, but even she was tired.

"Hey," he said, edging inside. He held a muffin, an apple, and a knife. Bjørn bounded into the room, sniffing everything in sight.

"Hi."

"I've been checking on you every few hours. It's been a day or so, so I thought you might want these," he said, holding up the food. "How do you feel?"

"A day or so?" she asked.

He nodded, then sat at the edge of the mattress. "Yeah, you've been asleep since yesterday."

Bjørn jumped onto the bed and lay across her legs. "And somehow I still feel terrible."

"Yeah, well, every time I came to check you were crying in your sleep."

As he spoke, tears welled in her eyes once more.

"Shit, I'm sorry." He leaned across the bed and pulled her to him, placing her head under his hand and against his chest. Her whole body shook. "I'm so sorry," he whispered.

"I just can't believe it." Her voice was unrecognizable.

"I know."

"I fucking saw it when we crossed over from Dewmort, and I hardly thought anything of it. This only happened because of me." Nyx cried harder.

Erebus shook his head. "You had no idea—neither of us did. This isn't your fault."

"What does Bellum even want from us?"

"From what Hans has been telling me, he's done this kind of thing for eons. Something about the Relics—Bellum's scared of them. They're the only things more powerful than him. But he needs them for something."

"But why Chasity? She would have been terrified."

"Shhh, no, no, you can't think of that."

"But why her?"

"She's a Seer, maybe she knew something. We don't know. But you can't keep thinking about it, Nyx. I know it's hard, but you can't do that to yourself." He paused. "I don't know if this will make you feel any better, but there was news from Dewmort. That girl—Kita—she's a lookout for the Council. She came back to the castle this morning—Chasity has appeared in Dewmort."

Nyx pushed Erebus away. "What does that mean?"

"She was taken to the Dewmort hospital. By the sounds of it, it was Damien, Mason, and Ridley who found her."

Her heart jumped in her chest. She stood and tightened her robe. Bjørn jumped up excitedly and ran to the door. Nyx wiped her puffy face. "We've got to go then."

Erebus shook his head. "I already tried. Ira said it was too dangerous. She thinks Bellum is going to try and find a way into the Nethers. She wants us here, where it's safer. Dewmort could be one of the first doors he tries—"

Nyx went to protest, but he spoke over her.

"—*but* Mortem is trying to sort something out. He wants to see if he can bring them here instead."

"He's going to bring her here?"

Erebus nodded. "It may take a few days or weeks even, but she'll be here. She's okay."

She smiled through her tears.

"Ira also wants to take us out tonight. Show us around, try to get our minds off of everything."

Nyx looked out the window, the tower so high that all she could see was sky. The sun was just about to rise—the Hallows would soon be asleep.

"Try to get a few more hours in." Erebus touched her face. She could only imagine how tired and red her eyes looked. He pulled his hand away and went to the door, slapping his leg for Bjørn to follow.

"I'm going to bed," he said. "I've had a big day—Hatter dragged me through every room of the castle."

As Nyx nestled back down into her bed she mustered a smirk. "How many were there?"

"Three hundred and thirty-seven, actually," he said. Nyx laughed. "Someone will come and wake you up tonight, okay? Help you get ready."

She nodded. "Thank you, by the way. For telling me about

Chasity. I'm glad your brothers were there."

"Me too." He closed the door behind them. Nyx stared up at the black marble ceiling and the lava veins running through it. She tried to think of Chasity being surrounded by new friends who would be able to help her.

Just as Nyx closed her eyes, there was a click in the room. The Banshee stirred and she bolted upright. Someone was at one of the windows, latching it closed, his back to her. He wore a hood that covered his whole head.

A sick feeling twisted and turned in her stomach. Her skin felt hot.

Reaper. Her insides hissed the word.

She kept her eyes on the stranger as she slid her hand across the bed, searching for the knife Erebus had brought with the food. She found it and quietly stood, then slunk across the floor toward the stranger. A growl vibrated up from her throat and Nyx stabbed at the Reaper in front of her.

Her attack would have landed firmly between his shoulder blades had he not swatted her hand away, forcing it back.

"*Don't,*" he growled.

The monster inside Nyx took over. Using her trapped hand as an anchor, she whipped around and planted her foot in his chest. Sent him flying back with a crack. He landed, rolled onto his side. Clambered to his feet.

The stranger stood tall in the center of the room. He stepped forward. "Nyx," he said.

Nyx tried to stop but the Banshee refused. She paced, agitated. The knife on the ground trembled.

The stranger stepped forward. "Nyx, you need to tell it to stop. Control it."

But the Banshee refused to cede control. The knife hovered above the floor now, its tip turning to the stranger.

"Nyx," the stranger repeated, raising his hands.

The Banshee snarled, and Nyx watched as her skin flashed from brown to the glow of her Underneath. She put all her strength into separating herself.

"Try to calm down, Nyx," the stranger said calmly.

"I'm . . . *trying*," she growled.

The stranger continued forward. "That's it . . ." The monster growled; the stranger paused. "It's okay, Nyx, it's only me."

"Only *who*?"

With one hand still raised in peace, the stranger slowly went for his hood and pulled it back, revealing a dark-haired boy with familiar blue eyes.

At the sight of Cole's face, the monster fell away. The rage disappeared and the knife clattered to the ground.

"Wha . . . what are you doing here?"

Cole smiled. "Just checking up on my favorite Relics. I heard about your cousin—I'm sorry."

"Are you from Dewmort?" she asked, confused.

He shook his head. "No, I just go there occasionally. I go everywhere. I'm one of the Council's scouts—their lookouts."

"So that's why you helped us?"

He sat on the edge of the bed. "Yes and no. I wanted to know if it was true or not."

"What?"

"If Erebus was really one of the Relics."

"You know Erebus?"

He didn't answer, reaching into his back pocket instead. "I also thought you could use a present."

"A present?"

He pulled out a woven silver bangle—like the chain of Erebus's necklace. "It's a dampener. To try and control the *other* you. So you won't skin every Reaper you see." Cole took her wrist and slid the band over her hand. It slithered and tightened around her arm like a snake. The initials C. S. were etched into it.

Cole noticed her looking at it. "A second-hand present, but still better than nothing."

"Is this yours?" Nyx asked.

He nodded. "Cole Salem."

She tilted her head. "But . . . that's—"

"Erebus. I know," Cole said, grimly.

She stared at him. The eyes. Of *course* they were related.

"Nyx," he started, "I can't say too much yet."

"Well, tell me just enough then."

Cole sighed. "He's my uncle."

Nyx scoffed. "Erebus?" Cole nodded. "How? You're, like, the same age."

"Nyx, Erebus hasn't aged in a really long time. I haven't either."

"How?" she demanded. "I thought you weren't dead."

Cole shook his head. "I'm called an Incubus. I have certain . . . talents—" He frowned at the word. "To take a little bit of life from others and keep myself young. It's the equivalent of a Necromancer's second gift."

"Yes, but you're a Reaper—Reapers don't *have* second gifts."

Cole faked a smile. "You can thank my special family for it."

"So . . . how old are you?"

Cole thought for a moment. "One thousand . . . *ish*."

"Ish," she repeated, jeering.

"Roughly," he added. "My father's name was—*is*—Keelie. He

was Erebus's older brother. I was thirty-one days old when they all . . . *went*. They made sure I was safely hidden until it was over, but no one ever came back to get me.

"I was only three days old when they discovered my incubi properties. Back then, a mere touch from me could weaken someone. So my father and my uncles made this." He tapped the band around her wrist. "It grew as I did, and now I want you to have it."

Nyx watched him expectantly.

He looked up. "Nyx, it was risky enough just coming to see you. You'll hear the rest soon, but please, for now, be patient. You can't tell Erebus about this—any of it. Ira has her own way of helping him remember, and she doesn't want us messing with any of it."

Nyx nodded.

"You have to promise me that you won't say a word of this to Erebus."

She looked at him. Erebus had no idea, she realized. No idea about Keelie—his brother. Or about his nephew.

"I promise."

Cole stepped back. "Look, I have to go. You need your rest. I'm sure Ira and Mortem have a lot planned for your first proper night."

"Will you come back?" she asked as he stood by the window.

He glanced over his shoulder as he swung a leg over the ledge, and smiled. "Of course."

CHAPTER THIRTY-FIVE

LACHANOPHOBIA — FEAR OF VEGETABLES

"*Nyx*! Hurry up!"

She opened her eyes. *Tellus*.

Nyx sat up. Her sister was leaning over her. They were in their usual spot, sitting on the grass under the dead tree next to the foggy river. Tellus crouched next to Nyx.

Dream Tellus had two distinct personalities. One where she was seminormal—someone you could have a conversation with. And then there was psychotic Tellus, who would kill animals while conversing. And, by the feathers and crusted blood trapped under her fingernails, this was the latter. *Great*.

Nyx was wary. "Tells . . . what's up?"

Tellus smiled as she tore at the gaping hole in her cheek. "I have something to show you." She grabbed Nyx's arm and hauled her to her feet. She spun them around, bringing Nyx face to face with a shimmering, watery screen. On the other side, instead of seeing more of the foggy meadow, she saw a bedroom and a large, old vanity.

"What? Whose room are we looking at?"

Her sister shushed her. "Just wait . . ."

Suddenly, a figure sat down at the vanity. The woman had her back to them, a large, dark-green cloak wrapped around her shoulders. Long white hair—not unlike Mortem's—spilled down her back. In the reflection, Nyx saw the woman's face: gray skin and white hair like polished silver. Her orange eyes were encircled with thick, dazzling kohl and shimmering shadow.

Nyx let out a breath. She was—in Necromancer eyes—stunning.

Tellus whispered, "Just waaaait . . ."

Looking back, the woman stood from her chair, makeup in hand. The cloak fell from her shoulders, revealing a low-cut gown. Her back was splayed with copper-colored tattoos.

"Oh, come on, I swear I just saw it," Tellus whined.

Then, as the woman adjusted her hair, Nyx saw her image flicker. For a moment the gray around her shimmered and seemed to glow golden. The closer Nyx looked, the more it glitched. Once more, a golden glow enveloped her. Her sickly skin became sun kissed. Her eyes changed to a wooden brown, her hair from white to golden blond. The twists of wire and pins in her hair changed to a beautiful crown of brightly colored flowers. The tattoos on her back disappeared and her skinny frame filled out. Her dress transformed, becoming a long-sleeved gown of the deepest red.

It was as if she was flickering between two different selves.

"Did you see it, Nyxie?" Tellus asked as the glitch settled. The Necromancer they'd seen only a moment ago had vanished.

She nodded her head. "What's her name?"

"She calls herself Ossa."

Ira watched Nyx's reflection, continuing to brush the tangles from Nyx's thick hair. "You okay, love?"

Nyx nodded numbly. Greta had woken her from her dream

with Tellus. She'd brought Nyx down to Ira's quarters and seated her in front of a black vanity to get her ready for the night. Nyx could feel the thick coverage over her skin. The heaviness of the hair on her head. The weight of her eyelashes. She could see glitter on the end of her nose, fallen from another place.

She kept a hand wrapped around Cole's band, all too aware of Greta being a Reaper. Bjørn sat at her feet the whole time, tail thumping against the floor.

Ira explained the people of the Hallows were throwing one of their annual festivals, but that this year they would also be celebrating the arrival of the Relics.

"It's going to be wonderful. Music, dancers, performers—*food*. It'll take your mind off of things, love. Help you settle in."

Greta pushed the final pin through Nyx's hair and they stood back.

"You ready?" Ira asked.

"I guess so."

Ira spun the chair back to face the mirror. Nyx's face glowed like an autumn sunset. Her eyes were painted with glittery bronzes. Lips, ruby red, her black hair braided and strewn with pearls, curled in a bun at the nape of her neck. Around her neck was a snug, multilayered necklace—four golden bands wrapped around her throat, above her detector.

Ira clapped. "Now for the dress!" She ran to her large wooden wardrobe and came back holding a flowy white frock. Ira held it against Nyx's body, smoothing it so she could see.

"It's a lace-up back, but we can help with that." Ira pointed to a paper dividing screen and handed Nyx the dress. The two left the room while she changed.

There was a knock, and then the door creaked open.

"Oh. Shit," Erebus whispered, seeing her silhouette on the divider. "Sorry, Nyx. I'll get Ira."

"It's fine!" she yelled over the screen. "You're in here now anyway . . . would you mind lacing me up?"

"Y-yeah, sure," he answered, after a moment's hesitation.

She turned her back to him. Erebus, feeling tentative, pulled the ribbon tight.

"So where are they taking us tonight?" Nyx asked over her shoulder.

"I'm honestly not too sure. Hans just said that they were going to introduce us to the people. Whatever that means. The Relics are a pretty big deal, I think."

He gently pulled the ribbon, making sure it was tight enough.

"How did you sleep?" he asked.

Nyx was reminded of Cole's visit—Erebus's unknown family. She wanted to tell him so badly.

"Hopefully it was a bit more peaceful, knowing that Chasity is being looked after?" he added.

"Yeah, a lot more, actually." Nyx turned and faced him, standing chest to chest. He wore an all-black suit, buttons done up to just under his Adam's apple, and smelled of cedarwood.

Erebus was lost for words at the sight of her. "Hatter told me to come and get you," he said, moving his eyes from her face.

Greta entered then. Her lips were a dark accompaniment to her mauve cocktail dress. She jerked her head toward the door. "We're ready if you are. The others are waiting downstairs."

Erebus waited as Nyx slipped on the shoes Ira had provided. Bjørn followed Greta out the door. Erebus took her arm as they left, heading downstairs. "You look gorgeous, Nyx."

"So do you, Salem."

The rest of the Council met them downstairs, each dressed stunningly. Mortem bowed and smiled, which Nyx returned. But she faltered when she saw the woman standing next to him.

It was the blond woman she'd seen with Tellus. She no longer flickered, and she definitely wasn't a Necromancer. She smiled, sickly sweet.

"Nyx, Erebus," Mortem said, "meet my wife, Aliana." Mortem placed a hand on the small of her back.

Erebus smiled, and Nyx caught a glimpse of Aliana's image faltering for a mere second—unsettled. Bjørn watched her warily.

The castle doors opened and Nyx saw two other Council members. One was dressed in a lavender and black pinstripe suit. Long hair stretched down his back. A small skull was pinned to the top of his tie.

This, she presumed, was Bayou.

The other was, in all seriousness, a walking scarecrow. They'd seen him before—in Kyra's town square, as the statue atop the fountain. Jack. His jack-o'-lantern face grinned kindly as they walked through the gates of Castle Monstrum. He, too, wore a suit.

Ira, leading, wore a long red dress that trailed behind her. The sky was darkening—sunset had passed and night was here. Nyx could see the specks of the town's lights in the distance. Arriving at the gravel path, Ira faced a large patch of round, orange pumpkins off to the side of the road.

The witch winked at Nyx before bringing her fingers to her lips and whistling. As if on cue, one of the pumpkins trembled then rolled to the center of the path, small specks of golden dust trailing after it. Bulging everywhere, it grew at a rapid rate. Ira walked around it as it morphed into something new.

Round wheels and railings appeared. Windows, carriage doors, steps. The stalk on top grew into a canopy of sorts. In a matter of seconds, the last of the fluttering dust vanished, revealing a ten-foot-tall pumpkin carriage.

Ira smiled at her handiwork. The door opened, revealing plush seats. The witch waved to the open carriage. "After you."

CHAPTER THIRTY-SIX
MYSOPHOBIA – FEAR OF CONTAMINATION AND GERMS

Inside the carriage, Greta beckoned Nyx to the window. Looking out over the tops of the forest, she saw the city—great shining buildings of all shapes and sizes. Marble white, red, or blue, like lapis lazuli, with fat, multicolored onion domes.

A flash of purple passed by as the pumpkin carriage wound through the forest. Nyx leaned forward in her seat. "What was *that?*" She stuck her head out the window.

It was a person, clad head to toe in Venetian-like carnival dress: a frilled and collared cloak the shade of eggplant, trimmed with swirling lines of golden thread. Their face was covered by a vibrant volto mask; feathers, silk, and beads wrapped around their head and neck.

They passed another two people, both dressed in orange. "What are they doing?" Nyx asked, pulling her head back inside.

"They're headed to the city center for the annual Martem Ball," Ira answered simply.

"Ball?"

Ira nodded. "It's in honor of the Mother Goddess. You and Erebus arrived just in time. But it won't take up too much of our night. After that, we'll head to the Grove." Ira smiled, as did Greta.

"The ball is an excuse to get dressed up, show off, and pester the Relics," Hans added, bored.

Hatter leaned forward and sneered at Hans. "It is not an *excuse*. It's *tradition*, bread boy. The people get to *celebrate* the Relics. We haven't been able to do this in ages, so don't be such a downer. *Jesus*."

"But before we worry about that," Ira said as the coach began to slow, "we need to get some masks."

The street reminded Erebus of the crowded lanes of Prague. Thatched roofs, street lamps drooping like bluebells. Brightly clad masked Hallowers were becoming more abundant, filling the streets.

Mortem and Ira led the group from the coach to an oddly shaped shop. It was painted black, the roof tiled and pointed, and leaning at the top. As they approached, Erebus could see a pentagram engraved in the wood of the door. Ira opened the door and ducked to enter.

There was a shove from behind as Hatter pushed Erebus through the door, eager to go inside himself. Erebus's eyes widened at his surroundings. Covering every space of the shop were thousands of porcelain masks. Everywhere he looked he saw empty eyes, painted lips, glitter, fabric, and beads.

"*Sahlie*," said a cheerful girl standing behind the counter, under a slanted staircase. Her bubblegum-colored hair was tangled with azure feathers, while her arms were tattooed with scenes of dragons and flowers. From her back hung two bat wings, and necklaces of teeth and bones wrapped around her neck.

Hans had explained basic Hallow language to Erebus the night before. *Sahlie* was a greeting: Hello, how are you?

"I don't understand—if it's a masquerade then why all the makeup?" Nyx asked as Bayou held different masks to her face to see which looked the best.

"The masks are only for the ball," said Bayou. "After that, no more masks, no more ball."

"They're so heavy," Nyx said, holding a porcelain mask to her face. "How are we supposed to keep it on?"

The girl behind the register demonstrated, holding one of the masks to her face. It suctioned into place with a *schlop*.

Erebus watched as Nyx found her reflection in the mirror on the other side of the room. She flattened the fabric of her dress, making sure it wasn't bunched anywhere. In that moment, studying herself like she wasn't gorgeous, Nyx Lahey had never looked so human. Erebus smiled at her mundanity—he was sure she was one of the prettiest things he'd ever seen.

"Oi," Erebus heard Ira yell.

Ira took Erebus by his suit and shoved a mask in his face.

"See if this one fits."

"What are you doing?" Greta leaned forward, whispering to the back of her brother's head.

Hans moved his legs in an attempt to stretch the material of his trousers. He pulled at his crotch, making an uncomfortable face. "I've got a wedgie, okay?"

Greta fastened her white mask over her face to hide her

embarrassment. The porcelain was decorated with silver around the lips and eyes, and painted with lilac flowers. Erebus inspected his black mask—a half mask with a curved beak. Nyx's was splashed with gold and black, to match her hair.

Black pavement was underfoot while towering palaces and homes rose from all corners. The masked Hallowers massed around them in the thousands. The crowd filed inside under a vaulted, golden ceiling. The checkered floor was a mix of sun and caramel. Twisting chandeliers covered in flowering plants hung down and tall stained-glass windows lined the walls, draped on either side with velvet curtains.

Fantastical Hallowers gathered in droves: hooves, horns, beaks, snouts, wings, antennae, claws, fangs, scales. The hall was buzzing.

Nyx scanned the crowd, catching sight of a large white horse. Its mane and tail were all the colors of the rainbow. A bow tie was fastened around its neck. She leaned over to Hans. "There's a horse in here?"

He leaned back. "That's Hector."

Greta leaned in too. "Unicorn," she said. "Snob. Social butterfly."

As she said it, the horse, who was *laughing*, turned and revealed its spiraling horn.

Hans put a hand to Nyx's shoulder. "You hungry?" She shrugged, and he led her to a long table filled with steaming food. Hans handed Nyx a plate, grabbing another to pass to someone beside her.

Aliana took it from him without so much as a thanks. Hans moved away to fill his plate.

Aliana refused to meet Nyx's eyes. "I don't know why they bother with all of this," she said, looking at the table. "I've seen enough of you Relics in the past to not get too caught up in all your wonder like the rest of these fools."

"Oh . . . right." Nyx was taken aback.

"So, you do *know* about the others, don't you?" she continued, turning to Nyx. "Not a single one of you has been strong enough to even stay alive. I mean, how many times must we pretend that you're all something special?" She looked Nyx up and down. "I'm sure it won't be long until you end up like the last Lahey we had. Can't even control yourself on your own," she said, her eyes falling to Cole's bracelet.

Anger bubbled in the back of Nyx's throat. "So, you *do* know about the stick?"

"What stick?" Aliana grumbled.

"The one up your ass? You should probably look into getting that removed."

Aliana frowned and walked into the crowd, leaving her plate behind.

"Could cause an *infection*!" Nyx yelled after her, pleased with herself.

"Really?"

Nyx spun around. Erebus.

"*What?*" Nyx exclaimed.

He laughed. "Didn't say a thing. It's about to begin, come on." He held out his hand.

The last of the chatter died as they went and stood beside Hatter. Nyx felt a knot in her stomach as she looked at the people around them, the room dotted with Reapers. She touched Cole's bracelet.

At the front of the ballroom, before the orchestra, an emerald-clad woman stood atop golden stairs. "Welcome, ladies and gentlemen," she said, "to the Martem Ball, in tribute of our Mother Goddess. But tonight's ball is not like the rest. Tonight, we have more than the goddess to celebrate. After hundreds of years, we've finally been blessed with not one but both Relics in our kingdom at one time. We've been waiting for this day for a long time, as I'm sure many of you are aware."

Murmurs of excitement filled the air.

"I'd like to welcome and introduce our Wraith and our Banshee: Erebus and Nyx."

Faces turned to them. Ira beamed, but Erebus looked like he wanted the ground to open up and swallow him.

"Relics," the woman continued, "our saviors, our heroes, your people welcome you."

"Welcome!" the crowd around them echoed, before bowing in unison.

"We are so honored to have you here for your first annual ball and we trust that you will enjoy your night. The Hallows has many things to offer, and I know that this Council will show you your way. The people here tonight will support you both throughout your journey. May our history books be blessed with your names for many years to come."

She held up a glass. "With that, let us begin this year's Martem Ball!" She clapped her hands and the orchestra began to play. Glitter rained down upon them. Nyx looked up and saw ribbon dancers performing from the ceiling.

"Quick!" Greta pushed Nyx to Hans. "The first dance is about to start, go!" Nyx gave her a questioning look as Greta took Erebus's arm. Greta rolled her eyes. "Well, neither of you know the dances!"

Hans smiled and led Nyx to one side of the ballroom where

others were lined up. Erebus and Greta lined up opposite them. Hans said, "Follow me," right before the music started and the room became a blur of motion. The music was fast paced, with fiddles and flutes, like an Irish jig.

Hans followed the line, twisting them between other partners. The two lines formed a circle that slowly turned around the ballroom. Hans spun Nyx around; they jumped and whirled, and he caught her, laughing.

"Okay, get ready," he said, panting, "we're going to swap." Hans twirled Nyx again, letting go and sending her into another set of arms while he caught the girl spinning his way. Another spin and skip, and partners were lifted from the ground and twirled in the air.

Nyx was passed from partner to partner—each as surprised as the last to be dancing with the Banshee. Eventually she landed in Erebus's hands, both grinning ear to ear.

He looked so . . . *lovely*, mask pulled down around his neck, hair slightly askew. His flash of a smile cut the slightest of dimples into his stubble-grazed cheeks. He lifted Nyx up, looking at her with so much joy that she felt something twinge in her chest.

Outside, the wind bit at Nyx's cheeks. Hatter, Hans, and Erebus were taking turns drunkenly swinging themselves around a lamppost. Ira had collected their masks, dropping them all into an endless, small velvet bag. Greta linked arms with Nyx as they started down the tiled street. Soon enough, the others followed.

Ira and Aliana were making small talk, although clearly neither wanted to engage the other. Nyx imagined Mortem standing awkwardly between them. Meanwhile Erebus, Hatter, and Hans were laughing about something to the point of crying. For hours they'd danced at the ball and been introduced to all manner of Hallower.

"Where are we going now?" Nyx asked Greta.

Greta leaned her head against Nyx's shoulder. "To the inner city, where the parties are starting. The inner Hallows is split into five regions. First, you've got the Grove—all rainforest and rivers, cities built on water. Next is the Duster—desert, lots of exotic Nether animals. The Hallows' largest trade route runs through there.

"Next to the Duster is the Den, so called because of the pack of Lung Dragons that inhabit the mountains and water caves. The hill tribes have a monthly lantern festival.

"Then there's the Willow. Real Victorian style. Horse-drawn carriages, museums, and archives." She paused. "And then there's the Pit—the Dark Forest. Where all of the . . . reclusive . . . creatures live. A lot of the land is marked by old battlegrounds or cemeteries."

Nyx paled at the sound of it.

"Oh, we won't be going there," Greta assured her. "Tonight's the Grove. And Grovers know how to throw an *amazing* party."

CHAPTER THIRTY-SEVEN

GELOTOPHOBIA – FEAR OF BEING LAUGHED AT

On the second floor of the warehouse, Ridley Channing, on his back in the middle of their makeshift lounge, stared at the ceiling. Damien was still banished from Ridley's sight they'd continued fighting over Erebus's disappearance, even after Die's reassurances.

Then a blue-skinned girl came with a letter signed by Mortem. She'd left them hunched over the note. Mortem expressed his deepest sympathies for Chasity's death and hoped she was settling in well. He explained that both Nyx and Erebus were safe and, when possible, Mortem would like to invite them all to the Hallows to visit.

They had rejoiced, the Laheys crying at the thought of seeing Nyx again. But something had been bothering Die. Ridley heard the distinct click of the front door opening and closing. He continued to count the bolts along the beams above until she appeared over him.

"What are you doing?" Die asked.

Ridley shrugged against the concrete. "Nothing."

"Then what do you want?"

"I need to show you something."

Die eyed the concrete floor with distaste. Ridley smiled and patted the floor next to him. Die groaned, swinging her legs out and lying back on the dusty floor next to Ridley.

Both stared at the ceiling, counting bolts in the metal beams. Die rolled her head to the side. Ridley lifted his hand and dropped an object into her palm.

"I forgot about it until we got that letter. Mortem knows who attacked Chasity, and it got me thinking: Mason was bitten by one of the Brauge. I found that stuck in his neck. What if the attack at the party and Chasity's death are connected?"

Die opened her palm—and on sight dropped the object and bolted upright. The girl hissed and scrambled away. "Where did you get that?!"

"I told you." Ridley jerked upright and cautiously picked it up. "Mason's bite."

Die grimaced at the sight of it—a large tooth. Pure white, proving the Brauge had been recently raised. Covered in tiny etchings. Symbols in a language Ridley couldn't understand.

Ridley stared at Die. "Do you know what it says?"

Die nodded stiffly, looking like she was going to be sick.

"What?"

"Well, for one, I know who raised your Brauge."

Back in her own home, the curtains drawn to let in only a sliver of sunlight, Die stared into the crystal ball in the lounge. In the crystal appeared the scarred face of Bellum the Young God. His black hair was streaked with silver, one red eye ravaged by a deep, wrinkled scar.

Beside him was Ossa, eyes wild with fire.

To the other side appeared a hazier image—the second sister,

Cutem. Short white hair and wide silver eyes. A streak of bronze across both of her cheeks.

The faces dissipated. Die looked at the large, carved tooth in her hand. It was Bellum. He'd sent an army of zombies and Brauge to kill someone that night. And it didn't take a genius to figure out who.

Seven children disappeared that week. Three in Berlin. Two in Munich. One in Stuttgart. The other was in Freiburg, on the edge of the Black Forest. The Blind Witches required certain *ingredients* for creating their spells.

Luto and Petram were brewing a cast for Bellum, to allow the Necromancer to enter the Hallows. A spell that would break even the great Mortem's protection shield.

So far, they'd required:

Eight wolf kidneys.

Two pairs of cobra eyes.

The tail of a young lion.

A vial of poison from a dart frog in the Amazon.

Four bear claws, which Bellum had to rip personally from the beast. It hadn't been pleasant for either of them.

Seven teeth from Mortem's collection of human skulls—for which, of course, they'd had to count on Ossa.

And, the last, the blood from seven innocents.

Bellum made sure to spread his takings so as to not draw too much attention.

As a young boy, he'd spent months living with Luto and Petram, training and developing his necromancy and witchcraft skills. He'd built his own brick cottage just down the trail. Built the furniture from the forest. Caught his own food, created his own potions and casts.

He'd even had a cat.

Bellum had been different then. Not old. Not ugly—the scar wouldn't come for a number of years yet. He was then still free to roam the Nethers. Not yet a havoc maker, he was inquisitive, almost normal.

Then he fell in love with a young, Horned Witch in training.

Ira.

Then came Mortem, a creature created by Bellum's own father. And just like that, Ira slipped away. The young Necromancer had been heartbroken. Which ultimately ended in a massacre and the Great Burning of the Hallows.

That was when Mortem constructed the barrier to protect the people from Bellum. And to also hinder Bellum's plans to get his father back.

Bellum followed the scent of the sisters to a large, dead clearing. They stood there, side by side, welcoming him as he stepped out of the trees.

Luto approached him. "We have finished the task."

Bellum dropped his head as Luto swung a cord over his neck. He saw a leather-wrapped pouch hanging by a dark strap.

"This will allow you entry into the Hallows." Luto stood back.

"Thank you, ladies . . . but why have you called me way out here?"

Petram smiled and turned her back on him. "You have worked well for us over the years, and we wish to reward you. A homecoming gift of sorts." She beckoned him over. The field before them was riddled with holes that burrowed deep into the earth.

Within slept an undead army, waiting to be awoken.

—

Mason pushed off the wall as Ridley exited the bathroom. "So, how was it?"

Ridley glanced back to the bathroom. "Brutal."

"I meant with Die. What'd she say?"

"She acted . . . *weird*. Told me she knew who made the Brauge but wouldn't give me a name. I let her take the tooth home so she could study it."

"That's it?"

"She mumbled things like Grim and Neco, Mortem and Martem. But I've no idea who they are."

Mason cocked his head. "You don't know Grim and Neco? Are you kidding me?"

Ridley continued, "She gave me a book. Told me to have a read. Told me it wasn't exactly a common-knowledge book." He led Mason into Erebus's room which still looked like a hurricane's aftermath.

"What isn't common knowledge? Was there anything about Grim and Neco?" Mason was confused.

Ridley nodded and pulled out Die's book. "I read the story about Grim and Neco. And then it had, like, family trees for each." He flipped to two specific pages. It was obviously hand drawn, looking like someone's notebook.

Mason studied the Necromancer's page, noting that Neco's first three descendants—his children—were named Bellum, Cutem, and Ossa, with no mention of their mothers. Ossa's branch connected with another name, symbolizing marriage— *Mortem*.

A note beside Mortem's name: Lord Neco spent his entire lifetime trying to perfect raising. He conducted countless experiments in which he hoped he would create the perfect soldier. It is uncertain whether or not he achieved this.

Ridley pointed to the other page. "Grim had at least five children, one of which was named Rego. Rego became a king but took his wife's name. When they had children, they were given that surname. Salem."

Mason followed the line from Rego and Regina to their four children.

Keelie. Erebus. Ander. Sage.

Grim's grandsons.

CHAPTER THIRTY-EIGHT
OCHOPHOBIA — FEAR OF ALL VEHICLES

The scenery around them changed. Instead of shimmering buildings and tiles beneath their feet, paved stones now led the way as rainforest grew thick alongside them. In the distance they heard music, singing, and boisterous laughter.

The Relics walked ahead.

"Are you cold?" Erebus asked quietly.

Nyx smiled and shook her head. The air had lost its bite, warming the closer they got to the Grove. "I'm just thinking about Chasity."

"Oh. Are you worried?"

"No, of course not. You said they'd look after her."

Erebus felt a twinge in his heart at the thought of his brothers. "Yeah, Damien and Mason had lots of sisters growing up. I'm sure they can handle her."

Nyx looked at Erebus. "So, how'd you all meet? How did they get to Dewmort?"

Erebus let out a long breath. He'd known his brothers for so long that sometimes he forgot that they'd had lives before Dewmort. His whole life, on the other hand, was Dewmort. "Ridley was the most recent. He came in the '70s. His family were Necromancers, but they didn't practice, and they never told

Ridley or his brothers what they were. They grew up thinking they were human."

Nyx pulled a face. She knew the dangers of not frequently releasing necromantic powers.

"One day, Ridley accidentally raised someone, and that same night he died of an aneurysm. Releasing his power after so long was just too much for his body to handle.

"Damien's family were Reapers, during the trials. They ended up being killed under suspicion of witchcraft, even though they were the ones protecting their town.

"And Mason was a Viking. His whole family were considered the sorcerers of their time, raising zombie armies alongside living ones to invade England. He died serving Ragnar Lodbrok."

"And what about your caretaker—Max, is it?"

"Yeah. I don't really know when Max came to Dewmort—he's never said anything and we never really pressed him for it. But he was there when I arrived. And he was already known across the whole city by then."

"So it was just you two for a while?"

Erebus nodded. "Max worked at the Dewmort hospital, where everyone is taken when they first arrive. He had me helping out with new patients and keeping the books and stuff. I'd go around and check up on everybody, and as others slowly got their memories back, they'd tell me stories about their families and their lives.

"And the others . . . we all just kind of gelled, you know? It was like we'd known each other our whole lives. We just fit into each other's stories. And Max fell in love with them too. We joined the Dewmort Legions as hunters and moved into the warehouse where Max lived, and that's just how it was."

Nyx smiled at him as they walked, shoulder to shoulder, noting how his face lit up as he spoke about his brothers. She felt a pang of sadness. Love seemed so pure when the person holding it had nothing else before them. Erebus came with nothing—no family, no memories, no stories of his own. He'd found his own family, though, made his own memories from scratch, and was so grateful for everything he'd managed to gather.

"What?" he asked, feeling bashful with her staring at him.

"Nothing." She looked away. "It's nice to hear you talk about them. Makes me feel good knowing Chasity is with them."

"Me too." Erebus smiled.

She took his hand.

They came to a stop where the road met a large body of water. Along the waterline bobbed red canoes. Tall, tanned men stood on them, long wooden rods in hand. Mortem approached one of the boatmen, exchanged words, then turned around and beckoned the group over.

Still hand in hand, Erebus and Nyx balanced each other as they walked to the front of one of the boats. The boatman used his rod to push them away from the dock. Nyx looked down and saw fish of all different sizes, patterns, and colors swimming beneath the surface. An abundance of plant life under the water glowed in myriad colors, creating a bioluminescent forest, and, below that, the sand shimmered with what looked like coins.

Rising from the water were towering stepped pyramids, temples, and buildings of topaz blues to crimson red, trimmed with gold. Most had been partially taken over by the jungle, vines and trees rooted into the brick. An ocelot sat at the water's edge while monkeys could be heard in the trees.

Music grew louder in the forest as the boatman pushed them along. The approaching shore was lined with lights and brightly dressed people excitedly waving and yelling. The air smelled of food and flowers.

The boatman looked down, smiling. He had a splash of red paint across his eyes, like a band. "Welcome, my friends, to the Grove."

A horde of vivid people swarmed the water's edge. Women and men adorned with silks and jewels, bangles, and headdresses. Children ran around laughing at one another, waving ribbons and bright banners.

They ushered them from the boat. One took Nyx's hand and led her from the canoe, pulling her into the crowd. The music grew louder as the temples around them curved to reveal an open city square filled with a sea of people. Overhead were paper-mâché lanterns; streamers and kites blowing in the wind as confetti fell.

A stage at the right of the square was lined with performers and lights. Market-like tents dotted the rear of the square, sheltering tables piled with dishes of food. The scents of chocolate and chili were carried on the wind.

Hans and Ira danced their way through, following the horde into the square. Someone came up from behind and linked their arm in Nyx's. Greta danced in time with the music, nudging Nyx with her hip.

The music quieted and a hush fell over the crowd as the Council was led before the stage. An old man stood upon the stage; a guitar slung around his shoulders. The curled ends of his moustache were streaked with gray. His face flickered, revealing golden eyes, scaled skin, and horns. His Underneath flashed for only a second.

He spoke with a voice thick as syrup. "I would like to welcome our friends to tonight's celebration. My fathers before me have had the honor of welcoming your predecessors over the centuries, and now that honor is mine. It is such a privilege to have you in our beautiful city, and on such an occasion as the night of Martem. I truly hope you enjoy your time here."

Cheers rose from the crowd. He continued: "Watch the drinks, enjoy the lights, love the music—and have fun." He stepped away and the musicians took their places, and the thrum of fast-paced guitars and drums filled the air once again.

A glass was shoved under Nyx's nose. She looked up to see Mortem, his long white hair now scooped into a thin ponytail.

She took the purple cup from him. "What is it?" she asked, sniffing.

"It's called *hueyatl*," he answered. "Their traditional drink."

The cup's contents cast a blue light. "It's glowing," she said bluntly.

Mortem laughed and took a sip from his own cup. "Indeed it is."

She eyed him suspiciously before taking a sip. A sweet flavor, then sour, then hot like cold chili. A bubbling, fizzing sensation, and then a blur—the night came in chaotic bursts of color and noise. Glowing faces and glimmers of Underneaths. Neon paint tossed through the crowd like a cafeteria food fight. Swaying bodies and laughter.

And then, somewhere in the middle of it all, Erebus picked Nyx up. He spun her around, and she laughed at the sight of his drunken, blue-streaked face.

He took her hand and whispered, "Come with me."

CHAPTER THIRTY-NINE
XENOGLOSSOPHOBIA – FEAR OF FOREIGN LANGUAGES

Eris had been watching the news a lot more lately. She'd heard of the missing children in Germany. The lion that had been butchered at the Berlin zoo, its tail nowhere to be found. The dead wolves found at the edge of a farmer's property in Turkey. The mutilated mother bear found in Slovakia, her cubs dead around her.

She hadn't missed those messages in the ticker that ran along the bottom of the screen. Nor had she failed to notice the raven in the trees outside her window every night. She'd seen it before, with its ugly scar and milky eye. It flew away each night at 10:06, swooping and scratching Eris's window as it did.

Lilith sat beside her now, in the kitchen, bickering with someone only she could see.

"No, Peter, what do you expect me to—" She stopped abruptly. Her eyes moved across the room as someone exited. The door slammed seconds later. Lilith dropped her head.

"What'd Peter say?" Eris asked.

Lilith sighed. "Fucking *nothing*."

"Well . . . what if there *is* nothing?"

"There has to be something, Eris." Lilith faced her. "I *know* he

knows something about Chazz and Nyx. He just won't tell me."
Eris went to speak but was cut off. "You know I saw him the
other day, out back, talking to himself. Like someone was actually
there. Someone that even *I* couldn't see. And then you know what
I noticed?"

"What?" Eris asked.

"Chazz's detector is missing."

"Where's it gone? It's not like anyone in the house would take
it." Eris paused. "You think Peter took it?"

"Who else would have? I love him, but the talking, the pendant,
all this weird behavior? Something's . . . *off.*"

Alice rounded the corner then, looking disgruntled and tired.

"How is she?" Eris asked.

"No better than yesterday," Alice said. "Or the day before that."
She dropped onto the stool next to Lilith.

Maura was the last Seer in the household. The last few days,
after losing her daughter and her niece, she'd started to change.
She'd locked herself away. Mae had entered to find her in the
corner, delirious, sweat dripping from her hair, mumbling about
monsters and invisible people.

"What was she talking about today?" Lilith asked.

Alice looked at Eris. "Ravens."

CHAPTER FORTY

FYKIAPHOBIA — FEAR OF SEAWEED

"Do you know how the humans at Pompeii were killed?" Erebus asked.

Nyx stared at him. "Didn't they suffocate?"

"Nope. *Actually*, studies have revealed that they were killed due to the immense heat from the ash, air, and gas. The ash pile settled over them long after they'd died," he stated excitedly.

"Who spends their time finding this stuff out?" She laughed.

"Me, because I have no life."

He'd led her away from the party, back toward the dock. Lanterns along the side of the path and the moon above provided the only light. Behind them, the music was still loud, the laughter shrill. The jungle was filled with its own sounds. The punch of the hueyatl had left them both slightly off balance—the only thing keeping them from veering off was their clasped hands.

"Hey," Erebus said, looking ahead, pointing with his free hand. "What's that?"

Nyx followed his gaze to a lump along the water's edge. "I don't know . . ." She pulled Erebus along to the bobbing canoes. As they neared them, she realized it was a fish—like ones they'd seen earlier. Only dead.

Erebus nudged it with his foot. "Ew."

Nyx crouched next to the fish and smoothed her hand over the scales. Its body was dry.

"What are you doing?" Erebus asked.

"Well, I'm not just going to leave it here . . ."

"Please tell me you're not going to—"

Nyx's hands were already reaching for it. The fish jumped under her touch. The pattern of its scales flared, rippling down its fins and tail in vibrant swirls of green and violet as it bounced back to life. The Banshee inside was completely in her zone. The fish writhed in the sand.

Erebus stumbled back. Nyx heard scuffling on the moss-covered bricks, then—

"*Shhhhhhit!*"

A splash and a burst of laughter. The fish squirmed in Nyx's hands as she shuffled closer to the water. Erebus, meanwhile, was drenched to his knees, looking less than impressed. The fish touched the water and swam away.

"Won't it eat all the others now?" Erebus asked, climbing from the water.

"Um, *no*. A zombie acts on orders, otherwise they act normal. *You* give *it* the orders."

"And what did you just order it to do?"

She smiled. "Don't eat the other fish."

"How many times have you done that?" he asked, watching it disappear into the glowing corals.

"What, raised something?" She wiped her slimy hands on her dress.

"Yeah. Like, I know your family doesn't do it conventionally, but don't you have to, you know, release the pressure?"

She nodded. "When we were little, we got to choose a dead

animal from the garden. We kept the bodies in jars and every few weeks were allowed to raise them, let them run or fly around the house for a bit, and then draw the life back out of them again."

"You can take life back?"

She sat next to him on the shore. "Most Necromancers don't know how, but my family does. It's taught to us more than the art of actually raising. You can only take away from what you create. We were taught it as a backup, in case we ever accidentally raised something and had to get rid of it."

Erebus frowned. "Wouldn't it be just as easy to take its head off?"

Nyx shook her head. "When you raise something, it's an almost maternal bond. Even though it's not biological, it's yours. Your magic. It would be like taking the life of your own child—it would just hurt too much. Does that make sense?"

"Yeah, of course. I didn't know that's how it felt. It's pretty interesting."

She smiled. "Interesting?"

Erebus laughed. "No, seriously, I like hearing about this stuff. The only Necromancers I know are Ridley and Mason. Ridley knows less about it than me, and Mason doesn't really talk about it. Plus, you know, with all of this Relic stuff, I guess it's good to know a bit about it all."

She'd forgotten about Relics for a moment. Neither of them really knew what it meant yet. "What do you think he wants with us?" Nyx asked, bringing her knees to her chest.

"Who?" Erebus asked.

"Bellum. The Council won't tell us why he's looking for us."

Erebus sighed groggily. "Honestly? Who knows. All these people and problems and worlds, living and breathing while we had no idea. Who knows what kind of issues he has with the Council, or past Relics. Give them time, they'll tell us eventually."

Nyx looked into the water. A fish at least thirty feet long, the color of flame, popped its head out. She was annoyed—at the Council for not just giving them the whole story, and at Erebus, because he had a point.

She looked back at him as paint dripped down his chin.

"Come on," he said, taking off his shoes and suit jacket.

"What are you doing?"

He grinned slyly. "You wanna take a swim?"

"Uh *no*, actually," Nyx said, eyeing the water.

"Sure, you do." Then, without warning, he picked her up and threw her over his shoulder. Nyx screamed as he waded into the water. "You ready?" he yelled.

"Don't you dare, Sale—"

And then Nyx received a face full of lukewarm water. She grabbed his collar right before going in and dragged him down with her. She surfaced and turned around, wiping water from her eyes as she laughed. Erebus's face lit up. The water began to glow. Nyx saw rocks on the riverbed, which was covered in plants of all shapes and sizes, each emitting their own vibrant tone—a bioluminescent forest.

The fish around them were large and uniquely patterned. Their scales glowed the same bright colors as the plants. Some were long, swaying slowly from side to side, whiskers and tentacles trailing behind. Others were smaller with large fins. There were mini whalelike ones and giant catfish, jellyfish, and sharklike-looking creatures.

"This is officially my favorite place in the world," Erebus declared, the light reflecting off his handsome grin. The zombie-fish circled

Nyx's legs. Its body had lit up like the others, violet and emerald. They stood there for a while, shoulder deep in the glowing water.

Erebus cleared his throat. "You know, a couple of months ago I didn't think I'd know you except as the girl who pistol-whipped me in a freezer."

She laughed as she swept wet hair from her face.

"But I'm really fucking glad I know you," he went on. "I would have never thought that you, of all people, would be the one with me here." *Here*, he thought to himself. Here he would find his family. Learn about his whole life. And somehow, it was Nyx beside him. Accidental friends.

Partners in crime.

He smirked at her, drunk. "You look lovely. You know that?"

She cackled. "Shut up, Salem."

"Hey, guys! Is that you? Wait for me!"

There was enough light around for them to see Greta kick her heels off and run into the water, soon followed by the stumbling, laughing pair of Hans and Hatter. Ira and Chef's silhouettes walked the path behind them.

The water erupted in color once more. Erebus's eyes remained on Nyx. He wrapped an arm around her shoulders and gazed into the water, glowing beneath them like a city.

"I like you, Lahey," he said. "I like you a lot."

She rested her head in the crook of his neck. "I like you, too, Salem."

CHAPTER FORTY-ONE

OPHTHALMOPHOBIA — FEAR OF BEING STARED AT

"You're not a Reaper anymore, Nyx," Mortem said.

Afternoon training consisted of being tipped out of bed at five o'clock and then running to Kyra and back. This was followed by a grueling sparring session in the courtyard with Thorn, the Head of Guard.

Now, Mortem held out his hand. "Hand me the scythe."

Nyx clutched the weapon to her chest, defiantly.

Mortem stepped closer. "You're the Banshee now. And for that, you need not a scythe but a Necromancer staff. So hand me your weapon."

Begrudgingly, she placed her scythe in Mortem's hands.

"Okay, close your eyes and feel your way around," Ira instructed.

Erebus had woken to Ira blowing purple powder in his face to rouse him as the afternoon sun filtered through the open windows. She had made him run from the mountaintop down to the mask shop in the village. On his way, he'd caught the shimmering figure of Aliana staring down from one of the towers. Something about her bothered him—made him uncomfortable.

He'd met Hans and Bayou at the castle's back entrance, standing in a gravel-covered courtyard. By then, night was settling in. Hans had tossed him a long, wooden pole before picking up his own. He'd swung at Erebus without warning.

Bayou had remained at the side, throwing fiery orbs at Erebus. Those that Erebus didn't bat away in time scorched his skin, and were often followed by a thwack from Hans.

"A bit ... unfair ... don't you ... *think*?" Erebus growled between slashes.

"War is unfair, Erebus," Ira yelled from the sidelines. "You're a Reaper, you will be trained as such. Necromancers use both their physical weapons and magic."

Erebus slashed out with his staff, which Hans dodged. He came back quickly, planting his boot in the Reaper's side.

"You can do this, Erebus," Ira said. "You've done it before. Your father and brothers taught you well. You just need to remember."

Erebus looked at her a moment too long—a quick, hard slap of a staff. Hans laughed.

Now, Erebus stood in a dark room. Adorning each surface were scythes of every color, size, and shape.

Behind him, Ira said, "The scythe will choose you."

Mortem held out his hands, revealing a bronze scepter atop which three long, curved blades reached upward. At their center was a large red stone.

"I was able to melt your scythe down. This is your Necromancer staff. It will act as a blade but also call forth your armies."

Armies. Zombies. Nyx regarded the weapon. It gleamed, and the stone pulsed like a detector. "Thank you," she whispered.

Mortem dusted his hands and walked to a table at the back of the room. Myriad blades were spread across its surface.

"Now," he started, picking up a black scepter much the same as hers. "When we train—" He cut himself short and cocked his head to the side, then pointed to her wrist. "Where did you get that?"

Nyx looked down. Cole's bracelet.

"Take it off," he said. "I need to teach *all* of you."

Reluctantly, Nyx dropped a hand to the bracelet. Upon her touch, the band loosened and dropped from her skin. Slipping it into her pocket, she could feel the Banshee slide back into place. She became aware of every Reaper in the castle: Hans and Erebus somewhere together. Greta in her bedroom. The guards and all other inhabitants.

She saw her reflection in the blades on the table—the beaten metal made her appearance bulge. Her hair turned white, stark against her skin. Silver lines ran down her face, eyes consumed by red. The white magnolias along her hairline bloomed.

The Banshee. Her Underneath.

Mortem watched her, gripping his scepter. "Are you ready, Banshee?"

She growled and lunged.

"Come on, Erebus," Ira yelled, holding her scythe steady.

Erebus's hands were sweaty, constantly slipping from the leather band around his staff. He'd spent an hour and forty-two minutes in the room of scythes, eyes closed, walking in circles. Eventually, he'd felt a pull. Following a ribbon of icy air, Erebus found himself staring at a tall, silver scythe. It was smooth and matte, with a single long blade etched with patina patterns resembling Celtic knots.

He stood opposite Ira, the two of them brandishing their weapons.

"You'll have to get used to attacking me, Salem. Just because I'm a woman it doesn't make me any less dangerous. Necromancers normally stick together in large groups—mothers and their children. You will very rarely find a father with the group, so it will almost always be a woman attacking you."

The two circled each other before clashing.

They trained every night.

Erebus and Nyx saw each other often over the next few days—at breakfast (which occurred around midnight) and after their training sessions. Days turned to weeks, which turned to months.

Some days, in the early hours before dawn, Ira and Mortem would let them study. Erebus and Nyx would hide in Chef's kitchen, books spilling across the table between them. They read up on the history of the Relics—Erebus had to learn about correct usage of his scythe while Nyx had to study how to command multiple bodies. There were even notes from Neco himself about how he preferred to raise, and different experiments he'd tried while attempting to create the perfect soldier.

Erebus would get bored and throw Chef's caramel popcorn at Nyx until she looked up. Sometimes they smuggled snacks up to one of their rooms, and spent hours lost in conversation. Erebus would talk about Dewmort. Nyx would talk about her strange family and their rules while Erebus snuggled with Bjørn on her bed.

Soon, Mortem and Nyx moved from basic scepter combat to raising. First, he took her through a thorough timeline of necromancy—from Neco, to the Roman emperor Nero, to Attila, to recent-day dictators and modern-day massacres. The world's most ruthless Necromancers.

"The higher the death toll, the larger the army. The more people dead, the more soldiers you have. That's how it works."

Simple.

"Okay, so by now you should be seeing something you wouldn't normally see," Ira said while studying Erebus.

They stood in the castle foyer. Alongside Erebus stood Ira and Bayou.

Lately, Erebus had been able to see things differently. The Underneath came to him a lot more easily. Mortem's face, for example, would sink, his eyes growing hollow. Ira's horns turned gold. Greta was a lot like Die—her skin turned the palest of greens, with two ram's horns curling around her ears.

The scarecrow didn't visibly change. When questioned, Jack laughed and replied, "I have a pumpkin for a head, kid. What else do you want?"

"You should be able to detect the Necromancers around you," Ira said. "Like with detector gems, though you should be able to do it on your own."

"Yeah, I can see them." He looked at the floor, watching lines. Three stood out from the rest.

"What do they look like?" Ira asked, watching Erebus with some degree of awe.

The flickering white lines ran from Erebus's boots and over

the tiles. "They're just lines . . . like silk. They look like silk." The brightest one danced to Erebus's right, traveling out the open door. Nyx.

The one running alongside hers was different. It had a feeling of wrongness—it jumped like a scratched disk. That was Mortem's.

The final one went in the opposite direction. He followed the pulsing white ribbon to the hem of a navy-blue dress—a visitor at the door of the training room. Someone stopping by to see how the young Wraith was training. Erebus raised his eyes. The visitor's eyes were fixed on the floor, slowly moving from Erebus's boots to the bottom of her dress. As if she could see the line too.

Aliana finally looked up. Face stoic, eyes hard. Superior and sure. There was a strange air around her. Mortem said she was a Fae, a species that included dryads, kelpies, and elves. Erebus had seen very few of them in Dewmort, but he understood why Nyx felt so uncomfortable around her.

You won't, Reaper.

"Erebus?" Ira said.

The ghost narrowed his eyes at the blond woman in the blue dress. He looked away.

Aliana didn't have an Underneath.

CHAPTER FORTY-TWO

MUSOPHOBIA — FEAR OF MICE OR RATS

Mortem, hoping to make Nyx ponder her existence, asked, "So, tell me, Lahey: What is a Necromancer?"

"We dig up dead people."

"No." Mortem beckoned her to follow him.

They started with a flower. Mortem sat the pot on the training-room table. The flower within was withered, dead.

He crossed his arms. "I want you to raise it."

Flowers were tricky. They weren't like animals as they didn't have brains to manipulate. But it *could* be done.

Nyx focused on the grayed petals, mangled stem, and faded colors. She placed a finger on one of the crumpled petals. It felt as though it would crumble under the weight. Then, spreading like shattered glass, cracks of deep pink traveled out from her finger. It felt like stitching fibers of sun and color back together. Magic engulfed the petals, the stem straightened and strengthened, leaves unfurling from its side. It took nothing to bring it back to life.

Nyx stepped away, the flower swaying to her movements, following her.

"Well done," Mortem said, standing before her. "Now, something a little harder."

—

"Rats?"

Mortem diligently stepped over the creatures as he spoke. "Yes, rats. One of the easiest animals to find in large groups. Perfect for this session. When you raise armies, you raise individual soldiers. You need to know where each is and conduct their souls back into their own bodies. This will help you practice multiple raisings."

Nyx buried her nose in her elbow and looked around the small room. In the moonlight she could see hundreds—maybe thousands—of tiny, shriveled rats. Some were on their backs, tails curled and brittle, small claws caught in a clench. If she looked close enough, she could see their gloomy green souls hanging above their bodies.

Mortem held his hands behind his back, a smug expression on his face as if to say *Good luck with this one.*

"Now, try to raise *thi*—"

Whoof.

The mischief wriggled, their thin, withered bodies filling out in a flash. Souls flew back to their bodies in a second. Teeth sharpening, eyes glazing over, claws growing. They scampered across the ground, taking position behind Nyx.

It took nothing. They were so tiny, Nyx felt only a *sliver* of her power slip away and travel across the room to their bodies. She felt a pulse in her feet as she and the mischief connected. It radiated across the floor as they stood straight, awaiting directions. She could feel thousands of small pinpricks at the back of her brain as their individual ties to her strengthened.

Mortem's smug smile was gone. "Not bad, Lahey. Not bad at all. Now this," he said, snapping his fingers. The rats disappeared, and in their place landed a hunk of bones and sparse brown fur. Nyx couldn't make out what it was.

She recoiled at the smell. "What is it?"

"Just focus," Mortem said, amused. "Feel it. Find out."

Nyx looked at the animal on the floor. Body sunken with time, bones white, fur fluffy brown. Above it, she saw the faintest glow of a soul—or multiple ones, she couldn't tell. The deeper she looked into it, the more it revealed: the scent of pine needles; clear, clean wind; fresh snow underfoot. Warmth. Love.

Nyx willed the carcass to rise. She felt her head tighten, a headache growing as she pulled the body up like a puppet with her mind. It was heavy. And as it lifted from the ground, she felt her way through its structure—bones and strong claws, thick skull, and daggerlike teeth.

She willed the bones to thread themselves together, cracking back into place. Muscle moved into place, stretching and relaxing for the first time in years. Energy and signal traveled through the corridors of the creature's empty mind, bringing life to dormant senses. Fur brightened and lengthened, filling in gaps in the creature's skin.

The animal stood, bones clicking as it did. It grew taller than Mortem and Nyx. Its fur was incomplete, leaving patches of bone visible on its cheeks and across both sets of front knuckles. Its eyes came to life, an eerie ghost green as it looked down at Nyx.

It was a bear. Towering and huffing as it stood on its hind legs. The other souls Nyx had seen had found their own bodies—at her feet rolled two cubs. They'd been hidden beneath the pile of fur and bones.

The bear was aware of them, and, despite being at Nyx's command, felt the faintest wave of maternal longing.

Nyx stood back and released her grip on the mother bear. The mother fell to all fours and her cubs tackled her gleefully.

"Very good, Nyx," Mortem whispered from behind.

The mother looked at Nyx, waiting for some kind of order. She stepped forward, her two cubs playing between her feet. She stood before her creator, her wet, half-decayed nose inches from Nyx's own. The bear gently nudged her face.

"*Very* well done," Mortem chuckled. "Now, I want to show you something." He turned to the door. "Follow me."

Mortem led her lower into Monstrum's depths, stopping in front of a small wooden door with a bronze pentagram on it. He swung it open and ushered her inside.

The room was dim, covered with cobwebs and dust like a skin. Rectangular windows had been painted over with black. Shelves and bookcases lined the brick walls, filled with vials and jars—of what, Nyx didn't know. Old books were piled atop one another. Dried plants and shriveled herbs hung from pots and hooks in the ceiling.

A large wooden table in the middle of the room was strewn with candles, a mortar and pestle, and a thick, open book.

"I take it you're familiar not only with a Necromancer's raising abilities but also with their limits too," he stated.

"Yes," Nyx answered.

"Good. So tell me: What are they?"

"We cannot *fully* rectify the dead. We cannot repair decayed matter, nor can we restore former thoughts. All we can do is place a soul back inside its body and control its actions."

He regarded her for several seconds. "Wrong."

"What?"

"There has been one full raising."

"By who?"

"Neco," Mortem answered calmly.

"On *who*?"

Mortem hesitated. "Me."

"What?" Nyx stared at him. He couldn't be serious.

She noticed the scars. Along his neck, crisscrossing his chest like stitches. And the wrongness of it all. The symbols on his stomach seemed to stir then. She sensed pain. Ripped flesh. Needles and wire. Stitches and scalpels. Scissors and skin.

"Nyx, don't freak out."

And then confusion. Disorientation.

"Nyx," Mortem said. "Neco learned the secret to a full raise. He was able to completely restore the soul, the body, *and* the mind."

"The perfect soldier," Nyx breathed, remembering the pages she'd skimmed, written by Neco himself. "You were Neco's experiment. To see if he could create life."

The Necromancer, or *zombie*—she didn't know what to call him anymore—sighed and nodded. "Tomorrow we're going to see if you can do the same."

I know you're tired of waiting. You're tired of not remembering. All I ask is that you have patience. Just continue with your training and you will be rewarded.

At first he hadn't been sure what Ira had meant. Then the dreams started.

He was a boy again, sitting in a room with lavish tapestries draping the walls. Hazy portraits hung upon hooks—too fuzzy for Erebus to make out.

He looked down. Chubby hands rested in his lap. Fingernails

bitten too far, feet swinging as he sat on the chair. His shoes were too big for him. His feet couldn't reach the ground.

Grown Erebus—dreaming, watching this memory—was aware of someone to his right, a tall swirl of colors in his peripheral vision. A door opened then, and the room filled with voices. A long, green dress approached through the haze. Red hair tumbling over a shoulder in a braid. Face indistinguishable. And, finally, a white bundle in either arm.

The figure to Erebus's right moved closer. The woman crouched in front of them—blue eyes, white teeth, pink lips, gold woven through her hair.

"Erebus, Keelie," she said, placing a bundle in each boy's arms.

Erebus looked down. He felt the bundle squirming.

"I want you to say hello to Ander and Sage, your new baby brothers."

Keelie was allowed to hold Sage on his own, but the woman crouched in front of Erebus, guiding his chubby hands so they cupped the baby's head. It was a tiny thing—eyes shut, only a few wispy hairs on his head.

"Which one is he?" Erebus asked, his voice small and foreign.

The woman smiled beautifully, the way only mothers do. She ran her finger along the baby's brow. "This is Ander."

The scene started to fizzle, growing hazier by the second. Voices grew muffled. The weight of the baby on Erebus's knees lifted and everything faded away.

"Your Highness," someone said, "the royal nurse is here."

The last thing Erebus saw before waking was a silver locket around the woman's neck.

CHAPTER FORTY-THREE

CHAETOPHOBIA — FEAR OF HAIR

Ridley shut the water off. Steam filled the bathroom, water slicking the walls. He heard Die and Chasity downstairs, probably cooking breakfast. Die had been coming over daily. They would all sit in the lounge and Die would tell them about the Hallows.

Exiting the bathroom, Ridley came face to face with something that shouldn't have been there—a person with yellow hair, orange skin, and cat's eyes. Stitches through the corners of her lips, pins sticking out from her cheeks, like industrial dimples.

"Gather your belongings, Ridley Channing," she said. "Gather your friends too. Your time in the Hallows awaits you."

Die appeared at the end of the hall. Her face dropped. "Clarissa," she breathed.

The mysterious woman smiled. "*Die* . . . well, I didn't think I'd see you here." She regarded her fondly, almost sadly, Ridley noticed. "It's good to see you again. We've missed you very much."

Die approached. "What are you doing here?"

"It's time to go. Your access to the Hallows has been granted. When you're ready,"—she turned her smile to Ridley—"follow me."

—

Ossa the Great had never known the love of family.

She'd been raised with Bellum and Cutem in the house of her father, Neco, but none of them had ever really *loved* each other. To Neco, his offspring were nothing more than servants. Soldiers. Brought into the world to serve him and bring pride to his name.

Ossa had been born as, and always would be, a loveless creature. From the time she could walk she had been trained— how to hold a war staff, how to cast a spell, how to slip through walls and unlock doors with a mere thought. The blood of her father made her more than just a Necromancer. But to him, that was all she would ever be. Something regular. Something below him.

Things changed when Bellum was born. Neco actually saw him. His eyes shone upon Bellum in a way they never did with Ossa. From the time he was born, ripping his way out of his forgotten mother, Bellum was Neco reincarnated. Ossa remembered peeping around a corner at Neco when he returned home holding a black bundle in his arms. A pale baby, sleeping.

Neco had looked up at his daughter then and, for the first time, Ossa saw real happiness. Her father lowered the baby to her, and Ossa had to hold herself to not recoil.

The baby had red eyes.

Her father's eyes.

As the baby grew, Ossa found herself hating him. At the likeness he shared with her father. At the way Neco was so *enraptured* by the boy. At the time, she couldn't understand why.

It wasn't until she was older and Cutem was born that Ossa understood. Because of what Bellum was born with. What both sisters lacked. Ossa and Cutem were trained by servants. And Bellum? Ossa's father always managed to applaud him—encouraged him as they trained *together*.

It was Bellum who stood by his father's side while he created Mortem. For months, locked in a room together while Neco stitched together souls and body parts. Ossa and Cutem sat outside the door, day in and day out, waiting for any news.

When Mortem woke, Ossa was sure he was the most beautiful man she had ever seen. He was like her: pale skin, pale hair, similar eyes. Both daughters were amazed at their father's work. But then, after being home for what felt like only a second, Bellum left and their father fell into his slumber.

Ossa wasn't sure what was worse: Bellum's departure or his return years later with a Horned Witch.

"Sister, this is Ira," Bellum had said, gesturing proudly to the beautiful creature by his side. She was tall, a pair of beautiful horns spiraling from her scalp.

"It's lovely to meet you," Ossa said, forcing herself to smile. How could Ossa be happy for Bellum's love when she had never experienced it herself?

Ira smiled, wide and glorious. She spoke with a voice like worn velvet. "Likewise."

Mortem rounded the corner then. He'd come far from the disorientated creature their father had raised, naked and afraid, a stranger to language and anything that wasn't the pain their father had put into him during his making.

Ossa and Cutem had taught him to walk, speak, eat, and sleep. They'd shown him the warmth of the sun and how to use clothes in the bite of the winter. They'd taught him to wash and helped him remember the names of the creatures that lived around their home. He'd learned to write and tie knots and cut vegetables from their garden.

He, too, came to a complete halt at the sight of the witch. Ira warmly extended her hand to him. "Oh, I'm sorry, I don't think I caught your name. I'm Ira."

Mortem took her hand. "Mortem. It's a pleasure to meet you. I've actually heard quite a lot about you—you're trying for a spot on the Hallowed Council, right?"

Ira's face radiated. "Yes! That's right. Where'd you hear that?"

Mortem smiled. "Oh, I'm trying out myself."

"You are?" both Ossa and Bellum said, surprised.

Mortem nodded. "Yes, the Council believes my abilities will come in handy."

Ossa nodded, cursing her father for creating someone like him. Someone who was sure to be stolen from her too. His abilities had proven themselves only days after his creation—he knew who was going to die, who already had, and the moment it was to happen.

Of course they wanted him. Who wouldn't?

Days later, Bellum woke Ossa in the dead of night. "We need someone on that council," he said, frantic.

Ossa rubbed her eyes. "What? What are you talking about?"

"We need someone on the inside."

Ossa glared at him. "I think your new lover can fill that spot for you."

Bellum sighed. "I'm being serious."

"So am I."

"You're angry because Mortem is going, aren't you?"

"No, I'm not." Ossa was angry about a lot of things. Mortem was just one of them.

"What if there was a way you could go with him?"

"What do you mean?"

"I mean, what if he took you with him? We need to know if any news of Grim comes in. Whether he's still awake or in slumber, we need to know where he is."

"Why would I go with him?" Ossa snapped. "It's obvious he likes Ira anyway. They'd be perfect together on the Council."

Bellum's face became stoic. "Then make yourself like Ira. Make yourself beautiful—make yourself an entirely different person if you must. You have magic, Ossa. I know you do. You can do anything."

For once, Ossa felt as if her brother was impressed. And he was right. She could do it. She could do it easily. He would be even more impressed when he saw what she could craft. And that was enough for her. For the next two weeks Ossa disappeared, remaking herself until she stepped back into their home an entirely different person. She returned home as Aliana.

She immediately drew Mortem's eyes away from Ira. She made small talk about her travel and the Council. She offered to sponsor their campaigns, claiming to be the daughter of a Fae fruit farmer involved with Hallows politics. She could be their sponsor, their chaperone, their campaign partner. Anything to weasel her way into their circle.

And so, for the next two years, Ossa lived within another body, by another name, traveling through the Nethers. And over time, Bellum fell more and more in love with Ira while Mortem spent many a night sneaking into Aliana's bed.

"Marry me," Mortem whispered one night, lips brushing against hers as he spoke. He wanted her to stay with him after the campaign was over. He didn't want her as a sponsor.

He didn't want her as a consultant. He wanted her, only and completely.

They married four months later, and both Ira and Mortem were accepted into the Council. Ossa helped Mortem create his plans for the Hallows. Whether it be rebuilding villages, planning new schools, or securing the many portals that ran through their world. It was everything Ossa had ever wanted.

And then it was gone.

Ira returned from the royal wedding of Keelie Salem, the eldest of King Rego's sons. She'd told them stories of the snowy northern kingdoms and how beautiful the event had been. Someone, confused, had asked who Rego was. Ira had laughed and replied that he was the son of the one and only Grim.

Bellum's eyes had snapped to Aliana from across the room.

"He still has *children*?" Bellum spat later, alone in the halls with his sister. They'd lost track of Grim's children years ago, thinking they were all dead. Ira seemed to think that one of Rego's sons was the next Relic.

Bellum wouldn't have it. He wanted the descendants gone. All of them. Every last descendant of Grim. But Ossa had everything she ever wanted, and he expected her to throw that away for a feud that wasn't even hers. She had love for once in her life.

"Trust me, sister, your love is wasted," Bellum had said, raising his palm and conjuring an image before them.

It was Mortem, smiling. Caressing the face of a woman. Ossa smiled, trying to place the memory of it happening. But the image shifted and Ossa found not herself beneath Mortem's caress, but Ira.

Pain exploded in her chest. Bellum smiled, looking more like their father than he had in years.

"I wage war on the Hallows, sister. Care to join me?"

And she had. They decimated all. Ossa would fight and murder and pillage in her true form only to return to Monstrum as Aliana, gathering information on the Hallowed Council.

Then the Salems were killed.

That had hurt Ira the most, Ossa thought. Bellum had gone after the family Ira had brought to their attention. Deep down, Ira knew that it was her fault. But Bellum had also destroyed Ira, and the one encounter the two had shared after that led to the scar that now ripped across Bellum's face. Ira had unknowingly initiated the downfall of the Salem kingdom, and she would never let the guilt escape her.

And oh, how Ossa could see the pain on Ira's face at every mention of the Salem family.

She reveled in it.

"It's time to leave," Petram said as she strapped blades to a belt around her thin waist.

Bellum had fastened the charm from the sisters around his neck, making sure the pouch was hidden by his coat. "What about the army?" he asked.

Petram smiled. "Don't you worry, dear Bells. Leave that to us."

"Where is the closest door?" he asked. He'd met them at the edge of the woods and did not favor tromping all over Europe with two witches and a trailing zombie army, searching for a red door. It had already been months spent raising his army—Bellum had been all but comatose in focus, crafting body by body, wicked soul by wicked soul.

"Italy," Luto announced, marching into the black woods ahead.

—

People were staring.

Not at their appearances—the three of them had made sure to hide their true selves. All people saw were three tourists with cameras and backpacks. That did not, unfortunately, hide the ugly scar that deformed Bellum's features.

Luto and Petram led the way through winding, cobblestone streets of Rome. The houses here were earth colored, windows dusty and water marked. They eventually stopped at a building, its windows covered by wooden planks nailed from the inside.

"Would you care to do the honors, Bells?" Luto smiled wickedly, swinging open the frail old door. Behind it was a rusted, grimy door that led to the Hallows. It should have been trembling at Bellum's presence.

But it was still—the necklace was working.

"Once you open that door, Bellum, Mortem's curse will be broken. All protection from you and your armies will be gone."

Bellum smiled and reached forward.

CHAPTER FORTY-FOUR
CLAUSTROPHOBIA — FEAR OF BEING IN
SMALL, ENCLOSED SPACES

"He wants you to do what?" Erebus asked angrily.

"He wants me to bring someone *back* to life."

"How can you even do that? It's impossible, isn't it?"

Nyx had gone straight to Erebus's room at dawn. It was much like hers, with lava beneath the floor, warming her feet. His scythe was on his bed, books stacked, armor lying on the floor.

Nyx sat on the edge of the bed, watching him pace. "Apparently not," she replied. He sat next to her and she caught sight of the serpent tattoo on his back, peeking out above his shirt. "Neco did it. He conducted experiments and raised a perfectly pieced-together soldier. Lots of dark magic and surgical procedures on corpses I presume, but he did it."

"On who? Does anyone know?" Erebus asked.

"Mortem. Mortem is Neco's soldier."

Erebus sat back. "Oh, *shit . . .*"

"He said it took Neco hundreds of years to do it. But since the Relic is as strong as Neco—perhaps even stronger—Mortem thinks I should be able to do it."

"That makes sense, you know?" Erebus said. "All the Necromancers in the castle, I can see their energies. It's a line from them to me. Mortem's has always looked weird." He looked at Nyx. "How do you feel?"

"I don't know how I'm meant to do it. I know how to catch souls and put them back into bodies. I don't know how to fix bodies or create consciousness."

"Did he say who you'd be bringing back?"

"He said he'd explain tomorrow. But, like, if he was Neco's soldier, how can the Council trust him? How can I trust him? What if he makes me bring back someone who shouldn't be brought back?"

Erebus touched her hand. "Like you said, Mortem is fully alive. He's not some puppet; he's his own person. Neco isn't around to control him."

She looked at Erebus's hand. "I hope you're right."

Ira knocked at Nyx's door later that afternoon, atop the ice-covered steps. "Where's Erebus?" Nyx asked, expecting the two of them to be training after they'd woken.

"He's still sleeping. I wanted to be there when you started tonight."

Ira led Nyx through the castle halls. They came again to the small wooden door with the pentagram. Ira opened it, revealing Thorn, Mortem, Bayou, Hans, and Aliana, who smiled coolly.

Nyx's eyes landed on the table in the center of the room. It had been stripped of the books and candles, and upon it lay a long, black sheet.

Underneath that, a body.

"Now, Nyx," Mortem started, "this particular raising process involves a lot of time. Once you begin, you will be locked in. You will not break from the raise until you finish. If for any reason the two of you are put in danger during this process, the Banshee'll stop at nothing to defend your subject."

Mortem caught her looking at the scars on his body.

"The duration of this raise is affected by one thing: the age of your subject. It's one day for one year. If you were to raise a three-year-old, your raise would last three days." Mortem leaned on the table and stared at her. "Your subject is sixteen years old."

"*Sixteen days?*" Nyx blurted. She wondered then how many days Neco had spent on Mortem.

"One of us will be stationed in here with you at all times," he said, like that made everything better. "You can choose who you want to be stationed with you first."

She caught Hans's icy eyes looking down. "Hans," she said.

"Is there anything else you want? Some water or—"

Nyx stepped forward. "I want to know who it is."

Glances passed around the room before Mortem lifted the top of the sheet. Beneath it lay a skeleton.

"His name is Ander," Mortem said. "He was killed by Bellum a long time ago. We've been keeping his remains safe for an opportunity like this."

Nyx felt a pinch in her chest. This boy was killed by the same man who'd killed Chasity. She wondered how he had died. If he was scared. If he'd been alone, like Chasity.

"All right, I'm ready," she stated, standing next to Mortem.

"Are you sure?"

She nodded. "Yes."

Mortem looked at Ira, who nodded. He moved away from the table. The others filed out of the room, leaving only the three of them and Hans.

"You're going to need to take that off," Hans said, touching the silver band around her wrist.

Nyx slid the band off, doing her best to stay glued to her spot— ignoring the growing urge to tear Hans's throat out.

"Okay, Nyxie," he said, squeezing her shoulder before stepping away. "Whenever you're ready."

She turned to Ander, smoothed her hand over the white of his forehead. She opened her palms over his ribs.

"See you in sixteen days, Lahey," she heard Mortem say.

Nyx took a deep breath, and the world disappeared.

CHAPTER FORTY-FIVE
KYMOPHOBIA — FEAR OF WAVES
OR WAVELIKE MOTIONS

The dreams were sporadic and never in any particular chronological order. This time he was taller. Hands not so chubby, legs longer. He was standing in an empty room—brick walls, a large wooden chandelier overhead. Three windows filled the room with a dusty haze.

Keelie was taller too.

Erebus became aware of something heavy in his hands. Looking down, he saw a long, dark scythe. Across from him, Keelie swung one of his own.

Erebus noticed the glare in front of him. Sleet coming through the open windows had coated the walls and the floor.

Someone coughed. A blond-haired boy sitting nearby with paper and colored chalk. Sage, maybe ten years old.

Keelie pointed his scythe at Erebus. "You ready?" Erebus nodded. Keelie braced himself, readying a lunge, then stopped, giving an exasperated look. He dropped his weapon and took Erebus's hands. "Remember, one hand up here, near the blade, the other"—he placed Erebus's right hand low on the staff—"down here. Okay?"

"Okay," Erebus said, nodding.

Keelie picked up his scythe again. "Are you ready now?" Erebus tightened his hands around the staff. "Don't slip on the ice, Eb." Keelie smiled, which he knew made Erebus nervous, and lunged, bringing the blade of his scythe down. Erebus held the staff above his head to block. The force of Keelie's swing was enough to almost shatter Erebus's knees.

Erebus watched as Keelie taught his younger self to fight—how to trick opponents, how to jab, how to lever their own weapon against them. Only Erebus wasn't exactly good at any of those things. And his weight was nothing compared to someone four years his senior—Keelie was basically pushing him around.

Sage's stomach hurt from laughing. Erebus was red cheeked, sweaty, and out of breath. Keelie, meanwhile, had nothing more than a blister on his hand.

"You did good," he said, smiling.

Erebus looked up at him. "I suck."

"Weeeell . . . can't argue with that, but you'll get better."

Erebus woke with a start. The sky outside was pitch black. He'd slept in. There was a knock at his door, and it swung open, Ira's silhouette filling its frame.

"Erebus," she said, "when you're ready, someone's here to see you." She vanished, and Erebus reached for his jeans. Minutes later, in the foyer, he found the Council awaiting him.

"What's going on? Where's Nyx?"

"She's doing some one-on-one training with Hans," Mortem said, glancing at Ira.

Erebus knew what that meant.

"But never mind that," Mortem continued. "Bayou and Ira

have finally been able to sort some things out for you two."

Ira placed her long-nailed hands on the brass handle of the door. She turned back around. "Remember these faces?" she said as she opened the door, smiling like a mother on Christmas morning.

A blur barreled into Erebus. He regained his footing and looked down to see Damien.

"*Heeeey!*"

Wide eyed, Erebus looked to the door again. "Holy shit," he said as Ridley and Mason entered the castle with packs, scythes, staffs, and clothes strapped on their backs. Damien moved on to the Council behind them, introducing himself.

"You fucker," Ridley said. "Don't ever disappear like that again."

Mason smiled devilishly before tackling Erebus. After Mason, Erebus spotted two others: Die and Chasity Lahey.

"Oh my God, Nyx is going to be so happy to see you," he said, smiling at them.

"Where is she?" Chasity's eyes searched the room.

"She's in training at the moment, I'm afraid," Ira answered.

Die looked at Mortem. "Can't she end training early? Don't you think she could cut it short tonight?"

Ira and Mortem exchanged another glance.

At that moment, an explosion rattled the sky, loud enough to shake the castle walls. Through the open door, lightning-like patterns retreated across the sky.

Four things happened then:

The red of Ira's eyes disappeared beneath a glossy black as dark veins spread across her face and neck.

Mortem doubled over as though he'd been shot.

Thorn and his men burst into the room, weapons at the ready.

And Aliana disappeared.

Chaos erupted. Alarms sounded, drowning out Mortem's shouts. Ridley and the others jumped at the sound.

Greta yelled to Ira, "Which door did he come through?!"

"The Roman Door!" Mortem yelled.

"Who is it?" Erebus yelled. "What's happening?"

"Go, get to Kyra!" Mortem said, and half the armored men fled through the door immediately. Swords, staffs, and bows appeared in the hands of Bayou and his brides. Jack descended the staircase holding a large pitchfork.

"*Who* is coming?" Mason demanded, reaching for his staff.

Ira reached the open door and hissed, "Bellum."

"What do we do?" Die yelled. Only she and Erebus knew the gravity of that name.

"Get your weapons!" Mortem looked around. "Where's Aliana?"

"What was the bang?" Chasity asked.

"Bellum breaking through the barrier," Die said, eyes on Mortem.

Mortem looked at Erebus. "He's coming for you and Nyx."

"What about her and Hans, shouldn't we get them?" Erebus asked.

"No," Mortem shot back.

"Come on, no fucking training session is that important."

"I'm sure you're already aware of what's going on with Nyx, Salem," Mortem snarled, a large Necromancer staff appearing in his hands. "She's only with us in body while this training is undertaken. Hans has to stay and look after her."

Another screech rattled the sky, followed by howls. Outside, the moon cast silver ribbons across the dark—it looked like it might shatter.

"He's brought an army," Chasity said, sensing the dead they couldn't see.

Mortem felt it too. "We need to leave," he said, strapping his staff to his back. He manifested Erebus's scythe and threw it to him before turning to those who'd just arrived. "I won't ask you to come, but your help would be very much appreciated."

Chasity and Die looked at one another. The boys nodded.

"Well, we're already dead. What's the worst that could happen?" Ridley said. Hatter looked at him and laughed.

Erebus and the others filed out, followed by the remaining guard, leaving only Hatter and Mortem.

"Hatter? Are you coming?"

"No," Hatter said, watching Die as she ran out the door. "I'll stay here with Hans and Nyx. I promised I would do better, and I intend to keep that promise."

Mortem nodded. "I'll send backup once we get to the square." He turned to leave. "If you see my wife, make sure she's okay."

CHAPTER FORTY-SIX

ALTOCELAROPHOBIA – FEAR OF HIGH CEILINGS

The ghoul watched as the ground churned. In the square, bricks cracked in on themselves, and the statue of Jack tilted as everything beneath it fell away. Howls could be heard from underneath the rubble.

Doors opened as people carrying pitchforks and blades emerged from their homes, their sickly greenish skin stretched taut over their cheeks.

The ghouls knew what was coming—what would soon be clawing its way from the ground—and they were prepared to fight.

Hatter burst into the room holding Hans's scythe and Nyx's staff.

"What's happening?" Hans shouted as Hatter kicked the door closed behind him.

"Bellum's here," Hatter replied, rounding the table where Nyx stood, eyes vacant and hands spread.

"*What*?"

"He just broke through the Roman Door And probably the sisters too—they're the only ones who could make a spell strong enough to challenge Mortem's."

Hans paled. The Sisters. The pair who had killed him and his sister. "Okay, okay," he said, taking deep breaths. "Where are the others?"

Hatter passed Hans his blade. "They've gone to Kyra."

Hatter leaned Nyx's staff next to her. He remembered what Mortem had said: if she or Ander were threatened, the Banshee would destroy anything that posed a threat. Hatter eyed the Necromancer scepter. *Just in case.*

Hans said, "So you and I are going to stay here and look after N—"

A crash shuddered through the castle. They looked at the ceiling where the wooden chandelier swung wildly from its chains. Hatter pulled a pair of knives from his belt.

The howls reached a crescendo.

A pale creature crawled from the churned earth. Spindly arms stretched taut, thin skin, veins visible beneath. The Brauge cried into the air. Others followed.

Mason went quiet as they neared the city. Ridley cast him fleeting looks, checking for a reaction. The memory of the frat party was fresh in his mind. There were very few things that could harm a dead man. One such thing was Reaper Iron.

Another thing? Brauge.

"Mason!"

Mason saw Mortem pushing through the crowd toward him. Ridley watched as the two exchanged hushed words before heading to the edge of the group.

"Wait," Damien said, "where're you going?"

Mason smiled as he pulled the staff from the strap on his back. "Don't worry . . . I'll meet you guys there."

Up high, there was less interference—fewer buildings to absorb the spread of a spell. Here, Mason could wake *thousands*. He'd never spoken much about his life before Dewmort, but to him, raising was an art. He'd fought with Vikings for years, and in battle, raising was the purest form of war art there was.

He climbed the stairs to one of the roofs, his coat billowing behind him. In the distance, atop a matching building across the city, he spotted the pale speck of Mortem.

Across the rooftops, Mortem raised a fist. Both men raised their Necromancer staffs, mirroring each other's movements. They spun their scepters, creating a windmill effect. Mason could feel the spell spreading. The sphere in his staff glowed an angry green. Faster and faster they spun, their barriers engulfing acres. Each could feel it as another soul within their influence stirred.

Mason recalled his childhood training. He made sure to find and hold each soul as he spun both his staff and his body, dancing his war dance. He danced closer to the edge of the roof. One, two, ten, thirty-five. Mason felt hundreds of budding souls within his sphere, each filling him with power, aching to return to their bodies.

Mason and Mortem halted midturn. In unison, both flipped from the edge of their respective roof, bringing the tops of their scepters crashing into the concrete of the street below.

A blinding green light shot out from both—a shock wave that rippled silently through Kyra and the mountainside.

The ground of the Hallows trembled, crashing horrifically and cracking as the earth heaved. Then—

Breaking through the hard surface of the local market.

Bursting through tree roots in the forest depths.

Struggling out of the mud at the riverbank.

From far and wide, two armies stumbled toward their masters. Another, made up of civilians, marched toward the sounds of screaming creatures. And, finally, a council of mismatched monsters, ready to protect their kingdom.

Four armies, come to defend their world from one man.

The Council descended on the village already beset with screams and smoke and fire. Ahead of them were a pair of green-skinned ghouls—one with a pitchfork, the other a shovel.

The one with the pitchfork pierced an invading creature, holding it to the ground by its head as the other leveled the blade of the shovel at its throat. Both ghouls jumped away as the head screamed, the body thrashing at them before dropping to the ground, smearing black blood against the bricks.

The ghouls eyed the Council suspiciously as they approached the town, more Brauge spilling from the pit behind them. Ira stepped forward. "We're here to help," she said, hoping the two would understand.

The Brauge continued to clamber over each other, ravaging anything in view. Behind Ira, Bayou raised his hands, purple smoke dancing between them, before flinging an axe at an oncoming Brauge's head. The creature was taken off its feet, landing on the cobblestones with a mighty *oomph*. The ghouls looked at the Council.

"We're here to help," Ira repeated.

Somewhere, in the almost-empty halls of Castle Monstrum, an orange-eyed trickster came out of hiding.

Ossa the Great could hear the thrumming of hearts. The most fragile one, a whisper being pieced together, belonged to the boy on the table. Ander knew who Ossa really was.

That boy could *not* be woken. That girl could not live.

Two birds with one stone, she mused as she moved, her long swamp-green dress trailing behind her. No longer would she have to bear the guise of Aliana. Nor would she have to tolerate Mortem and his Council. Not after tonight.

"How long has she been like this?" Hatter asked.

Hans leaned against the wall, arms crossed. "Not long." He watched as Hatter regarded the skeleton. "His name is—"

"Ander," Hatter answered. "Ander Salem. Erebus's baby brother."

Hans looked confused. "Did they tell you?"

"Oh, no. But I can feel him. He's here."

Hans smiled. Of course. Hatter was a Beacon. He would have sensed Ander's remains in the castle before anyone else.

Hatter looked at Nyx. "Does she know we're here?"

"I'm not entirely sure."

"Well," Hatter said, pointing, "she obviously senses something." Nyx's hands had begun to tremble. And, if they looked close enough, Hans could swear they were beginning to glimmer, the pearlescent sheen of her Underneath giving her skin a glowing coat.

Hatter's head twitched to one side abruptly. "Something's in the castle," he announced.

Hans backed away from the table. There was a bang at the door.

CHAPTER FORTY-SEVEN

PHOBOPHOBIA — FEAR OF PHOBIAS

Sometimes, when Lilith Lahey slept, she'd dream, and, when she woke, she'd find objects at the foot of her bed. Or in the palm of her hand. If she dreamed about a painter, she would find brushes and dried paint under her nails. If dreaming about dragons, she would find scales among her sheets. Sometimes, nightmares would run wild. An earthquake might leave rubble around her bed and mud on her scratched and bleeding skin. A tsunami could result in her waking up drenched, cold, dead fish on the floorboards.

Tonight, though, she dreamed not of trembling earth or soul-sucking waves. Instead, Lilith saw a great mountain range. Thick smoke coated her throat, and she saw an orange glow far below her vision. But she couldn't see *what* was burning. Atop a mountain, she saw a mighty castle with a winding path etched into the mountainside leading down into the fire.

She saw two sisters, surging through the crowds, appearing in flashes like black smoke as they cut down villagers. Witches. And a scarred man watching overhead from an alcove hidden in the mountains.

She heard howls. The roar of flames and the crash of wood and metal. The sounds of battle.

Then: lavender and lemongrass—Chasity. And the faintest scent of something she'd not smelled in an age, like gasoline and cheap Beyoncé perfume. Die had often come home late with mussed red hair, her boyfriend driving away in his Chevrolet as she strutted inside. The denim jacket that, in a few years, would be Eris's, thick with these near-forgotten smells.

Amid the smoke and perfume, the screams and the sounds of destruction, Lilith, the Artifex, began to conjure.

They were stumbling out of *everywhere*.

Thousands of undead tripped from the woods, scampering down roads and into the village, clawing out of the dirt to clash with the Brauge rising from the town square.

Ridley ducked as a Brauge swung a clawed hand at him. He and the other Dewmort boys, including Erebus, had burst in and out of the battle. Using their coats, they took to the sky as ravens to escape blows or find new targets before returning to the ground, slashing.

Swinging around as the creature stumbled, Ridley brought his scythe down, burrowing it deep into the Brauge's arm socket. He barely had time to retrieve his weapon before the Brauge was taken to the ground by an armada of zombies. "Jesus *fuck*," he spat, jumping away as the monsters ripped at the writhing white beast.

"They're not a fan of Brauge meat," Mason said as his sword sliced through a Brauge's abdomen, spilling its entrails. He plunged the blade through the creature's head and, with a flick of his wrist and a crack, pulled out the blade, and the Brauge went limp. "But they'll do it if I order them to."

Ridley nodded appreciatively to the zombies now feasting on the Brauge and yanked his scythe from the beast.

They aren't seriously throwing mangoes, are they?

Damien paused midbattle to look.

Atop one of the houses, scrambling on paved tiles, two young ghouls were using mangoes from a nearby tree as ammo against encroaching Brauge.

"*Denis, Denis, Denis!*" the smaller one yelled, pointing to where Brauge claws were tearing at the eavestrough.

Damien saw their weapons lost in the gardens below. The Brauge screeched as the two continued to hurl the large, orange fruits, which exploded on contact.

One of the boys looked up and yelled, voice ragged, "You know, you could help, Reaper!"

Damien leaped into motion. "I'm coming, I'm coming!"

The candles in the chandelier above blew out, casting the room into darkness.

Hatter glared upward until the flames returned. "Haaaans."

Hans raised a finger to his lips. "*Shhhh . . .*"

Hatter slowly backed away, standing by Nyx's table while brandishing a long, shining knife. *Not this time*, he said to himself. He listened, watching the door. Silence.

"*Hatter!*" Hans screamed suddenly.

A flash of white, then a ghastly, pale woman stepped out from the shadows next to the table. Instantly, they recognized her.

Ossa the Great.

Hans lunged forward but was tossed aside by a mere flick of her wrist. He slammed into the door, his vision briefly blackening. He opened his eyes again at a scream and the sound of metal clanging.

Hatter was in front of Ossa, blade hilt deep in her shoulder. Her eyes burned with rage. She screamed and thrust her hand at Hatter's chest, hurling him against the rear wall. He slumped to the ground.

Hans scrambled to his feet as the woman began to pull the blade from her sh—

And the spires of Nyx's Necromancer staff pierced Ossa's head, emerging out the other side. Hans gasped.

Nyx was shaking, consumed by her Underneath. She stood, silent, now-red eyes distant.

Hatter stumbled forward. "N-Nyx?"

"It's not her," said Hans.

It was the Banshee. She was protecting herself and the body of Ander Salem.

"If you get in her way," Hans continued, "she might lash out. Just let her do her thing."

The Banshee surveyed the body of the pale woman before lowering the end of her staff and using her boot to slide Ossa's head from the three blades. Ossa landed with a wet thud, her blood briefly spreading along the floor before she vanished.

"Where'd she go?" Hatter demanded.

"I don't know," Hans said, paying close attention to Nyx.

"What is she doing?" Hatter asked. The Banshee cleaned the blood from her blades on her jeans, completely calm. "Shouldn't Nyx just go back to what she was doing?"

"It's not Nyx, Hatter. There's no telling what she'll do."

And then, without provocation, the Banshee moved to the door.

"*Hans*," Hatter warned.

"Leave her," Hans shot back. "Mortem said she would only abandon the raise if she felt threatened. There might be something else in the castle."

"What if she goes out there and Bellum's right outside the front gate?"

"She can handle herself. We'll follow her, though. But hang back a little, in case she gets the wrong idea."

Hatter nodded, leaning against Hans. "Where do you think she's going?" he whispered.

"I *think* she's going down the mountain."

CHAPTER FORTY-EIGHT

ACAROPHOBIA – FEAR OF VERY TINY BUGS

Chasity stood still amid the chaos, head raised. Illuminated by the moon above, a slithering green mist began to spiral over the village. She shut her eyes and visions flashed before her: Lilith sleeping. Peter on the windowsill, staring outside, as a shadow appeared over her. Lilith jumping, eyes shut. Almost convulsing. Thunder overhead.

Chasity opened her eyes again and watched as the faintest strand of mist wafted into the streets, passing her face. A Brauge scampered around a corner, slipping on its long talons before running straight into the green mist. The creature stopped dead in its tracks, stunned, choking, then slumped to the ground.

Chasity approached it cautiously, expecting the creature to rise and resume its attack. Nearing it, she saw blank eyes and darkening limbs, and it exploded suddenly into a pile of ash and dirt. She smiled as the mist continued on, moving through the streets.

It was familiar. Smelling of cinnamon and palo santo. It was her. Lilith was dreaming.

Erebus would have blisters tomorrow; they'd been fighting for hours and it didn't seem as though they were putting a dent in the

Brauge army. His shoulders were heavy, legs almost limp, chest burning. Even in raven form, he hardly had energy to fly.

He swung his scythe through the necks of a group of Brauge. The headless creatures spasmed, scuttling away before falling over dead.

Mason's and Mortem's armies were wreaking their own havoc within the village—tackling Brauge like football players, tearing into them like starved dogs. Amid the smoke and rubble, Erebus spotted all manner of beings awash in dirt and blood, each wielding weapons: Women with the bodies of snakes swinging kusarigamalike blades on chains. Winged creatures of stone wielding great hammers, lashing out with a force strong enough to shatter Brauge.

"Erebus!" someone yelled.

Swinging around, Erebus saw Chasity covered in just as much grime as he was. She ran toward him, pointing to the sky.

"Look!" she yelled.

Erebus followed her gaze to what looked like an almighty storm cloud—a great spiral of mist circling above the village. It filled the narrow street around him, dropping three Brauge to the ground. They clawed at their necks like they couldn't breathe.

"What is it?" Erebus asked as creatures were reduced to dust and the mist moved on, bending around the corner to the next lane.

"It's Lilith," Chasity said. "Come on, let's follow it."

Something was wrong. Something was terribly, *horribly* wrong.

Maybe it was the searing pain in Bellum's head. Or the great, twisting cloud above him, killing his army. Or the fact that the Banshee was walking down the side of Mount Monstrum. He watched as the mist continued to sweep through the town, striking down every soldier in its path.

"Petram!" he shouted, and the frail witch appeared at his side. He threw up his hands in anger. "What *is* this?"

Petram shrank away. "Someone's interfering with the plan."

"*Really*? You think I didn't notice that? If you wish to keep your head, witch, I suggest you fix this quickly."

"B-but I c-can't—it's someone outside of this realm. Some kind of astral attack. I can't get to them from here."

"*What*?"

"Bellum, we cannot fix this." She gestured to the sky. "This is something *else*."

"Get your sister," Bellum shrieked. "We're leaving."

"But—"

"Either we leave and regroup or we stay here and die—take your pick."

The mist spread quickly, dropping Brauge by the dozens—thousands of the creatures had been turned to dust until only three remained, huddled in a home in the main square, past the debris of Jack's statue.

The Council had gathered there. Slowly, the rest followed. Mortem stepped forward, his leather armor in tatters. "Erebus," he said, "come with me."

Mortem led Erebus to the farthest house, where, hiding inside, they found the remaining Brauge soldiers. The last of an army of thousands.

Erebus peered at them through the window. "What are they doing?"

"They know it's over." Mortem opened the door and they stepped inside. The creatures raised their heads—nothing more. Mortem pulled out two simple knives. He handed one to Erebus. The creatures did nothing as Mortem stepped forward. Erebus followed. They took death willingly.

Erebus returned to the square as dawn broke on the horizon. He looked out over the crowd, spotting Ira. She seemed to be staring straight through him.

Erebus turned.

Nyx—the Banshee—was standing at the edge of the village.

Petram had cast herself invisible as she moved through the crowd, searching for Luto. Ahead of her, people were whispering about something she couldn't see. She was shaking. She couldn't get enough air into her lungs.

They'd been defeated. They needed to get *out*.

She stood on her toes, trying to see over the crowd. At the very front of the group stood Mortem and the Wraith, both staring at something out of Petram's view.

"*Pssst!*"

She could only make out a speck of white—

"*Pssssst!*"

The witch searched wildly before locking eyes with her sister on the other side of the crowd. Petram beckoned to her urgently. Luto shook her head.

No, I need a few more minutes, she said, her voice in Petram's head. *Ossa failed. I will not.*

And before Petram could do anything more, Luto disappeared in a puff of black smoke.

"What is she doing out here?" Erebus whispered to Mortem.

The Necromancer ignored him. He turned to the crowd and yelled, "Reapers, evacuate immediately!"

The crowd devolved into chaos as every Reaper ran for safety. Ira took Damien and Greta away.

"You, too, Erebus," Mortem said, facing him.

Erebus looked at him incredulously. "*Absolutely* not."

"Erebus," Mortem warned, watching as the Banshee approached, scepter in hand, "you're the Wraith, you stand out like a beacon to her. I know what she's capable of. You don't. She *will* kill you."

"*Mortem*, I am n—" Erebus stopped abruptly. "Who is that?"

Mortem turned. He spotted the frail, blond woman behind the Banshee—the gleam of a dagger in her hand. Luto—one of the Blind Witches. She raised her knife.

"*Nyx!*" Mortem screamed.

Instantly, the Banshee loosened her grip on the scepter, letting it swing in her hands. She spun and, in the blink of the eye, took Luto's head from her body.

The crowd gasped. Some screamed.

Mortem and Erebus rushed forward. The Banshee turned, shaking. Her skin flashed, eyes going from red to orange. Nyx shook her head as if to rid herself of the other. She screamed and clutched the sides of her head.

"Nyx?" Erebus said, keeping his distance as Mortem approached.

Her eyes opened—crimson, though her skin was once more her own. She shoved Mortem aside, launching him into the side of a building, and stormed toward Erebus.

Ira screamed at him to move.

Nyx raised her staff, blades to his chest. Erebus raised his hands.

"Nyx . . ."

Mortem got to his feet. Nyx blinked. Slowly, her eyes went from the glorious red of the Banshee to the orange of her normal self.

Erebus looked at her blade, resting at his sternum. "Nyx?"

She looked at him, and her eyes widened in fear. She dropped the weapon. As she backed away her eyes darted across the square—to the crowd watching her. She had no idea where she was or why Erebus was covered in blood.

"Erebus . . ." she said, voice cracking, "what's happening?"

CHAPTER FORTY-NINE

NEOPHOBIA — FEAR OF NEW THINGS
OR EXPERIENCES

"You did *what*?"

"Die, it was her choice."

"*No*, you told her it was a part of her 'training.'"

"It was an experiment she was willing to conduct—"

"A fucking *experiment*? Do you think that makes it sound any better?"

The Council and the ghouls had agreed to begin reconstruction of Kyra, starting the night after the battle. In the meantime, everyone had returned to their homes or, if destroyed, to the castle.

Erebus had carried Nyx back up the mountain. But as soon as they stepped inside the gates, she became engulfed once more in a trance and swept soundlessly upstairs, all eyes following her.

"What do you reckon happened?" Damien whispered, head pressed to the door, trying to hear.

"Don't know," Mason whispered back.

"Do you think he'll tell us?"

Ridley sighed. "Maybe if you stop being annoying as balls, then yeah, he might."

"Sixteen days, Mortem," Erebus said through the door. "Who is it?"

A sigh. Then: "Come with me."

Mason, Damien, and Ridley jumped away from the door and leaned against the wall, trying to act as casual as possible. Erebus, Die, and Mortem stepped out—still bloodied, clothes in shreds.

"What are you three doing?" Mortem asked, glaring.

"Nothing," Ridley said. "You?"

Mortem rolled his eyes. "I s'ppose you're going to find out anyway . . . come on."

Nyx was frozen, hands spread across a jumble of bones.

"What is she doing?" Mason asked.

Mortem leaned against the door frame. "She's going to raise him."

"What?" Mason snapped. "Another zombie?"

"No," Mortem said pointedly. "She's going to make him whole again. Body and mind."

Mason approached the table and stared at the skeleton. Power radiated from Nyx's hands—he could see it pulsing through the bones.

"How is that possible?" Damien asked.

"Just keep your distance, Reaper," Mortem said through set teeth.

"Nyx is the Banshee," said a new voice, answering Damien's question. The trio turned to see Chasity. She entered the room, eyes trained intently on her cousin, as were Die's. "It makes her stronger. Different . . . better. Those bones will be a boy in a few days."

"So, who is it?" Erebus asked again.

"That's classified," Mortem replied.

"What," Ridley said, "do you work for the fucking Avengers or something? What the hell is 'classified'?"

"It means the identity of the boy is best kept anonymous for the moment." Mortem looked at Die, who averted her eyes. Erebus saw it—she knew who it was. *Perhaps*, he thought, *if things were different, she would have been in Nyx's place.*

"How long's she going to be like this?" Mason asked.

"Fourteen more days."

"*What?*" Ridley, Mason, and Damien said in unison.

"What if she gets hungry?"

"What if she needs to pee?"

"What if she has an itch?"

"*She will be fine!*" Mortem yelled. "Her body will sustain itself until the process is over. She will be tired and possibly a little thirsty. But that's it. Her body will carry on like it always has."

Ridley approached Mortem. "And what about Bellum? We didn't find him. He could be in the castle right now and—"

"I assure you, Ridley Channing, no one posing any threat will make it through those gates. Thorn has doubled the castle guard and the cities have posted their entire armies outside." He turned his attention to everyone. "No one is getting in."

Erebus kept his eyes on Nyx. She was unresponsive in every way.

"Now," Mortem continued, "we're all very tired. It's time for some well-deserved rest. Nyx will be fine—Hatter will watch over her."

"She did *what?*"

Bellum had escaped to one of the southern mountains just as

the Banshee had stepped onto the field of battle. He'd signaled for his sister and the witches to follow, but none did. He'd spent almost an hour alone in a cave before a screeching Petram appeared. The witch crashed to her knees, mouth open in an ugly howl. She told Bellum what had happened—that Luto was dead at the hands of the Banshee.

"She was a fool for thinking she could take on the Banshee," Bellum said. "You needn't fret, Petram—it was obviously for the best."

Petram regarded him with disgust before sulking away.

"Your sister was never trained like Ossa and I. We were taught as children to hunt the Relics. They're the only beings strong enough to destroy an Original, like my father. But also the only things strong enough to bring him back. It was our duty, as his children, to learn how to protect him. Not yours or your sister's. She should have been smarter."

A thump echoed throughout the cavern as something landed behind Bellum. His sister, limp on the ground.

"I see that you failed," he stated bluntly. "You should know: Luto is dead."

Ossa groaned and rolled onto her back, physically exhausted. Her face was swollen, cheeks like bulging sores. Three distinct, angry red wounds dotted her face—the largest right at the bottom of her temple.

"I see your necromancy has been put to good use," Bellum said, kneeling down. He caressed her swollen cheek then grabbed a handful of her hair. "Make sure it was worth it, big sister," he sneered. "Because if you fail me again, your fate will be worse than death."

Ossa glared at him. Bellum shoved her away. "We attack again," he said. "We'll wait—Nyx is impossible to reach in her current state. She'll be much weaker *after* the raise." He turned to his sister. "Fix yourself and return to your husband—make up some excuse for your absence. Play it safe until I give the signal to move in. Just you and me this time, and some of Petram's magic. You'll take Nyx and I'll take Erebus, and we'll find out which one we need and which one we don't."

He smiled. "It's just a process of elimination, my dear."

"Hans," Mortem said, growing more irritable by the second. "What are you saying?"

"I'm *saying* that Ossa the Great just *happened* to appear only minutes after the castle was evacuated," he whispered.

Mortem stepped closer. "And what does my wife have to do with any of this?"

Hans raised an eyebrow. "Well, *Mortie*, multiple people standing in the foyer say that Aliana just *disappeared* as soon as the alarms sounded. And how would Ossa just *get in*? Don't you think that's a little suspect? And what about Die? Do you remember that night? When her goddamn throat was slit?"

Mortem failed to answer.

"No? Let me refresh for you. We were in the village; Die was tired so Chef brought her home. Aliana decided to tag along. Later, we find Die dead in her bed. The guards saw no one else that night, and we sure as hell know it wasn't Chef."

"How dare you," Mortem scoffed. "Lest we forget, it was a knife wound. Knives are his specialty, are they not?"

"If Chef was gonna *murder* someone, don't you think he would have been a bit smarter than to use his own tools?"

"*Hans.*"

"Well, where *is* she, Mortem? Where'd she go?"

"I don't know!" Mortem yelled.

"You should talk to Erebus."

"Why?"

"He knows something. More than he lets on—I can tell. Whenever she's around, he changes. Ask him."

In the dream, Erebus was older.

The edges of his vision were blurred, but he could still see his mother beside him as a group stormed down the halls. Red carpet underfoot, stone walls to either side.

It was late and there was an urgency in the way everyone moved. The fact that his mother wore a thin white gown suggested they'd been woken. The men around him wore chain mail; their faces were grimy and tired.

They rounded a corner and came to the end of the hall, a pair of dirtied knights standing guard. Both silently stepped aside as Erebus and his mother approached. The Salems were led into a cramped room filled with smoke, soldiers, and the scent of lavender. A table stretched before them, a body unconscious atop it—Keelie.

Erebus's stomach plummeted. His mother gasped. Keelie was bare from the waist up, his side covered in thick, white bandages, red seeping through.

"She just came out of nowhere, my queen . . ." said a soldier on the other side of the room.

My queen?

"He didn't have time to . . . her blade went right through and—"

Erebus approached the table. Keelie's dark hair was plastered to his temple, sweat beading his skin. His eyes darted behind his eyelids.

"We'd been hunting them for the last five months, following their havoc through every village they upturned. It was just a game to them. The sisters ambushed us," the soldier said.

Erebus took his brother's hand. Keelie's eyes fluttered lazily then he gripped Erebus's hand tight and his eyes snapped open.

"Y-you . . ."

Their mother leaned closer, eyes brimming with tears. "What, honey?"

Keelie took a long blink and whispered, "Y-yooooou . . . need t . . . to . . . g-et ooou . . . t. Th-they're go . . . *going* to come . . . for you. For . . ." Keelie sighed. "For everyone."

"Keelie." Their mother held his face. His eyes rolled back. "Keelie, look at me. Who did this? Who's coming?"

Erebus backed away as a woman approached the table, sniffling. Keelie raised an arm to her weakly. The woman pulled back the blankets in her arms, revealing a tiny, sleeping baby. Keelie let the baby's fist wrap around his finger as he spoke.

"You need to . . . get him out of . . . here."

A silver bracelet hung from the baby's wrist. It looked identical to the one Nyx wore.

Erebus turned to one of the knights. "Who's he talking about? Who's coming?"

And the soldier whispered back, "The Young God, Bellum, is coming, Grim Prince."

CHAPTER FIFTY

ALTUSSESSIOPHOBIA — FEAR OF
ANTIQUE FURNITURE

Erebus woke immediately from his dream as the last words left the soldier's lips. Something was wrong. Something *had* to be wrong. He must have misheard.

Bellum and Ossa had attacked Kyra only hours ago. Apparently, they'd also been at war with Erebus's father.

He took the corridors to the visitor's quarters—to Die's room. He bashed on the door but to no avail. He hit it again. A sleepy groan came from the other side. "Ridley Channing, if that's you, I swear to God I'll cut off your—" She opened the door. "Oh. What do you want?"

"To ask you something," Erebus replied.

"What is it, Salem? I'm tired."

"I want to know why Bellum was at war with my father."

Die raised an eyebrow. "And why would I know that?"

"You've been here before. You know the lore and history better than I do. My family's tangled in all this mess—I figured you'd know why."

Die crossed her arms. "Ira's already given you back some of your memories, hasn't she?"

"Yeah."

"What'd you just see?"

"My brother returning from war. He'd been attacked by someone. Ossa perhaps."

Die looked at him curiously. "So, you know about your brothers?"

"Keelie, Sage, and Ander. Though I've only seen the twins as kids—Keelie's the only one I recognize as an adult."

"And have you worked out who your dad was?"

"Haven't seen him yet."

Die stood aside, opening the door wider. "You might as well come in."

Erebus entered the room. It was much like the other visitor rooms—plain wooden candelabras, a simple bed, and a set of drawers.

Die closed the door behind him. "How much *do* you know?"

"Before the dreams, when I first came to the Hallows, I had flashes of my brothers. I think Keelie had a baby and a wife. I know my mother had red hair and blue eyes. And . . . for some reason everyone keeps calling her queen."

Die smirked. "Which makes you a prince, Erebus."

Erebus nodded, looking away awkwardly.

"Is that it? That's all you know?"

"Basically."

"Well, I guess there isn't anything I can tell you that you won't find out *eventually*. It's not going to hurt if you know a little sooner . . ." She rummaged through her backpack and pulled out a book. "Do you know about the brothers, Grim and Neco?"

"Well, yeah, everybody does," he replied.

"Well, something not everybody knows is that Grim had kids. One was named Rego. Rego married a woman named Regina and they ruled a kingdom in the northern Hallows. They had four children of their own: Keelie, Ander, Sage, and . . . Erebus."

Erebus straightened. "Wait, what—*what*?"

"You're Grim's grandson. And Bellum was at war with your family because he's Neco's son. They're the archest of enemies. Always have been. He's been out to destroy your family since his very beginning—he and his sisters. Rego killing Cutem only fuels Bellum."

"Cutem?"

"One of Bellum's sisters."

"Is that why he attacked?" Erebus asked.

"Well, it was definitely a perk, but no, it wasn't the only reason. Neco and Grim disappeared years ago—most don't even know where to."

"But you do?" Erebus asked.

"No, but I know there's a price for being immortal. You may live for thousands of years, but one day, eventually, you just fall asleep. Your body needs to recuperate. They're just stuck in this . . . *slumber*." Die ran her finger down the book's binding. "So, there are two ways to wake an immortal. Either wait it out and probably die of old age in the process. Or wake them with the blood of an Amare."

"A what?"

"*Amare*." Die leaned forward. "It's when two Relics form a love bond instead of one of hate, which is called an Odi. If you think finding two Relics is hard, try finding two Relics that are *also* Amare.

"There have been a few throughout history. Romeo and Juliet. Cleopatra and Mark Antony. Pyramus and Thisbe. But you know how those turned out. Bellum's been at this for centuries. Most Amare kill themselves before they let Bellum take them."

"So, what, you have to kill them to wake the immortal?"

"Well, it normally ends that way, but only one of the two will actually wake him. However, it's exceedingly hard to find out which one works without killing them both first."

"And Nyx and I are Amare?"

"Well, you don't have the bond of hate."

"That's why they came. They're going to wake Neco."

Die replied grimly, "They're going to try."

"Erebus!"

Exiting Die's room, Erebus saw Mortem hurrying toward him.

Mortem's expression faltered. "You were visiting Die?"

"And you're walking the halls like a creep. What's wrong?"

"There's just, uh, something I want to speak to you about."

Erebus waited.

Mortem hesitated. "Well . . . it's about Aliana."

"What about her?" Erebus stiffened.

"*Well* . . . there have been some . . . *rumors* going around the castle about Ossa the Great—the woman who attacked Nyx in the spellroom . . ."

Erebus knew exactly where this was going. "People think she's Aliana, don't they?"

"Well . . ." Mortem stammered.

"I'd start looking into that if I were you."

"What do you mean?" Mortem was taken aback.

"She's a Necromancer."

"What? No, she's not. She's Fae, from Blas—"

"I'm telling you: that's bullshit."

Mortem's mouth hung open as he searched for a retort.

Erebus pointed to the ground. "Every Necromancer has their own line leading from me to them. You have one. Nyx has one. Rid and Mason each have one. And so does Aliana."

"Are you *sure*?"

"Absolutely. I'm sure Nyx knows too."

"Why didn't you say anything?"

Why hadn't he? Erebus had only been a visitor in the castle. He would have never dreamed of levying such an accusation before. But things were different now. "Not my place. I didn't know if you knew already."

Morten took a step back. "What have I done . . ." He trailed off. "I should—"

"Actually," Erebus said, stopping Mortem before he could turn away, "there's something I needed to talk to you about."

The door swung open, revealing a messy-haired, drowsy-eyed, less than impressed Ira. "What in all the Nethers could possibly be so important for you to wake me?" she asked Mortem and Erebus, who were standing in the hall outside her room.

Mortem regarded her in her black bedgown, healing bruises and cuts visible along her skin. He cleared his throat. "He knows about Rego and Bellum—about everything."

Ira's eyes widened. "*How?*"

"Die?" Erebus said. It came out more like a question than a statement.

"Die. I'm going to skin her—"

Mortem caught her arm as she tried to barge past them. "Actually, I was hoping we could show him the . . ." They fell into whispers.

"Come in," she said finally, moving aside so they could enter.

An assortment of cloth hung from the ceiling: burgundy, rouge, dusky purple. Moroccan-style lamps and animal antlers were suspended around the space. The floor was ebony. The room smelled of incense and perfumes from hundreds of jars lining a black vanity.

Ira stood next to Erebus in the center of the room. "So, you wish to know the whereabouts of your family, Salem?"

"Of course."

The Horned Witch nodded, then turned to the far side of the room. Erebus eyed the tall, mahogany cabinet as Ira reached for its doors. At her touch, they popped open. Inside were shelves lined with corked jars, bottles, and small, ornate boxes. From the shelves, Ira pulled a triangular flask. Within it swirled what seemed to be snow, miniature pine trees swaying, and animals trotting across the white ground.

"Well then," Ira said, pulling the cork from the top of the flask, "let's go and see them, shall we?"

Ira blew into the flask, and the world went white.

As his vision cleared, Erebus became aware of two things: They were no longer in Monstrum. And his bare feet were very, very cold.

Around them, snow swirled through the air, a flurry of white. Great evergreen trees towered overhead, their tops capped, branches heavy. Through the trees, Erebus spotted the antlers of a deer as it clambered among the brush. Above them, the sky was gray.

"Where are we?" he asked, looking at Ira.

"A graveyard," she replied solemnly.

They stood in a snow-blanketed clearing—alone apart from

creatures that lurked nearby. Ahead of them loomed a row of colossal stone statues with elongated features. Each fit within the shape of an oval.

The center image depicted a man, a crown upon his head. He had a broad, curved nose, downcast eyes, chiseled lips. Billowing out over his rounded torso were stone robes and a chunky livery collar.

Next to him stood a woman, similarly plump. A long, twisted braid draped over one shoulder, fringe framing her round face. A twisting crown ran through her hair. Closed eyes and a peaceful smile, her hands palm to palm, resting against her cheek as though she were sleeping. Around her neck sat a simple oval locket.

Erebus felt a lump in the back of his throat. He tried not to collapse in a heap at the base of the rock.

"Only your mother, father, and sister-in-law are truly here," Ira said, walking forward. "It's your family tradition to be entombed in stone upon death." She placed a hand on one of the billowing lengths of his mother's dress.

Erebus surveyed the statues to either side of the king and queen. The innermost two were smaller but almost identical in design. Two boys with curls, swords at their side, boots and royal sashes across their torsos.

Ander and Sage.

The outermost two were taller. The first was Erebus, though his hair was shorter. The other was broad shouldered and stern, with a crown nestled in his mess of curly hair and a scythe at his side. He wore the livery collar, like their father, with cape and medallions to match. Beside him stood a smaller figure, a woman, and in her arms lay their child.

Ira looked at them. "Kaya, Keelie's wife. And their son, Cole."

Keelie. Kaya. Cole.

"So my brothers are alive?" Erebus asked, gesturing to the empty tombs.

Ira and Mortem exchanged looks. "Not exactly," said Ira. "Neco's children stormed your family's castle. They killed your parents. They took each of you and hid you away. Keelie is imprisoned in the mountains of Loish. Sage sleeps frozen under a lake in the Valleys of Smrik. Ander was the only one killed."

Erebus stood deathly still, eyes pooling.

"You, Keelie, and Sage had anti-aging curses placed upon you before you died," Mortem explained. "You were kept prisoner with Keelie for some time. But one night you broke out of your cell, freed Keelie, and fled, intent on finding your brothers. Bellum found you after only a few hours. He chained Keelie back up and then burned you alive in front of him as punishment."

Erebus felt like he couldn't breathe; like he could remember choking on smoke and the smell of his own burning flesh all over again. "What's in my stone?" he asked.

"What few ashes we could gather. Bellum left your body somewhere we would find it. Like a taunt."

Erebus hesitated. "If you know where my brothers are, why haven't you gone to find them?"

"We can't find them. Yes, we can see them via tracking spells. But no matter how many times we send out parties, they can never locate them. Bellum ensured their locations are ever changing. You won't get your brothers back until he's dead."

"And what about Ander? You said he was dead. So where is he?"

Ira looked pained. She chose her next words carefully. "Your baby brother is in the castle. With Nyx."

CHAPTER FIFTY-ONE
ALLODOXAPHOBIA — FEAR OF OPINIONS

For the next few nights, the Council traveled down the mountain path at dusk and helped with village repairs. Die and Chasity helped clear debris and bury the dead while Damien worked with the pink-haired shop owner—Marvel—as they repaved the cobblestone road, covering the gaping hole from which the Brauge had crawled.

Erebus didn't sleep. He preferred to sit next to Nyx, staring at the ivory bones of his baby brother. Meanwhile, Mortem tried to explain to the Dewmort contingent how Relics worked.

"Whereas Die lost her Relic abilities when she passed, you, Erebus, only received yours after dying. Ander was the Relic before you. The gift passed from him to you. The power followed you to Dewmort, reversing the normal processing. We've never seen it happen before. We expected Cole, Erebus's nephew, to receive it next. Your bloodline makes all of you slightly different than the average Reaper, which may explain why the strain reacted differently."

Damien paced the room, bombarding them with a barrage of questions:

"What exactly *is* a Relic?

"How come there're only two?

"What happens if they have a baby?

"Can anyone be a Relic? Or is it, like, some sort of genetic disease or something?"

Mortem held up his hands. "A Relic is the most advanced form of Reaper or Necromancer. They possess heightened abilities and unique skills. Some believe that, one day, it will be the Relics that unite the Necromancers and Reapers once and for all."

Hans continued, "There can only ever be two Relics at once—one Banshee and one Wraith. When they die, their power is passed to another member of the same family. If no relative exists, it's suspended until someone worthy is born somewhere else. When Die was killed, her powers went to Nyx, but before her, they seem to have come from outside the family. We're not sure where from exactly, but it obviously lay suspended for some time before Die came along. But in this instance, the power never left Erebus. It followed him. Never to be suspended or passed on. We wondered why we hadn't found a new Wraith in so long. We didn't think to look in Dewmort where Erebus has been for hundreds of years."

"Why Erebus then?" Mason asked, suspiciously.

Hans shrugged. "It could have to do with the fact that both Erebus and Ander are grandsons of Grim. But a Relic occurs at random. Like a genetic mutation. It can't be predicted or controlled."

Ridley pinched his nose in confusion. "So, why exactly is Bellum hunting them?"

One and a half days left.

Bellum sat at the edge of the cliff, his back to the cave's

entrance, icy wind in his face. Nyx had been under for fourteen and a half days. The image floating before him showed the bones of Ander Salem.

Only a few more sleeps until they would attack again.

The final battle was coming.

CHAPTER FIFTY-TWO

PHENGOPHOBIA – FEAR OF SUNSHINE

"Technically," Mason said around a mouthful of pastries, "I'm the eldest."

Damien made a face. "Well . . . not exactly."

Mason scoffed. "I was born in 826, Tate. You were born in 1676."

"I mean, I was *about* to turn nineteen too. We would have been the same age."

Ridley sat back in his chair, grinning. "Well, if it's like that, *I'm* actually the eldest. I'm almost twenty."

Damien gave him an exasperated look. "You were born in the 1970s, Channing. I'm three hundred years older than you—counting dead years."

"And you're *still* fucking stupid."

"To be fair," Greta said, "I think Erebus is older. Counting dead years. In the Hallows, his grandfather is ancient."

"Do you know how old he was when he died?" Mason asked.

Greta sat down and grabbed a mango. "Well, if I remember correctly, Erebus was about twenty, twenty-one. Prince Keelie was twenty-three and the twins were sixteen." She stopped abruptly, looking to the opposite end of the room as Thorn and his guards marched through the halls. Nyx would wake in a few hours, as would Ander Salem.

The castle guard had been tripled. Ghouls from the village, gargoyles from the mountain kingdoms—even castle servants had volunteered. Everyone was prepared for Bellum to make his move.

Mason rested his chin on his fist. "Mortem said Keelie had a wife and baby. What were their names?"

Ridley looked at Mason and Damien. Both reveled in the news of Erebus's family. They'd been together so long they'd forgotten what it was like to hear new stories. Forgotten about the nights they'd sat around the warehouse reminiscing about their lives. They'd grown used to the fact that Erebus never had anything to say.

But now, with the news of Erebus's family, they'd been ecstatic. He'd told them about his dreams. About his mother, his brothers, and the castle they'd grown up in.

On the topic of babies, Ridley knew how both Mason and Damien felt. Mason had lost his wife and unborn child. And the last thing Damien saw before being killed was his baby nephew being killed in Salem.

Greta told them about Keelie's wife, Kaya, and their baby, Cole. She told them about Cole's incubi abilities—something rarely seen among Reapers—and how, as a child, a touch of his hand could drain a man of life.

Mason and Damien sat forward, enraptured. Ridley couldn't help but smile.

Finally, Erebus had stories to tell.

Bellum sat at the mouth of the cave, watching as Petram fiddled with a short piece of thick, black hair—something she had all but *begged* from Ossa. She had been inspecting it for hours.

"Well," Petram mused, "from what I can see, the girl has ancestral ties to Turkey, China, even to the Berber tribes from Niger."

"How very interesting." Bellum wrapped his coat tighter around himself, unimpressed.

Nyx was due to wake any moment now, along with her soldier, but Bellum, Petram, and Ossa would still need a few more days to recuperate. Ossa especially. She'd spent the last week sulking deep in the cave—mourning her failure and disfigurement. But their plan was clear. They'd gone over it hundreds of times. They needed Ossa for her knowledge of the castle and its hidden passages. And they needed Petram for her magic.

Luto was dead because she was stupid and hadn't planned at all. Ossa was eternally scarred because she hadn't planned well enough.

Bellum would not make either of those mistakes.

That evening, Erebus dreamed about Keelie. It was his brother's twenty-third birthday, and their parents had thrown him an enormous party.

Erebus had seen his grandparents there. Kaya. Members of his father's guard—friends, boys he'd grown up playing alongside, wielding wooden swords together. He could name them all.

Later, Erebus and Keelie stumbled drunkenly from the castle and wandered into the village. Navy-blue banners lined the shops and houses outside, all in celebration of the crown prince's birthday.

Keelie pushed open a tavern door and golden light poured into the street. Inside the bar, the patrons raised their glasses to the two of them. For hours, they drank and laughed with people from the village.

"The serpent." Keelie made circular motions with his finger. "The one from the emblem, you know?"

A man at the back of the tavern nodded, prepping sharp stone and ink and wiping down Keelie's chest. Erebus knew. Their family crest was that of a large serpent biting its own tail.

Their mother had always said that the symbol would protect them from bad spirits. Its image could be found in every childhood memory Erebus had—carved into chairs and on beds and banisters. For her, it had been a symbol of protection, and she had passed that belief onto her sons.

Pain raked across Erebus's shoulders as one of the men from the bar continuously punched a needle in and out of his skin. Keelie, looking pained, laughed as another began making the image of ouroboros on the left side of his chest.

Finally, Erebus Salem knew why and when he received the ink upon his back.

Erebus had joined them at Hatter's table only to be interrupted by Ira standing in the doorway, head held high and horns raised. She motioned for them to follow her.

Ira led them through the castle, toward Mortem's spellroom. Erebus looked at the ground. Two Necromancer lines were visible: one, twisted, belonging to Mortem; the other, bold and pure white—Nyx. It flickered. *She's awake*, he thought as the guard opened the door. A fragile figure stepped out from within.

Erebus smiled and held out his arms. Nyx ran right to his chest but was all but ripped from his grasp as Hatter and Hans tackled her.

"Let's not ever do that again," Hatter said, squeezing her as hard as he could.

The Dewmort boys gave her a group bear hug, only releasing Nyx when she locked eyes with Die and Chasity.

"Hey, chicky," Die said, smiling, trying not to cry.

Nyx held a hand to her mouth before the three of them collapsed into one another in a teary heap.

"Erebus," Ira called. Erebus looked up. She stood by the open door to the spellroom and waved him over.

Inside, Erebus found Mortem and Bayou standing by the table, and more guards lining the walls. Ira stood at the opposite end of the table.

Sitting there was a boy with a brilliant crown of blond curls. He had freckles, deep green eyes, and a face that was an echo of Erebus's own.

Ander looked at Mortem, tears running down his cheeks. He pointed to Erebus. "This is my big brother," he told Mortem, his voice cracking. "This is my bi—" He put his hands to his face and started to shake.

Erebus didn't even remember walking over to him. He didn't remember taking Ander in his arms, or Ander wrapping his arms around him, holding on for dear life.

Ander was alive. Nyx was back.

Everything was fine.

CHAPTER FIFTY-THREE

EOSOPHOBIA — FEAR OF DAWN

The inhabitants of Ebony Manor had awakened the morning following the battle in the Hallows to a house filled with green mist. Peter had bashed on the walls to wake everyone. Searching each of the rooms, Mae and Marga had walked in to find Lilith convulsing on her bed, tangled in the sheets, surrounded by three dead Brauge.

Over the next few days, he noticed Lilith going into Maura's room a lot more often now. Maura had become delirious and unstable after her daughter's death. She whispered about ravens and dead men and Horned Witch covens and someone named Bellum, the Young God. She prayed feverishly to her altars of the orishas Ọṣun and Yemọja in hopes that they would protect the women she loved.

"Are you really never going to tell me?" he asked.

Lilith sighed. "What do you *want*?"

"I want you to tell me what the hell happened."

Lilith gave him a hard stare before looking away again. She wanted to refuse, solely because he had refused to tell her anything about Chasity. "I saw where she went."

"Who?"

"Nyx," she replied. "She's not here."

"Obviously I know she's not h—"

"No, I mean, she's not . . . it's like she's not on Earth?"

Peter raised an eyebrow; Lilith continued: "I could feel it when I was dreaming. I could see this town and all these people. But everything felt foreign."

"What was the mist?" Peter asked.

"I don't know. I could feel it *pouring* from me. In the dream I watched it spread through the streets, and the Brauge just seemed to drop dead."

"Could you see Nyx?"

Lilith shook her head. "I heard people shouting her name. Mae woke me before I could see her. But there were others."

Peter looked at her, confused. "What do you mean others?"

"I saw Chasity—she was there. And, at one point, I heard Die's voice. I wasn't just dreaming. They were there. I think Maura can see it, too, sometimes."

Peter looked guilty at the mention of Chasity. Lilith knew he had seen her. Or the ghost of her at least. She'd come back to the house a few times, once to take her detector. Only Peter and Lilith's other invisible creations had been able to see her, but Chasity wouldn't disclose anything even to them. She'd come and gone, and they were none the wiser as to why.

Until now, perhaps.

"What do you mean?" he asked, wondering how Maura and Lilith could have possibly connected to them, wherever they were.

"Everything she talks about, it all ties back. I could see—with my own eyes—Horned Witches and a man with runes on his stomach. People with skin that flashed different colors."

"Where do you think it is?"

Lilith looked at the wall and sighed. "You know those stories Mom used to tell us when we were little? The ones about the Hallows and the Horned Witches and that secret council?"

Peter nodded, remembering how Marga would sit the girls down and tell them hundreds of bedtime stories about the Hallows.

Peter had always suspected that she'd learned the stories from Lilith's father—the other Lahey women discouraged the telling of fables and stories of magic, preferring their daughters to stick to the same strict study and training style that they had been brought up with, and not be distracted by the wonders of traditional stories and lore.

"I know it's kind of a stretch," Lilith continued, "but you remember that one about the mountain castle and the five cities?"

"Yeaaah?"

"I saw them. The castle on the mountain, and behind it, the five cities."

Peter looked uncertain. "Aw, Lil, I don't—"

"The cities were the exact same colors as in the story. And the Council run by a monster and a witch . . . I *saw* them in battle."

Peter looked unsure. Lilith shook her head. "I think they're there, with the Council."

Ander spent the entire night talking. Erebus suspected that the years of silence would make anyone want to talk until their throat gave out. He showed Ander everything there was to see around Monstrum. Ander cried nonstop, saying over and over again, "I can't believe you're actually here."

For years, Erebus had imagined such a moment. And thanks

to his dreams, they were able to speak like no time had passed. Erebus knew him.

"You know Mom knew Ira, right?" Ander said, unleashing a litany of questions.

"Do you have any idea where Keels and Sage are?

"What about Bellum?

"How'd you meet Nyx?

"So, where are Mom and Dad?"

"W-what?" Erebus stopped and faced his younger brother.

"Mom and Dad, are they here? Are they staying in Monstrum—"

Erebus shook his head and stared at his brother. He was unable to even fathom how to say it.

"Ander . . . they're . . ."

"What?" Fear fell across Ander's face.

"They're gone. Mom and Dad have been gone for a long time . . . as long as you."

Ander stepped back. The look on his face was something Erebus never wished to see again: fighting the urge to argue or cry, heartbreak and denial warring across his face, his mouth finally hanging slack and his eyes empty.

That can't be right. That can't be right. That can't be right, Erebus imagined Ander's mind reeling.

The whole of Ander Salem's body would be at war with what it had heard.

They were just here. We were just here, he'd be saying it. *Over and over*, Erebus thought.

"I'm sorry," Erebus whispered, unable to muster anything else.

"Yeah . . . um . . . you know—" Ander looked toward the pink horizon—dawn was beginning to break. "I . . . think I might head to my room," he whispered.

Erebus nodded solemnly. "Okay." He wrapped an arm around Ander's shoulder, and they walked back to the castle in silence.

The streets of the Duster, one of the Hallows' five inner cities, were filled with light, music, and parades—one of their annual celebrations. Dancing men wore wooden masks with ivory tusks protruding from snarling, carved faces. Olive-skinned women with braided hair and dressed in brilliant shades of pink, orange, and gold twirled knives. Elephant-like creatures, their heads painted with flowers and their alabaster hides adorned with bronze chains and jewels, paraded through the streets.

Men stood on stilts blowing fire, while women below them with bare torsos and covered faces juggled it. Huge spotted cats, their heads decorated with gemmed helmets, walked alongside them. Children dressed in red *pagris* played ney- and oud-like instruments while teens behind them banged on bright, orange drums, filling the air with beautiful music as the sun crested the horizon.

Nyx zoned in on the fire dancer—a woman dressed in red, spinning two large fans. Flames licked the ends of the fabric until soon she was entirely engulfed.

An Ignis.

"Oh my God," Nyx breathed, smiling as she peered through a set of binoculars Hatter had stolen for her from Mortem's study.

There was a knock at her bedroom door. "Come in!"

Erebus stood on the icy steps outside, holding a tray of food. "Hey, uh, thought I should bring this up. You need to eat something."

Nyx smiled at the way he balanced the tray in his arms as he shuffled inside, trying his hardest not to spill anything. "Want to watch the parade with me?" She patted the cushion next to her.

Erebus smiled. "What parade?"

"Every year the Dusters throw their Albidaya Festival. It means beginning, and they do it right before sunrise, to mark the coming of a new day and a new year. Today's the first day on their calendar."

He raised the binoculars to his eyes, and she watched his face transform with wonder: his dark brows raised and the corner of his mouth lifted ever so slightly as he regarded some marvelous thing in the street. There was more stubble along his jaw than she'd noticed before falling into her trance. A darker shade than his hair, it constantly pulled her attention to the dimples in his cheeks.

She rolled her eyes into herself. *Yuck, Nyx, get a grip.* She regarded the plate of grapes and toast, then cleared her throat. "So, Ander's upset?"

Erebus lowered the binoculars. "How'd you know?"

"There's like this line that tethers us. We're connected now. I can slightly feel him, and he me. It's the same feeling I got when I used to raise that butterfly. Once you raise it, it's a part of you."

Erebus looked out the window. "What was it like?"

"What's what like?"

"Raising."

"I just stood in this white space. Ander was at one end; I was at the other. We got closer as the days went by."

Erebus tried to imagine what it must have been like. During the days Nyx was still in the raise, he'd remained alongside Hans or Hatter as they watched over her. She had been magnificent— white haired and shimmering like star matter, her warm skin shining like pearls in the moonlight. Even with her weapon against his chest in Kyra, Erebus had been floored by her brilliance.

"Weird," was all he could muster, finding himself distracted by the dark freckles across her nose.

"Yeah." Nyx broke off another grape. "So, what's wrong with him?"

"Ander? I, uh, told him about our parents. He didn't know they were dead."

"Oh . . . *shit*. I'm sorry."

He tried to smile. "It's okay. *I* should have realized that beforehand. I could have broken it to him better. Not the best way to break your baby brother's heart."

Nyx touched his arm. "You didn't know."

"I *should* have known that he wouldn't—he's been gone for all this time. He's still just a kid, and he still needs his parents. He still expects them. He had no idea, and I just blurted it out like a fuckin—"

Nyx leaned forward on her knees, hands on Erebus's leg. "He's lucky to have you as a brother, Erebus. At *least* he has that. You don't know how much he missed you. How much he needed you. He is so lucky to have you. Don't forget that."

Erebus felt something inside of him melt. The tears that had been stinging his throat burned as Nyx kissed his cheek. She pulled back, putting the plate of food between them as the sun turned the sky a beautiful golden red.

People cheered in the street below.

"Happy New Year, Salem."

He smiled. "Happy New Year, Lahey."

CHAPTER FIFTY-FOUR

HYPNOPHOBIA — FEAR OF FALLING ASLEEP

While the rest of the castle slept, Ander was restless. He and Nyx were situated on opposite sides of the castle, separated by thousands of bricks, but the bond they shared meant that if he was awake, she felt it. If he was upset, she felt it. When he laughed, when he dreamed, when he smashed his knee on the *same* corner of the bed each night—she felt it.

Nyx stared at the ceiling of the lava room, sheets tangled at her feet. As warm as she was, the part connected to Ander felt deathly cold.

Bjørn's tail thumped against the floor in his sleep. Nyx hauled herself out of bed and ventured across the castle to Ander's room. She knocked on his door. It swung open a moment later, and she went inside and sat at the end of his bed.

"Why were you crying just now?" she asked as he shut the door.

The question seemed to take him by surprise. "How did you even—"

"I basically created you. We're connected. I know everything you're doing. When you sleep, when you swallow food, when you scratch your elbow. Everything."

Ander made a face. "Does that get annoying? Like, is it all faint or is it like, *bam*, in your face all the time kind of—"

"Ander."

He sighed and sat down. "When I was little, Sage and Erebus found a baby cat. Well, not *exactly* a cat. It was as close to a cat as you could get in the Nethers. They've got antennas and saber teeth, and . . . anyway, they found it in the gardens one summer. This thing was dehydrated, malnourished, almost dead. They brought it inside, and one of the cooks made it some food and helped cool it down. I named it Dente."

"Dente?"

Ander looked at her like she was stupid. "Because of the saber teeth . . . You know, *dente*?" He waved a hand. "It's not important. This cat became a family pet. Followed me everywhere, even slept in my bed at night.

"One night, I must have fallen asleep before I felt him settle. I woke up the next morning, and he wasn't there. My mother said that sometime that night he'd been walking the halls—probably headed to the kitchen—and one of the guard dogs had ripped him apart."

Nyx grimaced.

"But, like, you know that feeling you get when you're so used to someone being around, and then you can't grasp it when you learn they're never going to be there again? Like, you can't really believe it?"

Die. Chasity. Tellus.

"When I died," Ander continued, "my parents were still alive. At least, I think they were—it's a bit hazy. But I wake up, and I'm told they're not anymore. I was so used to seeing them every day—and now they're just gone." He wiped his face.

"Trust me," Nyx said, taking his hands, "I've felt like this plenty of times. And it's horrible for a long time. For forever.

But it will get better—it just *does*." She paused. "For now, you need to remember where we are. The people who killed you, your brothers, and your parents, are here. *Right here.* They're going to attack again, and we need everyone ready to take them down— that includes you."

Ander nodded, looking off into space.

"They loved you, Ander. So much. I don't know a lot about your family, but I know that much. They died protecting you."

He tried to smile. Nyx wrapped her arms around him. "I'm sorry. Just think, in a few weeks we'll be on our way to finding your brothers. But for now, try to get some sleep. You're exhausted."

"You *shithead*," Ridley snarled.

Damien laughed as he played the Pick Up Four card. Ridley glared at him and did as instructed.

Mason had brought a pack of Uno, which they played during lunch while cleaning up Kyra—while Damien was trying his best to woo a local blacksmith. The boys had taught Marvel, the pink-haired girl, how to play. She was easily annoyed by it, and often threw her cards down before walking away.

Most of the debris had been cleared, new cobblestones laid, and a few houses rebuilt. New streetlights had been fitted, making work easier. Every day, parties were sent out to scour the surrounding land for signs of Bellum.

"Uno," Damien said, holding his last card to his chest.

"Shit, do you have anything to get him?" Mason asked.

Marvel shook her head, staring at her last three cards.

The statue of Jack was still being repaired. On the opposite side of the street, Erebus and Nyx were laying the foundation for a new house. Above their heads floated small orbs of light. Marvel had called them the spirits of Martem, the goddess of the Hallows. She said they came as answers to its citizens' prayers, to light the city again after the damage it had sustained. Marvel had coaxed one into her palm to show Ridley. Plump, glowy faeries. She said they would be drawn to the Relics, which reminded them of the goddess.

And she'd been right. A group of them tailed Nyx and Erebus wherever they went. Even now they floated around their heads— one sleeping in the hood of Erebus's jacket while others chased each other around Nyx's hair.

Marvel took her turn, putting down a red six. Damien's eyes brightened. He leaned forward and slammed down a yellow six, raising hands in triumph. "I win!"

"I changed my mind, I take it back," Marvel said, trying to retrieve her card.

"Uh, no, girl. You can't do that," Damien said.

Marvel glared. "Why not?"

Ridley and Mason threw in their cards.

"Because it's against the rules. You can't just take it back," Damien answered.

Marvel threw her cards down in disgust. "This is a stupid game."

"How was he when you spoke to him?"

Nyx and Erebus walked through a section of forest next to Kyra. Martem spirits followed low to the ground, their light filtering between ferns, bushes, and moss-covered trunks.

"Really upset. And I suck at comforting people."

Erebus smiled. Ridley had cut his hair earlier in the night. The sharp lines of his jaw cast a shadow over his neck. "I'd say you did an all right job. He seems in a better mood," he said. "I think he'll be okay. He's got me, and we'll get Keels and Sage back. Plus, he's got you supporting him now too."

A group of sprites dove in and out of a small, glowing creek. "Has there been any progress finding the others?" Nyx asked.

Erebus's smile faltered—only for a second, but she saw it. The look on his face made her chest hurt.

"Not yet. Ira sends out more parties every day. She hopes that Bellum was at least injured in the battle—maybe softening his magic, which is what keeps them hidden." He looked away.

Nyx touched his arm. "We'll find them. It'll be all right."

"I know. It's not that," he said. "I've just been having nightmares lately."

"About what?"

"They start off with Keelie and Sage. Keelie's chained to a wall. Sage is under ice somewhere. I try and talk to Keelie, but before he can speak, he disappears. Sage is screaming, bashing on the ice. Sometimes, another person's there. He's got black hair and eyes like mine. He looks so familiar; I just can't put my finger on who he is."

Faeries, from branches above, sprinkled flower petals over them, giggling as they walked past.

"A lot of the time he's screaming too—the other person. He's punching the ice, trying to get Sage out. And then you're there." His voice cracked slightly. "You're bleeding, you're chained up ..."

The look on Erebus's face then was one she'd never seen before. Fear, but ... petrified. Powerless.

"I hear you screaming, and there's pain everywhere. . . . And then I die again."

CHAPTER FIFTY-FIVE

RUPOPHOBIA — FEAR OF GARBAGE

Every day, the Monstrum search parties came closer to finding Bellum's hideaway in the mountains. They had limited time to act—a few days left, at most, to somehow get through the castle's walls and take the Relics.

Nyx and the boy had the bond of Amare. Bellum knew that as Amare, the Relics would give up everything to protect each other. And that *one* of them was the key to bringing his father back.

"What if they find us before we get the chance to kill the second one? What if the first one doesn't work and we don't even get to kill the second one?" Bellum questioned his sister.

Ossa's face had healed as much as it could, though she was still very much deformed. "How would they just *find us*? They don't know where Father is sleeping."

"You're a fool if you think they don't at least have an idea. Even if they didn't, that horned cow could muster up a tracking spell faster than Nyx could stab you in the face."

Ossa hissed. "Just remember, you and that 'horned cow' are the reason we're in this mess." She sighed. "What do you propose we do?"

"We need to find a Seer to determine which of the two we need to wake Father."

"And what do we do with the other? Leave them at the castle?"

Bellum gave her an incredulous glare. "Of course not. We take both. Leverage, sister. Plus, the Relics have a connection. Leaving one behind would only aid the Council in locating us. Taking them together gives us more time."

"I see," Ossa mused. "And who do you think would help us?"

Petram appeared suddenly. "I know exactly who," she said.

The Pit.

The dark stain. One of the five inner cities. It was home to the Hallows' most reclusive creatures, and dotted with forgotten battlegrounds and mass cemeteries.

Dawn was just breaking over the horizon as Bellum, Ossa, and Petram took their first steps on the black ground. Long-dead trees stood mangled and charred, and grass the color and texture of soot crunched underfoot.

"How do you know where you're going?" Ossa yelled at Petram, who stormed ahead.

"This is not my first time in the Hallows, child."

"Yes, I am aware. But you are blind."

"Not all need eyes to see."

They trekked behind her until Petram led them to a dead redwood tree. A flock of black birds spiraled out from its hollow trunk, which reached into the sky. A thin golden outline was charred into bark—a door.

"Here." Petram stopped.

Ossa stiffened, sniffing the air. "Whose house is this, Petram?"

The door in the tree opened then, and Bellum's heart stopped. When he'd been younger and in love, he'd learned of

Horned Witch heritage—an ancient, powerful race that had all but disappeared over time. But apart from Ira, he hadn't seen another of her kind in at least a hundred years. Until now.

Her skin was the darkest shade of onyx. Eyes the color of champagne and hair like wool. She wore a patterned ankara dress, a choker of fire opal, and a blue beaded necklace that fell to her sternum. In the tight curls of her hair nestled baby's breath and red orchids. A pair of ram-like horns grew from her head, curling back and around her ears.

The witch smiled. "Young God Bellum."

"Adama," he said with a nod.

Bellum had met this witch before. She'd been close friends with Ira during their schooling. He was surprised to see her in a place like the Pit.

The woman grimaced at Ossa, as if she could feel the pain of her swollen face. "Ossa, Petram, sahlie," she said. "I suppose you require my help. The whole kingdom's talking about you, you know?" She stepped aside and gestured for them to enter. "Well, come in."

"Why would I do that?"

They sat at a rough wooden table in Adama's study. Vials, stones, and dried plants littered one side, books and a small golden telescope the other. A male apprentice bought them tea and set it on the table.

"Thank you, Jackery," Adama said as the boy left the room.

Ossa cast Bellum a sideways glance. "Because," she started, "we need to wake our father."

"Why?" Adama pressed.

"He needs to kill Grim, the Reaper."

"Again: Why?"

Ossa's eye twitched.

"Grim is his sworn enemy—*our* enemy. If we wake Neco first, he can put an end to Grim. It's our duty, as his children, to do this for him. And we're asking for you to please help us."

Adama leaned back in her chair. "Neco is not my father, nor is he my duty. I have zero interest in your messy family squabble. What's in it for me?"

"We won't kill you when Neco takes over th—" Bellum slammed a hand over his sister's mouth. Adama smirked.

"Join us," Bellum said. "We'll take over the Hallows and overthrow the Reapers who hunt us. No longer will our kind have to fear for their lives. We'll take the Nethers, the next world, and the one after that."

The witch leaned across the table. "Young God, I do not pick sides. I'm not involved in this war, and I plan to keep it that way. You seem to forget that I am very good friends with many members of the Council."

"If you're such good friends, why are you speaking with us? How do we know that you won't stab us in the back?" Ossa spat.

"I haven't alerted the Council now, have I, child? I am willing to help but don't forget that you are but visitors here. You are the most wanted people in all of the Nethers." Adama held up a hand. "Here is my offer: I will tell you what you wish to know. But, in return, I will do the same for your enemies. I keep my place in the middle."

"What information will you give them?" Ossa asked, suspicious.

"Information as valuable to you as to them. Equal information of equal importance to each party. There's not a lot in this kingdom that I don't know."

"You keep your place in the middle," Bellum mulled.

"I have no place in this war. I may have loyalty to Ira, but I mustn't forget that I also have it to you, too, Young God. Despite everything."

This witch's word was her bond. Bellum extended a hand, which Adama shook. "Deal," he said.

The witch released his hand. "Give me a piece of each Relic."

Petram and Ossa reached into their pockets. Petram pulled out the lock of Nyx's hair. Ossa produced a single strand of dark, auburn hair that she'd taken from Erebus. They placed each in one of Adama's palms. The witch closed her eyes and wrapped her fingers around them. Her champagne eyes snapped open again.

A face materialized before the trio.

"This is the Relic who will wake your father, Young God." She snapped her fingers and the image before them vanished. "Although I'm afraid there's quite a catch."

His face wrinkled in confusion. "What do you mean?"

"Well"—a cigar materialized between the witch's fingers—"I absolutely hate to be the bearer of bad news, almost as much as I hate clichés." She took a long drag from the already-lit cigar.

"Cut to it, witch," Ossa spat.

"It seems that this season's Amare are . . . different." Adama blew pink smoke from her nostrils.

"How so?" Bellum asked.

"If you accidentally kill the wrong one, you, in turn, will also die. As will you, Ox."

"It's Ossa," she spat.

Adama shrugged. "Whatever you say, Octopus."

"How?" Bellum demanded. "How can they possibly—"

"They're special, darling. They're the strongest pair of Amare this world has seen in a long while. Frankly, they're the only couple to make it to this world in the first place."

Bellum looked at his sister. "We'll have to be cautious in how we deal with the one we don't need."

"So, we can't just kill the other one after we wake Father?" Ossa inquired. Adama shook her head.

"We can use the other for leverage," Bellum said. "But we mustn't harm them, do you understand?"

Ossa nodded begrudgingly.

"Oh," Adama said, standing. "One more word of advice: make your move with haste. You've all overstayed your welcome in these lands. The Council is catching up. You have maybe two days before they discover your hideaway—"

"How do you know where our camp is?" Ossa asked.

"Ostrich, there is nothing that goes on in these lands that I don't know. And if you interrupt me once more, I shall have to skewer you to the floorboards like the Banshee did. So please, shush."

Bellum pondered the information for a moment. Then he stood and pushed his chair in. "We do it tonight. We take them both."

Cole rubbed his hands together, tiny bits of ice sticking to the ratty cotton of his gloves. They'd stopped at the edge of the Lorin Forest, in the middle of the Valleys of Smrik. The land around them was towering evergreen trees; twisting, frozen rivers; and snow-covered mountains.

Ira and Mortem believed that they could find and kill Bellum, and that once he was dead, the curses placed on Sage and Keelie Salem would finally lift.

And Cole *needed* to be there when they were found. He'd raced from the shadows and merged into the search party ranks' clothes and armor; he even had a rucksack over his shoulder. He'd blended in perfectly.

They'd trekked over half of the eastern Hallows. Cole had befriended a group of younger guards. Only two had figured out who he was: West, a burly redhead with a beard and bright blue tattoos, and Kanium, a tall, dark warrior from the northern dragon tribes. They'd stuck with Cole, walking at his side, always setting their tents near his.

"We'll make sure ya get there, lad," West said with an accent that could have passed for Scottish. They sat around a pathetic fire. The sun had begun to paint the sky a deep lilac—dawn was fast approaching.

"So," West said, shuffling closer. "The new Relics in town, isn't one of 'em Keelie's brother?"

"Yep," Cole said.

"Have you seen 'im yet? I mean, like, gone and spoke to him?"

Cole thought about Erebus. He'd spoken to Nyx since coming to the Hallows, but he hadn't gone anywhere near Erebus. At the frat party, it had taken all of him to not freeze at the sight of his uncle. He also worried about Erebus's resemblance to Keelie. Cole had visited Ira before—he'd rewatched Erebus's memories over and over, drinking in every detail of his parents, grandparents, uncles. Cole had memorized his mother's voice, her smile. He'd learned all of his father's tendencies. He worried that if he saw those same tendencies in Erebus, he would break.

"Uh, no. No, I haven't," Cole answered, staring into the fire.

"For real?" West asked.

"Why? Why don't you go up and say hey?" Kanium added.

Cole hesitated. "I'll meet him when we bring his brothers home."

CHAPTER FIFTY-SIX

THEOPHOBIA — FEAR OF GODS OR RELIGIONS

After the parade, Nyx fell asleep on the cushions next to Erebus—falling and falling into sleep until she landed into a dream with Bayou. He lounged in a plush, red chair across from her, a large albino python across his shoulders, trying to nuzzle under his collar.

"Nyx, darling, I did not expect to see you here," he said, gesturing for her to sit in a newly materialized chair in the otherwise pitch-black room.

"Where exactly *is* here?"

A cigar appeared between his fingers. "This is my dream space, dear. When I sleep, I sometimes choose to come here. Today, I came here to speak privately with a friend of mine. Like an astral meeting place. But it seems that for some reason you have arrived here too." He snapped his fingers to light the cigar.

"Oh, I'm sorry," she said, starting to rise. "I didn't mean to—"

Knocking echoed throughout the small space.

Bayou held up a hand, pink smoke billowing from his nostrils. "No, child. Please, sit. They can wait."

"Are you sure? I don't want to interrupt anything." Nyx sat back down. The snake watched her intently.

"Please, you are most welcome. Would you like one?" He held up a second cigar.

"Oh . . . um—"

"These won't harm you, child. They're magic. Made by the finest witches. Try one if you like."

The cigar floated from Bayou's fingers to hers. "Thank you." She brought it to her lips and it lit itself. She drew—it tasted like raspberries and cotton candy, cold and sharp like ice.

"So," Bayou puffed out a cloud, "we haven't had much time to talk since you and your hero arrived, have we?"

"No, I guess we haven't."

"Do you know who I am?"

Nyx grimaced, embarrassed to say that she didn't.

Bayou smiled and waved his hand. "No, that's fine, child. Not many people do."

"How'd you get on the Council?" she asked.

Bayou sighed. "Well, I started off in the early days in New Orleans. Like yourself, my kin and I were Necromancers. Only I was a bit more . . . interested in the craft, I guess you could say."

Nyx appeared confused; he continued: "My family did only what they needed. Released only what had to be released every month or so. We never raised more than we needed. We didn't need any more attention on ourselves, if you understand. My mother and aunts did their best to keep me in line, but I always wanted to push it further. See how far I could take things—how big I could go before I ran out of juice.

"I, unknowingly, was following much in the same footsteps as Neco. I wanted to perfect the raise. I wanted to see how much personality I could put back in. Long story short, I caught the Council's eyes when I had a partially reanimated Marie Laveau walking the streets in '83—two years after she'd passed. But unfortunately, I also caught the eye of the local Reapers . . ." Bayou trailed off, grimacing.

"Needless to say, they quickly dispatched me. Luckily, Mortem had been keeping watch and brought me here. He thought maybe I could help create more like himself, maybe even help him understand himself better." He took a draw from his cigar.

"And did you?" Nyx asked.

He smiled and shook his head. "I was never able to do what you have done, child. Never quite that powerful. The 'brides' are about the closest we ever got to reanimation."

Nyx recalled the strange, colorful women that she'd seen throughout the castle. The women who had tended to her after the Banshee was released. And the one named Kita, who had told her Chasity was dead. Like a cross between faeries and mermaids, or angels and dryads. Some appeared held together by pins and metal while others had been stitched with golden thread.

"For the most part, they have free will. But, as I'm sure you can see, they're not without their scars. They were 'gifts' to a wealthy prince and were on their journey to his kingdom across the oceans when their ship capsized. We found them washed ashore on Maliakas Beach, on the other side of Duster, and gave them a second chance."

Nyx prayed Ander would be happy for his second chance. Coming back into the world parentless and, for the most part, brotherless . . . she hoped he could still find happiness here.

Bayou leaned forward, giving her a strange look as if he knew what she was thinking. "My girl, don't ever think you did the wrong thing. You gave him a second chance—that's more than most people get. And because of you and Erebus, his brothers will have their chance too. I know it. You are stronger than most. You can do this, child."

"Thank you, Bayou."

Bayou leaned back, drawing on his cigar. "You will never let anyone put you in your place, Nyx Lahey. I like that. You've got the fire of your ancestors in your blood and the Banshee beneath your fingernails. Don't let anyone change that. Not even that boy falling in love with you, you hear me?"

Knock, knock.

There was a flitter in her chest. "I won't."

KNOCK, KNOCK, KNOCK.

"Bayou! I need to speak with you! Adama got in contact with me!"

It was Mortem.

"I'll be a second!" Bayou yelled.

Bayou crushed the last of his cigar on his pant leg. He gestured for Nyx to pass him her nub. "Well, for whatever reason you came tonight, Nyx Lahey, I am very glad you did." He stood and bowed.

"Thank you, Bayou."

"I will see you at sunset, child."

When Erebus slept, he saw his mother's face.

Her brows conveyed sadness or anger or shock—Erebus wasn't sure. For a long while, the picture didn't move. All Erebus could do was analyze the agonized look upon her face. Something was wrong. He could remember most of his past now, so it puzzled him: What could this dream possibly be trying to show him?

His mother's face began to change. Lightning cracked, and he was plunged into darkness.

Then they were running. *Sprinting*. Flying as if Death itself was on their heels.

Rain outside thundered. Erebus's throat was raw, eyes stinging. *They're going to come. For you. For everyone.*

The castle halls were pitch black, only the lightning illuminating their path. But both Erebus and his mother knew this castle like the backs of their hands. They needed nothing to guide them.

He'd done this before.

They smashed open a wooden door as they ran. Ander and Sage were on the other side, drenched, their silver armor splattered with blood. Ander was cleaning a cut on Sage's neck when their mother and brother burst into the room.

Their faces paled. "They made it past the gates?" Sage asked.

Erebus caught sight of himself in the mirror there. He, too, was covered in a chunky mixture of red and black bits of flesh. As was their mother. He wore a beaten steel chest plate and leather on his forearms and thighs. His hair was longer, down to his ears, like it had been when he'd first met Nyx.

His mother yelled over the wail of the storm. "Where is Keelie? Where's Cole? We need to leave!"

The door swung open, revealing Kaya, Keelie's wife. Hair plastered to her forehead, blood ringing the hem of her blue dress. Underneath her shawl, baby Cole screamed. Kaya leaned against the door frame, trying to catch her breath.

"Where's Keelie?!" Ander yelled.

Keelie flew around the corner. His abdomen was still bandaged. Blood seeped through the white. He'd returned to them only days earlier from the front line, fighting the exact army overwhelming them now. He leaned against the door, weak.

"We . . . we need . . . to leave." In his hands, Keelie held two scythes, like axes. He tossed one to Erebus.

"Your father will be with us soon," their mother said. "Come on."

The twins gathered their weapons and followed them out of the room. Keelie took Cole from his wife's arms and she followed too.

Erebus went to do the same, but Keelie caught him by the shirt. "I need you to do something," Keelie said. His mouth twitched as if he was trying not to cry. "I need you to hide him." He placed the bundle of blankets in Erebus's arms.

"Keel—"

"I need you to hide him. My son will live, Erebus. If I take him, I won't be able to bring myself to leave. I'll lead them straight to him. I need you to hide him. Please, Erebus."

Erebus nodded, crying.

Keelie pulled his younger brother into his chest. "I love you so much."

Erebus hated it. Hated everything about this. The way Keelie spoke—as if already defeated. "Don't talk to me like that," he said.

"*So much,*" Keelie said one last time before letting go.

Erebus turned and ran up the staircases with a screaming Cole pressed to his chest and his scythe in his free hand. High up in one of the spires, he ran through room after room until he found a cluttered storeroom that would suit. He stared at Cole, his scythe slipping through his fingers. Erebus cradled his nephew in his arms, rocking until Cole stopped crying.

"I love you *so* much," Erebus blubbered as Cole stirred in his sleep. Behind a mountain of dusty furniture and paintings was an empty fireplace. Erebus gathered dust sheets and folded them into a cradle in the soot, then lowered the baby into it.

Erebus touched his face one last time. "*So much*, Cole."

Erebus left Cole there and ran back downstairs, passing narrow spire windows red with fire. He paused and looked out and saw only chaos as far as the eye could see. The armies had made it. Bellum, Ossa, Cutem. They'd arrived.

Erebus swung his scythe ahead of him as if cutting down a tree. His face was suddenly covered in something warm, as were his hands and neck. It seeped into his clothes, not having a chance to dry before more was added. Blood covered the stone floors. They sloshed in it as they fought.

Brauge and other creations surged through the castle. Erebus swung at them so hard he thought his arms would tear from his body. The creatures continued to fling themselves through the glass. One latched onto Erebus's neck, its fangs sinking deep into his skin, scraping against his collarbone.

Erebus screamed and Sage, appearing just in time, slashed the creature with his sword. Glass smashed on the other side of the room. Another creature, tiny and agile, raked the queen's body all the way to her face before she could defend herself.

King Rego snatched one away and crushed its body in his fist. More poured through the windows.

"Sage!" Erebus yelled, his throat burning. There was blood in his eyes. The room was filled with the screeches and wails of the undead.

Sage lay on the floor, an arrow sticking out of his stomach. Creatures leaned over him, clawing and stomping on his body. Ander and Erebus made it to him, cutting down anything that got in their way.

"Where did that arrow come from!" Ander screamed over the hell. Erebus crashed to his knees and tried to grasp the protruding arrow, the blood of his brother bubbling over his hand.

Ander held Sage's face. "Th . . . there . . ." Sage tried to speak, blood pooling in his mouth. He raised a finger to the window. Cutem. Pale blond hair, silver eyes, crossbow in hand.

She grinned. Blood in her teeth.

Pain exploded in Erebus's rib cage. He swung around and was suddenly facing Ossa the Great, his mother's crown crooked atop her head. She twisted a dagger in Erebus's side. He tried to strike but she vanished before he could make contact.

She reappeared behind the queen. And Cutem, midstrike, in front of Kaya.

Cutem's blade came down between Kaya's eyes. Kaya's scythe fell, and her body followed.

Keelie screamed and threw his scythe like a javelin, striking Cutem and driving her back into the brick. The center blade of Keelie's scythe pierced her stomach, pinning her to the wall.

Ossa paused.

Rego turned to the wall and, in one fluid motion, severed Cutem's head with his blade.

Ossa screamed. She found Rego's eyes as she plunged her dagger into the queen's stomach and dragged the blade upward.

"*NO!*"

Keelie and Rego lunged for Ossa. Sage and Ander slashed through the crowd, wilder than ever, to get to her. Sage was unstable, blood flowing freely behind him.

Keelie wrestled Ossa to the ground. Rego came up behind them both, raising his weapon as Keelie moved aside, giving the king a clear shot.

Then: lightning flashed and she was gone. And Bellum the Young God appeared behind Rego, elbow deep in the king's chest. The king's face twisted in pain. He fell forward onto his knees as Bellum pulled his heart out of the hole in his back.

Erebus had never known such horror, rage so white hot that he couldn't feel anything else.

Keelie lunged forward, grabbing his father's weapon. He scrambled toward Bellum but it was too late—the heart of the king fell to the ground, and Bellum was gone.

Sage dropped, losing more blood by the second. Erebus ran to him.

Ossa appeared, latched to Keelie's back, and smashed a brick against his head. Keelie crumpled and Ossa vanished as quickly as she'd appeared, then reappeared by the window.

Then: a knife soared across the room. Ander fell a moment later, the blade—Ossa's blade—lodged in his throat.

And Erebus was suddenly alone, standing before Bellum the Young God.

Bellum smiled.

And Erebus felt something smash into the back of his head.

Erebus woke to find Nyx staring at him. The pillows beneath his cheek were wet. He'd been crying.

"What happened?" she whispered, so quietly that Erebus almost didn't hear it.

"I know how we all died."

"Oh my God." Nyx pulled him into her. Something consumed her as she held him. She felt warm and light, like she'd been covered in pixie dust. He told her everything. She didn't say anything, only listened. Which meant more to him than any condolences she might've offered. He cried, and she cried with him.

"Thank you for bringing him back," Erebus said at the end. He didn't need to specify who. Erebus had seen the ground-shattering power of Mason, a mere Necromancer. Nyx was more than that.

The trees sang to her. Their leaves brightened and their flowers bloomed to please her. The creatures of this world drifted toward her without even realizing it. She was a beacon of life. Creatrix. She had brought his brother back to him.

"Don't thank me."

"I'm sorry if I woke you," he said, pushing a strand of hair out of her eyes.

Nyx wiped the last of his tears from his cheek, as she did with her own. "Don't be, I was already awake."

Erebus poured over her face. He pulled back. "Are *you* okay?"

Nyx smiled. "Yeah, I was talking to Bayou. Some kind of weird dream-meeting."

"About what?"

Nyx shrugged. "I don't really know. I think it was by accident. He told me how he came to the Hallows. Mortem thought he could be like Neco . . . and me."

"How?"

She told him about New Orleans, and the sisters he'd found drowned on the beaches, and how they had become his "brides."

Erebus rolled onto his back beside her. "Well, shit," he said, impressed by Bayou's story. Someone with power so close to Nyx's but not quite the same.

"You know," Nyx said, and he looked at her again. "I wonder

about the Banshee before me. Before Die. They say Ander was the Wraith, but who was the Banshee all those years ago?"

He smiled at her. Erebus couldn't imagine anyone else holding that kind of power. Surely no one had ever wielded the same magic that pulsed through Nyx. But still, he, too, wondered. Had they had the same fire? The same quick wit and the courage? Had they even come from her family?

"I doubt they would have been as delightful as you," Erebus joked. Nyx rolled her eyes. But it was true—they both knew that the ones who had come before had mostly been of the Odi pairing. Something hateful and horrid.

Not like this.

Nyx was saying something but he was busy watching her big sunset-like eyes. He wondered if other Banshees had had those signature orange eyes too. Or her lazy curls and tattoos and plump lips with freckles on them.

Nyx's cheeks reddened. "What?"

Erebus dragged his bright eyes back to hers. "What?" he asked in return, rolling closer to her. He smiled like he hadn't been caught.

"What are you looking at?" One black eyebrow raised.

For no reason at all, he reached out and traced the arch of it to her temple and then along her cheek. "Nothing," he lied, very quietly.

Nyx's skin was hot. She didn't move under his featherlight touch. He trailed his fingers from her cheek down to the corner of her jaw.

Her pulse was making her whole body shake. She said nothing as his fingers moved wisps of hair back behind her ear before cupping the nape of her neck. His skin was dull against her warmth.

Erebus found her eyes again and moved his face closer to hers. She could feel his heat radiating. *That boy falling in love with you*, Bayou had said.

Nyx's voice was a whisper: "That doesn't look like nothing."

He gave her a wicked smile, only for a second, before clutching the side of her face and bringing his lips to hers.

And as he lost himself in the warmth and wonder of Nyx Lahey, he realized: this definitely wasn't nothing.

CHAPTER FIFTY-SEVEN
CARDIOPHOBIA — FEAR OF HEART ATTACKS

Cole Salem dreamed of his father every night. He was distracted as the group of soldiers waded through the never-ending snow in search of a break in Bellum's curse—he was so excited he couldn't breathe. Excited that, perhaps, by this time next week, he might be returning with a father and an uncle by his side.

But above all was fear. Fear that they were *gone*. Never to be found. He couldn't bear the thought of it.

He lingered behind the group, a path of boot-stamped snow leading up the mountain before him. His throat hurt, and he wanted to cry. They were so close.

He closed his eyes, willing both the Banshee and the Wraith, a kingdom away.

Please hurry.

Beneath a castle carved into a great mountain, a phantom flashed in and out of the shadows. Gold dripped from her, becoming tangled in her silver locks, turning her knuckles into weapons, and wrapping around her slender throat like a python. She moved with grace, her heart in pieces within her chest. Were this phantom feeling poetic, she might have cried as she traveled the maze of tunnels underneath Monstrum for the last time.

For the husband she lost. Her will to love. To forgive.

Her very heart.

She might cry because, after so long, it was all finally coming to an end.

There would be no one left to hate. No more need to pretend. Ossa would be at peace. Her life back. Her brother and her father. Hundreds of years had guided her to this moment. She stepped through another wall, another locked door, like she was a wisp of cold air.

Revenge was like breathing, Ossa believed. Necessary. People had full control over whether or not they wanted to keep breathing. They could stop, hold their breath, if they wanted to. Revenge was like that too. Always there, whether or not you decided to act on it.

Ossa wouldn't leave it be.

Mortem hadn't slept for days. He paced the halls of Monstrum, imagining where Ossa and Bellum could be.

Trying to piece together how he'd missed it. How he'd let the enemy into their home—for years.

Aliana hadn't been seen since Bellum broke through the door. And Ossa's body had never been found. But Mortem knew that Ossa's powers were strong enough to raise herself from the brink of death if needed. He knew, also, that it would have been nothing for her to craft a body and a story for all these years. He felt so foolish. Bellum had always been one step in front of them. It all made sense now.

Mortem tied his hair back. Before him, the globe spun in the center of the room. Mist rolled off its sides. Within the sphere, the image of Cole Salem appeared, cheeks red from the cold wind of the northern kingdoms.

Adama, one of the Horned Witches of the Hallows, had contacted him to say that she had made a deal with Bellum, and that she would uphold her promise to remain impartial in this war by sharing information with the Council—information regarding the Salem princes. She knew their locations, but in order to actually free the princes, Bellum's curse still needed to be broken. He needed to be killed.

Nevertheless, Mortem had sent word to his generals, telling them to change their routes and prepare. He didn't want to get Cole's hopes up, but Mortem was leading the boy right to his father and uncle's location in hopes that Bellum would soon be dead.

Mortem admired how far Cole was willing to go for a family he had never even known. He sighed, unsure how long he could keep going with no sleep before he began to hallucina—

He froze.

A flash of red swooped down behind the globe. Mortem immediately wished away Cole's image, dropping the room into darkness.

"Who's there?" There was no reply—only the sound of dripping water. "Who is there?" he repeated, sternly.

Aliana appeared from around the other side of the globe, a red robe strung around her shoulders.

"Aliana," Mortem said. Her face was scarred. Faint and well healed, but the wounds were still visible. "Where have you been?"

"I got spooked when the Young God attacked. I went to check on my family. To see that they were okay."

Mortem felt sick. But he would play this game. "And you didn't think to . . . to tell me?"

"I'm sorry, my dear, I was in a rush. You were busy, and I had no way of getting in contact with you—"

"*Busy*? I was defending our home! And you decide, amid all of that, to go on a trip?"

Aliana's mouth was agape. "My dear, Mortem, I—"

"What happened to your face?"

Her visage flickered. "Horse carriage. I was behind it as it took off. Some rocks came back and hit me. My own fault."

"We've been worried—"

"We?"

"Ira, myself, the rest of the Council. The *family* you have been living with."

Aliana scoffed. "Ira? Really?"

"Yes, Ira."

"I highly doubt Ira would be too upset were I to disappear."

"What are you talking about?"

"Oh please!" she screamed. "I know about her! I know about you!" Her eyes filled with tears.

Mortem stepped back. "You . . ."

"Yes, I bloody know," Aliana spat, wiping her eyes. "I knew from the moment my brother walked her into our home. I knew when I lost our baby that you loved her!"

Mortem fell silent.

"Go on then, say something!" Aliana screamed.

The words coiled in Mortem's throat. "Your brother," he said, his own words seeming to cut him like a blade.

Aliana looked confused. "What?"

"You said 'my brother,'" he repeated. "You don't have a brother." He took another step back.

Aliana's guise fell away like dust, revealing a woven dress, high around her neck, and skin that matched her husband's. Hair like liquid silver, eyes necromantic.

And Ossa the Great revealed herself at last.

"How *could* you?" he said.

Ossa glared at him. "How could *you*? You were the only one I loved, Mortem. Out of everyone!"

"I'm sorry, I—"

Ossa laughed and shook her head. "It's a bit late for apologies, husband."

"Then why are you here?"

"I'm here to repay you." And suddenly, she was in front of him. A piercing pain shot through Mortem's stomach. He looked down.

A dagger, hilt deep, through his navel.

"For breaking the last piece of heart that I had left." She vanished, and Mortem crashed to the floor.

Miles away, a Young God stared out over a mountainous landscape. The sun was setting once more. Bellum could feel the thrum of his sister's heart as she worked her way, silently, through Monstrum. Of all the times Bellum had thought *This is it*, he was finally sure that this time he would succeed.

"What are you waiting for?" Petram sneered. The witch's blind eyes stared blankly ahead. "Are we leaving or what?"

"I wanted to make sure my sister got in safely."

Petram scoffed. "Since when have you cared about your sister's safety?"

He almost laughed. "You're right. If she doesn't get in, then it's up to me to make our father proud."

The witch held out a pale hand and her golden eyes brightened—like fireflies. Soon, both were enveloped in warmth. Bellum closed his eyes, feeling wind slashing at them from all angles, ripping through the fabric of their clothes as they traveled.

When all stilled again, he opened his eyes. "Perhaps you could just transport us into Mortem's bedroom so I could slay him in his sleep, yeah?"

They were in a rocky cavern. Enormous stalactites and stalagmites ruptured from above and below. All around, lilac crystals grew from the walls.

Bellum blew hard air from his lips. "I haven't been here in years."

Petram pulled her shawl tight around her shoulders. "Nor I."

Before them stretched a great room. The floor beneath was etched with thousands of interlocking patterns. In the ceiling, a single hole in the rock allowed for a thin beam of light to fall in the center of the room.

And there, a sarcophagus.

Bellum could feel his father's resting heartbeat echoing through the stone at his feet—as if the entire cavern were a part of Neco. He stepped closer. The heartbeat quickened.

Neco knew.

Bellum grinned. "Time to wake up, Father."

—

Ira was having trouble clawing her way out of sleep.

She'd dreamed of the Horned Academy—the school where she was trained while only a calf. Frail and pale, with stark black hair and short, stumpy horns.

In the dream, other young witches wrapped ribbons around their horns and tied flowers in their hair as they prepared for the Martem Festival. Her mother had been on the opposite side of the room, putting tiny Adama's hair into tight braids.

Ira felt a pain in her head, dull and pulsing. She passed it off as a flower thorn pressing into her hair. But it got stronger, hotter.

Something was wrong, and Ira needed to wake up. But it was hard. She tried to roll, lift her arms, open her eyes, move her head. The pain began to sear and burn. She writhed, trying to claw herself from sleep until, finally, she woke.

The first thing she noticed was the violet light of the evening filling her bedroom. The next was that her hands were bound to the headboard. She found her reflection in the mirror on the opposite side of the room. Her hair was gone, strewn all over the sheets and the floor beside her. Knicks and cuts on her head sent thin rivers of blood down her neck.

Her horns were gone. Severed and pierced through the mattress before her in a mighty cross.

Sickness swelled within her. From pain, fatigue. From fear— the gut-wrenching fear she felt as she realized: someone was inside the castle.

Nyx woke with a start, the feeling of a bad dream dissolving in her stomach.

The entire room was filled with an eerie, dull light. Erebus's spot on the bed was empty but still warm. Nyx rolled out of bed then tiptoed silently to the en suite at the opposite end of the room. She watched the stained-glass lanterns slowly spin as faint whispers of wind danced through the room. The bathroom was empty.

She went to the windows, but as she touched the thick velvet drapes, she heard a thump from the other side of the brick wall. Nyx peered out the window and, seeing nothing, made her way to the balcony door. Another thump sounded through the brick. Outside, ice and snow pelted past like bullets.

She pushed open the doors, fighting against the wind. The lanterns behind her danced.

Outside, everything was white. Until it wasn't. Red flickered in Nyx's periphery—a cape, billowing.

And there he was. Erebus, still shirtless. Hands bound; mouth gagged. He was standing there, barefoot and freezing, eyes wide and alert.

"Ah, Nyx, darling."

Aliana, as fierce and beautiful as always. Until she wasn't. Her robe coiled in the wind, and the woman changed: rose to gray, brown to orange. Another woman stood in her place, a hand on Erebus's shoulder.

"We're so glad you could make it," Ossa the Great said as she kissed Erebus on the neck.

Nyx tried to speak, bare feet stinging in the cold.

Ossa sneered, embracing Erebus from behind, pressing an already-bloody dagger to his neck. "I'm afraid Erebus can't talk right now, love. He's got somewhere to be."

And in a heartbeat, Erebus disappeared from Ossa's grasp. Like a light being switched off, he was gone.

Nyx's lungs burned like hellfire.

"*What did you do with him? Where did you take him?*" [screamed over the wind, her soul surging as the Banshee stirred

"Don't worry, little Banshee. He won't be alone." Ossa approached and, dagger to Nyx's face, whispered, "We're going too."

CHAPTER FIFTY-EIGHT

TYRANNOPHOBIA – FEAR OF TYRANTS

Nyx woke up.

She couldn't see. Couldn't move. She could feel that her feet were bound, as were her hands. She was gagged, her eyes covered, and she was lying on a cold, hard floor. The only noise she could hear was the sound of her own ragged breathing. She had never been so scared. Or so angry.

Something touched her hand, and she let loose a muffled scream and tried to roll away. Someone caught her fingers and held them tightly.

Erebus squeezed her hand.

"Ah, isn't that just lovely?" boomed a voice from above. Both Relics startled at the sound. Erebus held on to her like iron.

"Don't you think it's adorable, sister? Two Amare together like that?"

Ossa scoffed. "I think it's pathetic."

"Aw, don't be sour. You've no right to be a stick in the mud just because the Banshee ruined your face." The man laughed.

Bellum.

"Whatever," Ossa said, sounding less than impressed. "Just get on with it."

Nyx screamed as she was hoisted from the ground, hands snatched from Erebus. Bellum stood her up, gripping her hands tight behind her back with one hand and a fistful of her hair in the other.

"Get him up," Bellum grumbled. There were muffled protests as Erebus was wrestled up from the ground.

"Now, I'm sure Mortem explained to you the importance of the Relics and the power of the Amare pairing, yes?" Bellum asked.

Silence.

"Well, if not, today is your lucky day—we'll be having a live demonstration. Just for you two!"

The cloth over Nyx's eyes was pulled down. They were in a cavern. All around them, embedded in the rough rock walls, were gleaming, glowing crystals. She glanced down and saw, beneath their feet, deep, interlocking carvings on the rock floor.

Ossa held a blade of Reaper Iron to Erebus's throat and yanked the blindfold from his face. His eyes settled on something in the center of the room. Nyx followed his gaze, her heart almost bursting with fear.

One of the witches was there, the sister of the one Nyx had killed. She stood next to a large, stone sarcophagus etched with the same patterns as those on the ground. It glowed green. The witch whispered to it, as if in conversation.

"Welcome to your one true purpose, Relics," Bellum said.

Erebus found Nyx's eyes. She was shaking, as was he. His chest heaved with pain at the sight of her so afraid.

Nyx held his gaze. He shook his head. *Don't listen to him. Please don't listen.*

"Oh, what's that?" Bellum piped up. "You want to have a closer look?" Erebus shook his head. "Okay then!" Bellum shoved Nyx forward. She fell but he continued on, dragging her behind him by her hair. She screamed, unable to walk or stand.

"I can't drag you," Ossa said to Erebus, "so just walk." The ropes around his ankles disappeared as Ossa shoved him forward. Erebus lurched forward, trying to spit the gag from his mouth, arms straining against his bonds.

"Don't be a fucking hero." Ossa sneered. She caught him by the arms and yanked him back.

Erebus couldn't believe this was happening. He was going to lose Nyx, and no one was coming. He knew this was going to happen—he was the Wraith and he knew when someone was about to die.

And he hated it.

Bellum shoved Nyx to her knees before the sarcophagus. "How's it feel to meet your maker, Banshee? Look at it."

Nyx shook her head, tears dripping from the tip of her nose.

"*Look* at it!" he roared, lifting her face with a clawed hand. He squeezed her cheeks, leaning over her shoulder.

Nyx stared at it. Then she reared her head back and smashed it into Bellum's nose. He fell backward, and both Ossa and Erebus jumped. Bellum yelped in pain, holding his face.

"*Goddamit*," he cursed, spitting blood from his mouth. He got to his feet again and struck Nyx across the face.

Erebus thrashed against Ossa as Nyx fell to the floor.

"Enough, brother," Ossa yelled. "Get on with it already."

Bellum rose, wiping his face. "Amare blood is the key to waking an Original. Now, normally"—Bellum raised Nyx by her hair until she was back on her feet—"it'd be no problem to just kill *both* Relics. Only one of you is the key, after all. But it seems, dearies, that killing the wrong one of you could be quite detrimental for my sister and me."

Bellum retrieved a knife from the folds of his jacket. Erebus yelled through the gag, but Bellum merely smiled before bringing the blade to Nyx's throat and tilting her head back.

Erebus thrashed again, stuck in Ossa's impossibly strong grip. Nyx stiffened against the touch of metal. Erebus kicked backward and connected with Ossa's knee. There was a loud crunch and Ossa screamed in pain. She fell as Petram turned, palm raised to him. Erebus brought his boot to her chest, slamming her into the coffin before she could cast anything against him.

Ossa groaned. Erebus faced Bellum, ready to strike, but she quickly raised a hand and he froze in place. Ossa picked Erebus up like a doll and dropped him to his knees at her feet, replacing the bonds around his ankles.

"Next time," Ossa said, hissing in Erebus's ear as she brought her knife back around, "I'll cut your leg off." She shoved him to the ground.

Bellum cleared his throat. "*Anyway*, as we only need one of you, the other will get to live tonight. You'll be taken with us and used as leverage against the Council. Once my father is awake, we'll need to keep them at bay."

Nyx made angry, muffled noises.

"Oh, I'm sorry"—Bellum pulled the gag from her lips—"what was that?"

Nyx spat cotton fibers from her mouth, glaring at Bellum. "What makes you so sure the Council will even care? Why would they risk not stopping you and Neco for one of us?"

"Oh, trust me, dear, you're far more important to them than you give yourself credit for. It's not just because of your Relic title. I think they might actually *like* you." Bellum snorted.

"And why would you tell us your plan? That's just stupid."

It was Ossa's turn to laugh. "Because, darling, no one's going to find you here."

Little did they know, half a kingdom away, a young Salem boy woke to the screams of a Horned Witch. Ander rose from his bed at the last sliver of sun. He stood and—

He dropped his arms and stared at himself in the mirror. He placed a finger on his throat, swearing he could feel the cold touch of . . . of . . .

He felt his hands then. His feet. An invisible weight upon them, as if they were bound.

"*The Relics!*" someone screamed—it was Ira, howling from down the hall. "*They've taken them!*"

Nyx felt something stirring. Somewhere, miles away. She felt it touch her throat, beneath the dagger's blade. Her cheeks. Her bound hands.

Her heart quickened. As Bellum and Ossa bickered, she reached with bound hands and pinched the skin of her wrist.

One. Two. Three.

She let out a yelp when something pinched back.

One. Two. Three.

"So, how does it feel, Prince Salem, to have my dagger pressed to your throat once more?" Ossa ran her free hand through Erebus's hair. He ignored her. "Come on, love." Ossa pulled the gag around his neck. "Speak up."

"I've nothing to say." Erebus's voice was like thunder.

"Aw, no, really?" Ossa looked to Bellum. "No famous last words?"

Erebus had stopped crying. Nyx hadn't, though. It hurt more than anything to see him so lifeless. Erebus's eyes flickered down to her for just a moment. A second. No more.

"What about you, Banshee?" Bellum snickered, poking her head. It was a game to them. "Anything to say?"

Nyx willed Erebus to look at her. She had so much she wanted to say.

I wanted to help you find your brothers.

I wanted to be there when you took Ander home.

I wanted to meet Max.

I wanted to meet the boy Damien likes in the village.

Erebus wouldn't look at her —she wanted to die. He winced. Everything was being taken from him, *again*. He had to resist the urge to laugh at the universe for ripping his life out from underneath him once more. Damn the gods that ruled this world. Damn their vendetta against Erebus Salem.

Bellum tightened his grip on Nyx's hair, pressing the blade flatly against her throat—drawing the tiniest sliver of blood. She winced.

Erebus wanted Bellum to burn. The very hands that held Nyx in place—Erebus wanted them to melt, fizz, and peel. He wanted to turn Ossa into a pile of ash. He wanted to wrap around Nyx like fire and protect her from everything. But he couldn't. All he could do was watch Bellum draw blood from the woman he loved. And it—

Erebus paused, eyeing the blade. Bellum was drawing blood.

Bellum was drawing blood from Nyx. Yet nothing was happening to Erebus. He was merely being held in place. But Nyx. Nyx was the one being beaten and carelessly punished.

. . . killing the wrong one of you could be quite detrimental for my sister and me.

Nyx was going to die today. Nyx was the stronger of the two of them. It was obvious. She'd been able to bring a whole person back to life while Erebus felt like he was still only just coming into his power.

Nyx was the key.

"So, you know which of us it is then?" Erebus said.

Bellum nodded. "Sure do, lad. It was obvious, but we got a little tip-off just to be sure."

Erebus nodded and closed his eyes, shuffling forward. Nyx stared at the blade Ossa held to his throat, so very close to piercing the skin. One tiny move from her hand and there would be blood.

He opened his eyes again and sighed. "I'm sorry, Nyx. I—I'm going to fix this," he said, tearfully, finally looking at her.

Bellum laughed. "Ha! I'm afraid it's a bit too late to fix this now!"

"Erebus—"

Erebus smiled. "I love you," he said. And then he lurched forward and buried Ossa's dagger deep into his neck.

Everything stopped.

Ossa jumped away, blood covering her hand before she could snatch it away. Shocked, she threw her hands in the air like she was lost.

No. Nyx's voice boomed in her head, but she couldn't bring herself to speak the words.

Bellum *bellowed* in horror.

No no no.

Erebus's eyes stayed locked on Nyx as he slowly fell to his knees, his shirt growing dark with blood.

No no no no no no no.

Nyx couldn't breathe. Everything stopped. There was no noise. No sound of blood dripping. No breeze blowing through her clothes. Just stillness and silence in this void that Erebus Salem had created the moment he decided to die a second death.

And Nyx decided—with a single inhale, a single heartbeat, in a single, tiny moment—that there was nothing for her now. One last tear slipped from her eye as the Wraith's body hit the floor and Erebus Salem, son of King Rego and a prince of the northern kingdoms, turned to dust.

Nyx screamed. Only it wasn't Nyx. In her place, a glimmering, pearly goddess. White hair, glowing skin. Marks of the dead on her face and eyes like rubies. Magnolias in her hair.

The Banshee wailed the pewter thrum of a hurricane, turning all life before her to nothing.

In an instant, Bellum the Young God fell to his knees.

As did the witch.

As did Ossa the Great.

Her scream wrapped around the cavern like a hurricane, ripping everything within it to shreds. Ears covered, eyes squeezed shut as skin peeled from muscle, muscle from bones. Joints broke, cartilage shattered, blood boiled, and organs turned to tar.

They tried to scream through the anguish of it all as their bodies frayed like discarded denim. But no sounds filled the air—only tattered, pained souls as they were torn from their bodies and shattered, thrown into the ether.

And then there was nothing—only a hollow Banshee and a slumbering god.

A kingdom away, Cole looked out over a frozen lake with a bundle of firewood in his hands. He scanned the lake in passing and turned away, seeming to not even recognize it.

But he stopped. Looked again. And when he turned back, he saw it—a shadow under the ice.

He had never run so fast in his life. Never been so fearless of freezing water—of drowning—than in that moment. He landed on his knees and slid across the ice. The shouts of his friends were almost inaudible over the roaring wind.

"No, no, no, no, I know I saw you, come on," he said, swiping at the snow on the surface.

He raised his pickaxe and started to smash through the ice. And finally, after centuries, a young prince lost and trapped beneath the ice was awake and beating against the surface, trying to escape.

And finally, after centuries trapped in the mountains above, another prince fell to his knees in an empty cell.

Keelie Salem laughed as he rolled onto his back, crying at the ceiling.

He was free.

EPILOGUE

A girl sat alone in a cemetery. She was a beautiful girl. Skin like earth, eyes like fire, hair like the night, and with freckles that decorated her like stars.

She knelt in a white dress as she had done for the last twenty days, twenty-three hours, and fifty-eight minutes. She had no company but the wind and grass, and the occasional butterfly that would land on her shoulder. Before her stood eight giant stone statues.

One for a king.

One for a queen.

One for a princess and another for her son.

And the rest, four brothers—princes once lost to the world. Three of them had already been united. As had a son and a father.

Only one was missing.

An additional three hours and fifty-nine minutes before the Banshee set to work, Nyx Lahey had been found by the Hallowed Council, sitting alone in a bloody cavern. They had been led there by a boy—a prince named Ander. Ira, bleeding and almost unfamiliar, had fallen to her knees and held Nyx to her chest, sobbing—followed by the two other Lahey girls. And Mortem was there, pale, bleeding through bandages on his side.

Hatter, top hat in hand, had knelt down and gathered the golden dust of his friend.

Ridley had screamed and cried and slumped to the floor. A Viking had fallen mute, inconsolable as he knelt alongside the madman in the top hat and tried to help save the last few remnants of golden dust. The Tate boy stood on his own, face turned, sobbing harder than he had in hundreds of years.

While the Council cried their tears, somewhere in a forest, unbeknownst to them, another great king was rising from his slumber, climbing from a sarcophagus etched with scythes.

Meanwhile, Nyx sat in stunned silence until a man named Bayou scooped her into his arms and carried her back to a great castle carved into the side of a mountain.

That was where she had decided what she was going to do.

She had washed herself of blood and marched into a cemetery to try and create life from a pile of ashes and golden dust. She had to bring it all back. She had to weave muscle, skin, and soul back into a shell.

No one knew if it would work. No one *believed* it would. But Nyx Lahey was an incredible girl who could do incredible things.

And so, as her time before the eight ancient statues clicked over to twenty-one days, she finally opened her eyes. She breathed with uncertainty. She didn't dare move.

And then a prince took the first breath of his new life.

ACKNOWLEDGMENTS

This book has been a beast.

I started off with nothing, just another fourteen-year-old posting little bits of a story to Wattpad after school when I should have been studying. Fast forward a year: I'd been featured, hit over a million readers, won a Watty, and had an inbox that was backed up with letters and fan art. So, I think the first people I need to thank are the people who decided to give this book a go. Thank you to everyone who read this story and loved it. Thank you to Alessandra, I-Yana, Deanna, and Monica at HQ especially, and to all the amazing editors I've had the privilege of working with. From getting me featured in the very beginning to working with me these last few years to get this story polished and perfect, I've been so lucky to have such amazing people on my team.

Thank you to my massive, insane family. I kept this secret for a long, long time. When I said I wanted to write there were so many of you who doubted me, but I thank you for that because when I finally revealed what I'd been up to, you guys turned into my biggest supporters. Thank you for being my go-to advice team and my first contract readers and being the people willing to fight tooth and nail for my dreams.

Thank you to Blackwater Mine CHPP B Crew for being the best people I've ever worked with, even though you drive me absolutely fucking insane. Thanks for all the writing tips and for being my biggest and best critics. Thanks for all the "brainstorming" and listening to me bitch and whine. One day maybe we'll get to that wash plant novel you all want so bad but no, I will not do crib-time reading for you.

Thank you to all my beautiful friends who have supported me through this journey from start to finish. Thank you to every person I've loved and every stranger I encountered who left a piece of themselves with me. I love you all endlessly.

ABOUT THE AUTHOR

Wendii McIver is an Australian author born and raised in Queensland. Between her career as a miner and being a university student, Wendii spends her time traveling and collecting plants, crystals, and books. Wendii began her writing journey at age fourteen, posting stories on Wattpad that have now accumulated over five million reads worldwide. *Relic & Ruin* is her first novel. Wendii can be found on Wattpad @spite- and on Instagram @wendiimac.

RELIC
AND
RUIN

Turn the page for
exclusive bonus content!

LIST OF PHOBIAS

COULROPHOBIA – fear of clowns

ONEIROPHOBIA – fear of dreams

PHASMOPHOBIA – fear of ghosts

DIDASKALEINOPHOBIA – fear of school or going to school

EPISTEMOPHOBIA – fear of knowledge

WICCAPHOBIA – fear of witchcraft

AICHMOPHOBIA – fear of sharp objects

AGYROPHOBIA – fear of crossing streets

SOMNIPHOBIA – fear of going to sleep

PIGMENTUMPHOBIA – fear of paint

DECIDOPHOBIA – fear of making decisions

NYCTOPHOBIA – fear of the night

HYLOPHOBIA – fear of forests

APOTEMNOPHOBIA – fear of persons with amputations

HEMOPHOBIA – fear of blood

ALGOPHOBIA – fear of pain

TERATOPHOBIA – fear of monsters

ECCLESIOPHOBIA – fear of churches

ANATIDAEPHOBIA – fear that you are being watched by a duck

TETRAPHOBIA – fear of the number four

LEPORIPHOBIA – fear of rabbits

ANGROPHOBIA – fear of anger or becoming angry

BASIPHOBIA – fear of not being able to stand or walk

ANTHOPHOBIA – fear of flowers

DEMENTOPHOBIA – fear of going insane

BAROPHOBIA – fear of gravity

HIPPOPOTOMONSTROSESQUIPEDALIOPHOBIA – fear of long words

PYROPHOBIA – fear of fire

NYCTOHYLOPHOBIA – fear of forests at night

ILLYNGOPHOBIA – fear of vertigo or dizziness when looking down

ARACHIBUTYROPHOBIA – fear of peanut butter sticking to the roof of your mouth

CARTILOGENOPHOBIA – fear of bones

CRYSTALLOPHOBIA – fear of crystals of glass

HYPSIPHOBIA – fear of heights

LACHANOPHOBIA – fear of vegetables

MYSOPHOBIA – fear of contamination and germs

GELOTOPHOBIA – fear of being laughed at

OCHOPHOBIA – fear of all vehicles

XENOGLOSSOPHOBIA – fear of foreign languages

FYKIAPHOBIA – fear of seaweed

OPHTHALMOPHOBIA – fear of being stared at

MUSOPHOBIA – fear of mice or rats

CHAETOPHOBIA – fear of hair

CLAUSTROPHOBIA – fear of being in small, enclosed spaces

KYMOPHOBIA – fear of waves or wavelike motions

ALTOCELAROPHOBIA – fear of high ceilings

PHOBOPHOBIA – fear of phobias

ACAROPHOBIA – fear of very tiny bugs

NEOPHOBIA fear of new things or experiences

ALTUSSESSIOPHOBIA – fear of antique furniture

ALLODOXAPHOBIA – fear of opinions

PHENGOPHOBIA – fear of sunshine

EOSOPHOBIA – fear of dawn

HYPNOPHOBIA – fear of falling asleep

RUPOPHOBIA – fear of garbage

THEOPHOBIA – fear of gods or religions

CARDIOPHOBIA – fear of heart attacks

TYRANNOPHOBIA – fear of tyrants

If you loved *Relic and Ruin*,
check out *Crossbones* by Kimberly Vale!

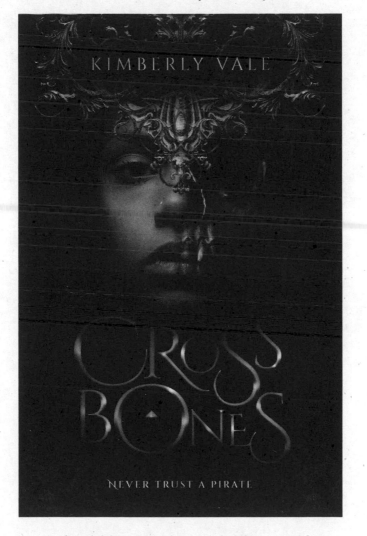

Available now, wherever books are sold.

CHAPTER ONE
CSILLA

Port Barlow

Late Sunspur

I will not die today.

Csilla's unspoken words crowded her mind. She never dwelled on death—there was no reason to in the life she lived. Death came, it took, and it did not give back. She hadn't given much thought to how she would die, but she assumed it would be bloody and brilliant. *Not like this.*

As she walked through the crowd with her wrists tied tightly behind her, her fingers ached for the leather hilt of her sword. If she could, she'd fight until every Incendian soldier lay dead or until her last breath wheezed through her bloodied lips.

Around her, the weathered courtyard overflowed with unruly harbor-folk who'd normally be selling wares or watching the soldiers' demonstrations. On this day, however, they'd be witnessing her execution.

The soldiers marched before her, parting the path like a sword through the sea. To onlookers, she was a stain on their garments they couldn't scrub out, a plague they couldn't be rid of. Every time their eyes ran over the scars along her skin, the piercings that lined her ears, and her one blind eye, their anger flickered with fear and their shouted insults grew louder.

Csilla ignored them. The distant crash of waves and the briny scent of the sea was enough to calm the frenzied beating of her heart—for now. It was impossible to truly be calm when a storm was on the horizon.

Time was running out. The noose loomed across the courtyard.

If the Incendian Navy thought to humiliate her in her last moments, they would fail. She held her chin high and stepped with grace. No one would see her falter. No one would see her break. She'd show them only a girl who was proud of her pirate heritage, who preferred to die and be seen than to waste away, hidden in a cell.

"Filthy pirate!" a woman's voice yelled, her words slicing above the crowd's jeers like a sharpened blade.

Csilla glanced to her right, her good eye coming to rest on a woman whose worn face snarled at her. The woman wove through the crowd, following as the soldiers pushed Csilla forward. Then the woman stopped, slipped off her shoe, and hurled it, the shoe smacking hard against Csilla's cheek. She ignored the searing pain as well as the taunts and laughter that rose from the crowd.

Rage burned through Csilla like wildfire. They could rot in Limbo for all she cared. She stopped walking, pulled against the rope binding her to the soldier, and cut her sight to the woman. When their eyes met, the woman shriveled back, averting her gaze to the ground. It wasn't the first time Csilla had received this reaction, which was why she usually wore a scarf to cover her white eye, but today she embraced her difference. Today, she was glad the soldiers wouldn't let her wear it.

"*Sobel liitena shobenasku,*" Csilla said, repeating the same words that had cursed her half blind. "*Sobel miitesa jaharren eto.*" The woman's face went as white as merchant sails, her eyes growing wide and frantic as she realized Csilla's incantation was a curse. There was no magic in Csilla's veins to fulfill the venomous words, but the woman didn't know that. A glimmer of satisfying warmth spread through Csilla even as the soldiers dragged her forward, their fingers digging into the muscle of her arms and adding more bruises to her body.

"Witch!" the woman screamed. "Pirate witch! You'll waste away in Limbo!" The Harbor of Souls. Once a lost soul docked there in the afterlife, it never left again. It could very well be where Csilla's soul was heading today.

"See you there." Csilla locked gazes with the woman, her lip twisting into a smirk.

The sky was a blanket of clouds but the heat of the sunspur season still hung in the air. Sweat from the dense humid air gathered at the nape of Csilla's neck and traced down her spine like a river snake gliding over water. She wore only the filthy rags that the fort had *graciously* provided after they'd ripped her from the bed of her betrayer and stolen all her gear and armor. Though she hated the way the fabric scratched her skin, there was a twisted satisfaction in knowing that the soldiers, clad in their military trousers and multiple frilly layers, had to withstand the humidity. Sweat dripped down their temples, soaked their collars, stained their underarms.

One soldier shoved her forward into step again. The crowd

parted and Csilla's face went cold when the gallows came into view. She swallowed, her insides on the edge of heaving the small piece of bread she'd eaten yesterday. The noose swayed back and forth, a pendulum ticking down her last moments, and all previous confidence drained from her like blood from a fresh wound. The raised wooden scaffold with the dangling noose was a vision that reignited her darkest nightmares, her deepest unspoken fears. She shivered as she imagined her flailing body, her fingers clawing at her neck . . . her eyes, which would remain open long after her soul departed.

A soldier nudged her forward again until she was at the foot of the wooden stairs.

The world tilted—she blinked, but even in her good eye her vision didn't clear. A scream suffocated in her throat, her stomach turned to rock. She tried her best to remember her grandmother's training on the deck of the *Scarlet Maiden*: *Live fearlessly. Face every threat with a wicked smile and a sharp blade.* Yet as her gaze trailed up the scaffold, she struggled to lift her foot. Fear was an anchor that held her firm against the tide.

A drop of warm rain fell, splattering onto her cheek as she took the first step up and toward her death. By the time the soldiers corralled her directly in front of the noose, the clouds had opened up and showers poured down, cool against her skin.

Observers below pulled their hoods over their heads but Csilla embraced the rain. As the executioner looped the noose around her neck, she tilted her face back, letting the rain wash away the dirt and grime that had collected on her skin during her days in the cell.

The rope binding her wrists cut into her skin, but it didn't stop her from testing the strength of the soldier's knot. She wriggled her arms, attempting to free herself until a sharp blade pointed into her back, making her freeze.

"As issued by the king of Incendia," a soldier announced. His eyes trailed over the scroll as if he was reading the words, but the ink dripped in dark droplets from the edge of the rain-soaked parchment. He must've hanged so many pirates he knew the words by heart. His voice boomed across the open courtyard. "Any persons associated with piracy will be charged without trial."

Csilla scanned the upper level of the fort, searching for Rhoda or other Scarlet Maidens. She'd hoped her sister and her crew would come for her, like Csilla would do for them, but their absence proved that not everyone supported the youngest captain on the Sister Seas. Her crew had given up; and worse, they'd left her to die in this forsaken kingdom. Her gaze darted left and right, down by the stairs, by the doors, around the stage, anywhere, everywhere. Hoping she was wrong. Wishing she'd catch a glimpse of her sister's tightly woven braids or her friends' devious smiles.

But they truly hadn't come. It was a stab to the chest that left her knees trembling and filled her with a deep and cruel loneliness.

Then, her eyes fell upon someone in the crowd below, unhooded, rain dripping from his light hair with a smile that she knew too well split across his lips. The sight of him set her stomach on fire—an anger nearly strong enough to cover the ache in her chest.

In another time, in a place she'd buried deep within her memories, she would've been relieved to find his familiar sea-green eyes in this crowd, and perhaps, she would've allowed herself to get lost in them as he saved her from this unjust death.

But in this moment, in this turn of events, he wasn't there to rescue her. In fact, he was the reason she was facing death.

Flynn Gunnison—*her betrayer.*

It may as well have been him tying the noose around her neck. And after how he'd betrayed her trust, their friendship, and the possibility of what could've been between them, he had the gall to look her straight in the eyes. She lifted her chin. She would never let him see how much he'd shattered her.

She partly blamed herself for being so foolish, for letting the warm flame of his touch pull her into bed with him a week before. Maybe it was his charm. Maybe it was the rum. Whatever it was, the cost was her life.

Csilla's stomach twisted. She tore her gaze away from her betrayer as the soldier spoke once again.

"Csilla Abado of Macaya," he announced. "Captain of the *Scarlet Maiden*, conspirer against the Crown, pirate by choice, and pirate by blood, has been sentenced to hang by the neck until death."

The soldier rolled his drenched scroll back up even though it tore at the edges, then retreated down the stairs. No one cheered. No one clapped. The pattering of rain continued, seeping through Csilla's clothes, dripping off the tip of her nose. The fall through the gallows would break her neck, and if by some chance that didn't kill her, she'd choke to death soon after. This didn't stop her fingers from digging desperately at her neck for a grip around the rope.

Csilla closed her eyes once more, sending her last prayer to the Sea Sisters. She asked Anaphine to guide her soul with grace through Limbo and into the After. She prayed to Talona for strength for herself in her last moments, and even though they'd abandoned her, she prayed for her crew and for Rhoda, who had to go on without her. Finally, she pleaded for Iodeia to avenge her and smite Port Barlow with vicious waves taller than any tower they could build, taller than the Obsidian Palace in their capital city.

Maybe Csilla's dying wish would stop Incendia from encroaching any farther on the island kingdom of Cerulia. If the Incendian king had his way, the pirate fleet of Cerulia would be buried at the bottom of the sea, along with everything they stood for. Except for the gold. The greedy king would keep every coin for himself.

The footsteps of the executioner echoed behind her, thick heavy slaps against the creaking platform. Her chest fell in heavy pants and she counted every last breath. Her hands clenched into fists, her fingernails cutting crescents in her palms as she held on to every last second.

Then the lever clicked, and the wood below her dropped.

Everything stilled for a moment, a breath taken before the leap.

Csilla's heart fell first, then her legs followed. The blur of the crowd and their angry screams made her wish that the force *would* break her neck. A quick death. This hungry mob didn't deserve to watch her struggle for air.

It was just a blink of time, but in that moment, memories wisped through her mind, blowing past her like leaves in the wind. The flowered jungle treetops of Macaya. Her grandmother's sharp and commanding bark on the deck of the *Scarlet Maiden*, still able to be heard over the sea's crashing waves. The sparkle in her mother's deep-brown eyes even as she lay in her bed, frail and dying. And Rhoda's softness with her, which she never gave to anyone else.

All of it there, a beautiful painting, then a faint whir cut through the air above her and instead of jolting to a violent stop, she kept falling, the rope never tightening around her neck. She hit the ground hard, her legs crumbling beneath her weight, her head knocking into stone.

A thick tang clouded the air around her, making her throat itch. Maybe she'd died and the fall had broken her neck. Was this what death smelled like?

She opened her eyes but the cloud wouldn't clear from her vision. She blinked several more times before realizing it wasn't her eyesight—it was smoke. That was what she was choking on. Somehow, by some miracle, she'd escaped death this time.

Her left ankle throbbed unmercifully as she tried and failed to sit up with her hands still bound. Biting her lips shut to keep from groaning, she rolled onto her knees, careful of her ankle as she gazed out from under the gallows.

The crowd before her was a frenzied mob. Women screamed, tripping over their muddy skirts, clawing at each other to escape the possible danger first. Most of the men attempted to run for the fort gates, too, their eyes wide as they searched the area for threats. Soldiers swarmed in from their positions throughout the inside of the fort, their swords at the ready. They tried to reach Csilla but the panicked crowd's momentum pushed them back.

Csilla glanced at the end of the noose that still hung around her neck. The rope laid limp on the stone, severed and frayed. The smoke around her thinned, and her gaze trailed up the wall to see a small dagger wedged between two stones. There was only one person who could throw a dagger with enough accuracy to cut a rope. The same person who used to practice throwing her daggers at Csilla's dolls when they were children.

Her sister.

The weight that'd been suffocating Csilla was gone and she

could breathe easy again. She should've known Rhoda would be too dramatic to take out the guards as they escorted Csilla to the fort, or to break her out of her cell the night she got arrested. It was just like her sister to wait and make a scene out of saving her so that she could be applauded for the show later. Rhoda might've been brash and selfish at times, but they were family and all each other had left. Csilla should've never doubted her, but Rhoda could have at least saved her *before* she was dropped through the gallows.

"Csilla," a harsh whisper sounded from behind her as a blade cut her wrists free. "Get your lazy ass up. We've got a grand escape to make."

Csilla pulled the noose from her neck then whipped around to glare at her elder sister, wincing as she forced her body to stand, her ankle buckling beneath her. "We won't be going anywhere fast. My ankle's shot to hell."

"Don't be such a baby." Rhoda trudged toward her, eyes widening as she glanced to the side. Then she reached behind her back, withdrew a dagger from her leather belt, and threw it in Csilla's direction. The blade whizzed by her ear, followed by a thud and gurgle from over her shoulder. Rhoda had taken out a soldier, but Csilla still wasn't happy with her.

"You couldn't warn me?" Csilla asked as her sister yanked her dagger out of the guard's chest, wiping his blood off it with the crimson scarf that dangled from her belt. Csilla finally managed to stand alone without her sister's help and placed most of her weight on her right foot, allowing only the tip of her left boot to touch the ground.

"Are you finished griping, little cub?" Rhoda asked back, adjusting her daggers, then reaching for her cloak's tie and unraveling the knot. She pulled the scarlet cloak from her shoulders and draped the fabric around Csilla, lifting the hood over her soaking hair. Rhoda pulled another hood from her blouse and covered her own two braids before wrapping an arm around Csilla's waist and moving them both forward.

"Thank you, Rhoda," Csilla said as her sister helped her limp to the edge of the gallows' shadow.

"You didn't really think I would leave you to hang, did you?" Rhoda asked, the taunting sneer gone from her tone. She leaned forward, turning her head left, then right. "You're my sister. I'll always be there to rescue you when you get yourself into trouble." Csilla took notice of how she didn't address her as Captain; she likely never would.

Csilla braced herself as they left the cover of the platform and pushed into the chaotic crowd toward their escape. Soldiers still fought to get through the swarm of people while others searched for the one who had cut the rope. Smoke continued to clear, and the soldiers took the opening to shoot straight for the gallows, where Csilla and Rhoda had been a moment before.

"She's escaped!" a soldier yelled from behind them. "The pirate has escaped!"

Rhoda picked up her pace, practically dragging Csilla along. Csilla put as much weight as possible on her left foot, trying to ignore the sharp pain that shot up her leg with each step. *I will not die today*, she repeated over and over in her head. *Rhoda will not die today. I will not die until Flynn Gunnison has paid for what he's done.*

"Where are the others?" Csilla whispered to her sister.

"The twins are here," Rhoda whispered back. "They have more smokers ready if we need them. The rest are with Nara and the ship."

Csilla nodded, gripping Rhoda's waist tighter as she bit back her cry. Her ankle twisted again beneath her. The world spun, her vision spotting. She needed water. She needed food. She couldn't remember when she'd last had a good meal. But she didn't dare give up hope or Rhoda would use her instead of her old dolls for target practice. Just a bit farther and they'd be home free. If they could just get through the open doors and to their ship, then she could rest her ankle as long as she needed to.

"Find her!" someone yelled. "Find her allies! Do not let them leave this fort alive!"

Soldiers swarmed through the crowd, a few brushing past her in the chaos. Csilla always preached to her crew to remain calm in the worst of situations, to raise their chins against the biting wind, to grit their teeth and breathe deep when they wanted to scream and give up. Her girls never surrendered, never raised a white flag.

But there she was, their captain—her ankle throbbing, her spirit broken, tears pricking at the corners of her eyes like a weak little doe.

A soldier combed through the rushing men and women and stopped directly in front of Csilla and her sister. His brow turned down and his curious eyes flicked between the two them, their faces shrouded in shadow.

"Remove the hoods," he ordered, stepping even closer when they tried to shuffle past. When they didn't comply, he pointed his sword at Csilla. "I said, remove the hoods."

Rhoda sighed, then a hiss filled the air. Thick, white smoke rose in plumes from multiple spots in the crowd, unleashing more screams and yells among the harbor-folk. Smoke engulfed them almost immediately, shielding them from sight. Rhoda used the opportunity to hoist Csilla's arm over her shoulder, taking some relief off her ankle. Another body pushed in at Csilla's right, lifting her other arm. The scent of the mint leaves that Serafina liked to chew calmed Csilla's heart a beat.

Soldiers yelled orders but their confusion made them incapable of doing anything. They were birds flying blind. Smoke billowed up into the sky and out of the gates of the fort, masking their group as they continued forward through the sea of people. Soldiers yelled from behind, their curses fading the farther Csilla and her crew trekked down the hill to the harbor.

Cutting from the crowd, Rhoda and Serafina guided Csilla down a side path. Serafina's twin, Rosalina, darted in front of them, her dark ringlets bouncing as she led the way. She placed her hand idly at her back, ready to unsheathe her hidden blades if need be. If it came down to it, by Maiden's honor she would protect Csilla before her own blood.

A small farmhouse stood in a field off the path, surrounded by tall grass and little white flowers. Csilla thought someone stood in the open doorway, long dark hair blowing with her skirts as she watched the Maidens run like the wind toward the sea. She knew the watching stranger didn't matter in the scheme of things, but something in the back of her mind made her glance over her shoulder at the girl before they rounded the hill.

The sea finally came into view, followed by another glorious sight—the *Scarlet Maiden* with her crimson sails flapping, ready for departure. Csilla had never been so delighted to see her ship, even when she had set foot on it for the first time as captain. The deck had been her home since she was a little girl, more a home to her than anywhere else in the world. She needed the scent of the wood, the wind blowing against her cheeks, and the sun on her skin out in the open water.

Hidden by a short peak of land, the ship was unable to be seen from the busy harbor and its nosy inhabitants. Csilla and her girls neared the edge of the cliff, the *Scarlet Maiden* waiting below in the water.

Csilla peered down at the waves crashing against the jagged rock. Freedom was within reach, but first a high drop off a sharp and terribly intimidating cliff. "You just *had* to make this escape as dramatic as possible, didn't you?" she asked Rhoda as she cocked her brow. She remembered the time Rhoda blew up a military ship at a trading harbor just because she could.

"Oh, shut up about it," Rhoda grumbled, "We jumped higher cliffs than this in Macaya when we were kids. Now, do you need me to throw you over, or are you going to be a big girl and get your ass in the water?"

Csilla shot her own daggers at her sister with her eyes and moved back to make room for a grand swan dive. The sound of someone clapping stopped her as she bent at the knees.

"Well done," a familiar voice rang out behind. She would recognize that smooth honey tone anywhere. It was the same one that had coaxed her into bed, along with the soft eyes and even softer lips.

Csilla spun around to glare at the captain of the *Anaphine* and the one she'd almost let shatter her. She'd never developed a liking for killing, despite how many had died by her sword, but she would enjoy ripping Flynn apart piece by piece.

How could she have let him lure her to this in the first place? She'd been so gullible, so naive; she'd never make the same mistake again.

"You son of a—" she started.

"Ah, ah, ah." Flynn cut her off. He smiled and wagged his finger at her. "Our mothers have nothing to do with this, so please leave mine out of it. I could rattle off nonsense about your mother, but I'll bite my tongue for your sake."

There were shouts in the distance, coming closer every second. If she could somehow drag him with her to the *Scarlet Maiden*, she would, but she'd be lucky enough to get to the ship herself with her brokenness.

"I'll kill you, Flynn Gunnison." The words tasted delicious on Csilla's tongue. "When you least expect it, I will be there, waiting in the shadows. *And I will end you.*"

Flynn chuckled, as if knowing she wouldn't follow through on her threat. "You can hate me all you want, but I count on seeing you again very soon." Her stomach twisted at the reminder of a time when she would've been excited for that moment, but now she only felt the thrill of avenging his betrayal.

Without another glance at him, she turned around and flung herself from the cliff. Her hood fell away and the wind cut through her hair, billowing her cloak behind her, and when she hit the water, it engulfed her like a blanket. She came up for air, glancing back at the cliff as her crewmates made their own leaps.

Flynn stood at the edge, waving good-bye. For now.